Flint Bluff

An American Saga

Other books by James Duermeyer

Heroes in Obscurity
Market Time Conspiracy
Trail of the Outlaw
Singing Creek

The Capture of the USS Pueblo: The Incident,
the Aftermath, and the Motives of the North Korea.

Flint Bluff

An American Saga

James Duermeyer

SPEAKING VOLUMES, LLC
NAPLES, FLORIDA
2019

Flint Bluff

Third Edition Copyright © 2019 by James Duermeyer
Second Edition Copyright © 2012 by James Duermeyer
First published in 2011 Copyright © 2011 by James Duermeyer

ISBN 978-1-64540-095-0

Introduction

During a trip to visit the Vicksburg National Military Park and Cemetery in Vicksburg, Mississippi, my wife and I were intrigued by the many stories of drama and hardship endured by the people of Vicksburg during the Civil War. Shortly thereafter, I began writing *Flint Bluff*, building the story and weaving actual events in history into the story as I wrote. A small part of the story takes place in Vicksburg during the Civil War. The bulk of the book is set in the southeast section of the fledgling Iowa Territory, later the State of Iowa, in the town that would become Burlington, Iowa.

Many of the names, locations, and events in the book are based on fact. Some of the characters associated with those events are also based on fact. In writing about factual people and events, I attempted to adhere to the actual dates and facts regarding the events. When using the name of actual historical figures, I attempted not to attribute any action to that character unless those actions were verified in my research. All other characters, names, and events are fictional.

FLINT BLUFF: Principal Characters

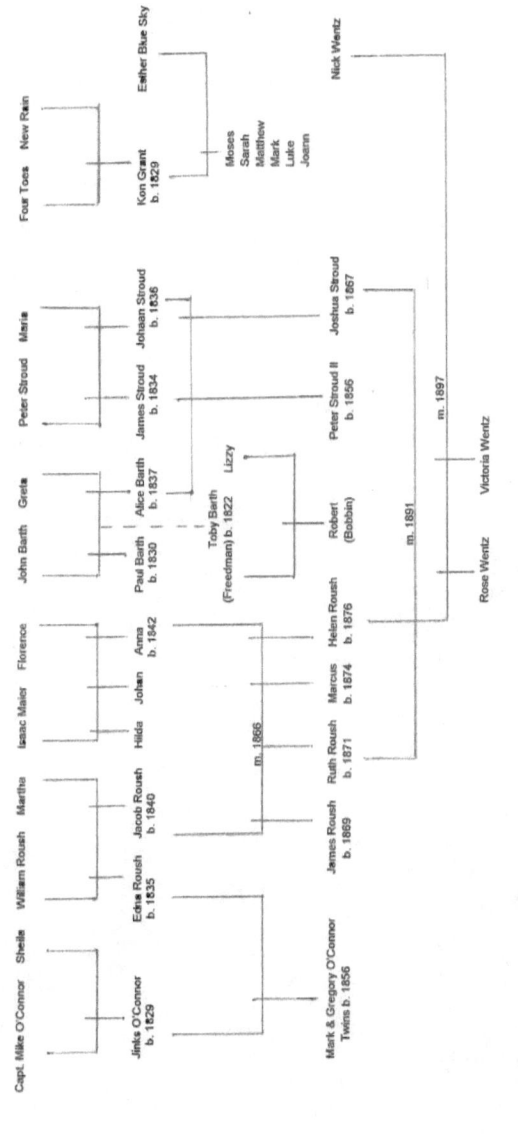

Part One

The Journey
and Settlement

Chapter One

The Journey
1833

Most of the time, the tune was recognizable. Other times, raspy shrieks were interspersed, making the music a bit comical. Yet, even with the imperfections, Martha loved the sound of the calliope. The sometimes screechy, noisy, yet gay music filled her with joy. She had loved music all of her life and could sit for hours watching the garishly dressed deckhand, who also served as the boat's calliope player, on his red bench in front of the instrument, as his hands moved rapidly across the keyboards bringing forth magical sounds from the various steam pipes and whistles. She sat on the main deck of the paddle wheel steamer as it wended its steady course north on the great river. Each afternoon, she made her way to the same location following the shipboard announcement from the captain reminding all passengers of the concert.

As she sat idly listening to the closing strains of the afternoon's performance, she gazed on this foreign country as the riverboat glided past lush green forests and occasional hand-built, ramshackle cabins. Her mind wandered to the whirlwind which had been her life for the past eighteen months. She still struggled to grasp all of the events which had taken place in that short span of time.

Back in the old country, where her given name had been Herta, it had been understood, ever since she was ten years old, that her father, with her mother's blessing, would arrange for a proper traditional suitor and eventual husband for her. This was the manner in which conventional

Jewish families carried out the task of seeing that their daughters were wed to a suitable man, and that families expanded. In most instances, daughters had no influence in the matter. The match-making which would affect a young man and woman for the rest of their lives, was in the hands of the respective parents. Therefore, the parents of Wilhelm Raach and Herta's parents held many meetings with each family lauding the qualities of their respective marriage prospect. The discussions were friendly, since the families had known each other for many years. Yet, it was expected that the girl's family would provide a dowry to sweeten the negotiations. Dowries could be comprised of money, land, livestock, or other items held in esteem by the parents. When values of the dowry were discussed between the two families, the women would leave the room to drink tea in the kitchen, while the men drank their schnapps and continued their discussions. The two fathers trusted each other, as they were old friends, and both families were considered "well-off" financially, but certainly not rich.

Herta had known Wilhelm in school in Minden, Germany, but Wilhelm was two years ahead of her in his studies. She knew him to be bright, cheerful, and handsome, and like several of her girlfriends, she had admired him from afar. After their families had reached an agreement that the two of them would wed, Herta and Wilhelm began spending more time together to nurture their friendship and respect for one another.

Wilhelm was an outgoing, optimistic dreamer, yet, a hard worker. Herta was more private in her aspirations and dreams. As their friendship and admiration for each other slowly grew, Herta was shocked and dismayed to learn that Wilhelm held an unwavering desire to leave Germany and go to the fledgling democracy, the United States of America, to build a new life there. Unbeknownst to Herta, her parents were aware of Wilhelm's adventurous dream, because the subject had been discussed at length in the marriage negotiations. This aspect of the future nuptials had not been revealed to Herta for fear of causing an immediate breakdown in the negotiations. Herta was fearful of leaving her family and the comforting familiarity of her village and friends. After the marriage negotiations were concluded, there were many nights she cried herself to sleep, overwhelmed with the uncertainty and fear of the unknown wilderness of America.

As the young couple's love for each other grew, Herta became cautiously optimistic and intrigued by the idea of traveling to a far-off land and building a life with her soon-to-be husband. In addition, she had recently bid a tearful farewell to her best friend Maria, who with her new husband, Peter Stroud, had departed to emigrate to the United States. Maria promised that if Herta and Wilhelm later came to America, she would meet Herta and Wilhelm when they arrived.

Wilhelm had completed his schooling and was apprenticed to a successful merchant. He learned the business quickly and was proficient with sums and merchandising. Herta had one more year of school to complete, and on her seventeenth birthday, her family announced her engagement to Wilhelm. The couple was married one week after Herta completed school, and they moved in with Herta's parents. Herta went to work for her mother in her seamstress shop, and the couple saved every bit of money possible for their passage to America.

Wilhelm kept scrupulous records of their earnings, exchanging their earnings to silver Vereinsthaler coins and other gold coins, while counting the weeks and months until they would leave. In late fall of 1829, the day finally came when he told Herta that they would leave in the early spring for America. Herta was dismayed. Now that there was a certain date for departure, her trepidation returned.

Anguished packing followed, with both the newlyweds forsaking many personal possessions to travel with the minimum freight and baggage. Their entire travelling luggage consisted of two large traveling trunks and several large carpet bags.

After tearful, wrenching good-byes were made with their families and a bit more travelling money was received from the parents, the couple's rented coach took them to Hamburg. Passage was quickly booked on a sailing schooner bound for the United States.

Herta's mother had sown small pockets into Herta's corset. These small hidden pockets held the gold and silver coins which Wilhelm had received at the Warburg Bank in Hamburg. He also deposited a portion of their funds in the bank and obtained a letter of credit for those funds. They were ready to leave on their sea voyage.

Their sailing ship held sixty immigrant passengers who had all booked passage to America. Wilhelm and Herta had been told by both sets of their parents to keep to themselves on the boat and not to trust strangers. They heeded this advice and only spoke to other passengers when necessary. Both Wilhelm and Herta were violently seasick for the first two days of their voyage, which added to their angst in making this drastic change in their lives. They both cried, consoled each other, and wondered aloud if they had made the right decision. To a twenty-one-year-old and a nineteen-year-old, life now appeared greatly daunting.

The ship moved north into the icy-cold North Sea, and then set a course for the English Channel, followed by the Atlantic Ocean. Having grown up in a land-locked city, neither Wilhelm nor Herta had imagined that there could be so much water in the world. When booking their passage tickets, the couple had been told that there were two major ports in the United States for immigrants to enter – New York City or New Orleans. They had chosen New Orleans because their friends, Maria and Peter had journeyed there. The monotonous days crossing the Atlantic were interrupted only by the varying degrees of sea-state and weather. The couples grew tired of this leg of their journey and were anxious to see their friends. Their ship would stop in New York City for provisioning and then immediately resume its journey to New Orleans.

As they neared New York, the ship tacked back and forth several times to properly align itself for the run into the New York harbor. A pilot boarded the ship as it came slowly into the harbor. The pilot and the captain barked orders to scrambling deckhands, and the sails were slowly lowered. Several small boats, each with a crew of oarsmen, then towed the ship to a berth. After docking, the couple marveled at the industry and skyline of the city. They were also greatly encouraged by the fact they observed no previously rumored savage natives roaming the harbor area. Passengers were told to remain on board the ship while it was fitted out, because the ship needed to be ready to leave again at any time, depending upon provisioning progress and the condition of the tides.

The next morning as they dozed in their small cabin, the couple awoke to the ship's gentle rocking. They arose and upon reaching the main deck, they watched as the skyline of New York City slowly faded from view.

After a few days, they stopped very briefly in Charleston, South Carolina, passing formidable Fort Sumter, with its bristling array of visible guns. While their ship took on water and supplies, they stood on the deck watching the busy port activities. After watching a few moments, Wilhelm asked one of the deckhands about three, strange dark ships moored at a separate pier from the other ships. They appeared to have no activity and no visible cargo.

"Them are slavers," replied the deckhand. He continued, "Slavers bring the Africans to America."

Wilhelm and Herta listened as the deckhand told them that the Africans were then sold as property to wealthy plantation farms, where they would work for the rest of their lives. This concept of slavery was unknown to the couple, and was so unimaginable to Herta and Wilhelm that they doubted the truthfulness of the ship's deckhand, but held their thoughts to themselves. After all, how could it possibly be true that in America people could be bought and sold like a bag of potatoes.

A few days later, their ship entered the Mississippi River delta and continued to the port of New Orleans. The first thing the young couple noticed was the oppressive, stagnant heat of the Deep South. It over-whelmed them, making it seem difficult even to breathe. After the ship was properly berthed, customs officials boarded the ship to determine and examine the ship's cargo and the passenger manifest. Presently, all immigrant passengers were escorted into a small, stiflingly hot, smelly building, where they were told to stand in line, waiting their turn to speak with the immigration officials. The heat sapped the couple's energy. Herta held her scented handkerchief to her nose, but the human stench of unwashed, sweaty people was overpowering. She was afraid she would swoon, so kept a firm hand on Wilhelm's arm and stared at the filthy floor. The line moved ever so slowly.

Finally, they reached the table where an uninterested immigration of-ficial sat. They stood politely in front of the table without speaking. The official, with a permanently sweat-stained government uniform, looked at the papers on his table and glanced up at the young couple. He then picked up a pen, dipped it in an inkwell on the table, and began speaking to the couple. Neither Wilhelm nor Herta spoke English, but the immi-gration man continued to pepper them with questions. The couple's hearts sank. Was this an unknown requirement to enter America – that they be able to understand the questions being asked of them? No one had told them this. To their relief, a well-dressed woman in line behind them quietly asked them in German if they spoke English. They an-swered no. The woman then offered to act as their interpreter. They quickly agreed. The woman explained to the immigration official, and the questions started again. When the woman was asked the names of the couple, she conferred with them. She then turned and spoke with the immigration worker, who scowled as they continued to talk. The discussion became more heated in nature. Finally, the exasperated woman turned to Wilhelm and Herta and told them that the immigration official had changed their names to Martha and William Roush because their names needed to be "Americanized," making them easier to write and understand. Herta and Wilhelm looked at each other in disbelief.

"What kind of country is this that you cannot keep your own name," cried Herta. Her tears began. The remaining questions were then completed, and the immigration official heavily stamped the papers in front of him and handed a small sheaf of papers to Wilhelm. They were free to leave, and turned and thanked the woman in line behind them.

As they hurried from the immigration building, they caught sight of Peter and Maria Stroud waiting for them. The excited couples laughed and hugged. Martha then tearfully explained to Maria what had happened in the immigration process; the fact that their names had been changed on their papers. Both Peter and Maria expressed their concern, but then informed Martha and William that this was a common practice. They explained that in their German Jewish community in New Orleans, there had been many name changes by immigration officials. Apparently, the names were changed to more common American names that the immigration clerks knew how to spell and were easier to pronounce.

In the days that followed, William was hired by a large dry goods firm, and Martha resumed her sewing, acquiring work at a small dress shop. They rented a small furnished room at a boarding house and settled into the Jewish German community. Learning the English language was a necessity, but it was a painstakingly slow ordeal for them. Ever so slowly, they replaced the guttural German inflections with the slower, quieter, Southern American manner of speaking. When they spoke with their friends in the community, Yiddish words often replaced English words that they did not yet know. But it was not long before they could converse and easily carry out business in English.

When they were not working, usually only on Sundays, William and Martha explored the city and were amazed at the lush flower gardens in the gated yards of the wealthy. They also marveled in the quantity and variety of fresh fruits and vegetables, which were not as common in the old country. One day they decided to stroll to the fish market for fresh fish. The stalls were set up near the fishing docks, and they watched in amazement as the shirtless, ebony-skinned men unloaded the heavy crates of fish from the deck of one of the boats. Suddenly, one of the black men stumbled and fell with the case of fish, spilling the fish onto the dock. Instantly, a white man, carrying an evil looking, multi-thonged quirt, ran off the boat and began whipping the black man who had spilled the fish. Martha turned away and could not look as the whipping continued. William pulled his wife away and started for home. As they passed another pier to go home, they stopped when they saw a small crowd of people standing on the pier. Close by was a ship tied up at the pier that looked very much like the slave ships they had seen in Charleston. As they watched, black-skinned people with shackles on their wrists and ankles were being brought up onto the deck of the ship and pulled out onto the pier. As these people stood on the pier, wealthy plantation owners inspected the shackled black people. The males were stripped of their clothing and inspected by pulling their lips to reveal the condition of their teeth, and their muscle condition was closely scrutinized. The women were stripped of all clothing to ensure that they were sturdy enough for childbirth, field work, and housework. A few of the women carried babies, some of whom had been born on the ship while it was in transit from Africa.

When the inspections concluded, an auctioneer began his sing-song chanting to begin selling these black people. The landowners raised their hands to bid as they participated in the auction. William and Martha were aghast. At no time in their lives had it ever occurred to them that people could be bought and sold. In their childhood religious studies, they were aware that slaves had been kept in ancient tribes in the Holy Lands. But this was America, the country where many of their acquaintances from the old country had come for the freedoms that were crafted by the men who had formed the new American government. This scene, which they felt was so morally wrong, of men brutalizing and selling other men, made a lasting impression on William and Martha.

The weeks and months passed and the couple was happy. They had good friends, and they were once again saving money for the future. But they each disliked the steamy, muggy weather of the Deep South. They were also uncomfortable around wealthier acquaintances, who had succumbed to the local custom and had purchased one or more slaves to work around their homes, doing the cooking, laundry, or gardening. William and Martha were in agreement that owning another person was simply not acceptable.

***

William loved to talk to customers in the store. He was always fascinated with their life stories – how they had come to America and the opportunities they had experienced. In listening to them, he learned more about America's history and the men who had formed this young nation.

William developed a rapport with many of the riverboat captains who came to the store to trade and purchase. They told him of the Mississippi boat traffic and the adventures of traveling in the less inhabited northern mid-section of the country. The tales of the army fighting bands of marauding Indians, the remarkable fur industry, the logging industry, the fertile farmland, the abundant wildlife, and sheer beauty of the country intrigued William and tugged at his heart. At home in the quiet of the evening, he retold Martha all of these wonderful and exciting stories.

One of William's favorite boat captain friends was Captain Michael O'Connor, a fiery, red-bearded Irishman, not a great deal older than William, who owned an odd little steam powered packet boat. The two men developed a bond and confided in one another. While Mike related his adventures on the northern Mississippi, William mentioned to Mike that one day, he would like to leave the South and go North to start his own business. On a cool day in early November 1832, as William was filling an order for Captain Mike, they laughed and told jokes to each other, ribbing each other as young men will do.

Then Mike became serious, and asked, "William, have you ever heard of the Black Hawk Purchase?"

After William said no, Captain Mike told him another story. He told William that nearly thirty years ago, in 1803, the United States Government had purchased a huge amount of land to the west of the Mississippi from France. It was known as the Louisiana Purchase. This territory was so big that it more than doubled the size of the United States.

"We heard of the Louisiana Purchase in the old country," replied William.

Captain Mike then told William that the Black Hawk War, which had extended from the Michigan Territory, through Illinois, and west of the Mississippi had finally ended in defeat for the Sauk Chief, Black Hawk, and that following the war, there had been another land purchase by the government in September 1832. That purchase was called the Black Hawk Purchase. Mike told William that the land acquired in the Black Hawk Purchase was being opened up for settlers. Mike said he made periodic stops at a trading post called Flint Hills, on the river in that territory. He said the land was beautiful, with rugged rolling hills, lush, black earth, and farmland to the west. At Flint Hills, he had seen numerous wagons ferried across the river going west. The wagon trail ran right beside the boat landing and the trading post. William listened intently, when Mike said that on his last visit to Flint Hills, it appeared that the old store owner was not in good health. The old trader had told Mike that this winter would be his last at the landing. He would not stay for another winter and therefore, needed to sell out.

During the remainder of the day, William's mind was not on his work. He was thinking of Captain Mike's stories. He had made up his mind that the stories foretold his future. He wanted his own business and was intrigued by thoughts of exploring the northern wilderness. His mind wandered, weighing the possibilities, and he reached a momentous conclusion. He would somehow purchase the Flint Hills trading post. That evening, he barely said a word at supper with Martha, but afterwards, when they both sat on the swing on the front porch of the boarding house where they could be alone, William began to stammer out the story Captain Mike had told him about Flint Hills. He had been unsure of how Martha would react when finally, he told Martha that he would like to move to this new territory and purchase the trading post. Martha had stared straight ahead and said nothing.

After several minutes, during which William had quietly fidgeted on the porch swing, Martha raised her head and looked at William, and said, "I love you, William, and I believe you should follow your heart. I trust you, and I would follow you anywhere. You know that. We will build our life in this new land. Now, let's go inside. I'm chilly." William hugged his wife, and the couple retired to their room.

***

Captain Mike O'Connor had provisioned his boat and planned to leave New Orleans in two days for his last trading run of the season on the upper Mississippi. He would need to time his trip so that he could return to New Orleans before the bitter cold settled in the North.

While filling provision orders for Mike and helping him stow the supplies on the boat, William told Mike of his wish to examine, and possibly buy, the Flint Hills trading post. Mike knew that William and Martha were comfortable in their jobs and in the community, so at first he did not believe William and laughed. William then told Mike that he was dead serious. He explained that he saw this as a great opportunity to experience the life of an adventurer settler and a chance to own his own business.

"Mike, I want to come work for you on your boat and go with you to the North Country," said William. After some discussion, the men came to an agreement, and in two days, William bid a tearful Martha good-bye as she stood on the dock with Maria and Peter Stroud. They would be separated for six weeks or more.

"Hurry back to me, William," Martha said tearfully.

Captain Mike and his packet boat, along with his new deckhand, William, plied their trade on the river as they steadily moved northward. The two men made a successful team. They spent several days in the bustling river port of St. Louis, selling their wares and provisioning for further travel. The early December weather was turning ever colder, and Mike told William that Flint Hills would be their last stop before turning south for the remainder of the winter. On a bright, clear, and crisp morning, as they avoided the numerous and perilous sand bars in the river, Mike pointed out the huge bluffs on their port side and said that Flint Hills was just ahead. As they neared their destination, William could see the open area between proud bluffs on each side of the landing. He could also see a grey, low, log shack sitting next to a rutted wagon road leading up the riverbank landing and continuing westward. Just north of the trading post, and across the rutted road, was another ramshackle building which housed a small, flat-boat ferry business. Further west on the road appeared to be a few more shacks, including a smithy and stable, a combination shack and tavern, and a couple run-down houses. It was just as Captain Mike had described. To a casual observer, the scene was one which would discourage anyone considering moving to such a place. But this pathetic appearing little settlement did not deter William, and he struggled to hold back his excitement.

The little packet boat carefully maneuvered up to the small, rickety, Flint Hills dock and tied up. Captain Mike sounded a short, shrill, steam whistle from the pilot station of the boat, and the two men left the boat and walked toward the trading post. As they neared the building, William was startled to see an Indian, dressed in a combination of common clothing and Indian wear, furtively come out of the trading post door and slink around the north side of the building and walk west on the rutted road. The trading post door opened further, and a stooped, gray-bearded, man with a walking stick emerged. He slowly hobbled toward them and called out, "O'Connor, ye rascal, you're a sight for tired eyes." The old man was a French trader named Jacque Laguire, who had been a fur trapper in his younger days. As he aged, his health deteriorated, making it impossible for him to continue the arduous livelihood of winter trapping. Laguire then started the little trading post. As he became more frail, he now wanted to return to the French community in New Orleans to live out his final years.

Mike and William off-loaded the meager Flint Hills cargo and loaded the skins, hides, and other goods that Laguire had for them.

"The stew pot is almost ready," said Laguire, "and I 'spect you'll keep me company tonight." As they ate, neither Mike nor William could discern what ingredients comprised the stew, and they were afraid to ask what type of critter had given up its life to become hot stew. But Laguire had given the concoction plenty of seasoning, making it palatable and tasty to the hungry men. After supper, Mike and Laguire smoked their pipes, and sipped a small glass of whisky.

"Laguire, you heathen, where did you get this rotgut? It's awful!" said Mike, after he had downed several sips of the whisky.

"Yah, I know," said Laguire. "Captain Bill was through here a few days ago and I bought this from him. He said it came from a miner's still up at Julien Dubuque's lead mine. I think they must have made this stuff out of the lead drippin's. It could kill an alligator," said Laguire. But then he laughed and gulped down another swig of the brew.

Laguire and Captain Mike teased and good-naturedly poked fun of William because he did not smoke and refused to drink the homemade whisky. William didn't mind. He told the other two men they would probably go blind drinking that poison, and they all laughed.

"Mr. Laguire, who was that man that came out of the cabin just as we were coming in this afternoon?" asked William. "Was he an Indian?"

Laguire then told him about his Indian visitor. "Oh, that's just my friend, Four Toes. Yep, he's an Indian all right. After old Black Hawk and his Fox warriors lost the war, Black Hawk's Sauk people moved farther west. I should say they were pressed west by the Army."

Laguire paused for another draw from his pipe and another sip of whisky. "I don't really know why, but Four Toes didn't want to move. He hid out in a cave up on the south bluff, and has been living there ever since," said Laguire. "Mostly he just fishes and traps, and we trade vittles and gear for his fish and hides. When he isn't busy, he comes in to chew the fat with me," said Laguire. He continued, "He got the name Four Toes, because as a young lad, he filched a metal trap from one of the trappers and was showing some of his little friends how it worked. He was holding the jaws of the trap open with his feet while he tried to set the trap. But as he set the trap, it sprung shut and clean sliced off one of his toes. From then on, he was known as Four Toes, a handle he doesn't like a whole lot. But he and I get along just fine, and since he speaks passable English, he is company for me."

Laguire then told them the history of the original trading post cabin. It had been built by a small fur trading company. They had used logs from the surrounding forest to erect the walls and roof runners and split shingles for the roof. The cabin was well built, but rather small and dark. Laguire had kept his eyes open, and when the trading company abandoned Flint Hills, Laguire acquired the property from them at a near-giveaway price.

As the evening wore on, the conversation turned to business, and William asked a great number of questions about how the trading post operated. He was concerned about obtaining supplies in this remote outpost, and with having enough traffic to sell his goods. Although young, William had a good business head, and could tell from looking around the post that Laguire was not in business to get rich. Huge gaps in the shelves where goods should be displayed attested to the fact that Laguire had lost interest in being a frontier merchant. In fact, goods in the store were so sparse that he was sure Laguire was just hanging on, waiting to leave. They began talking about what Laguire wanted in exchange for the business. Naturally, Laguire thought the place was worth far more than it was, but after another glass of rotgut whisky, he began to mellow. The price drifted downward. Before the men turned in for the night, William and Laguire had reached an agreement on the price. They sealed their bargain with a handshake. The plan was that William would return to New Orleans with Captain Mike and come north in the spring with Martha and the money for Laguire. William did not sleep much that night. He wrestled with his thoughts, hoping that he was doing the right thing with his life, and with Martha's life.

***

After nearly six weeks without William, Martha was overjoyed to see Captain Mike's packet boat slowly easing up to the pier in New Orleans. As the gangway was laid across to the pier, she quickly crossed it and ran to William.

As they held each other, she whispered, "I've missed you so!" William smiled and kissed her warmly.

"Now come on. We're stopping at a tonsilorium on the way home," said Martha. William had not shaved in six weeks.

That evening, William broke the news to Martha, saying, "Martha, we own a trading post!" Knowing William as she did, she expected this. During his absence, she had steeled herself in preparation for facing another move that could very well be much more dangerous than their sea voyage to America.

The following evening they invited Peter and Maria for dinner and told them of their bold new plans.

"You'll be eaten by savages and I'll never see you again," wailed Maria. She burst into tears and sobbed, "You simply cannot go!" Her outburst, in turn, got Martha started, and she too began blubbering. At this point, the men adjourned to the front porch.

Peter looked searchingly at his friend. "Are you completely serious about this plan?" he asked.

William smiled slightly and replied, "I've given this a lot of thought. I can't get used to this infernal New Orleans weather. Both Martha and I are distressed by the horrendous heat, humidity, and overabundance of vile bugs. In addition, we don't want to remain in New Orleans, a place where people are bought and sold. I understand the need for laborers on the plantations and farms. But I also firmly believe that no man should be able to purchase another man as property. I detest this practice and believe it is morally wrong. With my work experience, I have come to realize that I could run my own business." He paused, then went on.

"The thought of going to this new Black Hawk Territory is daunting and somewhat frightening, but I'm willing to take the chance to live my dream. Frankly, Peter, I am a bit scared, but I'm going to do it."

"Well, William, my friend, I too, do not wish to stay in New Orleans, and I see no real future here for me in the banking business," said Peter. Peter was not exactly telling the whole truth, since both men knew he was doing well in the bank and had already been promoted once and would have a bright future at the bank if he chose to stay.

"With the number of older men who will not soon retire, I am not certain that I can be promoted in the near future at the bank," said Peter. He continued, "William, would you consider taking on a partner in your business?" William had never considered such a prospect, but the thought of having his friend to assist in the problems he would certainly encounter, was attractive to William.

"But Peter, you must realize the risk. There might not even be profit enough for both of us in this venture," said William.

"I'm willing to risk that if you are," said Peter. "And the worst that might happen is that we have to return to New Orleans to resume making a living." They faced each other and laughed quietly.

They continued their discussion, specifically on how the responsibilities and finances would be shared. The discussion was easy because they trusted each other and had been friends for many years. Once again, as he had done at Flint Hills with Laguire, William shook hands with Peter on their new, shared business venture.

"I don't envy you, Peter. You still have to talk with Maria," said William.

"I'll take care of that and see you in the morning," said Peter.

The wives had composed themselves and dried their tears. The Stroud's then left to return home. After the Roushes were in bed, William cautiously told Martha about the agreement he had made with Peter.

To his surprise, Martha was overjoyed. She loved the idea that their best friends might go north with them. She was excited to hear the outcome of Peter's discussion with Maria and would anxiously await tomorrow morning. Just as the couple was about to blow out the candles, there was a quiet rapping at their rooming house door. William carefully opened the door and saw a young black man holding an envelope in his hand.

The man said, "Mistah Stroud say to give you this," and handed the envelope to William. The young man then left.

William closed and locked the door, then walked over to sit on the edge of the bed. He opened the envelope and read its contents aloud to Martha. The brief note simply said, "We're going with you! Love, Maria."

Martha danced from the bed, hugged William and said excitedly as tears of joy trickled down her face, "Oh, William. This is so exciting. I will have Maria with me to share our great adventure." Once again William went to sleep, wondering and hoping that they were doing the right thing.

The two couples would have the remainder of the winter of 1832 to prepare for the spring trip to the north. They worked hard, saved their money, and as much as possible, William once again continued to convert their cash to gold coins. Martha sewed several more small pockets onto her corset to accommodate the coins and showed Maria her little secret for traveling with money. Maria quickly followed the example and began sewing pockets on her underclothing. They laughed with each other and called themselves, "The Corset Bankers."

Chapter Two

The Upper Mississippi

Captain Mike O'Connor had also not been idle through the winter. His river trade had been extremely lucrative, and he sold his packet boat and purchased a small steam paddle wheeler, which would double the cargo and passenger capacity he could carry on his river runs. The little paddle wheeler had some years on it, but after many hours of laboring on the machinery and a sparkling new coat of paint, the boat was well prepared for its new tasking. Surprisingly, the steam-powered boat also had a calliope, which Mike had refitted and put into working order. He hired two deckhands to help him, one of whom could struggle through a few well-known tunes on the boat's calliope, albeit with quite a few squeaky, screechy, dissonant, and often missed notes. Mike thought this was hilarious and encouraged the pseudo-musician to play the old instrument. Mike even acquired a garish band uniform for the deckhand to wear while playing. As the men continued to complete the maintenance and refitting of the new boat, Mike looked forward to a new year on the river.

The damp, gray, foggy days of winter in New Orleans finally gave way to partly cloudy and sunny mornings with warmer temperatures. Vegetation which had lain dormant in the cooler months began sending tender green shoots to reach the sunlight. The Roushes and the Strouds were nearly ready to begin their journey. Captain Mike had been consulted, and the couples would be traveling with him as he made his way north. The little paddle wheeler left its mooring and began steaming up the Mississippi at the end of February 1833. As the boat churned its way up river, they stopped at settlements along the riverbank, where a few passengers would depart and new passengers would board. Mike and his deckhands supervised the off-loading of various types of freight, and the on-loading of goods that would continue on the northern run. They observed fewer slaver packets on the river as they moved north and saw only two of the ugly brown boats on the river after their provisioning stop in Memphis.

***

As Martha listened to the fading squeaks and tweets of the calliope, she was so deep in her reverie she did not realize that William had sat down beside her. He kissed her cheek and offered her a penny for her thoughts.

"Oh, William, you know very well what I'm thinking about. I just cannot imagine what we will find at Flint Hills and what sort of life we will have. Truthfully, it scares me," Martha said. "I only hope I am strong enough for you," she continued.

William chuckled and said, "You worry too much. We'll be fine; just wait and see." He then pointed out to Martha that they would soon be landing in St. Louis and reminded her that Captain Mike had promised to stay for three days so that the couples could purchase everything they would need for the trading post. It would be a chance to walk around the city, mingle with other people, and complete their purchases.

As the river port buildings of St. Louis appeared off the port bow, the couples' excitement grew. They could not wait to stretch their legs and explore the city. After the boat was moored, the couples went for a much anticipated walk. To them, St. Louis had a very different feel to it compared to New Orleans. They knew they were now in what the river captains considered to be the North. Customs were different, commerce moved more quickly, and as the ladies observed, the clothing styles were also different. The influence of French fashion was evident, but not nearly as prevalent as in New Orleans. Weather that could be much cooler played more of a role in the ladies' clothing. Martha and Maria had been tasked with finding the more feminine goods to be sold at the trading post, while the men searched vendors for staple goods and hardware items. William and Peter had also been conferring in confidence about ideas for improving the little post to make it more habitable for two couples. To this end, they found vendors for the lumber, tools, nails, and hardware needed to build onto the trading post. Their goal was to have these improvements completed before the next winter.

While in St. Louis, the couples had an opportunity to visit a Jewish Temple. As they sat in the service, they marveled at being able to sit together as a married couple, unlike the synagogues in the old country where the women sat apart from the men. After the service they spoke with some of the attendees and learned that there was a small group of Jewish people up the river at Keokuk in the Michigan Territory. No one at the temple had heard of Flint Hills, which was a bit daunting to the couples. They were wished well in their journey and were told they would always be welcome to return. The four young people were quiet as they returned to the boat, each with their private thoughts, hoping that their lives would be safe and happy in the northern territory.

Captain Mike stopped for trading in Hannibal, Missouri; Quincy, Illinois, and subsequently in Keokuk, where the couples had dinner in the home of a lay rabbi. The older gentleman encouraged the couples to settle with the small Keokuk group, but the four young people agreed that they were so very close to their destination that they wanted to keep going to Flint Hills. Therefore they politely declined the offer to stay. As the boat continued traveling north, Mike's last stop before Flint Hills was Ft. Madison. Mike skillfully navigated the boat past the treacherous rapids at Venus, Illinois, as he deftly guided their approach to Ft. Madison. Mike explained to his passengers that this was the first army fort on the upper Mississippi, and the site of Chief Black Hawk's first battle with Union Soldiers. The couples marveled at the abilities and knowledge of their friend, Captain Mike O'Connor. As immigrants to a young country so full of rapid change, they also were anxious and humbled to join the ranks of thousands of settlers who were forming the character of this nation.

After leaving Ft. Madison early in the morning in a drizzling rain, Captain Mike announced that they were approaching Flint Hills. Because William was the only person in the group who had been to Flint Hills, Peter and the two wives could not make out the small ramshackle buildings in the gray distance. Mike slowed the boat and began a slow sweeping turn to port. The trading post became visible through the rainy mist, and no comment came from Peter, Maria, or Martha. The disappointment was evident by their silence. One of the deckhands slowly cranked the bow gangway down as the boat neared the shore. The old rickety dock could not accommodate Mike's larger boat; so instead, he eased the boat to the riverbank where it could be moored nose in, with the front gangway used for disembarking, unloading and loading. Spring lines were staked into the riverbank to hold the boat steady. After making certain that his boat was secure, Mike gave a loud, short blast on the ship's whistle and the two couples and Captain Mike walked ashore at Flint Hills.

Jacque Laguire gingerly ambled toward them, leaned on his stick, and stuck out his dirty paw to shake hands with everyone.

"Laguire, this is my wife, Martha, and our friends Peter and Maria Stroud. They are going to be staying with us," said William.

"Pleased to meet 'ya," said Laguire. "Feel free to look around," he said.

While the men conferred on preparations for off-loading the cargo that would remain at Flint Hills, the women ventured forward to the trading post. They opened the door, peeked in, and entered. Within seconds, both women ran screaming and shrieking toward the men.

"There's a dead savage of some sort in the trading post," wailed Martha. "He has black hair with a scarf around his head, some sort of beaded belt and shoes made of animal skin," said Martha.

"And he stinks!" added Maria, "I think he's dead."

Peter and William were about to run to the cabin, when Laguire began laughing.

"Nah, he ain't dead," said Laguire. "That's just Four Toes, and he's sleeping off a half bottle of Captain Bill's rotgut. He'll be all right in another hour or two," said Laguire.

The women had seen and heard enough. They pointedly marched back across the gangway to the safety of the river boat.

The shriek of the boat's whistle and the noise of the hysterical women must have roused him, because just then, the hung-over Indian ambled out of the cabin and trudged west up the road. Peter stared at the departing fellow. William explained to Peter that Four Toes lived in a cave close by and could usually be seen fishing at his favorite spot on the riverbank just north of the road.

Off-loading of the supplies from the boat and stocking the cabin took the remainder of the day, and most of the next. The lumber, made up of various sized boards and shingles, was stacked next to the cabin, with a resultant pile that nearly reached the roof. Martha and Maria did their best to clean some of the filth and debris out of the cabin, as Laguire casually watched all the activity from the small front porch.

That evening, Mike invited Laguire and the two couples aboard the boat for supper. William and Peter paid Laguire for the cabin and its inventory, and a bottle of wine was shared in celebration. Still, Martha,

Peter, and Maria had made no spoken comment about finally seeing the run-down trading post.

While finishing supper, Peter finally said, "Well, I guess we have considerable work to do to this place," and raised his glass. The others burst out laughing, but they, too, raised their glasses. The tension had been broken, and all agreed that they had a daunting task ahead. As only a true friend would do, Captain Mike agreed to stay and help them for three or four days. His muscular frame and the help of his deckhands would make the initial work go much faster.

The next morning, a most important task was begun. Laguire had not seen the necessity of having an outhouse on the property. He had simply wandered back into the adjoining woods for necessity purposes, but William and Peter knew this was not appropriate for the women, and frankly, they were also not inclined to simply wander into the woods. So the digging began, and following excavation, the lumber and tools were used by the men to complete the upper portion of the outdoor privy. Again, Laguire casually observed the work, making no effort to assist.

While the men worked outdoors, Martha and Maria continued their work indoors, and with Laguire's none too eager help, they began carrying Laguire's possessions out of the cabin and onto the boat. They were determined to get Laguire and his mess moved out of the cabin as quickly as possible.

During the following day, the outhouse was completed, and large stones were hand carried from the bank of the river to the back side of the cabin. The stones would soon form a foundation. Framing was laid on these stones for a floor which would then be the base for a second large room to be added to the cabin.

While the group labored, they had visitors. Two brothers who ran the ferry on the north side of the road ambled over and introduced themselves. They were Aaron and Robert Quinn. Captain Mike knew them and vouched that they were "good Irish boyos." The Quinns were especially happy to see the two young wives.

"Mrs. Barth is the only woman hereabouts, so we sorely needed some more womenfolk," said Robert. Later, the smithy and his wife also paid a visit. John Barth, the village blacksmith, and his wife Greta were from the old country and were delighted to "talk to some other Germans besides old Vogler."

Thomas Vogler was the owner of a dilapidated shack wherein he sold homemade liquor from the front door of the abode. According to the Barth's, he was not around very much and was not the most sociable fellow in town. Sure enough, late that afternoon, as the group was about to quit work for the day, a swarthy dark haired man carrying a rifle and wearing a pistol belt came upon the group.

"Name's Vogler, Thomas Vogler," he said. He did not offer his hand.

William and Peter offered their hands and introduced themselves and their wives. Vogler did not shake hands.

William said, "I see you are armed. Have you had some trouble?"

Vogler replied, "If you know what's good for you, you'll get a gun too. I'm just protecting my property, and every now and again, we get an Indian hunting party passing through that will rob you blind. They know me, and they don't mess with me." He continued, "You don't aim to sell liquor here, do you?"

The question took them somewhat by surprise. Peter replied that he had no intention to sell liquor.

"Well, see that you don't. I don't need you cutting into my business," said Vogler. He then turned and walked away up the road.

"Not a very friendly man, is he?" said Maria.

They all agreed.

"Where does he get his liquor?" William asked Laguire.

"Oh, he's got a still hidden somewhere up in the woods, and he don't want nobody snooping around his place. And I believe that's the real reason why he wears them guns," said Laguire. The group continued with their work.

The dingy, dark interior of the cabin was laid out with a long wood plank counter running across the cabin, just a few feet inside the front door. Behind this counter were shelves on the two side walls of the cabin, where Laguire had stacked his goods for sale. Free standing shelves were placed well in front of the back wall of the cabin, and behind those shelves was a small living and sleeping area, with a door on the back wall. The merchandise shelves were nearly empty; in all likelihood because Laguire had known he would soon be leaving. All of the dry goods, canned goods, and hardware items that had been purchased in St. Louis were stacked on the floor and would soon need to be stocked on the shelves.

When the women were satisfied that they had cleaned the cabin as well as they could, they began placing merchandise on the shelves, while the men completed the floor of the addition and began framing the walls. That evening, the tired party again boarded the boat for dinner and slept soundly on the boat.

The next morning, as the group groggily walked to the cabin to continue their work, they noticed an open can lying by the north side of the cabin. The canned peaches had been crudely opened and the contents devoured. Upon closer examination, it appeared that the can had been opened by a knife.

"Four Toes," they all said in unison.

No one had thought to barricade the doors of the cabin, and it appeared that the curious Indian had been watching when they retired to the boat. Part of the business of the day would then be installing hasps and locks onto the two cabin doors.

That same day, the Quinn brothers ferried a group of two large wagons with teams across the river. This was no small task, as the large flat bottomed, deck boat had to be hand rowed by the Quinns across the river. But during each crossing, the southward flowing river carried the boat to a landing south of where the boat would need to begin its return trip. As a result, the men on the riverbank would pull the boat north up the river by means of ropes until they reached their designated departure point to return to Flint Hills. Travelers would then be loaded onto the boat, and it would be rowed across the river to Flint Hills. If all went well, the combination of rowing and the flow of the river would bring the boat correctly back to the landing at Flint Hills. Wagons and travelers would be taken on the boat first, and the horses and livestock would be taken on a subsequent trip. At times, the Quinns were also able to use a rope and pulley system to bring the boats across the river. But often times, the system, while more efficient than rowing and poling, would strain and break under heavy loads and a high, fast-running river.

After the travelers crossed the river, they stopped in the road by the trading post, and a man climbed down and walked to the cabin. He was followed by four rambunctious children who swarmed out of the two wagons. The man greeted the group and asked if they had any axle grease that they might sell. Peter ran inside the cabin and came out with a small sealed cask. Peter knew what the cask had cost and told the traveler the price.

The traveler hesitated a few minutes, then continued talking, and asked Peter, "Say, you wouldn't have any use for that young'n over there would you?"

Peter was confused and asked the man if he was trying to sell one of his children.

The man burst out laughing and said, "No, no, not the kids, that little filly over there that just got weaned by its momma. She's about seven months old. Her momma is one of my team. But we've got a fur piece yet to go, and I can't be looking after that little girl."

The group had not seen the little horse tied on the far side of the lead wagon. She was a little deep red roan with white stockings and a white blaze on its forehead. Strangely, the blaze was almost round, with six equidistant points on the circumference. It looked eerily like the Star of David.

Peter answered, "No sir, I don't believe we have a need for the pony right now."

The group had not noticed that Martha had slipped away and was behind the wagon intently peering at the filly. The little filly, on her lead, calmly walked to Martha and put its nose next to Martha's belly. Martha rubbed its nose and stroked its neck.

Martha asked, "Mister, how much does a little horse like this cost?"

The traveler scratched his chin and replied, "Well, I don't rightly know, but if you don't charge me for this axle grease and throw in a piece of candy for all the kids, I reckon we could call it even."

Peter and William looked at each other and knew what was coming. Martha and Marie were both grinning as they looked at the men and nodded their heads affirmatively. The men were not so sure. Here was their first sale, and it was being traded for a horse. This did not seem to be the way to run a fledgling business.

William said, "Now Martha, you don't know anything about horses. What would you do with this animal?"

Martha did not respond. She just looked at William and smiled. The men looked at each other, and then back at their grinning wives. Peter pulled a white handkerchief from his back pocket and waved it back and forth above his head.

"Martha, I guess you've got a horse to take care of," said William. Martha giggled and jumped up and down.

"Her name is Becca," said Martha, "short for Rebecca," and she untied the lead rope and led the little filly over to the two men.

The hard peppermint candy was distributed to the children. The traveler laughed and climbed back up onto the wagon seat, followed by the chattering children. He waved cheerily, and the wagons slowly rumbled west.

Captain Mike said, "Looks like we're building a corral." The men all shook their heads and walked back to their work behind the cabin.

With Captain Mike's help, the framing was completed and the shingles attached to the roof of the addition. William and Peter would have to finish siding the addition because Mike needed to resume his travels up the river. He had been with the couples for five days and needed to get underway. Before he left, the men completed a small corral for Becca. All of Laguire's possessions had been moved onto the boat, and he had been living aboard awaiting departure. The mooring lines were taken in, and with a sharp blast from the ship's horn, the paddle wheel began a backwards rotation. Captain Mike backed out into the river and turned the boat to the north. The group would miss him.

The couples were now on their own in the wilderness. The building continued as the days went by and was completed in mid-summer. The group fell into a routine with the women doing the cooking, and the men continuing to make crude furniture and conduct trading with the numerous travelers being ferried across from Illinois each day by the Quinns. Once in a while they would see Four Toes fishing, but it was several weeks before he finally brought a string of catfish over to the cabin and haltingly asked to trade them for flour and salt. Peter agreed, and Four Toes shyly grinned, tucked his acquisitions under his arms, and trudged up the road. The couples had a catfish feast that evening.

They learned something from every traveler who came by the trading post. All the visitors were asked about news of the nation, where they were from, the weather, hostilities with Indians, and other topics of interest. While most travelers had some silver coins to purchase goods, many had other items for barter. Bartered chickens were soon in a coop behind the cabin, and the resultant eggs were sold to travelers. Families with a cow sometimes had butter or cheese to sell in exchange for eggs or canned goods. To replenish their dwindling stock of merchandise, the couples bought goods from packet boats or an occasional paddle wheeler. In addition to staple items and hardware, the cloth, ribbons, and sewing materials also sold well. Peter kept meticulous records, and by fall, he knew exactly what was needed for replenishment, and what items had been repeatedly purchased and requested by travelers.

It became nearly a daily occurrence to see Martha in the little corral with Becca. Martha had not known a great deal about horses, but there was something in her calm demeanor that the little filly loved. With her own novice methods, Martha worked the horse daily so that it was so gentle that a child could work with it. As time passed, Martha strapped a blanket on Becca's back so the little horse would get the feel of a foreign object on its back. With the blanket attached, the little horse moved around the corral without protest. It would be some time yet before the filly was old enough to have a rider. After their training sessions, Martha would attach a lead to the filly and stake her to the grassy riverbank where there was abundant forage and water. William was amazed at the progress of training the little filly and saw the unusual bond between the horse and his young wife.

In August of 1833, another adventurer, Dr. William Ross, came to Flint Hills. Dr. Ross was a welcome addition to the little community, as a doctor was sorely needed. Dr. Ross, a devout man, also opened a small store, practiced medicine, and became the druggist for the village. Although the retail competition was not necessarily welcomed by William and Peter, they truly liked Dr. Ross and became friends with the scholarly gentleman.

By late fall of 1833, the weather had begun to turn much cooler. The cabin addition was completed, with a walled partition in the middle of the additional room so each couple had its own small living and sleeping room. Shuttered windows provided light for each room. The old back door of the cabin was removed, and it and another door were installed in the back wall of the addition for access to the outdoor privy by either couple. Yet another door was cut into the original back cabin wall, so each couple had an entrance to their respective rooms from the trade area. The men had felled several trees in the nearby woods, and the wood supply was ready for winter.

Business had been good throughout the late summer and fall as the last of the westward travelers for the year passed through Flint Hills. As a result of their hard work and good fortune, the couples decided to go to St. Louis at Thanksgiving time. They would ride with Captain Mike as he made his way south for the winter. They needed to conduct banking business and buy new merchandise. They arranged for the Quinn brothers to look after their property and take care of Becca and the chickens in their absence. They also told the Quinn's to help themselves to the eggs and to sell the eggs they could not use. Captain Mike arrived just before Thanksgiving, and the group moved down the river to St. Louis. The two couples would stay in St. Louis several days to complete their shopping. Captain Mike left them and proceeded south on the river.

Thanksgiving in St. Louis was a festive time with brightly decorated store windows that lured the many shoppers. Their time in St. Louis afforded the couples a much needed chance to mingle with hundreds of other people while shopping, and to allow hotel staff to look after and pamper them at the hotel. It was a luxury not having to rise early and work.

While in St. Louis, William and Peter called on Jacob and Samuel Hawken at their firearm manufacturing company. They purchased a dozen of the new percussion, 50 caliber Rocky Mountain Rifles. The Hawkens' also provided twenty of the new percussion pepperbox multi-barreled revolvers. The couples would rely on these firearms for their own protection and sell the remainder in the store. Plenty of lead and powder was also purchased. Before they left the Hawkens' factory, the couples were taught how to load, aim, and fire the weapons. This training could prove invaluable for their very survival.

After all of the purchasing had been completed and arrangements made for delivery of the merchandise to Flint Hills, the couples found a packet boat that was making a quick run north before winter settled into the upper Mississippi. With mixed emotions, they gazed at St. Louis as the packet moved from the landing and turned north. Once again, they were leaving a civilized city for the daily unknowns of the wilderness.

Two days later, the packet boat arrived at Flint Hills, and the couples were met at the landing by the Quinn brothers. Martha quickly peered past the landing to the trading post cabin and spied Becca in the corral. As she ran to the corral, the little mare whinnied in recognition.

Chapter Three

The Frontier Village

All of the men pitched in to unload the packet boat, and as they worked, they talked. The Quinns assured William and Peter that there had been no trouble, but a few wagons had ferried across and headed west while they were gone. These were late season travelers who would join wagon camps to the west and bivouac near wooded areas for the winter in hastily-made temporary shelters. But the biggest news from the Quinns was that there had been additional settlers in Flint Hills. Three wagons had camped together up the road, and they had begun building winter shelters. They had told the Quinns that they would be settling here.

The following day, before beginning in earnest to stow all the supplies, and as they watched the packet boat steam out of sight, the couples walked up the road to greet the wagon encampment. There they met Clarence and Alice Baily, John Gray, and Caleb and Susan DeGroot. Clarence Baily was a wood crafter. John Gray was an engineer, and the DeGroots would be farming. Dr. Ross had previously begun surveying and plotting the town, and John Gray had purchased the first lot in the town for $50. As they all talked and became acquainted, the Quinn's and Barth's walked up and joined the group.

Greta Barth smiled and said to Martha and Maria, "Isn't it exciting to have these people join us. We're going to be a real town one of these days."

As the group continued their informal meeting, it was decided that since he had purchased the first platted lot, John Gray would have the honor of picking a real name for the town. Flint Hills was the English interpretation for the Sauk and Fox word "Shoquoquon." The group felt that the little town needed a more proper name. John Gray had moved across the country from his hometown of Burlington, Vermont. He suggested they call the little town Burlington, and the group agreed. Flint Hills was now Burlington, still a part of the Black Hawk Purchase. Before the group broke up to go back to work, they agreed to have Peter be the recorder and keeper of the funds received for purchasing the land. In addition, Dr. Ross showed the group his progress in plotting out the properties in the town. When the group broke up, William and Peter were dumfounded. So much had happened in the village while they had been away for such a short period of time.

While they had been purchasing lumber in St. Louis, William and Peter had had also included a small supply of glass panes of various sizes. They wanted to install three windows in the cabin; a larger one in the front wall of the cabin, and a smaller window in each living room. After asking Clarence Baily for advice, the two smaller windows were quickly framed and installed. The front window was much more difficult because they needed to saw through the log exterior. Almost an entire day was spent cutting the opening, framing and installing the window. After this tedious installation, the couples admired the bright interior of the cabin, knowing that they had the first glass windows in Burlington.

Winter set in on the Mississippi, and business came to the expected standstill. No wagons would come through in the winter, and boat traffic slowed considerably. But the couples stayed busy making improvements to the trading post cabin and helping the wagon settlers set up their temporary winter shelters for their families and animals. William and Peter were also using the available time to begin drawing plans for construction of a small warehouse facility for storage of merchandise. This would begin in the spring.

Mysteriously, throughout the fall and early winter, Thomas Vogler would only appear sporadically, and no one knew where he was when he was absent from the community. The colder weather did bring more trappers to the trading post, exchanging hides for canned goods. Four Toes could be seen fishing, but he had also constructed an ingenious snare on the riverbank to catch ducks making their migratory flights to the south. He then sold the ducks to the settlers and traded dressed-out fowl to the trading post for the two couples' eating pleasure. Each time Four Toes ventured to the cabin for trading, he admired and remarked at the beauty of Becca, the little filly.

The approaching Christmas season was strange for the two couples. The wagon settlers and the Quinn's were excited about Christmas, while the Roush's and Stroud's would privately and quietly observe Hanukkah. In their festival of lights, they would use candles in the cabin, and exchange small gifts. Early on Christmas morning, the wagon settlers and the Quinn's came to the trading post and fired off their rifles outside the door. When William peered out, the outdoor group yelled, "Merry Christmas," and laughingly shoved their way into the cabin. They said they knew the two couples did not observe Christmas, but they wanted to share a drink of friendship. Aaron Quinn opened his coat to reveal two bottles of wine and John Barth produced two more bottles, and Clarence Baily brought forth yet another bottle. Corks were extruded, and glasses were filled. The friends toasted each other and wished each other the very best in the year to come. Greta Barth taught them all to sing "Deck the Halls," and with much laughter and friendship, they all struggled to sing the holiday song. This informal get-together served to bring the friends all closer in their bond as pioneer adventurers. They had become an extended family. William and Martha, and Peter and Maria were blessed to have such caring friends.

***

The morning dawned bright, but icy crisp, with a slight skiff of ice on Becca's water bucket. William and Peter had gotten up early and had gone to the south bluff to gather more wood. On their way to the woods, they borrowed Caleb DeGroot's rock sled and a horse to drag the loaded sled back to the cabin. They also would cut more wood than they needed as payment to Caleb for the use of his sled.

Martha and Maria were up and dressed. Martha put on her coat and went to check on Becca to ensure the mare had grass and water. But as she came around to the south side of the cabin, she literally ran into three mounted Indians and a fourth Indian pony. The Indians were wrapped in winter blankets, with their arms free for holding their weapons. Their faces were painted, and with their long black hair, they were a menacingly frightening sight. Martha gasped as she saw them. Then she caught sight of the fourth Indian in the corral with Becca. The Indian had attached a lead to Becca's halter and was dragging at the pony, trying to get it to the corral gate. Martha was shocked and so frightened that she could not speak. Regaining her composure, she loudly and brusquely asked the four Indians what they wanted. She was told in broken English and by gestures that the Indians wanted Becca.

Martha loudly responded, "She's not for sale. You need to go away now!"

She had made it clear that Becca was not for sale or bartering. The Indians became more vocal, with raised voices and threatening gestures. The Indian in the corral came out and menacingly advanced toward Martha, while another one dismounted and also came toward Martha. The Indian who had been in the corral pulled a knife from beneath his garments and began waving it wildly while advancing on Martha.

Martha stumbled backwards, tripped, and was thrown to the ground while loudly screaming. The Indian quickly jumped down on Martha, straddled her, and covered Martha's mouth.

Just then Maria came from around the corner of the cabin. In her hand was a raised pepper box pistol. The Indian kneeling over Martha saw Maria and watched, but then raised the knife above Martha. As the other dismounted Indian advanced toward Maria, she fired the pistol. But, there were two loud explosions at the same time. The Indian on Martha fell to the side, blood flowing from a bullet wound to the head. The second Indian slumped to the ground with a lead ball in his chest. Witnessing the death of their two accomplices, the other two mounted Indians let out a scream, wheeled their ponies, and raced up the road to the west, where a third shot was heard momentarily.

As Maria helped Martha sit up, she noticed the blood on Martha's coat and dress. Martha struggled to her feet and managed to sit on the porch. She was wan, with almost a yellow tinge to her face, and she shook uncontrollably. Her teeth were chattering, and she wrapped her arms around herself and rocked to-and-fro. William and Peter, with axes in their hands came running around the side of the cabin to see the two women sitting on the porch. At almost the same time, John Barth came running from the road to the cabin with a rifle in his hand. Maria told the men the story, and John confirmed that two Indians had galloped up the road after two shots had rung out. He had taken a shot at them as they rode by, but had missed them. Peter was examining the pepper box pistol that Maria had used.

"How many times did you shoot, Maria," asked Peter.

"Only once," she replied.

Now the group had a mystery. There had been a third shot, and no one knew who fired it. William and Peter went to the side of the cabin and looked at the two fallen Indians. Maria described where Martha had been while on the ground, and where the Indians had been. After looking more closely at the Indians, the shot that killed the Indian kneeling over Martha had come from the southwest, up on the bluff by the old cave. The two men looked at each other, and simultaneously whispered, "Four Toes." The two ponies ridden by the dead Indians were put into the corral with Becca. William and Peter dragged the dead Indians into the woods and buried them where the graves would not be seen by Martha or Maria.

Maria helped Martha into the cabin and took her to the back, where she helped Martha remove her clothing. As she got to the undergarments, the evidence became clear.

Martha whispered, "I lost the baby, didn't I."

"Yes," replied Maria, "I'm so sorry, Martha."

Martha then told her that she was not sure she had been pregnant, so she had not told William. She asked Maria to keep the secret from William and Peter, and Maria agreed. Maria hid the bloody clothing and later burned it in the outdoor burn pit the couples used for trash and garbage. The next day, William told Martha the story of how the second renegade Indian had been killed, telling her that it had to have been Four Toes who had fired the rifle that saved her life. The couple would remember this event forever and began to nurture a new respect for their reluctant friend Four Toes. Maria was keeping a secret of her own, and she felt that this was certainly not the time to share it with Martha.

***

As Martha recuperated in the following weeks, the men had begun another building project. They were hauling large flint stones from the bluffs and riverbank. They had built their own rock sled, and with John Barth's help, they had broken the two reluctant Indian ponies for general riding and pulling the sled. The rocks would form the foundation for a new, small warehouse for the post's surplus merchandise, and for goods waiting for transport south. They had carefully chosen a site that was higher and further from the river in case of spring flooding. While Maria watched the trading post and conducted business, William and Peter also consulted with Dr. Ross as he continued his surveying and plotting of the property within the village. William and Peter purchased more property to be used for future expansion of their business and discreetly purchased other property on the north bluff. While exploring the local area and cutting wood, they had located property on the north bluff that would be ideal for building homes. They each intended to build on those sites, but would keep the secret of this purchase for a later surprise for their wives.

Because several people had been up and down the north bluff with sleds for wood and stones, they had made a path from the road level to the top of the bluff. Dr. Ross incorporated this path as a street on his survey, and other worn paths used by the settlers on both the north and south bluff were also added as streets to the plat. The Baily's had also purchased property a bit further west on high ground, and Clarence had purchased lumber from the trading post. He was in the process of building a cabin with a woodworking shop attached. This would be Clarence's start of a small factory for making furniture, which was certainly in demand by the settlers. Peter was recording the property transactions and was holding the money from all the land purchases. He was worried about the security for the cash and important documents. He and William resolved this issue by designing a secret, floor trap door in the warehouse for the money, and for the proceeds from the trading post, keeping its existence to themselves. Peter casually remarked to William that a bank would soon be needed in the village.

During the same winter, Dr. Ross saw the need to begin a church for the village. He corresponded with the Methodist Conference in Illinois, and a representative was sent to Burlington to help Dr. Ross start a new Methodist Church. The fledgling church and its members began meeting for services in Dr. Ross's cabin. Because there was no Jewish church in town, the Stroud's and Roush's privately practiced their religion, but struggled with questions of their faith. They had heard that the small Jewish contingent in Keokuk had disbanded and moved farther north to Dubuque, which was too far away for the couples to travel for religious services. As a result, the couples would periodically join Dr. Ross's group to gain a perspective of the Christian faith, and they were made welcome each time they attended. But because of their early religious training in the Jewish faith, they could not yet bring themselves to truly change religions on a permanent basis.

In the beginning months of 1834, winter extended its icy talons on the village, and trade at the post dwindled to the occasional fur traders. William and Peter, with help from John Barth, took advantage of the slow time to build a three-sided shelter for the horses and continued work on the warehouse. The Quinn brothers also decided to move further from the riverfront. They tore down their small shanty and moved higher up the road. The Barth's, too, were enlarging their shanty and making it more sturdy and permanent. The wagon settlers camp had grown in late fall and early winter, and many of those people were purchasing property with the intent to stay and build. Ever so slowly, the number of permanent settlers in Burlington was growing.

The mysterious Thomas Vogler was seen only occasionally as he rode his horse while leading two pack horses into town. In the intervals when Vogler was in town, he would open the door of his shack to sell his home-made whisky. He had few retail clients and no friends in the community, because of his antagonistic attitude. Strangely, he was never seen leaving town.

***

In January of 1834, the village was surprised to see a small group of eight mounted U.S. soldiers ride slowly into town. The Army, at that time, was stationed at Fort Madison and patrolled the Black Hawk Purchase to maintain peace with the Indians and for the security of the settlers. The Black Hawk Purchase, sometimes known as Scott's Purchase, was comprised of six million acres on the west side of the Mississippi, from the northern boundary of Missouri to the upper Iowa River. General Winfield Scott had represented the United States government when the land was purchased from the Sauk, Fox, and Ho-Chunk tribes. The sheer magnitude of the area made it very difficult for the Army to oversee.

The small group of soldiers was led by a captain and a sergeant, and they dismounted at the trading post. The curious villagers gathered around the men in uniform.

The captain introduced himself. "My name is Captain Deke Monroe," he said. "We have been sent here under orders for two purposes. First, we are looking for some Indians. We understand that some renegade Potawatomi braves have been seen in this area. They have been scaring and robbing settlers, and they have also injured some folks."

Captain Monroe watched the faces of the Burlington settlers as he continued.

"The renegades were old allies of Black Hawk during the war, but apparently stayed behind when the Indians were moved west. We need to find them and push them west to the reservation." The captain continued. "We also heard a rumor that there was still a Sauk brave living somewhere in these parts, and we need to find him too."

The small group of villagers then told Captain Monroe about the incident of the four braves coming into the village, attempting to steal a horse, and almost killing Martha Roush. They described the incident in some detail and described the dress of the Indians.

Captain Monroe nodded his head and said, "I can't be positive, but from your description, I would venture a guess that those Indians are part of the renegade Potawatomis."

Captain Monroe was then shown the graves of the Indians who had been killed and was told that the remaining two braves had gone west after the incident.

The captain looked at Maria and said, "And you shot both those Indians?"

Maria looked down and stammered.

William quickly looked at her, and then the captain, and lied, saying, "She sure did. She got both of them with a pistol. It's a lucky thing she had that pistol."

The rest of the villagers knew the true story, but they also knew that Four Toes had saved Martha's life. They nodded their heads in assent and kept quiet.

"OK," said the captain. "We'll move west looking for the rest of that band." But he was not finished. "Our second reason for stopping by is that we are also looking for a man who is rumored to be selling liquor to the Indians up west on the Des Moines River. We don't know much about him except he sneaks into the Indian camp at night with a couple pack horses loaded with home-made whisky, which is against the law. The Indians then all get crazy and ride around trying to burn settlers' cabins. That's got to be stopped."

The captain paused and put his finger in his mouth and fished out a plug of tobacco, which he threw a few feet away. Wiping his hand on his britches, he continued.

"We aim to catch him and toss him in jail back at the Fort. Have you seen anybody like that around here?"

The villagers were in a real quandary. They all knew that the captain's story sounded familiar. But they also had a healthy respect for Thomas Vogler. He was an unpredictable, short-tempered man, and they did not want to cross him.

William finally spoke up and said, "We'll keep our eyes open for this character, Captain."

After the troop watered their horses and purchased a few supplies from the post, they headed west out of town.

The villagers had waited on the porch of the trading post until the cavalry troop was gone. They knew that they had not exactly been truthful with the Army and were all concerned of any possible consequences. Everyone began talking at once.

As the heated discussion calmed, Peter spoke up. "Folks, we must be united in our course of action for our little village. From what I hear among you, I believe that we are together in this. We owe a lot to Four Toes for saving Martha's life, and he has helped us in many other ways. I don't believe we should give him up to the Army. But our bigger problem is Vogler. I think you would agree that we don't want his kind in our town. Do you all agree with me on this?"

The group mumbled and nodded its assent. After a great deal more discussion, a village committee was formed from volunteers. The committee would meet regularly and begin to manage the affairs of the little village. It would also confidentially take up the matter of Thomas Vogler.

Later in the day, Martha completed some baking and told William to take a loaf of bread and a can of peaches and place them at the entrance to Four Toes cave. William did as he was instructed and trudged to the mouth of Four Toes' cave, where he placed the gifts.

***

The spring of 1834 slowly and methodically pushed green into the dour gray fields and trees. The rolling river rose as the northern snow fields and ice succumbed to the warmth. Soon the river traffic would increase, and the little mercantile company would be busy again. Predictably, spring also brought a change to the normally docile Indian ponies. The Indian stallion continually pestered the Indian mare, even though she was not yet in season. Becca, of course, was too young to breed. Fearful that Becca would be injured, Martha moved her into her own, new corral, out of sight of the stallion. The DeGroot's and Baily's had three heavier, draft-type mares that came into season, and the stallion was moved to a corral with them. It was hoped that the number of horses suitable for wagon and farm duty could be increased. The stallion was moved back to the corral holding the Indian mare, as the mare came into season. In the chicken enclosures, the roosters strutted around all the hens, acting as if they owned the place. Sparring matches between the roosters went on throughout each day, while the unconcerned hens ignored the raucous roosters and continued scratching the ground in their never-ending search for bugs and tender grass shoots. As if in response to the springtime cycle of life, a smiling Maria finally broke the news to Peter, William, and Martha that she was expecting, which was certainly a cause for celebration for the couples. Spring had, indeed, descended upon the little village.

As the springtime warming progressed, the first river boat paddle-wheeler calling on the trading post arrived. It was piloted by Captain Mike O'Connor. The couples were overjoyed to see their old friend after his winter absence. His boat was loaded with goods to sell, and he would be buying all the hides stored in the warehouse for sale down river.

While Mike unloaded lumber and supplies, he marveled at the progress the village was making. The number of homes had increased, and other small business ventures were appearing. Captain Mike stayed for two days, and during that time he walked the length and breadth of the little village, meeting all its inhabitants, including Dr. Ross. In addition, he spent several hours alone with the Doctor, but told no one of his conversation. When the time came to depart, Captain Mike eased his boat away from the riverbank and turned north to continue his trade run.

The population of settlers in the Black Hawk Purchase land area continued to grow in 1834. Because of this, the land included in the Black Hawk Purchase was incorporated into the Michigan Territory. Burlington was now officially a part of the Michigan Territory.

***

In the late spring of 1834, the wagon traffic increased, and the Quinn's ferry boat business was once again busy nearly every day. As the travelers came across the river on their Westward quest, they stopped and bought and sold at the trading post. The couples' business was hugely successful. A larger, more robust dock was built to accommodate the ever-increasing boat traffic, and soon, even the paddle-wheelers could tie up without beaching their boats. The number of permanent Burlington inhabitants continued to grow steadily. There were now several businesses, and plans were already under review by Dr. Ross for building a permanent Methodist church, the very first in the Michigan Territory. Very soon they would need a school for the many children that ran freely throughout the village.

By relative standards of the time, it could be said that the couples were now wealthy. It was at this point that the relationship between William and Peter became strained.

For some time, Peter had seen the need for a bank in the village. Peter approached William one morning and broached a difficult subject.

"William, you are my best and most trusted friend," he said. "I don't wish to strain our friendship and partnership, but I truly believe that we can enlarge our business by starting a bank here in Burlington. Furthermore, with my background, I would like to run the new bank. With all the business we have, it is time to hire one or two people to help out in the business, so this seems like a good time to discuss this with you."

For some time William was silent. On the one hand, he did not want to lose his partner and best friend. He had also seen the need for the bank, but kept putting it out of his mind, because he knew this day would come. Still, he felt like he was being abandoned. On the other hand, Peter was like a brother to him, and he knew if the town was to have a bank, there was no one more qualified to run it.

William slowly turned to face Peter and said, "Peter, I also have a plan of my own I have been considering, and I guess this is a good time to discuss it with you." William continued. "First, I want to get our houses completed up on north hill. Then, I want to abandon the old trading post and cabin and build a much bigger mercantile on higher ground."

He paused and looked at his friend. Seeing no response, he went on.

"Peter, if you can make a financial plan and a timetable for this plan, which incorporates adding a bank into our enterprise, I will support you. You would be the perfect person to run the new bank."

He continued, "I want to make it clear, though, that I will need your help to fill the void for someone to help us run the retail business, and help both of us with the problems of enlarging the joint venture."

Peter was immediately disappointed. It almost sounded like he was being given conditions to meet before he could open the bank, and he did not like the inference.

For two days the men barely spoke to each other. Mealtimes with both couples, which would normally be very vocal with laughter and discussions of many topics, became strained and quiet. Martha and Maria were distraught. They felt sure the rift would heal, but they were concerned that it was taking too long. On the third day, the men confronted each other again.

Peter had given the situation a great deal of thought the past two days. "William, I agree that your plan is sound. I am just impatient. With our population growing, we already have the labor available to build the mercantile, and we can build the bank in the same construction."

Peter continued, "I have devised a plan for the financing of the enterprise. In fact, we can almost pay for the whole project with our savings. And I will not leave you alone in the mercantile until we are ready to open the doors to both the new mercantile and the bank."

With just those few words, William's concerns were eased. He was not being abandoned by his partner and friend. They were simply branching out the business. Their strong friendship and trust in each other would get them through the growing pains of the larger venture.

"Let's go see Dr. Ross," said William. "We need to get the property purchased and recorded." The stress and tension between the two men evaporated. The couples were, once again, at peace.

While their business flourished, the men made their long-held secret announcement to Martha and Maria.

"Ladies, we have an announcement to make, but first we need to take a walk," said William.

The couples set out on foot and climbed the grade up to the top of north hill. Upon reaching the top, they all looked out at the Mississippi churning along far below them to the east. Martha and Maria noticed that the ground in the area had been disturbed, and there were several wooden stakes driven into the ground at various places on the property.

"Come with me Martha," said William, and they walked over to a spot amid some of the wooden stakes. Peter and Maria also walked a distance away in the opposite direction, also within the boundary of other wooden stakes. Both men then leaned down and whispered to their wives. The ladies gasped, grabbed their husbands and then ran to meet each other.

"Houses, Maria," squealed Martha. It was several minutes before the two women regained their composure enough to talk calmly and begin discussing all the small details that women so artfully add to the construction of a home.

The two men stood side by side and both mumbled their usual response to new endeavors, "I hope we're doing the right thing!"

Work began on the new higher ground, larger mercantile building, and the new bank, while construction of the two homes on north hill moved forward. In the meantime, the town committee continued to meet every couple of weeks. The committee came to the conclusion that they must begin a city government. All citizens were informed, and an election was held for mayor and two council members, one to represent the north side and another from the south side of the city. Over his objections, William was elected mayor. He argued that he was far too busy, but he was nearly unanimously voted into the office. Although there was no official title yet, Peter was made the treasurer of the little town.

***

In a couple weeks, Captain Mike returned to Burlington from the north and snugged his boat next to the dock. The back-breaking work of off-loading and loading the boat began. After completing the work, Mike brought the couples onto the boat for dinner in his cabin. They ate splendidly, with everyone sitting around the large captain's table in Mike's onboard cabin. Buffalo steaks and boiled potatoes, followed by a blueberry pie which he had purchased the day before at a market in Muscatine, satisfied everyone's hunger. With after-dinner wine, Mike told the group he had an announcement.

He told them, "I have purchased some river front property from Dr. Ross. He has been holding the funds until I returned. I had to tie up some loose ends in my business and complete my circuit to the south, but since I really didn't have any property in New Orleans, I've decided that I can run my boat out of Burlington just as well as New Orleans."

This was wonderful news to the two couples, and the laughing and drinking continued.

Mike then said, "You folks have been like family to me. And the upper river is exploding with traffic and settlements. I think my future is here. Oh, by the way gentlemen, since you are moving the mercantile, I would like to propose that you sell me the trading post cabin and property, and your small warehouse and its land. This will give me enough room on the waterfront to operate my business. The cabin will become my home, and I will need the storage for my business."

William and Peter looked at each other and nodded. They both wondered why Mike needed this much property, but his idea certainly fit in with their plans.

Peter spoke up, "Now Mike, you understand that we need to wait until the new mercantile is done, and we have moved into our own houses. Is that OK with you?"

The agreement was made, and that meant another new resident and business would be coming to Burlington.

***

He was still seen periodically arriving in the early dawn with his empty pack horses. Thomas Vogler would then stay around town only for a few days, selling bottles of home-made whisky out of the front of his ill-kempt shanty, and then he would mysteriously disappear for several more days.

While still nearly dark, on a warm, early summer morning, as John Barth stoked his forge for the day's business, he saw Vogler riding into town from the west. His tired, over-worked pack horses, with their necks parallel to the ground, trudged along behind him. The horses were without cargo. The light was still dim in the early dawn, but John's eyes picked up another shadow. Trying not to be noticed by Vogler, John stood quietly in a shadow and soon made out the shape and color of a young, ebony-skinned African boy walking along behind the third horse. The young man's hands were tied together, and a rope led from his wrists to the pack tree of the horse he followed.

John did not know what to make of it. Nothing stays quiet for very long in a small village, and later in the morning John had the opportunity to mention his observations to his fellow villagers. Word spread to members of the Village Committee as they quietly gathered to talk informally, recognizing that something would need to be done about Mr. Vogler; but what? And who was the captive boy that Vogler had brought into town? The Committee was not really sure they wanted to pursue the answers to these questions. But they were certain that the only safe way to confront Vogler was in a group.

As fate would have it, a few days later brought the arrival of Captain Deke Monroe and his small army patrol. The tired, road-weary soldiers dismounted at the trading post and made a point of finding William and Peter.

"We have not found the rat that has been selling the whisky to the Indians," said Captain Monroe. "But we know who he is. With a little friendly persuasion, one of the Indian trouble makers finally spilled his guts. We know the man's name is Vogler," said Monroe. "And we trailed him to just west of town and then lost the trail in a shale creek. Strange prints in his trail, though. It appeared to be three horses and a man walking. We haven't figured that out yet," said Monroe.

John Barth touched the Captain's arm and asked to speak with him in confidence. The troopers stepped away and began watering and graining their mounts before settling themselves down to eat. The Captain, John Barth, William, and Peter sat on the porch of the cabin.

"Vogler lives here, Captain," said John. "I saw him ride in this morning with his pack horses. He usually takes the horses back into the north woods, but I know he is in his cabin." John continued, "But the strange part of this is that he had a colored boy tied up and following him on foot."

"Hmm, that would explain the footprints," said Monroe. "Do you gentlemen know how much whisky he is making? Have you ever seen him packing it out on those horses of his?"

He was told no to both questions.

"Well, I guess it's time to pay a call on Mr. Vogler. Here's what we're going to do," said Monroe. He then told the men of his plan for confronting Vogler. After the men were in agreement, Captain Monroe called his troop together and spoke very quietly to them. The men then mounted and loped west out of town.

In exactly two hours, Captain Monroe, his sergeant, and one of his troopers quietly walked out of the woods south of the trading post cabin. The troop had ridden in a circle to the south. Captain Monroe and his two accompanying men left their horses with the rest of the patrol, which was hidden in the woods. The three soldiers entered the rear of the cabin and repeated the plan to William, Peter, and John. Martha and Maria then left the cabin and retraced Captain Monroe's path to wait with his patrol in the safety of the woods.

William and John left the cabin and walked to Vogler's shack. They called out to him and rapped on the shack's door. To their surprise, the door was flung open, and Thomas Vogler faced them with a loaded pistol in his hand, and another one tucked into his waistband.

"What do you want," growled Vogler.

The two men were taken aback by the confrontational attitude of Vogler. But William swallowed the lump in his throat and replied, "Mr. Vogler, we just wanted to give you the courtesy of letting you know that we are having an informal town meeting at the trading post and wanted to invite you to sit in. Since you are the only liquor establishment in town, we thought you might want to give us your thoughts on the future direction of Burlington. Would you like to come with us?" asked William.

Vogler looked the three men up and down and smirked. His arrogance was then demonstrated by his response, when he answered, "You're damn right I'll come over there. I've got a few things I want to tell you pompous jackasses. I'll be over at your place in a few minutes," and he slammed the door.

As he closed the door, William had noticed a slight movement behind Vogler, but he could not make out the source.

William and John moved away from Vogler's shack and returned to the trading post. They related their conversation to Captain Monroe and his two troopers, who quickly took their places behind the doors to the rear living rooms. In a few minutes, Vogler entered the cabin, still wearing the pistols.

He immediately groused at the men, "All right, what's so all-fired important?"

William tried to be as calm as possible, and answered him, "Mr. Vogler, we don't want any trouble with you. We just wanted to talk to you about your liquor business. We have had other settlers who have asked about starting a liquor business in town, and we wanted to get your thoughts on how competing merchants can make this work."

Vogler savagely lashed out at them, "There ain't gonna be any competition. The liquor business is mine, and that's the way it's gonna stay. Who are these other folks? I'll make them see the light that they ain't gonna sell liquor in this territory, and that's that."

John then spoke up and said, "Mr. Vogler, you don't sell that much liquor anyhow, and the town's growing. What's the harm in competition?"

Vogler had had enough. He was livid, with his face a deep red purple. He pulled one of the pistols and waved it in front of the three men and said through clenched teeth, "Listen here you prissy little bastards. I've got a great little business here, and I don't need you or anybody else telling me how to run it."

But then his arrogance got the best of him, and he made a mistake and blurted out, "I've got some mighty good Indian friends that like my liquor just fine. And you jackasses better not stick your noses any further into this, or you'll all be dead by morning. Is that clear enough for you?"

Vogler was about to turn to leave, when Captain Monroe and his sergeant came from behind one of the living area doors. The third army man came from behind the other living area door and stood to one side.

"Mind if I stick my nose into it, Vogler," said Monroe, "As a representative of the United States Government, I am arresting you for selling liquor to the Indians. Put down that gun!"

Vogler glared at the Captain, and said, "Go to hell, soldier boy."

In that instant, he pointed the gun and fired at Monroe. The shot went wide, but struck the sergeant at Monroe's side in the upper arm. Vogler then began to draw his second pistol. But before he could free the pistol to fire, Captain Monroe fired his service pistol. At the same time, the other trooper also fired his rifle at Vogler. Mortally wounded, Vogler crumpled and fell, but as he fell his second pistol discharged, with the ball grazing Peter's thigh and lodging into the merchandise shelving. Peter howled and gripped his thigh.

The smoke and the smell of spent gunpowder filled the cabin. With smoke still wafting from the gun barrel, Captain Monroe holstered his gun, walked over and checked the condition of Vogler.

"Good shooting soldier," he said to the trooper with the rifle.

Vogler would not be selling any more liquor to the Indians. He was dead. Monroe then turned his attention to the wounded sergeant and to Peter Stroud. Ripping some material from a cloth bolt he found on a merchandise shelf, the captain tied tight bandages around the men's wounds. Monroe then told the other trooper to bring the rest of the squad and horses out of the woods. Monroe and John Barth then dragged Vogler's body out through the front door, and unceremoniously dumped it in the dirt on the north side of the cabin.

When the troop arrived, accompanied by Martha and Maria, clean dressings and ointments were applied to the wounds of the sergeant and Peter. Maria kept up a steady sobbing as she helped dress Peter's wound.

Captain Monroe, seeing that the wounded were bandaged up, said, "Gentlemen, let's go have us a look at Mr. Vogler's place."

Leaving a couple of troopers to tend the horses, and Maria clucking over Peter and the wounded soldier, the rest of the party walked west to Vogler's shack. Captain Monroe gingerly opened the cabin door and peered inside. As he imagined, the place was in shambles, with trash and debris strewn about the cabin. Leaving the troopers outside, the Captain, William, and John stepped through the door and moved into the cabin. Full liquor bottles were on the floor next to the door. A small, wood-burning cook stove and bed were at the rear of the cabin, and a hand-built table with two chairs was in the center of the room. The men looked around the room but found nothing of value or interest.

But then William heard a small sound which he could not identify. He grabbed Captain Monroe's sleeve and hand motioned for him to be quiet. The men stood for a moment listening and then heard a small scratching sound. It came from under the bed. The men peered under the bed. A small Negro boy stared back at them with fear in his eyes.

Monroe said, "Whoa boy, what are you doing under there? Come out here."

The boy replied, "I can't. I's chained to this bed."

The men looked more closely, and the boy was, indeed, chained to the frame of the bed.

"Oh lordy," said Monroe, and he summoned a trooper.

"Go over to Vogler's body, and go through all his pockets and bring me everything you find."

In a moment the trooper was back and dumped his find in Monroe's hand. Among the articles were two keys. Monroe tried both keys on the locks holding the boy, and one of the keys unlocked the chained lock. The boy rubbed his wrist and looked at the Army Officer.

"What's your name, sonny?" asked Monroe.

"Toby, sir," answered the boy.

"Where'd you come from?" asked Monroe.

"Mastuh Vogler done bought me and brung me here," replied Toby.

Captain Monroe showed the other key to Toby and said, "Toby, what's this other key belong to, do you know?"

Toby replied, "Yassuh, that key belong to the box."

"What box?" asked the captain.

"The box under the bed," said Toby.

The men dragged the heavy, iron-framed bed to the side and examined the floorboards. Sure enough, two of the boards were loose and when they were pried up, there was a rusty metal box underneath the floor. The men took the box into the light of the open door and unlocked the box. The rusty hinges protested as the lid was lifted. Inside were a sheaf of papers, two bags full of coins, and several small gold nuggets.

"Looks like the Indians paid in gold," said Captain Monroe. "But I sure don't know where they got it. There isn't any gold around these parts. I guess they could have gotten it by raiding other tribes."

Monroe then started reading the papers that had been in the box. Among them was a bill of sale made out to Vogler for one Negro slave boy, signed with a signature that meant nothing to any of the men. It had a recent date, but there was no location mentioned. It was a mystery where the sale had taken place.

Monroe asked, "Toby, where did you live before you came here with Mr. Vogler?"

Toby replied, "I don't rightly know, but I heard people say something about Memphis sometimes."

"Figures," said Monroe, "anything in the world can roll up and down that river." Monroe then asked, "How old are you, Toby," to which the boy replied, "I ain't sure, but I think I'm twelve years old."

The Captain continued, "Toby, did you ever help Vogler in the woods?"

"Yassuh," said Toby.

"Take us to where you helped him, would you?" asked the Captain.

The boy led the way and followed well-concealed paths for nearly a mile into the woods to a small clearing littered with corn cobs and debris. Captain Monroe speculated that Vogler had gotten the corn in trade during his dealings with the Indians. To the side was a small corral with Vogler's scrawny horses casually observing the men's arrival. The smoky black still sat in the midst of the mess, with a small fire evident at the base of the contraption. The smoke from the fire curled up and was held within a thick canopy of vine and trees, thereby concealing the still's location. In a few minutes after being summoned, the troop of soldiers joined the men at the still. Following orders from the captain, the still was soon destroyed, leaving only pieces of metal lying about, and a stinky, smoky fire which was slowly dying. Everyone walked back to the road, and Monroe, William, and John walked to the trading post with the box and the young Negro boy. Peter joined them on the porch of the cabin.

"Well gentlemen, my men are burying Vogler over yonder, and we are about ready to leave. I'm sorry, but I have to leave the boy with you folks. Since Vogler is dead, I guess young Toby is now a freedman. If you will give me a paper and pen, I will write a letter to that effect. I figure that Vogler's money should go to the boy, what do you think?"

Everyone mumbled and nodded agreement.

"Now, what do you intend to do with the boy?" asked Monroe.

John Barth had seen the horrible living conditions of the little slave and spoke up. "Captain, I have a place for the boy. Me and my Greta only have one little boy young'n, Paul, and I can use help with my horses and the business," said John. "My stable has a dry hay loft where we can make up a bed for Toby, and give him a decent life, if that's OK with you."

Captain Monroe was pleased at this turn of events, and said, "Barth, that's a fine thing to do. But I will be through here periodically, and if I ever hear you have abused the boy, it won't set kindly with me. Do we understand each other?"

"Yes sir," replied John.

The Captain went on, "Mr. Stroud, since you are the treasurer for this town, I suggest you save and protect this money of Vogler's for Toby, to be given to him when he's of age. Can you do that?"

Peter answered affirmatively. "When the bank is completed, Toby will have his own account for the money," said Peter.

"That's fine," said Monroe. "I guess we'll be on our way. You folks did some fine work here today and helped the Army take care of a bad man. I appreciate it."

Captain Monroe finished the letter and a copy attesting that young Toby was a freedman, and signed both copies. He gave one copy to John Barth and would take the second copy to the fort for their records. In a few moments, Captain Deke Monroe and his little Army troop slowly headed out of town.

***

As summer crept toward the fall of 1834, business in Burlington continued its steady churn with new enterprises, including a small hotel, and the established businesses greatly thriving. The Roush and Stroud homes and the enlarged business sites were taking shape rapidly. With the influx of new residents, there was no shortage of labor. Carpenters, masons, and other laborers worked and consulted daily with William and Peter regarding the homes and the enlarged mercantile and bank, while other construction projects around the town also forged ahead. At times there were as many as fifty craftsmen working on the houses at the same time, and even more laboring on the completion of the new store and bank. William and Peter had set a target date for completion of all of their construction projects by Thanksgiving, when Captain Mike would arrive for the winter in Burlington. In the midst of this prosperity, the little trading post and small warehouse were bursting with merchandise, which, no sooner than it was arranged on the display shelves, was sold.

William and Peter finally recognized that the magnitude of their business enterprises had outstripped the men's abilities to operate them by themselves. They began to hire additional staff for the mercantile, and Peter would do the same for the bank prior to its opening. With their combined expertise, the two men had no trouble training new employees.

***

With a great deal of family fanfare, anxious moments, and help from Greta Barth, a very vocal and healthy James Stroud was born to Maria and Peter on a cool late August evening. While Greta, Martha, and other neighbor women waited on Maria, the men all congregated outdoors around the front porch. As the men cheered the news of baby James, John Barth appeared with a celebratory jug of home brew. After a quick prayer of thanks for the vibrant vocal baby, the jug was passed among the waiting men, and Peter was slapped on the back by his friends so many times that his shoulders ached. But he did not care. Like all first-time fathers, he was in awe of the miracle of a new human life and could not wait to see his son. Inside the cabin, Martha knelt down by her friend and told Maria that she was so happy for her and Peter. Then she told her best friend, "Maria, little James is going to have a play-mate soon. I am also expecting." The two women were ecstatic, crying joyful tears. Greta Barth then asked Martha if she could share the exciting news and was told that it would be all right. Greta moved to the front door of the cabin and told the men the wonderful news of Martha's pregnancy. A second cheer went up from the men, and the jug made another round. The day was surely blessed for the two young couples.

The Indian summer days of bright blue skies, crisp air with cool evenings saw a flurry of activity in the village, with new houses, shops and business, and scores of new residents. The feverish pace of tradesmen and craftsmen resulted in a nearly completed mercantile with a large warehouse, an adjoining bank, and the Roush and Stroud homes ready for move-in. Interior work would continue, but the couples were elated because they could finally move out of the cramped trading post cabin. The houses were next to each other with a stable and corral between the structures where Becca and the livery horses would be safely kept. High on the bluff on 4th Street, the couples had a breath-taking view of the river far below. William and Peter had agreed that the bank and mercantile would open together, with a gala grand opening in the fall.

In the late fall of 1834, as Four Toes tended his duck snares on the riverbank, Captain Mike O'Connor was making his way up the river. Mike shrieked the boat's whistle several times and then cautiously but skillfully landed his boat head-in to the landing. He was not alone. A second boat also moored alongside the paddle wheeler. Mike had acquired a second boat, a slightly smaller packet boat similar to his first boat. Mike then oversaw the secure mooring of the two boats. Heavy hawsers, nearly as big around as a man's fist were dragged from the sides of the larger river boat, up the riverbank. Stout timbers were then sledge-hammered into the riverbank, and the hawsers were then tied to the timbers. Four such lines, two on each side, ensured that the river boat would remain stable. The smaller boat was then tied off to the side of the larger boat. Mike moored the boats in this manner so that the larger, front gangway could be used. Knowing the nature and the weight of his cargo, Mike knew this method of off-loading would prove to be the most advantageous.

A lone passenger, Mr. Cletus Miller, walked up to Mike and shook his hand.

He said, "Thank you Captain O'Connor. It was a pleasant trip. I will be at the hotel. Just come fetch me when you are ready to off-load our cargo."

With that, Mr. Miller walked off the boat and headed for the hotel.

As he came ashore looking for his old friends, Mike walked to the trading post, only to discover that the trading post was nearly empty. He then walked over to the little warehouse, where he found William and Peter, amidst goods stacked up to the ceiling. They were completing the arduous task of moving all of the retail goods by wagon from the little warehouse to the new facility.

Mike was delighted and immediately had his deckhands join him to assist in the moving of the goods to the new mercantile building. Mike could very soon begin altering the trading post and warehouse to better suit his lifestyle and business. As the men toiled and the work proceeded, William, Peter, Martha, and Maria with baby James, all gathered around Mike and peppered him with questions. They wanted to know the latest news that travelled on the continent's main water artery, and a report of what was happening in other parts of the country.

While the group talked, Martha's gaze happened to settle on a small boy seated beneath a tree watching the men work. Martha's curiosity peaked, and she asked, "Do any of you know that little boy over there. I don't believe I have ever seen him before."

The others, except Mike shook their heads. Then Mike burst out laughing.

"Jinks, come over here," he shouted. The little boy obeyed and came up and wrapped his arm around Mike's leg, staring up at the group.

"Jinks is my boy, said Mike. The others looked at him in disbelief.

"There's a bit of a story here, considering I didn't even know I had a son."

He continued, "For several years I've been keeping company with a fine Cajun gal in New Orleans. Her name was Sheila. Oh, we talked many times about getting married, but never could seem to get real serious about it. I hadn't seen her for a while in my travels, but I heard some time back that she had passed away. Something about typhus, or some such thing, common in those damn Louisiana swamps. Anyhow, on my last trip down there, I was visited by Sheila's sister, and she brought Jinks with her. She said she had been keeping Jinks for the past few years. Sheila did not want it known that she had a son, and that I was the father. So it was a secret that had been kept by the sisters. Well, Jinks' aunt showed up and told me the whole story. She said she and her man didn't have the means to keep the boy any longer. I told her not to fret. I would take the boy. And well, here's my boy Jinks," said Mike, as he laughed again and tousled the boy's hair. The two women began oohing and aahing over the curly-haired little boy, and giggled as they asked Mike how Jinks got his name.

Mike explained, "Sheila used to get so mad at me when we would fight, and she always told me her life was jinxed because she had taken up with me. Well, she was probably right, and because she had the boy while not exactly in a proper state of matrimony, she named him Jinks, even though she wasn't sure how to spell the word jinx."

Mike looked down at the little boy, and then looked at the couples and said as he grinned, "Ain't he somethin?"

Even though he had been an absentee father, it was plain to see that Mike was taken by the small boy. The feelings appeared to be mutual as Jinks continued hugging Mike's leg while studying the other adults.

"I reckon he's about five years old," said Mike.

***

It took nearly two full days to move the mountain of merchandise from the small riverfront warehouse to the new mercantile. Part of the shipment stayed in the warehouse for Mike's business, and the other supplies had to be transported to the mercantile. Horse drawn wagons shuttled the merchandise to the new store, where the men then had to off-load the wagons by hand. At the end of the second day, the men were exhausted, but there was only one item still to be off loaded.

"OK boys, we'll tackle that job tomorrow," said Mike.

The next morning, all the men gathered at the river boat. John Barth now joined them. He drove a two hitch team of very large draft horses close to the river boat. The horses were pulling a very large and sturdy, flat-bed wagon. John left the horses in their collars and hitch gear, but unhitched them from the wagon. He then staked the docile animals where they could reach some grass. Finally, he put blocks under the edges of the wagon wheels to keep the wagon from rolling.

A short, wiry man dressed in a suit had walked down to the landing and watched as John Barth worked with the horses. He and John and the other men walked up the gangway onto the boat to join Mike. Onboard, they all looked over the main deck hatch into the cargo hold below. Crated and braced into the hold of the paddle wheeler was a very large, walk-in bank vault. Peter had ordered the vault from a St. Louis distributor. The distributor had given Peter the name of Mr. Linus Yale, Jr. Mr. Yale was a renowned locksmith and inventor. Peter had telegraphed Mr. Yale regarding the vault's purchase. That message was followed by a number of wire dispatches going back and forth between the two men. Subsequently, Mr. Yale's brand new prototype vault, with a newly patented combination lock, was shipped to St. Louis, and then on to Burlington on Mike's river boat for use in Peter Stroud's Burlington bank.

"Gents, this here is Mr. Cletus Miller. He is from the Yale Company, the outfit that made that safe you see in the hold. He is here to advise us on how best to move it," said Mike. Mike could barely hold back a smile. Mr. Miller shook hands all around.

The incredulous working men were sure that this little fellow would certainly be of no help in the task ahead and would probably just get in the way. But Mr. Miller was full of surprises. He removed his felt homburg, whisked off his suit jacket, and carefully laid them to the side where they would be out of the way. He then rolled up his sleeves. To the astonished surprise of the men standing near him, Mr. Miller grabbed a sheaved rope dangling from a block hanging from an overhead spar, swung over the side of the hatch, and quickly lowered himself hand over hand on the rope into the hold to stand next to the safe. Mike was probably the most surprised. He had figured Miller for a little dandy who would contribute nothing to the problem of moving the heavy piece of cargo.

"Well, I'll be damned," mumbled Mike.

Mr. Miller looked up at the men above. "C'mon down, gentlemen. Let's get this vault to the bank," he said.

The men scrambled down ladders to the hold. They stayed by Mr. Miller's side as he pointed out the manufacturer's specific lifting points and explained how the cargo rigging should be attached. As he talked, Mike sent the deckhands scrambling for the required cargo block and tackle to be fastened to the boat's main boom and then attached to the lifting point ropes. After ropes were attached to all of the lifting points, he instructed the men to join the ropes at the top of the safe. The main boom block and tackle, with ropes running through a multitude of sheaves, was then lowered through the main hatch. A large steel hook on the lower pulley was then slid under the ropes that were joined on top of the safe. Mr. Miller said they were almost ready.

Mike had gone to the main deck and was watching John Barth coax his draft team to back up and stand on the front gangway of the boat. When the team was finally in position and standing quietly, the main boom hawser was fastened to the team's harness. The horses were moved forward only enough to take up the slack in the lifting lines.

Down in the hold, Mr. Miller then gave the order to begin removing the wooden braces and crating from around the vault. Hammers and axes flew as the framing was removed. After a short time, the safe stood unsupported on the cargo deck. It was ready to be lifted.

"Everybody out of the hold!" shouted Mike.

The men scrambled up the ladders and stood to the side. Mike began giving orders to John and the team of draft horses. The horses strained forward and took a few steps. John held them in this position while Mr. Miller looked down at the safe and gave a thumbs-up sign. The two beasts began moving slowly forward. Every rope, every pulley, and even the main boom creaked and groaned under the load. Everyone observing feared that a broken rope or pulley could result in a catastrophe. By contrast, Mr. Miller was not the least fearful. It was apparent that he had experience in delivering his company's safes.

Sure enough, the safe soon reached the proper height. The main boom with the safe attached was swung out over the front of the boat so that the safe was directly over the flat-bed wagon. When Mike gave the signal, John Barth began slowly backing the team of horses. The safe dropped ever so gently onto the wagon just over the back axle.

The men all gave a cheer. But almost immediately, they began wondering how they would get the safe into the bank building, which was still under construction. But Mr. Miller and John Barth already had a plan.

Two of the men scrambled onto the wagon to remove the block and tackle from the top of the safe. The deckhands then scrambled onto the main boom of the boat with wrenches and other tools. In a flurry of activity, they soon had all of the pulleys removed from the boom, and the large hawser with the block and tackle was then placed on the wagon. The lumber that had been used to pack the safe was quickly brought up from the hold of the boat and loaded onto the wagon.

The team of horses was again hitched to the wagon and all of the men scrambled onto the wagon. Very slowly, the horses made their way down the street and stopped in front of John's blacksmith shop. With John's direction, a strange contraption with three long timbers for legs was loaded onto the wagon, followed by many straight, large diameter poles. The men returned to the wagon and the group slowly moved to the location of the new bank. John backed the wagon to be near the gaping opening in the front of the building where a future door and window would be located.

The men scrambled off the wagon and pulled the contraption with three legs off the wagon. John explained that the device was called a gantry. The three long legs of the gantry were joined at one end with heavy steel straps and bolts. The men set the gantry up with two legs on one side of the wagon, and the third leg on the other side of the wagon. With John's direction, the large block and tackle taken from the river boat was now fastened at the top of the gantry and the large steel hook once again was attached to the ropes which crossed over the top of the safe.

While the gantry was placed, John once again unhitched the team from the wagon and brought them to the side of the wagon. The hawser from the block and tackle was then fastened to the horse team's hitch.

With suggestions from Mr. Miller, John slowly moved the horses ahead bringing the safe up from the deck of the wagon. The rest of the men then pushed the wagon out of the way and began bringing the large supply of poles.

Meanwhile, two men were making a sturdy platform out of the packing timbers. The platform would soon become the base on which the safe would rest. The poles were placed on the ground under the swaying safe. When the right number of poles was on the ground, the platform was placed on the poles. The horses were directed to slowly back up until the safe rested on the platform, which was resting on the poles. The poles would now serve as rollers, and the block and tackle was removed from the top of the safe.

The real muscle work for the men now began. Every man had a stout timber that was wedged against the safe and the rollers. By sheer, back-breaking work, the men rolled the poles forward with the safe riding atop the platform and rollers. As the rollers were passed over by the platform, the back rollers were moved to the front of the path of the safe as it moved slowly forward. Hours of work finally resulted in the safe sitting in its place at the back wall of the bank. After the work had been completed and all of the materials loaded on John Barth's wagon, Peter went among the men handing out cash and thanking them for their effort. From under the seat of the wagon, John pulled out a jug of his home-brew, and it was passed from man to man. The bank now had its new, combination lock, safe.

**

The gala grand opening of the much larger mercantile and the bank was held about two weeks later. To the delight of the entire village, free sausage, beans, biscuits, and beer were distributed. To Peter's surprise, nearly half the population of the village signed the necessary documents to open new individual bank accounts. Nearly everyone wanted to go into the bank and marvel at the large, shiny, black, walk-in vault where the bank's funds would be safely stored. To hard working, common people, this aspect of the bank was extremely important. Peter happily pointed out the safety features of the vault, including the new combination lock. He assured everyone that this was the latest design in monetary security. He also showed them the rows of deposit boxes that were available to the public for a modest fee. This was certainly a far cry from the little hiding place cache in the old warehouse that he and William had constructed in secret some time back. The city funds, as well as many business and individual funds were now safely ensconced in the new repository, aptly named the "Flint Hills Bank."

Depending upon one's point of view, the highlight of the day occurred shortly after the majority of depositors had completed their transactions, and a feeling of well-being had spread throughout the crowd attending the festivities. From a path southwest of the gathering, a familiar figure emerged from the woods. Wearing a red plaid flannel shirt with a strange pouch hanging from his neck, Four Toes approached the bank as the crowd parted to let him through. But the real surprise was the woman and small boy dressed in Indian attire, who were accompanying him. No one had ever seen them, nor did anyone know who they were.

Four Toes approached Peter and said, "I have money to put in your bank."

The strange pouch around his neck was actually a raccoon skin from the head of a coon. It looked like the head of the animal had been skinned, and made into a pouch, with the mouth being the opening of the pouch, and the neck and chest sewn shut to create the purse. The buzz in the crowd was very audible, with ladies pointing at the three Indians.

Four toes opened the pouch and showed Peter. Peter's mouth dropped open, and he asked Four Toes to come inside the bank with him. The woman and boy followed. The door of the bank remained open and quickly filled with gawkers watching the business being conducted within the bank. But Peter had taken Four Toes into his office and closed the door. After carefully opening the small pouch, Four Toes turned the pouch upside down on Peter's desk. When the pouch was emptied, there were nearly one hundred solid gold coins on the desk. Peter was at a loss for words. He carefully examined the coins. They appeared to have writing on them, which Peter thought might be French.

Finally, Peter asked, "Do you want to keep them in our bank?"

Four Toes responded affirmatively. Peter then helped Four Toes complete the necessary paperwork to rent a safe deposit box, and then walked the three Indians into the vault and placed the coins into Four Toes' new deposit box. As he handed Four Toes a key to the box, Four Toes examined the key, showing his pleasure with a smile.

At the conclusion of the deposit, Peter asked Four Toes where he had acquired the money. Four Toes did not answer and turned to leave. Peter then asked him about the woman and boy.

"Who are your friends, Four Toes?" asked Peter.

Four Toes responded, "Not friends, wife and son. They are called New Rain, and Kon."

Peter was dumbfounded. No one had known that Four Toes had a wife or son. After Peter regained his composure, he told Four Toes that he was pleased that the Indian brave had chosen to bring his wife and son to the celebration.

Peter was still curious though, so he asked Four Toes how Kon had gotten his name. Four Toes looked directly into Peter's eyes and held the gaze for several seconds. He was mentally weighing whether to answer Peter's question. Most importantly, he was measuring Peter, deciding just how much he could trust Peter. When he finally made the decision, he began telling Peter the story about his participation in the Black Hawk War in 1825. As a young brave, he had been fighting along with his Sauk band, and other tribes had joined in the fight, including the Potawatomis and members of the Ho-Chunk nation. The women and children followed the battles and stayed in encampments while the warriors fought the army. The camps would follow the battles as they moved up and down the northern frontier, always close to the Mississippi. New Rain was a member of the Ho-Chunk nation. During one battle, Four Toes had been severely wounded and was left for dead. He was later found by other braves and taken to the encampment, where the women would attend to him. One of the women was New Rain. Later, the Army located the encampment, and the soldiers charged into the camp and killed and wounded a large number of the people.

After the killing of the women and children was nearly completed, a young Army lieutenant ordered his attending sergeant, "Sergeant Conn, go over and kill that woman and any other Indian still living."

"Yes sir," Sergeant Conn responded.

New Rain was soon held at gun-point by the seasoned sergeant and assumed she would soon die. But the sergeant motioned to her that he meant her no harm. He then fired his pistol next to her head to make it appear that he had shot her. New Rain immediately understood the actions of the soldier, played her part, and fell to the ground. The sergeant then walked back to his waiting men.

The lieutenant ordered, "Sergeant Conn, form up the men and prepare to move out. Our work here is done."

The soldiers mounted their horses and slowly walked out of the camp. New Rain pretended to be dead, but as she lay on the ground, she repeated the name to herself, Sergeant Conn. She would never forget the name of the man who had spared her life. As she furtively watched the Army leave the camp, she glanced over at Four Toes who was also feigning death.

After hiding for several days, when Four Toes was able to travel, the pair made their way to Flint Hills to live in peace. They had been hiding and living in the cave to the southwest of Flint Hills for several years. When their son was born, he had appropriately been named after the sergeant who had spared New Rain's life, Conn. The name would subsequently be spelled Kon by the Indians.

Peter was astounded that Four Toes had the courage to tell him such an amazing and personal story. He recalled how helpful Four Toes had been when he and the others had been new settlers in this wilderness. Peter now saw Four Toes in a new light. In addition, the Indian was a wealthy bank customer.

Peter and Four Toes were interrupted in their conversation by sounds outside the front of the bank. Members of the crowd outside the bank were now angrily talking among themselves. Remarks such as, "I don't want my money in any bank that has redskin money in it," and "Where did a damn Indian get that kind of money?", and "I'm going to go back in there and get my money!" were heard loudly from the crowd. Peter and Four Toes, New Rain and Kon, all walked outside the bank where Peter addressed the crowd.

"Friends, not all of you may know my friend Four Toes. He has been a friend to us, and this is his wife, New Rain, and their son, Kon. As my friend, his money is welcome in my bank and any of you have the right to keep your money anywhere you like, but I wish you would stay with our little bank and offer your hand in friendship to these fellow citizens of our settlement."

At the end of the speech, several angry people proceeded to step forward to withdraw their funds. Most of the others grumbled and walked away.

When the refreshments were finally gone, the grand opening festivities ended abruptly, and the crowd members dispersed to their homes. Peter, Maria, William and Martha watched as the Sauk brave, Four Toes and his wife and son trudged back through the woods to their stone home, the cave in the woods at the far end of South Hill.

The main street heading west out of town that Dr. Ross had named Division Street on the city plat, now had businesses, a bank, and other ventures, including a hotel and boarding house. There was no indication that the progress of the village of Burlington was complete.

The following day, Peter walked into the assayer's office. He handed one of the coins Four Toes had given him to the assayer, with whom Peter was familiar.

They exchanged pleasantries for a moment, and then Peter said, "I ran across this old coin, and I would like to know what it is and what it is worth."

The assayer palmed the coin and turned it over in his hand. Then he took the coin and weighed it on his scale. Next, he took the coin and dropped two drops of liquid acid on the coin and watched it for a moment. Then he polished the coin and again examined it. And finally, he pulled a hardboard folio from among several on his bookcase and opened it. He leafed through several pages and found what he was looking for.

"Here it is, Peter," said the assayer, as he turned the book so Peter could see it. The page contained a crude drawing with several paragraphs of text. The drawing, although black and white, bore an unmistakable likeness to the coin the assayer held.

"It's called a Louis d'or, and it's a French coin. France has been minting these coins since late in the 1600's. So how did you come across such a coin?" he asked.

Peter lied and said, "It is an old coin that Maria had, and I'm quite sure she got it in some shop in New Orleans before we moved to this area. But she had forgotten all about it until she was looking through some of her mementos the other day. She wanted me to ask you about it."

The assayer then said, "Well, that figures that she got it in New Orleans. There have been several French explorers who explored all the way up the Mississippi. I think one of the more well-known gents was called

La Salle. So probably one of those men used it for payment long ago, and it ended up in a curio shop in New Orleans."

"Sounds reasonable," said Peter. "What do you suppose it is worth?"

The assayer took the coin to a bench behind the counter and performed another test on the coin. Walking back to Peter, he said, "Well, with today's rate for gold, and the purity of this coin, I would say that it is worth about five U.S. dollars. But I have no knowledge of what it might be worth in France. But I guess we don't really care about that anyway."

"Well, thanks for helping me out. I'll give this back to Maria and tell her what you told me. Thanks again," said Peter, and he shook hands with the assayer and turned and walked back to the bank. Four Toes had given the bank nearly a hundred coins, so his deposit was worth nearly five hundred dollars. But the secret was safe with Peter. He smiled and put the coin back into Four Toes' deposit box. But it was still a mystery as to where Four Toes had gotten the coins.

Travelers and visitors came through the town daily. One group arrived in the village in 1835. Lieutenant Colonel Stephen Kearney and his First Regiment, U.S. Dragoons, made a stop in Burlington. They were blazing a trail through Iowa, following the Des Moines River. The Dragoons were a lightly armored cavalry unit that got its name from the short, large bored muskets, called dragons, carried by these units. Authorized by Congress, this regiment blazed roads to be used by settlers in Iowa. They also accompanied and afforded protection to settlers as the settlers moved westward. They built a 200 mile corridor for the settlers to follow. After an overnight stay, the regiment split up, leaving one company in Burlington, while the other dragoons moved on to continue their road building. Mike O'Connor had been asked by Colonel Kearney for permission to allow the remaining regiment to camp near the levee on Mike's property. They were to wait for and accompany a large wagon train of settlers that would be moving to a location near a newly-built fort, called Fort Des Moines. The fort was built at a location known as "The Narrows," which lay between the Des Moines River and the Skunk River.

Mike curiously watched as the soldiers meticulously set up their encampment. The small tents were laid out in order, and a large cooking fire was set up away from the tents. The horses were hobbled in the grassy field, and sentries were posted. Mike's curiosity took hold, and he strolled to the camp. As he passed one of the tents, he noticed a few soldiers standing outside of it. Soon, a young captain emerged from the tent, and seeing Mike, he walked over and shook Mike's hand.

"I understand you are the owner of this property, is that right?" said the officer.

"Yep," said Mike.

"Well thanks for letting us camp here. Hopefully our wagon train will come in tomorrow, and we'll be on our way."

"I was just watching your men as they prepared camp. Looks like a fine bunch of men," said Mike.

The captain stuck out his hand once again. "My name is Boone, Nathan Boone," said the captain.

The men shook hands, and Mike eyed the young officer. "My name is Mike O'Connor. Boone, you say. Say, you wouldn't be any relation to that Kentucky fellow, Daniel, I think is his name."

The captain grinned. "Yes sir. That would be my pa. I'm his youngest son, and he doesn't live in Kentucky any more. Our family now lives in Missouri."

"Well, I'll be," said Mike. "I'm proud to have you boys for the night. Make yourselves at home, and if there is anything I can do for you, just come and find me. So you're waiting on a group to take up to The Narrows?"

"Yes sir. It's a group of Quaker settlers, and our scouts report that they ought to reach the ferries some time tomorrow."

"Well, that's fine. I won't bother you anymore, and good luck to you," said Mike, and he turned and walked away.

It took most of the following day for the entire wagon train to be ferried across the river. Captain Boone and his dragoons then led the wagons west out of town toward The Narrows, an area that would very soon be platted as a town called Oskaloosa.

***

Like all good parents, Four Toes and New Rain worried and fretted over Kon. The boy had been born in the cave where his parents lived, and for all of his six years, Kon had lived in the confines of the cave and the adjacent woods, with just his parents for company. He had learned the ways of his parents and could hunt and fish with his father, but only away from the eyes of the white settlers. In the Indian culture it was not unheard of for rival or marauding tribes to kidnap small children from other tribes and force them to become slaves or full members of the renegade tribe. Four Toes and New Rain were afraid of this happening to their son. They were not yet familiar with the ways and culture of the white settlers and held a belief that the settlers, like rival tribes, could very well take Kon away from them. Four Toes and New Rain also knew that all of their tribal families had been taken away to live on reservations mandated by the white people. They knew that they could also be hunted down and forced to move from the peaceful stone cave, the location that they loved. For these reasons, the small family had kept very much to themselves, not risking exposure to the white settlers. But through his interactions with the former trading post owner, Jacque Laguire, and the subsequent friendly relations he had developed with William and Martha

Roush and Peter and Maria Stroud, Four Toes became better acquainted with the white settlers' customs.

Four Toes was very astute. He had conducted business for several years at the trading post and thoughtfully watched as progress was made in the village. He clung to his beliefs in what was right and wrong and was bringing Kon up to hold the same beliefs. Four Toes would not be subjugated, nor put himself in a position to be duped by the white settlers. But seeing the rapid progress of the village and the cleverness, skills, and sheer numbers of the white people, he became fully aware that in order for his beloved son to survive, Kon must somehow meld into the white settlers' culture. He and New Rain were at a loss as to the best method to make this occur. But sometimes, the nature of small innocent boys takes its own course and charts the later lives of the boys.

Jinks O'Connor had been unknowingly, but aptly named. In short, he was a rascal, but a lovable rascal. With his sparkling brown eyes and curly hair, he could melt a heart, even when his mischief got him in hot water. As a precocious five-year-old, he loved to wander around the village, where everyone knew him, and if he became lost he was soon returned to his father. But his precocious adventurous spirit would again cause the little boy to wander away, exploring a very large world.

One day, Jinks was again on the loose. He had wandered into the woods on the southwest side of the village following a rabbit that he had seen hopping into the woods. Each time he approached the rabbit, the animal moved away from him, farther into the woods. Suddenly, from a tree above, the *scree* sound from a red-tailed hawk was heard, and the rabbit bolted into the underbrush. Jinks followed the rabbit, but by now the rabbit was long gone. Jinks sat down and then began to look around. The briars and brush were now all around him, and he had no idea which way to go. The world was suddenly far too large for a boy of five, and he began to cry. His dismal wailing could not be heard in the village. But it was heard. Following the sound, it was only a few minutes until New Rain and Kon found the little boy. New Rain picked up Jinks and comforted him, slowly retracing her steps to the cave. Jinks quickly dried his tears as he became intrigued with Kon. Here was another little boy, like himself, yet very different. New Rain sat Jinks on the ground and went to find Four Toes who was cleaning some catfish outside, behind the cave. She told Four Toes of her discovery, and as they talked, they did not notice the two little boys wander off.

Kon knew the way to the village because he had accompanied his father many times to go fishing, always skirting the people as they made their way to the river. But Kon saw no reason to avoid people this time, and they made their way out of the woods toward the landing where Mike O'Connor would be. But before they could reach the landing, Mike O'Connor and five frantic local mothers who were helping him search, came running down the street and gathered around the two boys. A great deal of fuss was made over the two boys, while another father emerged from the woods. Four Toes calmly walked over and examined the two boys as he joined Mike and the women. While the neighbors and the Indian continued their conversation, Jinks and Kon wandered off again. As the conversation waned, the adults suddenly looked around for the boys who had wandered off and spied the youngsters sitting in the dirt by the street, throwing dust and dirt clods into the air to watch the breeze take the dirt away in a cloud. They were laughing and having fun being little boys. From that day on, Jinks and Kon were inseparable. They became best friends and could always be seen together. Mike, New Rain, and Four Toes knew the boys were either wandering around the village or up at the cave together. Kon would become assimilated into the white settlers' world.

***

As the winter of 1834 loosened its cold grip on Burlington, the first wedding of the year took place at the Ross cabin. The Illinois Methodist representative officiated at the wedding of Aaron Quinn and Mary Smyth, a daughter of one of the settlers. The young couple's friends all attended, including the Stroud's and Roush's. Knowing the proclivity of some of the attendees to avoid alcohol, the after-ceremony festivities adjourned to Captain Mike's River Boat for a grand party. The calliope was fired up, and the happy whistling tunes spewed forth from the old instrument. Wine was passed among the friends, and the exuberant singing could be heard for hours. It was a fine way to break the winter doldrums.

Unfortunately, the first warm weather also brought to life some unpleasant life forms which had been dormant in the cold weather. Highwaymen, thieves, and other low-life individuals began to make their presence known on the roads to the west. For the first time, the city council began to discuss the need for a dedicated sheriff or constable, but because there had not yet been any significant problems, the idea was discussed and shelved.

In the early afternoon on a dreary gray day in March 1835, two strangers rode slowly into town from the west. They rode tall, strong horses and their garb was that of men who placed appearance very low on their priorities. Both wore beard growth of many days and had slouched well-worn hats on their heads. Their clothing was worn and showed signs of never having been laundered. Their boots were dirty and scarred, and severely needed new heels and soles. They slowly walked their horses down Division Street and cast glancing looks at the homes and businesses as they rode by. Presently, they stopped their horses in front of the bank, slowly dismounted and removed their rifles from their saddle scabbards. There were no customers in the bank as they entered. The only occupants in the bank were Peter Stroud and a teller. Peter looked up as the men entered the bank and did a fast mental analysis of the two strangers.

He did not like what he saw, but said, "Can I help you gentlemen?"

One of the men looked at Peter, and the other walked slowly toward the teller.

The man looking at Peter suddenly leveled his rifle to Peter's mid-section and said, "Yea, you can help us, you can help us clean out that big shiny safe you got back there. Get up and start moving." Peter knew they meant business and slowly made his way to the vault, which was standing open. In the meantime, the other stranger had leveled his rifle on the teller, who was visibly shaking. Peter and the man moved to the vault.

Peter tried to make a plea to the men, "You understand that you want to take the life savings of this town? Please don't do this to us," he said.

"You're making my heart bleed, little banker man. Knock off the crybaby crap and start loading those canvas bags in the vault with the cash," he said, and painfully whacked Peter on the back of his head with the gun barrel.

Peter and the man entered the vault, and Peter filled three canvas bags with cash. The two gunmen lifted the bags and backed toward the front door of the bank. Unseen, Peter reached a pistol that was kept behind the teller's counter. But as he raised it to shoot, a rifle barked and sent a ball into Peter's upper arm, breaking the bone and knocking Peter to the floor. As the two men hurried to their waiting horses, the teller yelled for help and shouted at the men through the front door. A shot rang out from one of the gunmen, but the bullet harmlessly entered the door frame next to the teller. At the sound of the first shot, several of the merchants on the street came out to the street with rifles in their hands.

"They robbed the bank," screamed the teller, as the felonious duo turned their horses to the west.

Several shots rang out as the merchants fired at the pair. To avoid further fire, the felons turned their mounts and burst into the dense woods and disappeared, heading south. The townspeople swarmed the bank, where they found a distraught teller, and Peter Stroud lying wounded on the floor of the bank.

One cantankerous merchant shouted out, "You damn fool; you just let those two bastards take all our money. We ought to string you up."

This misguided citizen was soon calmed down, and Dr. Ross hurriedly entered the bank and began probing Peter's wound.

"You gentlemen there pick up Mr. Stroud and bring him to my cabin. He's going to need some work done on him."

Peter was being lifted up just as Maria rushed through the bank door. Her sobbing and questions were the only things heard for the next several minutes, until Dr. Ross told her that Peter would live, but he needed to get his arm worked on.

Dr. Ross worked on Peter at his cabin. He was able to stop the flow of blood and splint the broken humerus. He then tightly strapped Peter's arm to his torso to keep it immobile.

"Sorry Peter, but you won't be using this arm for quite a while," said the doctor.

The mood in Burlington was somber. The bulk of the citizens had put money in the bank. Many of them had entrusted their life savings to Peter and the fledgling bank, only to see it fly out of town in possession of two ne'er do well, bank-robbing scoundrels. The more adventuresome among them wanted to get a posse formed and go after the two men, but they were not having much luck convincing enough men to mount up and pursue the gun-toting outlaws.

Dusk fell on the sad village with no progress made on forming a posse. Discussions would resume the following day.

***

Unlike the tiny bit of cloth he found on the protruding briar bushes, his deerskin shirt and leggings would leave no trail. He avoided all deadfall, making no noise as he moved through the woods. His buckskin moccasins left no footprints. He stopped every few minutes, crouched, and listened intently. By next day's light, the Sauk warrior would find them. He crawled beneath a fallen log to rest for a couple of hours. For three full days Four Toes had been running, carrying a rifle and pistol, along with a honed hunting knife. He would need some rest for the final push. He pulled another piece of rabbit jerky from his pouch and ravenously ate it. He then laid down and closed his eyes.

After two hours of much needed sleep, Four Toes rose, and once again listened intently. Light was beginning to fade, and he would need to hurry. He knew the direction of the sloppy men who left a trail that a blind man could follow, so he began running again; this time in a long arduous circling path. It would take him to a point that he would meet the two men as they made camp for the night. He labored through the dense woods, being extremely careful not to make any telltale noise. As he stopped to listen once again, he heard them. They were approaching the spot where he lay in hiding. As they passed, one of the men glanced directly at him and still did not see the Indian. The two men on horseback continued on until they located a small clearing beside a nearly dry creek, a perfect place to camp for the night.

They had determined that there was no pursuing posse. The outlaws had let down their guard and leisurely went about the business of making camp, unsaddling their horses, and starting a small fire. As the evening wore on, they decided that one of them would stand watch while the other slept, and then relieve each other later in the night. The Indian watched patiently while one man drifted off to sleep, and the other man propped his rifle up against a tree and mindlessly whittled a stick. After a time, the whittling slowed, and the look-out also nodded in and out of sleep. It only took a few seconds, and with the flash of a knife, the whittling look-out would never whittle again. But the sound of movement from his companion had roused the sleeping man. He groggily looked up to see the Indian lowering his dead companion to the ground. He grabbed the pistol that had been by his side during the night and pointed it at the back of the Indian. The pistol exploded, and the Indian spun around and fell on his back.

The outlaw rose and strode over to the prostrate Four Toes. He kneeled over the body to verify the death of the Indian. But just as he leaned down to look into his victim's face, a knife flashed, cut the femoral artery in the outlaw's leg, continued up the groin, was withdrawn, and then plunged into the chest of the outlaw, just below the sternum and entered the outlaw's heart. The outlaw fell to his side, went into a convulsive tremor and subsequent immobile stupor, and quickly bled to death.

Four Toes was injured badly, but not mortally. The bullet had been fired, but had apparently been seated on a charge that had not been maximized with powder. The trajectory was at an angle, and the ball had hit him on the left shoulder blade. From there it ricocheted through the upper shoulder muscle, exiting at the front of the upper shoulder. The shoulder blade was chipped, but not broken, and no vital blood vessels were severed. Four Toes could very painfully still move his left arm. In the dark, he staggered to the feebly flowing creek and washed the wound as best he could. He covered and stuffed the wound with cloth ripped from one of the outlaw's frayed shirts, and exhausted, he lay down to sleep until first light.

As the first sunlight filtered through the canopy of the woods and into the clearing, the wan, aching Indian once again moved to the creek and removed the dressing and washed the wound. He then began searching the surrounding vegetation. Finding what he needed, he ground the various leaves with water to make a paste, which he then applied liberally to the shoulder wound. He then tied more pieces of the outlaws' clothing together to make a shoulder wrap. The effort was exhausting, and he sat down to rest. After retrieving some food from the outlaws' belongings, he again rested while he ate the hard biscuits he had found. While he gnawed the biscuits, he debated whether to leave the men in the woods or take them back. After a brief rest, it took every bit of strength he could muster to lift and tie the two men to the back of one of the horses. Exhausted, Four Toes sat on the ground next to the horses, waiting patiently for the pain to subside. The whole left side of his body was on fire with pain. After a time, audibly groaning from the pain, he slowly saddled and mounted the other beast and slowly headed north.

Two days later, William Roush walked toward the bank to open the door for business. Peter was still recuperating and would need several more days before he could resume his banking duties. The brave teller who had yelled out the alarm during the robbery was coming toward the bank from the opposite direction. Almost simultaneously, both the teller and William noticed the two horses resting with their heads down in front of the bank. Each horse had a load. As they neared, they saw the two men lying across the back of one horse, and a rider in the saddle, but bent over the neck of the second horse. Approaching nearer, they could see that the rider was Four Toes, and the bank's canvas bags were tied to the saddle behind him. William shouted an alarm and cry for help, and other citizens including Dr. Ross rushed to the bank. Four Toes was lifted from the horse and taken to Dr. Ross's cabin, where bone chips and a bullet fragment were removed from his wound. Dr. Ross carefully installed a considerable number of stitches and dressed the wound. Four Toes was extremely dehydrated and had lost a fair amount of blood, but Dr. Ross was amazed by the good condition of the wound with the herbal paste dressing. Four Toes, the hero of the village, would be up and able to return home in just a couple days, where he could recover comfortably from his wounds. Nothing was ever again said in the village about mixing an Indian's money in the bank with other citizen's money. Following his recovery, Four Toes was offered a job with many businesses in Burlington, but a free spirit is hard to tame, and the Sauk brave turned them all down to remain with his wife and son in their cave refuge.

Chapter Four

Becoming a City
1835-1843

Later in the spring, healthy baby Edna Roush was born to a jubilant William and Martha Roush. They had been waiting for quite some time for a child, and their prayers were answered. Baby Edna was baptized by Dr. Ross, and it was at this point that William and Martha began regular attendance at the Methodist Church. Not to be outdone, Becca, who had been bred to one of the Barth studs, had her first foal, another roan filly just like her dam. Martha could not contain her joy of having little Edna, and now her sweet mare Becca had also become a mother. Springtime was truly a season full of wonder.

The warmer days also brought a resurgence of westward traffic moving northwest toward Mount Pleasant and Oskaloosa. The rich black soil of Iowa was luring hundreds of German, Dutch, and Scandinavian farm families. The back-breaking labor of plowing through the thick, native prairie-grass vegetation would yield soil that could grow almost any crop, and the grassland was perfect for cattle and hogs. But many of the immigrants were also moving toward the Oskaloosa area to work in the newly created coal mines. The abundance of coal opened up a three county area with coal production that would be transported to Burlington and other river communities, to be sold as fuel for the multitude of river boats plying the Mississippi. Quaker farmers and craftsmen moving west from their initial settlements in Pennsylvania were passing through the village to take advantage of the fertile farmland west of the Mississippi. The Quakers had already established a small community called Salem, which was south of Mount Pleasant. Burlington residents overheard the conversations of other Quakers as they discussed their dreams of farms and an eventual Quaker college.

The ensuing years brought more change to the bustling little village of Burlington. With the voracious need for fuel and building material, the timber and lumber business exploded. Logging in the far northern regions of the river to meet this demand grew more innovative. Entrepreneurs, using lashed together rafts of logs and river barges began the transport of logs down the Mississippi to the towns desperate for building materials and fuel for the hungry river craft boilers. The market, thus, opened a new business in Burlington. The logging, timber, and lumber need saw John Barth and Aaron Quinn partner in business, purchasing the logs from the north and opening a new sawmill for processing the logs into building lumber. The lumber was used locally or shipped west to settlers in the Iowa plains, where forests were scarce. In addition to the lumber business, the coal business in the Oskaloosa area grew rapidly to meet the demand for fuel. Captain Mike O'Connor foresaw the need for fuel on the river and built up the business of freighting lumber from the Barth and Quinn sawmill to the western settlements, returning to Burlington with his freight wagons filled with coal purchased in the Oskaloosa mining camps. Mike transformed the river front area that he had purchased into a freight company with huge mounds of coal, waiting for sale to the river steam ships. His property also held many freight wagons, and corrals of draft animals to pull the many wagons. Mike had come to the conclusion that a man with a son needed a proper home, so he purchased property and began construction of a new home on the north hill, not far from the Roushes and Strouds.

***

Mike began to hear rumors from his drivers who called on the little Quaker village of Salem, south of Mt. Pleasant. They told him a story of other wagon drivers passing through and stopping at Salem. But their wagons always seemed to be empty, and as Mike's drivers and the other drivers spoke to each other in passing, those wagon drivers always seemed to mysteriously reveal nothing about their business. On occasion, Mike's drivers also had noticed Negroes walking quickly in the streets of Salem, only to disappear into homes in Salem. This all seemed mysterious to Mike, but it gave him no cause to dwell on the matter.

Predictably, Burlington's population continued to rise with many young children seen scurrying about the village. In 1836, Peter and Maria Stroud also added a new son, Johann, to their family.

***

When a Federal Territory reached a prescribed population, the territory could apply for statehood. During the year of 1836, Michigan gained its statehood, and the entire Black Hawk Purchase land, which included Burlington, was subsequently made a part of the Wisconsin Territory. The capitol of the territory was Belmont, Wisconsin, certainly a considerable distance from Burlington. The Federal Government was of no particular concern to the residents of Burlington. They were much more concerned with their own daily lives, the well-being of their neighbors, and their fledgling businesses operating in the town. However, Territorial Governors were appointed by the President and changed with changes in administrations. Soon, government became a factor in Burlington.

In 1837, Wisconsin gained statehood, and the Iowa Territory was formed, with Burlington named the territory's capitol. As a result, the Iowa Territorial Government needed a place to meet in Burlington. Dr. Ross had spearheaded the drive for a new Methodist Church. He had purchased the land for the church, and it was under construction on North Third Street. The church would be known locally as "Old Zion." As construction progressed into 1838, the Territorial Government selected Old Zion as its meeting place, and the church was able to collect rent from the governing body for its use of the church. William Roush and Peter Stroud had both offered their services, and both served on the governing body.

With its new Territorial status, Iowa now, more than ever, needed some inland transportation routes. The Iowa Territory's first governor, Robert Lucas, approved the establishment and construction of Iowa's first official road, which would run from Keokuk to Iowa City. Later in 1838, Governor Lucas approved a second road, designated as a Military Highway, to run from Iowa City to Dubuque. The governor had also stipulated that the road must run through as many county seats as possible when it was built. To achieve that goal, a contractor was hired to mark the path of the road. Mr. Lyman Dillon, a Dubuque merchant, hitched up a team of five oxen to a heavy plow, and plowed a furrow from Dubuque to Iowa City passing through as many county seats as possible. The furrow would be the guide for the road builders to follow, and was called "Dillon's Furrow."

In the same year, Captain Mike, with his keen business sense, had the foresight to see the need for passenger land transportation. Not only that, but he also acquired the U.S. Mail contract to deliver mail on the same wagons. With clever modification to some freight wagons, he was able to equip them with awning covers and seats, and started the first stagecoach service in Iowa. Mike ran his passenger service from Burlington, south through Ft. Madison and Montrose to St. Francesville, Missouri. This forty-five-mile trip took eighteen hours. Passengers suffered the unsprung, jolting wagon rides and were asked to bring a lumber board with them. The boards were used by the male passengers to help pry the wagons out of mud when the wheels bogged down. Small towns along the route benefitted from the passing passenger wagons as they provided food and overnight lodging to the passengers. Stagecoach travel was not ideal. Rains, snow, mud, poor roads, and bandits all added to the discomfort of the passengers.

An important item discussed by the new Territorial Legislature was the need for defense of the territory. The Union army was spread quite thin in its duties to cover the huge territories. As a result, the legislature approved the formation of an Iowa militia, but the appointments to the militia were actually not made until 1839. These appointments were quite haphazard, with members of a community nominating an individual to lead their local militia. The name was then sent to the legislature, which then conferred the rank of Captain, Major, or Colonel on the nominee. The formation of the rest of the militia unit was just as haphazard. Men would form a group, give the group a name, and send that information to the legislature, which rubber stamped the recommendation.

No sooner had the militia been formed in 1839 than it was called upon to go to war against Missouri. Known as "the Honey War," the dispute centered on a disagreement between the two territories as to the exact location of the southern border of the Iowa Territory. Those southern counties had an abundance of honeybee hives, apparently a commodity worth fighting for. The Iowa militia appeared at the border with weapons such as blunderbusses, flintlocks, and old ancestral swords that had probably adorned someone's wall. One man even carried a sausage stuffer for a weapon, while another carried a six-foot sheet iron sword. 1200 men in various semblances of uniforms showed up at the border. Luckily, cooler heads on both sides prevailed, and the affected legislatures agreed to defer the issue until the U.S. Congress could survey and set the border correctly. Even then, the issue was finally decided by the Supreme Court.

With Burlington being the capital of the territory, the Catholic Diocese in Dubuque saw the need to bring Catholicism to Burlington. Father Samuel Mazzuchelli was dispatched from Dubuque to Burlington to form a nucleus for a new Catholic church. Burlington's first mass was held in the home of German immigrants, the Thollmans. But it was not long before the actual construction of a church was begun, and in 1840 St. Paul's Catholic Church was completed except for a proper bell and bell tower. Father Mazzuchelli would happily take delivery of the new bell which had been cast in Pittsburgh, Pennsylvania, and delivered to Burlington in 1842 by the riverboat, *Iowa*. After a few days, the bell pealed from the steeple at St. Paul's, beckoning worshippers to the church. The first church bell in the Iowa Territory sounded the call to Sunday worship in Burlington.

Burlington's designation as capitol of the Iowa Territory would not last long. President William Henry Harrison was elected President of the United States in 1840, and he appointed a new governor. For political reasons, the capitol was moved to Iowa City. In the same year, William and Martha Roush welcomed their new son, Jacob, to the family.

***

Like all families, Martha and William believed that Jacob was a very special baby. He had black hair and brown eyes that from birth seemed to follow the family activities. He was a quiet baby, and Martha was firmly convinced that little Jacob was destined for greatness. Big sister Edna, who was now five, pestered Martha constantly, wanting to hold baby Jacob. She thought he was ever so much more fun than her dolls, except when it came time to change his diapers. She watched adoringly as Martha nursed and cared for little Jacob. She couldn't wait until he was old enough to play outdoors with the other children as they explored the village and played hide-and-go-seek in the woods. Edna had many friends. There were all sorts of adventures that the playmates enjoyed. James ("Jimmy") Stroud, Johaan Stroud, Claire Bailey, Edna, and little Alice Barth could usually be seen together, closely watched by one of the mothers of the children. The older children, Kon, Jinks O'Connor, and Paul Barth were usually close-by, playing ball or exploring. The village of Burlington was a grand place for children to grow up in 1840.

But a settlers' life was demanding and difficult. Death from disease, childbirth, and the elements was common. As a result, the community saw death on a regular basis. A young settler from Ohio named Isaac Newton Prugh was an accomplished wood crafter and furniture maker, and was well regarded by his neighbors. On many occasions he had been asked to construct wooden coffins for use in the burial of fellow settlers. Before long, he became so busy in this endeavor that he reduced his furniture business, set up a shop on Jefferson Street, and changed his vocation to become the official undertaker for Burlington. But space for the burial of the deceased became a problem. A city committee drew up a petition to the Iowa Legislature, and permission was obtained in 1843 to establish a city cemetery called Aspen Grove. One of the first settlers to be interred in Aspen Grove was Mr. John Morgan, a veteran of the Revolutionary War who had seen action at the battles of Brandywine and Germantown.

Chapter Five

Jinks and Kon

It had rained for five consecutive days throughout the Iowa Territory. The blessed moisture followed a worrisome drought that had slowed the growth of the corn and oat crops of the settler farmers west and south of Burlington. Due to the high temperatures and drought conditions, ears of corn already were showing signs of "tipping back," a condition where the ears of corn were not filling in completely with kernels to the ends of the ear.

Five days of rain, while needed greatly, was almost too much in such a short time span. The fields were awash, and oat crops were nearly underwater. There was now some talk of possible oat blotch, or blight, which could develop and harm the oat crop due to the excessive moisture in such a short time. Nothing was easy for these early farmers eking out a living on the prairie, and their success in making a living and caring for their families was always subject to the weather conditions. The excessive rain had also raised the levels of the rivers in the Territory, with roiling tributaries crashing their waters into the Mississippi resulting in an angry roiling river, much higher on its banks than normal.

They built the raft from old packing case lumber from the O'Connor transportation yard. Jinks and Kon were proud of their handiwork and spent hours on the river poling the raft from trot line to trot line to collect their fish and re-bait their hooks. Under normal conditions this process would take the twelve-year-olds about two hours. They would then pole the raft back to the Burlington landing, drag their raft far enough up the bank to keep it high and dry, and then go sell their fish to the Roush Mercantile.

On this early summer day in 1841, the boys watched the river as it rushed by at a frantic rate. The boys had played on or near the river for years and were both strong swimmers. While not afraid of the torrid waters, Jinks and Kon had a healthy respect for the river, especially in its present condition. The boys dragged the raft to the river's edge, put their bait bucket and gear on the raft and poled the raft into the water. Their trot lines were anchored to the riverbank, and they strenuously poled to the first anchor and secured the raft while they pulled the lines in hand-over-hand. They soon had their fish and had re-baited the hooks. They shoved off for the second anchor. But as they approached the second location, they were not watching upriver. From behind them came an entire up-rooted elm tree with a trunk three feet in diameter. It had toppled in the rain, and most of the smaller branches had slowly sloughed off as the tree turned round and round while being washed down the river. The huge tree slammed into the boys' raft and sheared the raft into two pieces. As the tree sliced the raft, Jinks' lower leg was caught beneath the tree as it moved over the raft. The leg was crushed and one of the lower leg bones was broken and the other was cracked. The broken bone was a compound fracture leaving bone protruding through the skin of the right leg. Jinks screamed in pain. It now appeared that the raft would be forced under water as the remaining branches of the tree bore down on the raft. Water cascaded over the raft, and it was soon under water with the boys still clinging to the partial raft. For what seemed an eternity to the boys, the tree moved with the river and the raft was catapulted from beneath the tree branches and bobbed to the surface of the river. As the tree continued past the raft, a branch caught one of the raft poles and it was taken away into the maelstrom. The boys clung to the half raft as it was forced away from the bank into the deeper water by the passing tree. They were now in water too deep for the remaining pole to be of any use. They were at the mercy of the river. The frothy, roiling brown water pushed the raft at ever higher speed, further away from Burlington.

As had happened many times before, Jinks and Kon were missed later in the day when they did not come home. Four Toes and Captain Mike sought each other out and learned that their sons were not at the home of either family. The fathers began the hunt for their sons, soon discovering that the boys' raft was missing. Dusk and then dark fell on the village, and panic set into the fathers, and now into New Rain, who had joined the hunt. With darkness upon them, the search for the boys would have to wait until morning light.

The day began with the fathers rousing friends to assist in the search. There could be only one explanation for the absence of the boys and the raft. It was obvious that they had gotten caught in the raging flood waters and been swept away. The search party mounted horses and began following the riverbank south. As the party moved south, the going was tough. The normal, north and south, traffic-carrying road was not close to the river in most places. To be near the river, the search party had to go through brush and brambles, and slog through the mud to be near the riverbank. It was extremely slow going to coax the horses through the soft, sticky mud. The search party was worn out in a few hours. They made camp for the night and built a roaring campfire. They reasoned that the fire would dry out their clothing and gear, and serve as a signal fire that could be seen from the river if the boys were anywhere nearby.

After another exhausting, mud-caked day of slogging through the riverbank vegetation, Ft. Madison came into view. As they made their way into town, they asked everyone they met if they had seen the boys. They proceeded to the fort and again asked if anyone had seen the two young boys. There was no success, as no one could claim seeing the boys. The following day, the search party turned back. The consensus among the party was that with the condition of the river, the boys had been caught in a dangerous eddy that was so common on the river, and had been submerged to their deaths. The tired men and horses moved north on the road to Burlington. Four Toes and Mike rode side by side as they trailed the group, but did not speak to each other. After all, what was there to say? They were convinced they had each lost their son, and both men grieved horribly within themselves.

A week went by with no further word on the boys. After two more days, a brief funeral service was held at the Methodist Church. The attendees then made their way to a small grove on a piece of property that Mike owned, where a graveside service would be held. New Rain was dressed in a ceremonial robe, and the two fathers stood side by side. The sun was shining, and the neighbors marveled at the beauty of the day after so many days of torrential rain. Two temporary wooden markers had been placed in the ground. The names of the boys were clearly written on the markers.

The pastor cleared his throat, but just as he was ready to begin, two strangers were outlined in the glare of the sun as they rode their horses toward the gathered friends. The sun was at the riders' backs, and their identity was unknown until they were closer to the crowd. It soon became apparent that the two men were Army soldiers. Captain Deke Monroe and an Army trooper dismounted from their horses. The captain approached Mike O'Connor. He and the trooper removed their hats.

"Mr. O'Connor," he said. "I believe you have a son, is that correct?"

In his grieving state, Mike stammered his answer, "I used to have a son. He was killed on the river. We are holding services for him, can't you see? I don't see that I have any business at this time with the Army. You are welcome to stay, if you like, but we need to continue our service."

With that, Mike turned back to the minister. "Please proceed, pastor," said Mike.

All this time, Four Toes and New Rain slowly moved to the back of the crowd, staying out of sight behind their friends.

"Mr. O'Connor, you don't understand," said Captain Monroe. "We found your boy."

With a look of stern disbelief on his face, Mike whirled to face the Captain. "What are you saying," he said.

The Captain responded, "I should say that our mail packet found your boy on the riverbank just south of the rapids at Venus. He was unconscious, lying on the riverbank, with a broken up old raft next to him. He had swallowed a great deal of dirty water and was in bad shape. He has a severely broken leg, but he is alive. He is being cared for by our doctor at the fort. With his fever, he is in and out of consciousness, and isn't making any sense. For instance, he mumbled to us that his name is Jinks. Is that possible?"

Mike O'Connor, the robust riverboat captain, fell to his knees and began a combination of weeping and laughing. The days of pent-up grief, anger, and foreboding finally surfaced, and Mike cried with relief.

"Yes, yes, that's his name, and he sure earned that name," said Mike.

"Now, Mr. O'Connor, there's another matter I need to talk to you about. Along with your son and the busted up raft, we found an Indian boy who appears to be about the same age as your boy," said the captain. "Would you know anything about that boy?" he said.

Mike slowly rose to his feet and pulled a handkerchief from his pocket. He didn't know what to say, and continued to blow his nose while he stalled. The gathered crowd was lowly murmuring. While Mike looked down at the ground, and slowly replaced the handkerchief in his pocket, Four Toes sidled up next to him.

"The Indian boy is my son," said Four Toes.

"Well, who in blazes are you?" said Captain Monroe.

Mike finally found his voice, "His name is Four Toes, and he is my friend. In fact, he is a friend to everyone here. He lives with us in Burlington."

"Well, where did he come from," said the captain.

Mike replied, "He didn't come from anywhere. He has always lived here."

It didn't take Captain Monroe long to put two and two together and remember that several years ago, he had been looking for a stray Sauk brave who was rumored to have remained behind when the tribe had been driven to their reservation to the west. Now it was Captain Monroe's turn to be bewildered. The Indians were at peace at this time, and there was no trouble for the Army to address. He would like to keep it that way. He had also heard stories of other Indians living peaceably among the settlers, adopting the white men's customs. With those Indians, the Army's policy was to let them alone as long as they caused no trouble. He made his decision.

"Gentlemen, it will be some time before we can bring the boys back to Burlington. The Indian boy is recovering nicely and has told us the story of how they were hit by a tree on the river. He also confirmed that the white boy's name is Jinks. But Jinks has not been lucid since we brought him to the fort and is in pretty bad shape. Just thought I would ride up this way and give you this news in person."

He shook Mike's hand, stared at Four Toes, and turned to leave.

He then turned back and said, "You two can come to the Fort and see the boys if you like."

He and the trooper remounted their horses and slowly rode south.

The following day, Mike rode to Fort Madison. Four Toes had seen the Fort from the distance in his travels, and there was no way he was going to willingly enter the home of soldiers. He trusted Mike to bring him news of the condition of Kon. Mike entered the fort and was directed to a barracks where the two boys were housed. As he entered the building, he noticed a gentleman with a white duster coat on, and he was introduced to the fort's doctor. Jinks and Kon lay next to each other on cots. Kon acknowledged Mike as he bent over the cots, but Jinks lay with his eyes closed. Mike watched as the doctor slowly removed the wrappings on Jinks' leg to reveal a raw, angry red wound with multiple stitches closing an opening on the leg. The unmistakable, strong smell of sulphur, from the sulphur powder used in the treatment of the wound quickly permeated the room. Splints with wraps held Jinks' leg in position. The doctor then told Mike that he had done the best he could to set the leg bone and was hoping that further surgery would not be necessary. He was giving Jinks medication to mask the pain and fight the fever. But he also said that Jinks might not heal, and if the leg became infected, it might need to be amputated. Mike quietly gasped.

For the next two days, Mike stayed with the boys. Jinks held his own, but was not improving. Kon, however, was ready to go home. On the third day, Mike had seen enough. He had an idea.

"Kon, we're going home," he said.

With Captain Monroe's help, Mike borrowed another horse, and he and Kon hastily left the fort. But on the ride home, Mike discussed his plan with Kon, and when the two riders reached Burlington, Kon left Mike and went home. Later that evening, there was a knock on Mike's door.

Four Toes stood at the door and said, "She will go with you."

Mike reached out and embraced Four Toes. "Thank you so much, my friend," said Mike.

Early the following morning they started out. New Rain did not say a word and was dressed in a combination of Indian and Western garb. She rode another of Mike's horses, and they led the Army pony on a lead from Mike's horse. They rode briskly and reached Fort Madison in the evening. As they entered the fort, a sentry stopped them and asked them to state their business.

"We are here to see Captain Monroe," said Mike.

A trooper was sent to find the captain, and soon Captain Deke Monroe came to them.

"I understand why you are here," said the captain, "but why is she here, and who is she?"

"She is the Indian boy's mother, and my friend. But even more important, she is Jinks' friend."

Monroe looked at the Indian woman, and finally said, "OK. You know where the boy is."

New Rain was visibly distraught to be among all the soldiers. Her only life experiences with Army soldiers had been most unpleasant. Mike had some trepidation that she might not help after all. But he and New Rain made their way to the barracks. Jinks appeared much the same, but even more red with fever. He was hot to the touch. Mike and New Rain looked down on him lying on the cot. Then New Rain got on her knees next to the cot. She looked closely at Jinks. She lifted his eye lids and looked at his eyes and laid her hand on Jinks' forehead. Then she leaned further over and smelled Jinks' breath. She then lifted his shirt and examined Jinks' stomach. Finally she slowly unwrapped the dressing on Jinks' leg. She grunted to herself in reaction to the sulphur smell, and then gently probed the tissue at the wound site.

"Could I have a pan of water?" she said to Mike.

Mike left the room to get the water.

Before he could return, however, the fort doctor entered the barracks, saw New Rain, and shouted, "Who are you. Stop what you are doing!"

New Rain shrank from the noise and never took her eyes off the doctor. As the doctor strode over to the cot, the barracks door again opened and Mike entered with the water.

The doctor turned and said, "Mr. O'Connor, I caught this Indian looking at your son. I'll get her thrown into the brig."

"No you won't, doctor," said Mike, "she is here at my request. I have asked her to help my son, who does not seem to be getting any better."

"You did what?" shouted the doctor. He continued, "Just what is she going to do that I haven't already tried?"

Mike responded, "I don't know just yet, but I intend to let her try to make my son better, and I will thank you, sir, to stand aside and watch."

Mike moved to New Rain and asked her to go ahead. A visibly shaking New Rain took the water, and on the top of a nearby table, she poured a small amount of water. Then from beneath her dress, she removed a small deerskin pouch. From the pouch she removed three different plants and placed them in the puddle of water. She replaced the pouch inside her dress, but as her hand returned, it held a hand-made knife, its hilt carved from a deer antler. The doctor was alarmed, but held his tongue. New Rain used the knife to chop the herbs into small pieces. Then, with the hilt of the knife, she began to grind the herbs into the water. Slowly she kept this up, adding a bit of water and continuing until she had formed a paste. Using the knife, she then carefully cut a few of the stitches, thereby opening the wound on Jinks' leg. She then carefully spread the herbal paste into the open wound.

The doctor became livid.

"O'Connor, you damn fool. This filthy Indian is going to infect your son so badly that he may never get better. I will not condone this, and I wash my hands of you and your son. I will not be held responsible if your son dies," he raged. He then shouted for the guards.

Mike turned to the doctor and said, "I will also not hold you responsible."

Mike turned back to New Rain. "Please try to make my son well, New Rain," he said.

The Indian woman turned her attention to her deerskin pouch. She retrieved two more dried plants, again used the table to crush the plants, combining the ingredients and grinding until she had a powder made up of the two plant leaves. Carefully she repeatedly picked up the powder on her knife blade and dumped it into her open palm until all the powder was in her hand. She then moved over to Jinks' cot.

"You must lick all the powder out of my hand and swallow it," she told Jinks.

"Now just a minute," blurted the doctor. "You can't just give the boy some sort of unknown plants without harming him. I refuse to allow you to do this," he said.

"Jinks, do as New Rain said," Mike told Jinks. He then turned to the doctor and said, "Doc, we're going to see what this native medicine will do for Jinks. It sure as hell can't do any worse than your ministrations. The boy needs to break that fever and infection, and you don't seem to know how to do it. At this point, I believe I will place my faith in my friend instead of in you." Mike placed his hand on the handle of the pistol in his belt. "Now, why don't you just scurry on out of here and leave us be," said Mike.

The doctor snorted and left the room. As he was leaving, New Rain was giving a large drink of water to Jinks. Later, as Jinks lay gently snoring on the barracks bed, Mike spent the night on a bed next to Jinks. New Rain slept on her blanket on the floor.

The following day, New Rain repeated the treatments for the wound and for the fever. For the next two days, Jinks went in and out of fever deliriums. At times he moaned and screamed and called out that his friend Kon had been killed. New Rain and Mike tried their best to calm the delirious boy. Jinks' fever rose and fell. On the fourth day, Jinks slowly opened his eyes and looked into the face of his father and New Rain. Jinks immediately began sobbing.

"Dad, Kon is dead," wailed Jinks, "I'm so sorry. We never should have gone out on the raft."

Mike replied, "Jinks, you damn little fool, you're right, you shouldn't have gone out on the raft. But the good news is that Kon is alive and at home. And more good news, it looks like you are going to make it too."

Mike hugged his son, crying tears of joy, and then turned and gave New Rain a hug and thanked her over and over.

The adults were interrupted by, "Dad, do you think I could have something to eat?" said Jinks. The adults both laughed.

The pompous Army doctor was astounded, but his arrogance would not allow him to make an apology to Mike and New Rain. He simply harrumphed loudly each day when he came to check on Jinks. Jinks' leg was knitting nicely, and the wound had lost its angry, red look. After another five days, Jinks had progressed to the point that he could be moved home. Mike and New Rain returned to Burlington. The next day, Mike prepared one of his wagons by placing heavy multi-layered padding in its bed, and returned to the fort. Jinks' leg bones had not fully knitted, but with the tightly secured splints, he could travel lying on his back in the well-padded wagon. The fort doctor had the final word after Jinks was loaded into the wagon.

"Mr. O'Connor, I don't know if that boy will ever walk properly again. But I am mighty happy to see him alive and on the mend." The doctor continued, "I never would have subjected a son of mine to native healing, but I must admit that I have gained some respect for that Indian woman. Have a safe journey."

***

Mike had been scheming. Each time he had returned to Burlington after tending to Jinks at the fort, he had met with many of the village members and planned to show his gratitude to Four Toes and New Rain. Mike and Jinks' house on north hill was completed, and he had moved his and Jinks' personal possessions to the new home. He had also hired a woman to help with nursing Jinks. After getting Jinks settled at home, he went looking for his co-conspirators. With Greta Barth, Martha Roush, Maria Stroud, Alice Bailey, and Mary Quinn, Mike made his way through the south woods to Four Toes' cave. The five women knew their part in Mike's plan. Upon reaching the cave, they soon gathered around New Rain, and asked her to come back into the village with them. Four Toes stood and watched the women leave with his mouth agape, not knowing what was happening. Mike calmed him, and he and Four Toes sat down and began smoking two of Mike's cigars.

After the cigars had burned to a nub, Mike rose and said, "Four Toes, my friend, our village owes you and New Rain so much. But I owe you much more. New Rain saved the life of my son. You will always be my friend. Now, please come with me. I have something to show you."

Four Toes now was wary. But he accompanied Mike as they walked into the village. They walked down the street, past the shops and businesses to Mike's old home, the trading post. The six women who had left the cave were giggling and laughing on the front porch of the cabin. By now, New Rain had been informed of Mike O'Connor's scheme.

"Four Toes, please go talk with your wife," said Mike, and he stayed a distance from the women.

Four Toes approached the group of women and spoke in his native tongue to New Rain. They spoke only briefly, and as they spoke, Four Toes became more agitated, his voice rising, and his arms waving. Then the six women gathered around Four Toes and escorted the Indian brave into the cabin. The ambush of Four Toes was complete.

Martha then spoke, "Four Toes and New Rain, this village owes so much to you. Your good friend Mike O'Connor has built himself a new house and has no need for this cabin. For all that you have done for us, and especially for Mike, he wants you to have the cabin as your home."

New Rain was smiling as she looked at Four Toes, but the brave had absolutely no emotion on his face. He looked at New Rain, and at the other women, and slowly walked out the door of the cabin. He sat on the porch step for a long few moments, and while he was there, Martha walked over to the waiting Mike.

"Mike, you've got to do something. I don't think he wants the cabin," said Martha.

"I figured this would happen," said Mike. "Give Four Toes and me some time and then walk New Rain back to the cave," he said.

Four Toes rose from the porch and began walking back up the road to return to his home. Mike joined him, and as they walked, Mike said, "How do you like the cabin, Four Toes?"

Four Toes responded, "Can't take a house from a white man."

Mike knew this was coming and respected the fierce independent attitude of the Sauk brave.

"Four Toes, it does not matter that I am a white man. If you wanted to show your friendship by giving me a horse, would you be offended if I refused to take the horse? If you gave me a hunting knife, and I threw it away, would you be offended?"

Four Toes looked at Mike. He did not have to answer, it was evident.

Mike then pleaded with Four Toes, "Please do not offend me by refusing my gift. I also want you to think about New Rain and Kon. I believe they are anxious to be members of the village. I think they would like to live in a house and participate in the village."

Mike knew this argument was weak, and that Four Toes would give the first argument much more consideration. In his culture, it was dishonorable to refuse a gift from a friend.

"I will dream about what you say," said Four Toes, and continued up the path alone.

Six days went by. On the seventh day, Four Toes, with New Rain and Kon called on Mike O'Connor.

"My friend, Mike," said Four Toes. "I have waited for the spirits to tell me the answer. They have made their wishes known to me. For you my friend, and for my wife and son, I will accept your gift. But I have no gift to give in return, and that troubles my spirit," said the brave.

Mike smiled, held out his hand to Four Toes and gripped the Indian's hand. "Your friendship is the only gift I would like," said Mike.

Four Toes lowered his head, and as he raised his head again to look at Mike, there was a distinct, moist sparkle in the eyes of the Indian.

"Friend," he said.

The deed on the property was changed, and mysteriously, the property taxes were paid in full every year without the Indians' knowledge. Four Toes, New Rain, and Kon would move their meager belongings into the old trading post cabin. How ironic that a small part of the land that the Indians had so freely roamed in years prior to settlement, and which had been ceded to the white settlers as a cost of war, was now officially owned by Four Toes and his family.

Chapter Six

Toby Barth
1843

He was now twenty-one years of age. For the past nine years he had learned the trade. He had studiously and quietly watched the most important man in his life, John Barth, as hooves were cleaned, trimmed, and made ready for the forged steel shoes. He had learned the intricacies of tending the temperamental forge fire, fanning it with the large overhead bellows to make it white hot, hot enough to soften the steel used in the horseshoes and other metal equipment. His ebony upper body rippled with muscle, and the sweat rolled on his arms from the effort of swinging the heavy, shaping hammer. His wheelwright skills enabled him to craft new spokes and hubs, and to shape the steel hoops encircling the wagon wheels and smaller carriage wheels of his customers. Toby Barth (with John and Greta Barth's permission, he had taken Barth as his last name), the former slave boy, was now a full grown man running the blacksmith shop for John Barth.

John had branched out a bit in the business. The livery side of the business had increased greatly with the need for horses, mules, and wagons to haul lumber, coal, and supplies in the territory. John also had an on-going contract with Mike O'Connor to provide wagons and livestock for Mike's transportation company. He spent far less time at the blacksmith shop.

But the customers liked the young man who was now the village smithy. Toby got along with everyone, and there was not a job too large or small for the accommodating blacksmith. Over the years of working for John, Toby had saved every penny he could, and after many discussions with John, in 1843 he purchased the property and smithy business from John Barth. Nine years ago he had been a slave, a piece of property. Now, he was a freedman, a property owner and businessman.

Toby was a listener with a carefully hidden keen intellect. He paid attention to the conversations of his customers, and through those conversations he had learned of the Underground Railroad. He had also quietly allied himself with other people in the community who were sympathetic to the purpose of the Underground Railroad. It followed then, that almost immediately after purchasing the business, Toby began constructing a special horse drawn wagon. He told no one of his secret, but was often seen driving the wagon out of town to the west and returning to Burlington the following evening when he would park the wagon behind the shop and cabin. On most return trips, Toby's wagon would contain blacksmith supplies or coal for the unending hunger of the forge's fire. But many times, Toby would return with an empty wagon. A day or two after making these mysterious, empty wagon trips, a stranger driving another wagon would stop at the blacksmith shop, appearing to require minor repairs to his wagon. After it appeared that Toby worked on the stranger's wagon, the stranger and the wagon would then be on their way, usually after dark in the evening.

When work was slow at the smithy shop, Toby would disappear for a few hours and could usually be found north of town, sitting at the riverbank fishing. At least that is how it would appear to the casual observer. In truth, Toby was not fishing. He would prop a fishing pole or two into the riverbank, furtively dig into the bank, and quietly throw buckets of dirt into the river. His location on the riverbank was well camouflaged by vegetation, trees, and the rough hill. So he was seldom seen, except from the river, where it appeared there was a fisherman digging for worms to be used for bait. Toby had a purpose in his digging. He was actually digging a tunnel. He had held many secret discussions with the Reverend William Salter, a Congregational Minister who was building a new church in town. Unbeknownst to anyone in town, except Reverend Salter, Toby was a conductor on the Underground Railroad.

Toby's wagon trips out of town in the evening took him to the little Quaker village of Salem, where he would meet with one of several trusted senior Quakers. Toby would then assist the Quakers by transporting runaway slaves, who were fleeing from the South. Toby's special wagon had a false floor in it, and when the tailgate section of the wagon was removed, a hidden compartment was revealed where up to four people could lie side by side on the padded compartment bottom. Toby would then make the return trip to Burlington and hide the runaways in the woods behind the smithy shop. The next night, a stranger would come with the same type of wagon, pick up the runaways, and take them to Davenport for further transport to northern cities.

The tunnel that Toby was diligently digging would eventually link up to a special, hidden basement room in the new Congregational Church. Runaway slaves using the river to transit north would be able to enter the tunnel and stay in the church basement until further transportation could be arranged for them. Reverend Salter, then, with the help of his Conductor, Toby, was a Burlington Station Master on the Underground Railroad. Very few people knew about the work of these two men because the work was so dangerous. Wealthy Southern slave owners would send search parties to retrieve their "property," and those who had aided in the escape of the slaves could very easily have been killed. Toby's role in the Underground Railroad was, indeed, a very small part of a vast network of "railroad lines" leading from the South to the North of the United States.

All along the highways, freight trails, and river circuits, there was more and more talk of abolishing slavery. The strongest supporters of this concept were known as abolitionists. The Iowa Territory did not condone slavery, but the neighboring territory to the south did include some slave owners. The settlers and leaders of the village of Burlington had mostly all come from free states, and therefore did not hold slaves.

***

Very early on a hot, muggy summer morning in Salem, Toby was ready to load four runaway slaves into his wagon for the all day trip back to Burlington. Three men had been loaded into the wagon. Toby was then told there was a fourth person, a young woman, but that the woman might be too sick to make the trip. Two men carried her out of the Salem "station" house and brought her to the wagon. She was hot, and feverish.

"I believe she is too sick to make the trip," said one of the Quaker elders.

The attractive, young, black woman tightly gripped the arm of the man and hysterically whispered, "I have to go. If my mastuh finds me, he will kill me!" It was readily apparent she was terrified.

"What's wrong with her?" asked Toby.

"We don't rightly know," said the elder, "but she says she was bit by a snake, and I believe, since she came out of Texas, it was probably a copperhead."

He continued, "Them copperheads won't necessarily kill you unless you get a big dose of the poison, but I don't know if this girl will make it or not. Lucky it wasn't a rattler or she would be dead by now."

The men were in a quandary. But they decided that the girl could not stay in Salem where she might be seen, and she continued to plead that she must go on. In the end, she won out and was helped into the wagon compartment. Later that evening, when Toby arrived home and placed the wagon out of sight, he opened the wagon compartment. He asked the three men if the girl was all right. They told him they were not sure she was alive, but under cover of darkness they helped Toby place the girl on Toby's meager bunk in the cabin. The next day, another wagon came to Toby's blacksmith shop and drove away in the night with the three runaway men safely hidden in the wagon. The young black woman seemed no better, but Toby knew a man he could trust.

After the wagon left, and under the cover of dusk, Toby went to Dr. Ross's home. The doctor followed Toby back to the cabin.

"Here's the snake bite mark on her ankle," said Dr. Ross, as he examined the young woman. "Toby, I don't know if she will recover or not," said the doctor, "but you must continue to make her drink lots of water to flush her system out, and give her a bit of this powder every few hours for the pain and fever. That's all we can do for her," said Dr. Ross. "I'll check in on her tomorrow."

On the second day, the woman's ankle had swollen to nearly twice its normal size, and ugly dark veins protruded up her calf.

"Toby, we've got to do something for that swelling and infection," said Dr. Ross. "Have you got some clean old feed sacks out back?" he asked.

Toby went to get them.

"Put them under her leg here," said Dr. Ross.

He then gave the woman two pills from his bag and waited for an interval of time. The girl's eyes glazed over and she soon was quietly snoring. Dr. Ross produced a scalpel from his bag and held it in the fire of Toby's wood stove. He then carefully wiped it off and told Toby to hold the woman's shoulders down onto the bed. He then raised the scalpel and made an incision from the swollen ankle upward about three inches. The woman lurched awake and screamed in pain. A cascade of yellowish red blood spewed from the wound and flowed onto the feed bags below her leg. The doctor then continued to massage the skin and tissue to purge the remainder of the fluids. He then carefully applied medicinal powder to the incision and carefully wrapped the open wound. The woman returned to her stupor.

"Keep giving her fluids, Toby, and don't let her move around on that leg. I'll see you tomorrow," said the doctor.

The next day as she opened her eyes, she saw the black man standing over her, looking at the cloth wrappings on her ankle and leg. He turned his eyes and looked at her.

"What's your name, girl?" asked Toby.

She replied, "I'm Lizzy."

For three days Toby, with the help and advice from the doctor, nursed the young woman while continuing to help his customers. He was exhausted from lack of sleep. But so far, no one knew Lizzy was there except Toby and the doctor. Very slowly and subtly, an inseparable bond was forming between the young black man and the runaway slave woman. Very quietly, the doctor called on Toby each day, and the angry redness of the swelling on the young woman's leg and ankle drew down. Lizzy would live, thanks to Toby and Doctor Ross.

As Lizzy regained her strength and began to appear hobbling about at the blacksmith shop, the story around town in the fall of 1843 was that a young, black woman had been accompanying a wagon and teamster that came through Burlington, and while work was done on the wagon by Toby, an agreement had been reached with the wagon owner, that the young girl was given to Toby for payment for repairing the wagon. As a result, the young woman would stay in Burlington with Toby. At least that was the story that was carefully leaked by Dr. Ross.

John Barth was the best man, and Greta Barth gave the bride away. On a fine, bright summer morning, as the new day's sun lifted gloriously above the trees on the east side of the river, the wedding party stood on the deck of Captain Mike's paddle wheeler. Surrounded by their closest friends, the muscular former slave, Toby Barth, and the runaway slave woman, Lizzy, were united in marriage by Reverend Salter.

***

The Congregational Church was completed in 1844, and the tunnel that Toby had so diligently labored to complete was finally connected to a hidden room in the basement of the church. Scores of runaway slaves were helped to the hidden room by entering the secret tunnel from the river side, and by conductors such as Toby Barth, who secretly brought people in from the surrounding countryside to the church to await movement to an Underground Railroad Station farther to the North. Some estimates claim that as many as 100,000 slaves were brought out of the South on the nation's Underground Railroad in the mid-1800's.

***

1846 began with a great deal of news from south of Burlington. Disagreements between members of the Latter Day Saints community and other settlers in the area had come to a head. In February, members of the Latter Day Saints Church in Nauvoo, Illinois, had reached a decision that all members of the church would leave Illinois to head west. Wagons began crossing the Mississippi, landing at Montrose, from where they moved across the Iowa Territory to the west. News of their departure and adversity traveled to Burlington and other communities up and down the river. Under the leadership of Brigham Young, nearly 17,000 people made this initial trek in 1846, and would be followed by other members of the church for the next twenty-three years. It was hard to imagine a wagon train of this size crossing the river. The wagons followed old hunting and Indian trails, moving across the southern border of the Iowa territory. The first groups of travelers faced great difficulty with rain, mud, swollen streams and rivers. Initially of Jewish faith, the Roush's and Stroud's were empathetic to these caravans moving westward to practice their religious faith in freedom.

In 1846, there were approximately 100 people of Jewish faith in the entire state of Iowa. Most temples or synagogues were not located close to the Jewish people, who were spread around the state. The Roushes and the Strouds had previously kept their faith in their homes, and the families often got together on special holidays to celebrate their faith. But without a Rabbi and formal teaching the parents worried about the religious education of their children. For lack of formal Jewish teachers and a formal place to worship, the Stroud's began attending Dr. Ross's Methodist services with the Roushes. The concept of religious freedom in the United States was not lost on the two couples.

The Federal Government required that a territory have a population of at least 60,000 before the territory could apply for statehood. The Iowa Territory far surpassed that figure in 1846, and after completing all requirements in addition to the population figure, Iowa became the 29th state of the United States in December 1846.

While becoming an official state was cause for celebration among the friends in Burlington, the growing momentum of abolitionists throughout the nation caused deep concern for the safety of the states and their citizens. Radicals on both sides of the issue fanned furor among the populace. Many years before, the colonies had formed militias that played a key role in the Revolutionary War. After the war, the forces had dissolved. But most states, including Iowa, worried about their safety, followed the revolutionary precedent and formed state militias once again. It was not long before the majority of states had their own citizen armies. Little did they know that these small efforts to keep the peace were the harbingers of an approaching dark chapter in American history.

Chapter Seven

The Six Musketeers

Around town they were humorously known as "The Six Musketeers." Ten-year-old Jacob Roush was the unofficial leader of the gang. The other boys were two of the Quinn boys, Patrick, 11, and Robert 10; and Horace Bailey, 8. These four boys were much the same age, with the same interests. The other two youngsters were younger and tagged along with the older boys. They were Mikey Quinn, 6, and Robert (Bobbin) Barth (the son of Toby and Lizzy), also 6. Bobbin had gotten his nickname from his habit of never staying still. He was constantly running, jumping, and skipping. Even when he stayed in one spot, he hopped from one foot to the other. His nickname certainly fit.

When they were not in school, the boys might be found anywhere within the village. Jacob did not recognize himself as their leader, but he was the one who held the effusive exuberance of the Quinn boys in check when their mischievous ideas tended to cross the line. There were times when the older Quinn boys wanted to ditch the two younger boys, especially Bobbin, because he was the only Negro boy hanging around. But Jacob kept the group together through the strength of his personality and the goodness in his heart. Mikey Quinn and Bobbin Barth simply idolized Jacob and would follow him whenever they could, just to be near the great adventures of the older boys. Sometimes, however, trouble found the older boys, especially the Quinns, as they investigated the mechanics of how things worked, or just from their own impish personalities.

Nearly every home in the village kept a small supply of black gun powder for use in hunting rifles. A favorite place for the boys to meet was the vacant property behind the old Vogler shack. It was wooded and secluded, and the boys could run wild without getting into too much trouble. One day the boys met there to plan their adventures for the day. But Patrick and Robert Quinn came with a surprise. They had sneaked almost two cups of gun powder and some fuse from their house and were anxious to experiment. The Quinn boys had watched their father use the powder and fuses to blast rock and soil for enlarging their ferry boat landing. Thus, the ten-year-olds thought they had a semblance of knowledge of how these ingredients worked. All of the boys gathered around and made suggestions on how to make a giant gunpowder firecracker out of the smuggled ingredients. What they failed to recognize was that two cups of gun powder is a considerable amount. At the same time, they tried to figure out what they would do with the firecracker after they made it. Thirty minutes of work in wrapping the powder tightly over and over in old newspaper, finally resulted in a crude, large firecracker.

"I know," said Patrick, "we'll put it in the old Vogler shack."

Well, it seemed like a good idea at the time, and the boys wedged the firecracker into the board siding, next to a horizontal support beam in the side of the shack.

But Jacob then objected and said, "Are you sure we should do this?"

To which Patrick answered, "Oh, you old scaredy cat, just watch."

And with that, Patrick lit the fuse, and the boys scattered to what they thought would be a safe distance from the shack. The sizzling, smoky fuse edged closer to the powder cache. Suddenly there was a giant, deafening blast. Every single boy was bowled over by the blast, but they soon scrambled to their feet to see what the damage had been to the shack. That is, all but six-year-old Mikey Quinn. He was still lying on the ground and had begun crying loudly. As the boys gathered around Mikey, they could see blood on his shirt on his chest. Mikey was wailing now. Jacob knelt down to look more closely at Mikey. All he could see was something brown and rusty sticking through Mikey's shirt. All of the sudden, there was a high screeching sound. As the boys looked back, the sound became louder, and the entire shack slowly leaned, wobbled ever so slightly, and then deafeningly crashed to the ground with a belching of clouds of dirt and dust. The boys were in shock. They had blown up a house! Merchants on the street were running from all directions to the tumbled mess of the former shack. When the boys were spotted standing to one side of the old shack, it didn't take the merchants long to put two and two together to get Six Musketeers. But then little Mikey was spied lying on the ground, and the adults began looking him over. Mikey didn't seem to be hurt very badly, but soon Doctor Ross appeared. He looked at Mikey's wound and probed with his fingers. Soon, he plucked a rusty nail from Mikey's sternum. Being only six years old, Mikey's bones still had a portion of cartilage. In addition to flying bits of wood from the blast, a flying nail had struck Mikey in the sternum, but had stuck in the surrounding cartilage. Mikey was extremely lucky. The doctor dressed the wound and turned little Mikey over to his mother, Mary. She gathered the little boy in her arms and headed for home.

As Aaron Quinn rushed to the scene, he realized what had happened and quickly grabbed the ears of Robert and Patrick, and pulled them, not too gently, toward home. After appropriate sessions of discipline by all parents involved, in a few days the boys were once again seen roaming the village. They were all good boys, but once in a while, their exuberant youth got the better of their good sense.

On another occasion, the villagers had decided to hold a May fest celebration; a celebration of spring and the progress of the small town. A pleasant, grassy area overlooking the river was found and on a beautiful bright sunny Saturday, expansive board tables were arranged on sawhorses for a feast for the village. Two large kegs of beer were on support stands to the side of the food tables. Small vendors had craft tables arranged, and the day promised to be great fun for everyone. There was even going to be a puppet show.

The day started off as planned, with families arriving and bringing food to be placed on the tables in anticipation of the forthcoming feast. There were two full tables of home baked cakes, pies, cookies, puddings, and candies; and four full tables of main dish entrees were laden to the maximum, waiting for the go-ahead to begin eating. Neighbors gathered in groups to visit and tell stories. Children scampered everywhere, chattering and giggling as they chased each other around the open field area.

Well, not all the village children. The Six Musketeers had all gathered at the Quinn home to walk to the picnic together. And thus, the adventure began. Jacob, Patrick, Robert, Horace, Bobbin, and Mikey gathered around a wire cage trap.

"Ain't he somethin," said Patrick. All the other boys agreed; he was something special. Small squeaks, hisses, and scratching noises were coming from a large, and very unhappy, raccoon, that repeatedly paced the inside perimeter of the cage.

"My dad caught him last night in this trap," said Patrick. "The coon was getting under the house and making noise at night. So dad set up this trap, and here he was this morning."

The boys continued to marvel at the raccoon, but then Robert Quinn set the stage.

"I know," said Robert. "Let's take him to the picnic so all the kids can see our new coon."

Of course, Jacob was the only one of the group to stand aside and think about that idea.

"What do you think your dad will say?" asked Jacob.

Patrick replied, "Aw, he won't say nuthin, as long as we don't let the coon out of his cage."

So the boys picked up the four corners of the cage, and off they went to the picnic. William Roush and Aaron Quinn both spotted the boys as they approached the food tables, and intercepted them.

"What do you think you are doing?" said Aaron.

"Jacob, was this your idea?" asked William.

"No Dad," said Jacob. "Patrick and Robert thought the other kids would like to see the raccoon," said Jacob.

Just then, there was a loud whistle to get everyone's attention. Father Mazzuchelli, the Catholic priest who had been instrumental in founding the Catholic Church in Burlington, was visiting St. Paul's minister, Rev. George Reffe. Rev. Reffe asked everyone to bow their heads in prayer before the meal would begin.

"Put that cage under the dessert table, and don't touch it until it's time to go home," sternly hissed Aaron to the boys.

They quickly complied. As Father Mazzuchelli began his prayer, little Mikey sat down on the grass next to the raccoon cage. The prayer droned on. Mikey fidgeted and absently played with the latch that secured the door of the cage. All at once the cage door sprang open, and a terrified Mikey screamed. The raccoon saw the opportunity for freedom and darted from the cage. The priest's prayer came to a sudden halt, and everyone in attendance looked up to see a raccoon jump to the top of the dessert table. The coon then raced down the length of the table, becoming covered in cherry pie filling, peach pie filling, meringue, and pudding. At the middle of the table, the raccoon slipped and rolled over into a blueberry cobbler, adding to the rainbow of colors adhering to its normally brown fur coat. The raccoon quickly regained its feet and continued to run the length of the dessert table. It then made a flying leap and landed on the top of one of the large wooden beer kegs and stood looking at everyone. But the mad leap from the dessert table had upset the balance of the table, and it came crashing down. As it fell, it struck the wooden frame structure holding the beer keg on which the coon sat. The keg's support gave way, and the keg began its fall to the ground, while the raccoon jumped free and sped away to the woods. The wooden beer keg hit the ground and smashed open, with beer spewing in all directions, drenching Father Mazzuchelli. A huge gasp went up from the crowd, and then it was deathly silent.

As the beer slowly dripped from the good priest, he said very loudly, "Amen!"

Aaron and Mary Quinn sprang into action. While Mary grabbed little Mikey, Aaron grabbed two ears belonging to Patrick and Robert respectively, and the embarrassed Quinn family marched toward home. Alice Bailey also grabbed hold of young Horace, and the march began to the Bailey home. Bobbin had moved over and was hiding behind Jacob. William then marched Jacob home, with Toby and Bobbin bringing up the rear. The older boys would not be seen out of the house except for school for several weeks. It had been a Mayfest that would not be forgotten.

The Musketeers also spent a great deal of time on the riverbank, fishing, catching crawdads, or searching for duck eggs. But every mother in Burlington knew the story of Jinks O'Connor and Kon and their near death on the river nearly nine years ago. The boys were sternly lectured to by their parents that the river was no place to play. The boys took this warning seriously and remained on the bank. However, there was a hollow in the riverbank near the village that was safe for swimming, and because there was no current, the boys spent many warm summer days swimming there.

One drizzly fall day, the Six Musketeers were at the blacksmith shop watching Toby shoe a mule that was owned by John Barth. The old mule was used for shuttling wagons from the wharf area for John and Mike O'Connor's business. The mule was not cooperating with Toby, and Toby was devoting his full attention to the mule, not paying any attention to the boys' conversation. That conversation centered on which of the families had the best and fastest horses. The talk took a turn then, and the boys began boasting about which of them was the best driver of horse teams. Patrick, of course, was goading the rest of the boys, telling them that he could outdrive any of them and could handle any horses they had.

Jacob then spoke up and said, "Patrick, you couldn't even drive an old farm wagon."

An offended Patrick replied, "I sure can. I'll show you. C'mon," he said.

The boys made their way to a wagon that was parked on the far side of the blacksmith shop, out of Toby's view. There was a very large draft horse hitched to the wagon, and the wagon was full of hay shocks. Unbeknownst to the boys, the wagon was owned by a farmer who had brought the wagon in for repair to a front wheel that had a worn axle, causing the wheel to wobble. The farmer had gone down the street to eat while waiting for Toby to complete the repair.

The boys all climbed into the wagon, and Patrick jumped up on the driver's seat. The draft horse lifted his head. At the same time, Patrick kicked the toggle on the foot brake, and without a hand on the brake lever to ease it back, the brake handle sprang back to its stop with a bang that sounded like a gun shot. This so startled the draft horse that it jumped from all four feet and charged ahead at full speed. The wagon took off with a mighty lurch, and Patrick was thrown backwards off the seat and into the back of the wagon with the rest of the Musketeers. The horse and wagon then shot up the main street, with six terrified youngsters hanging onto the inside of the wagon. Meanwhile, the defective wheel wobbled at an ever increasing frequency, and while the horse continued running full speed, the wheel flew off the axle and rolled down the street on its own. The wagon, sans wheel, then fell on the axle, plowing a furrow in the muddy street as the wagon continued forward. At that point the fastening chains on the harness tree broke, freeing the horse which by now was thoroughly spooked. (The horse was found later, two miles out into the country.)

The wagon now veered and headed straight toward Isaac Prugh's undertaking shop, where the wagon finally broke through a fence and came to rest in a rear storage area among an assortment of wooden coffins. Wood and broken coffins lay strewn in the street, and six terrified boys climbed down out of the wagon.

"Geez Patrick, you've really done it this time," said Jacob. But he was already thinking of what his own dad would say when he found out.

The boys' memories of the pain of their fathers' leather belts warming collective buttocks was refreshed, and the boys were once again not seen on the streets for several weeks except for helping Mr. Prugh straighten up his storage area, and walking to and from school. The fathers of the boys soon decided that it was time for more constructive use of the boys' time, and all four of the older boys were put to work after school and Saturdays doing small chores in their fathers' businesses. The activities of the Six Musketeer were greatly diminished.

Even though there were four years difference in the age of Jacob and Bobbin, a special bond was formed between the older white boy and the younger black boy. No one could figure out why. Jacob had taken Bobbin under his wing, much as an older brother would do. He taught Bobbin various games, and also taught Bobbin to read. Allowing a Negro to learn to read was almost unheard of, and when it was learned that the young Negro boy could read, many of the village adults were not sure this was a good thing. Many spoke to William about this situation, but William saw nothing wrong with Jacob's actions and kept his own counsel. While Jacob worked for his father, William, in the mercantile, sweeping floors, stocking shelves, and running errands, Bobbin would also hang around to talk to Jacob and watch the work. Soon the day came when Bobbin, too, was old enough to help Toby in the blacksmith shop. The Musketeers' childhood faded as all the boys became young men.

***

At twenty-one years of age, Jinks O'Connor had completed school and now played a key role in Mike's transportation business. He had learned the business thoroughly and would inherit the business from Mike when the time came. Four years later, in 1854, Edna Roush announced to her parents that she intended to marry Jinks O'Connor. This statement rocked the Roush household. William and Martha did not even know that Edna had been seeing Jinks. Edna was nineteen years old, and Jinks was twenty-five. Edna's news was deeply troubling to William and Martha.

While William and Martha had been attending the Methodist Church, they could never forget that they were brought up, and professed to be Jewish. The religious lineage of Jinks O'Connor was a mystery to say the least, but probably leaned toward Catholicism. This was simply beyond comprehension to Martha and William. When this thorny subject was brought up to Edna, and later to both Edna and Jinks, the young couple already had an answer. The couple would attend the Congregational Church after their marriage. They had already spoken to Reverend Salter, and the minister had agreed to perform their nuptials. This was yet, another blow to Martha. To see her daughter married in a church that she had never even stepped foot into was unheard of. Martha was distraught.

Understandably, Mike O'Connor, who had never practiced any religion, had no concern over where his son and his fiancé would be married, so long as it would be a festive occasion. And he could think of nothing more festive than a wedding between two of the wealthiest families in town. He certainly thought a great deal of his best friends, William and Martha. So, he made arrangements to meet the Roushes for dinner at their home. And true to his character, he carried two nice bottles of wine in his coat pocket. While the Roush's cook labored in the kitchen, the three adults sat in the parlor, sipped their wine, and discussed their concerns regarding Edna and Jinks.

The discussions continued for thirty minutes before the cook finally announced that dinner was ready. Martha ate little, but did ask William to pour her another glass of wine. In fact, she asked William a third time to fill her glass. At last, Martha resigned herself to the fact that she really did not have a good argument for objecting to the marriage of her only daughter. Jinks was reasonably well educated, wealthy, and was of good character, albeit the rather unsavory circumstances of his birth. But she and William only wanted what would make their children happy, and with the final glass of wine, she began to formulate details of the upcoming wedding ceremony. She then stated that she would call on Reverend Salter the next day. The two fathers breathed a sigh of relief, and once again filled their own wine glasses.

The wedding in early fall included a guest list of all friends and business associates of the two families. As a result of the large number of guests, and as a concession to Martha, the actual ceremony was held on the lawn of the Roush's north hill home, with the reception following. It was a beautiful affair on a bright sunny day. The guests all marveled at the beautiful bride, the handsome groom, and the spectacular view of the Mississippi River far below the bluff.

Through tears of happiness, Martha bid farewell to the happy couple as they left for their St. Louis honeymoon. The host of friends, and the happy fathers, William and Mike, got happily "tight" and strolled around the affair with their arms on each other's shoulders the entire afternoon. It was, indeed, a festive occasion.

Chapter Eight

Crossing the River

The invention of the huge, black, belching steam engine that could pull a score of loaded freight cars resulted in vast amounts of money going to many Americans from the difficult labor of millions of men. The steel rail tendrils of the monster soon covered the land between centers of trade. The few railroads competed with one another to gain the rights for their lines and by 1850, most of the land east of the Mississippi was interlaced by the rail lines. But a formidable obstacle stood in the way of the westward expansion of the rail network. Old Man River, the mighty Mississippi, had not yet been forded by the railroad. The task would be monumental, and it was even thought that it might be impossible.

The Chicago, Burlington and Quincy (CB&Q) railroad terminated on the east side of the Mississippi. No viable plan had yet been designed to move rail freight across the formidable barrier. But in 1855, an ingenious plan was put into effect. A large barge with a section of rail on its top side was constructed and christened "The President." The barge could ferry locomotives and rail cars across the river to meet up with movable track on the other side in Burlington. It was in this manner that for thirteen years, hungry merchants on the west side of the river received their rail-shipped goods. The Roush's and Stroud's were able to enlarge their warehouses to accommodate the larger freight shipments, and their mercantile business kept growing.

Although the railroads were rapidly making inroads in the transportation industry, it would still be a few years until they would dominate the industry. In the meantime, water transportation thrived and provided livelihood to thousands of watermen. Captain Mike O'Connor's trans-portation business continued to grow, making him a very wealthy man. Mike had enlarged his operations to ply his trade on other rivers that emptied into the Mississippi. His boats ran up the Des Moines River into Iowa to Fort Des Moines, and even as far north as Fort Dodge, if the river level was high enough. Mike had invested heavily in purchasing larger fifty-foot flat boats that could haul grain and supplies. These boats could travel on the Iowa River, the Cedar River, the Skunk River and other tributaries to the Mississippi. The boats would then return to Burlington, where their cargo would be consolidated onto paddle wheelers for distribution north and south on the Mississippi. Where boats were not able to go, the heavily laden wagons of the O'Connor Transportation Company could haul freight from Burlington to the hinterlands through-out the eastern half of the state.

Twenty-six-year-old Jinks O'Connor was actively involved in the transportation business. With Mike's wealth, Jinks had received an excellent education from the Jesuits at St. Louis University. He had studied mathematics, accounting, and commerce. Jinks was Mike's right hand in the business and kept the financial records for the firm. After his boyhood accident, Jinks had regained the full use of his right leg. But the knitting of the bones had caused an imbalance in the normal bone lengths. Therefore, Jinks walked with a slight limp, which did not affect him in the least. His father, Mike, was over fifty years of age, and some day, Jinks would inherit the business.

Jinks and a very pregnant Edna were in the process of building their own home, so were currently living with William and Martha in the large Roush home until their home was completed. They were hoping their house would be finished before the "big event." But Mother Nature has a mind of her own, and the Roush home became a bit more crowded and hectic, as Edna gave birth to twin boys, Mark and Gregory O'Connor in late 1856. Grandma Martha was ecstatic. Her old concern about Edna marrying Jinks a couple of years back suddenly flew out the window. The sight of two wondrous little beings put her motherly instinct on full alert, and with twins, she and Edna had their hands full. As a teen-age uncle, Jacob merely watched in amazement as the two women cared for his new little nephews. On the day of the birthing, after the hard work by Edna had been completed, Jinks and Grandpas William and Mike adjourned to the kitchen for a small "dose of ambrosia" and took their drinks outdoors to accompany their cigars. Like all fathers, they marveled at the seemingly impossible miracle of birth.

*****

The nearly inseparable friendship between Jinks and Kon continued into adulthood. While Kon did not have the benefit of higher education past the eighth grade in the public schools, Mike O'Connor had found a place for Kon in the company. Kon started out in the maintenance sheds, helping with the service on the company wagons and tack gear. By the time the railroads began creeping across the river, Kon was head of all vehicle maintenance for the company. This included all land transportation vehicles, and the river craft. Mike and Jinks trusted the twenty-seven-year-old Indian as a key player in the burgeoning company. However, at times there were problems with this relationship. Occasionally a wagon driver would make a snide comment about the ethnicity of the chief of maintenance. Kon had been given strict orders that when he had a problem of this nature, he was not to fight the driver, but was supposed to bring the situation to the attention of Jinks or Mike. The normal result was that the biased driver would discover that he suddenly had a need to find employment elsewhere. Replacement wagon drivers were easy to find. Watercraft captains would also occasionally make the wrong comment. With that group, it was a bit more understandable, since many of them had been attacked by Indians in years past as they plied their trade on the river. Mike, an old river captain himself, gave those men only one more chance after threatening them with their livelihood.

Jinks and Mike could see the future of transportation in Burlington. The father and son team called on the CB&Q officials to arrange transportation contracts with the railroad that would allow their company to bring freight to the rail centers and also distribute goods delivered by the railroad. The lengthy and tedious work of drawing up the contracts between the railroad and the O'Connor Transportation Company was finally completed, and the O'Connor transportation company's revenue increased immensely.

Construction of rail lines moved rapidly across the state, usually following river courses and old roads. Towns and services sprang to life along the rail lines to service the railroad and the rail passengers. Most of this commerce was a great benefit to the small towns and for travelers. But, as is the case of most new enterprises, an undesirable element tagged along. Shady gambling halls and houses of prostitution often took root near train depots. The criminal element sometimes lurked in the shadows of these low-life enterprises to relieve unsuspecting travelers of their personal items of value. Travelers needed to be vigilant while traveling by rail.

In many cases, the trains carried cargo in demand by ingenious train robbers. When train robberies in the frontier became a problem, the railroads formed their own railroad police forces, and many of these men rode the trains to protect the passengers.

With the increase in travelers and settlers, more Jewish settlers came into Iowa. A synagogue was established in Davenport, and temples were built in smaller towns, such as Oskaloosa to the west. This caused some angst in Martha and Maria. They felt some guilt that perhaps they should attempt to reestablish ties to the Jewish faith. But by this time, the Strouds and Roushes were firmly established in a Protestant church, and raised their children as Methodists. In addition, the distance to the new Jewish churches was still too great. They would remain supporters of the Protestant faith.

Part Two

Jacob

Chapter One

1855-1862

As the son of one of the most influential families in Burlington, Jacob Roush wanted for nothing. He lived in the finest home, was given money to spend, had his own horse, did very well in his studies, and was sought by every young damsel in the area. Yet Jacob was an anomaly. Although he had many good friends and was a very popular young man, in truth, he would many times prefer to be by himself. He received an invitation to every young adult social event in the area, and yet he turned down most of them. He was not necessarily aloof, nor was he antisocial; he just preferred to be able to think, read, dream, and be by himself. He was gifted in his life. Yet, he was not necessarily happy. He much preferred walking in the woods, exploring, or lying on a riverbank fishing, while reading a good book.

William kept him busy at the mercantile, and by virtue of his many hours at the business, at the age of fifteen, Jacob had a knack for working with customers and vendors, and understood the cash flow of the business. William said, "He had a good business head." His father had made it very clear to Jacob that at the appointed time, Jacob would need to enter the business full time in order to one day take over. Jacob was unsure whether he even wanted to be in the business. William wanted to ensure that his son would have the finest education possible, and to this end, Jacob attended Jesuit, University High School in St. Louis.

Being away from home for three years of high school was only made a bit more bearable by the fact that Aaron Quinn also wanted the best for his oldest son, Patrick, and also sent him to the Jesuit high school in St. Louis. Jacob liked Patrick, but did not remotely think the same way

Patrick did. Patrick did not like school and would rather pursue extracurricular activities that were not always tolerated by school officials. Needless to say, Aaron Quinn made many trips to St. Louis to meet with school officials and court judges to bail Patrick out of his latest scrape. Jacob, on the other hand, excelled at school and was highly regarded by school officials. Yet through it all, given the glaring differences in the two boys, they remained friends. Patrick was astute enough to recognize the leadership traits in his friend and thought the world of Jacob. Patrick also knew when Jacob was not pleased with something that Patrick had done. Jacob would become very quiet and serious, and not talk to Patrick for a few hours. As soon as Patrick made amends, the relationship resumed where it had left off. Jacob always thought that Patrick would learn from his misadventures, but he never did.

For example, just three days prior to their graduation, Patrick hatched another plan of mischief. Four Jesuit priest robes mysteriously disappeared from the school's laundry. Four wrought iron campus benches also disappeared. Late on the night before graduation, a silent group of students led by none other than Patrick Quinn, hoisted the four benches to the open belfry tower in the common park area in the center of campus, and placed one bench facing outward, on each of the four sides of the open tower. The benches were lightly tied, and had another rope tied to the bell yoke which held the bell. On each bench, they crafted a scarecrow, dressed in priest robes, with a pumpkin for a head. Crude wind vanes were then attached to broom handles and the other end of the handles were attached to the clapper of the tower bell. This meant that each time a strong breeze moved a wind vane, the bell would ring. Another rope was tied to the clapper so it could not move, and the rope was led to a stake on the ground below.

Graduation was to be held at eight a.m. in the aforementioned park. Visitors were seated facing an outdoor stage, away from the belfry tower.

When all of the guests had been seated, the school staff and priests took the stage. An invocation was read, and other remarks followed. The ceremony continued with the first few graduating students coming to the front for their diplomas, while an unseen accomplice untied the rope that was holding the bell clapper still. With an intermittent brisk breeze that morning, the bell began its clamorous ringing. All eyes turned to the belfry to see the priest scarecrows rocking back and forth on their respective benches while the bell continued its joyful ringing. The headmaster of the school and his staff were not amused. Staff members finally ran to the tower and again secured the rope to hold the clapper from ringing.

As the name of graduating student Patrick Quinn was read, he jauntily ascended the stairs of the stage. The headmaster stared daggers at young Patrick as he graciously accepted his diploma and left the stage. All of the accomplices in the audience held their heads down to avoid anyone seeing the huge grins on their faces.

***

Following high school, William wanted Jacob to continue his education and attend St. Louis University. But Martha had put up with having her son away at school and only home for holidays for the past three years. She made her feelings known to William that a closer university would allow Jacob to come home a bit more often. While many colleges and universities were available to the family, the small community of Mt. Pleasant, Iowa, was approximately thirty miles to the west. Iowa Wesleyan College had been in operation there for over thirty years, and Dr. Ross highly recommended the Methodist school. William did not favor this idea, but finally conceded to Martha's wishes. He reasoned that it was not so important where Jacob went to school, as long as he received a good education in order to eventually take over the family business.

Where Jacob's universe was centered, Patrick Quinn could be found close by. Aaron Quinn also insisted that Patrick further his education, so it naturally followed that Patrick, too, was destined to pursue an education at Iowa Wesleyan. Patrick really did not want to attend college, but in his estimation, it sure beat working all day, every day, with his dad.

The two families went together to purchase a hand-made, sturdy, carryall carriage with a double tree for two horses. It took quite some time to locate and purchase two well-built, sound horses that could double for riding and carriage use. The horses would also need to be strong and fit enough to cover the thirty-mile distance in one full day on the occasion of traveling between Mt. Pleasant and Burlington. Jacob and Patrick would use the carriage for taking personal goods to and from school, and the horses would then be used for individual riding while at school. The boys were both excellent horsemen, and with their horsemanship skills, their animals would be well maintained.

The college setting may have been different, and the discipline not nearly as severe, but the scenario changed little for the two young men. Jacob applied himself to his studies, excelling in all that he endeavored, while Patrick exerted only the effort required to pass his subjects. There was one huge difference between Jesuit high school, and the college environment. Iowa Wesleyan, since its inception in 1842, allowed the matriculation of females and was the first coeducational college west of the Mississippi. Patrick was in heaven. A different lady was on his arm for each social event on the campus. His impish, roguish ways charmed a number of women, but he was forever, "playing the field." On the other hand, Jacob was sought out by social leaders on the campus and had the eye of a good portion of the women students. He attended many of the social events, but was never very serious about a relationship with a woman student. That is, until he met Georgia Hume.

Saturday afternoon teas were held every two weeks at the college president's home. Their purpose was to allow the president to mingle with the students and to become better acquainted with them. Secondarily, the gatherings would allow students to get to know one another in a "proper" setting. Jacob had attended a couple of prior teas and socialized with fellow students, but usually could be found conversing with a knot of male students, only occasionally wandering among the larger group or speaking with women students. On one particular Saturday afternoon, Jacob had spent nearly an hour socializing and had finally decided that the get-together was of no further interest. In the crowded parlor, he was attempting to make his way to the host and hostess, the college president and his wife, to thank them and make a departure. But as he moved in their direction, a young lady whom he was passing suddenly twirled around with her teacup and saucer in her hands. The cup and saucer bumped into Jacob, the tea spilled onto his waistcoat, and the cup went clattering to the floor. All eyes turned to the couple, but Jacob and the young lady were oblivious as their eyes met and apologies were effused by both.

Georgia was the daughter of a wealthy Quaker land holder in the Oskaloosa area. She was the third generation of a Quaker family who had settled in Iowa to avoid religious persecution. She had been sent to college for "finishing" and would most likely return to her family upon graduation. She was blue-eyed, with dusty blond hair. Her eyes sparkled as she talked with Jacob for the last half hour of the tea. Jacob, who heretofore had not taken much interest in the opposite sex, was smitten. Georgia was smart and could almost read Jacob's thoughts. Jacob found her to be very fascinating, indeed. Their relationship would continue during their college days. The couple could be found together at all of the chaperoned social events of the college and at chapel on Sundays. They had both spoken furtively about marriage, but neither was anxious to make that final commitment. They greatly enjoyed each other's company, but both were independent thinkers and were not yet ready for marriage. In addition to a more amorous interest, they became best friends and could often be seen strolling the college campus hand in hand, which raised many, more "proper" eyebrows. The romance blossomed to the point where both professed their love for each other. Friends of the couple believed it was inevitable that the couple would someday wed.

Chapter Two

Winds of War

It resulted from a truly remarkable set of circumstances. From the humblest origins, born into a poor family of settlers in Illinois, he was mostly self-educated. He became a small town attorney, was elected to the Illinois legislature, and later to the U.S. House of Representatives. Abraham Lincoln was an outspoken opponent of slavery. Against long odds, he was nominated by the Republican Party to be their presidential candidate. During his presidential campaign, he made few campaign promises. His campaign slogans included, "Vote Yourself a Farm," referring to the governmental land grants being made to settlers of western states. He also advocated leaving the states that practiced slavery alone, but making it unlawful for any new state to adopt slavery. At all times in his candidacy, Mr. Lincoln made it very clear that he was against the practice of slavery. Facing a great hurdle and against all odds, Abraham Lincoln was elected President of the United States in 1860.

Residents living on the Mississippi River continued to receive their news from river craft captains and settlers passing through the river communities. Knowledge of the rising tide of abolitionists had been circulating for years, with pundits on both sides of the issue only serving to raise the emotions of the opposing side. These burning embers were finally fanned into flames. Under the guise of states' rights and interference by the Federal Government, South Carolina seceded from the union in December 1860, and was soon followed by Mississippi, Florida, Alabama, Georgia, Louisiana, and Texas in January and February of 1861. In total, thirteen states and two territories soon formed the Confederate States of America.

The formidable Union Fort Sumter sat ominously in the Charleston, South Carolina harbor. To the recently seceded state of South Carolina, this edifice was a personal affront to the people of South Carolina, and only served to symbolize the intrusion of the Federal Government into states' business. During negotiations, Southern demands that the fort be abandoned by the Union Army and given to South Carolina came to a standstill, and at 4:30 a.m. on April 12, 1861, the Charleston artillery batteries began firing on Fort Sumter. By virtue of a southern blockade around the fort and the depletion of Union ammunition and food supplies, defending Union Army Major Robert Anderson had no choice but to cease fighting. The fort was surrendered to Confederate personnel on April 14, 1861. The Civil War had begun. The economy and industry of Iowa did not rely on the labor of slaves. This fact, along with the moral issue of slavery itself, kept Iowa loyal to the Union.

Residents of Iowa may have believed that this conflict was far afield, and would not affect them in their remote location. But following the fall of Fort Sumter, President Lincoln called for raising an army for the defense of the Union. That army would be comprised primarily of residents loyal to the Union cause, and that included Iowa. At enlistment rallies in the larger cities of Iowa, volunteers were signing up for duty in the Union Army.

In Mt. Pleasant, Jacob and Patrick would very shortly complete all requirements for their graduation. In the fall of 1862, they had both resigned themselves to the fact they would return home and work in their respective fathers' businesses. Both young men struggled inwardly with the prospect of being tied down so early in their lives, doing work for which neither had a burning desire. Jacob was also being torn by an affair of the heart. Although he had made his love clear to fair Georgia Hume, he could not bring himself to imagine being married. Georgia had made it evident that she would like to marry and for him to return with her to Oskaloosa and enter into farming with her father.

***

The men had ridden most of the morning and were resting themselves and their horses as they sat on the bank of the Skunk River. As the hobbled horses grazed, the men had fishing lines in the water, but were paying absolutely no heed of the cork bobbers. On this rare occasion, even Patrick was absorbed in the conversation. He was listening to Jacob.

"I'm miserable, Patrick. As a gentleman, I simply don't know how to gracefully break the news to Georgia. I love her dearly, but I do not want to marry her at this time. Not only that, but I am not looking forward to a life in the mercantile with my dad," said Jacob.

Patrick replied, "I don't envy you." A bit flippant as usual, he continued, "I've never had to break off a relationship. Usually the girls move on to other fellas when they realize I'm not too serious," Patrick said, laughing as he said it.

Jacob replied, "Dad will be very disappointed if I don't work with him, and I don't wish to disappoint him."

"Well, I have the same problem there," said Patrick. "As the oldest son, Dad wants me to take over the business and have my younger brothers work for me. I guess it's something I have to do," he said.

After more melancholy discussion, the men had talked themselves out. They gathered in their fishing gear, removed the hobbles from the horses, and began the ride back into Mt. Pleasant.

As they rode into town, they passed by the downtown shops and businesses and approached the town square. A great number of people and a small brass band were milling around a temporary sawhorse table.

At the table were seated a number of men dressed in Union Army uniforms. One soldier standing at the table was speaking.

"Gentlemen, our great United States of America is under attack. One of our forts has been taken by the enemy, the secessionist Confederate States of America," he said. "President Lincoln and the United States Congress have authorized us to be here today to ask for volunteers to join the army. We need to build an army of size to ensure that our Union remains safe. The army will pay wages while you serve, and at the present time we expect no further hostilities from the confederates. But President Lincoln wants us to be prepared. Now step forward and sign up right here."

Jacob and Patrick watched as a small line formed in front of the table.

One of the soldiers in a Union Army Officer's uniform next spoke up and said, "My name is Lieutenant Samuel Kirkwood Clarke. I am Colonel George Stone's adjutant. We are forming the officer cadre here for the next two days, along with the enlisted soldiers. If you believe you want to be an officer, you will need to speak personally to Colonel George Stone down there at the end of the table. The rest of you will need to speak with me and the sergeant here."

Jacob said to Patrick, "I recognize that name. Clarke is the son of the governor."

Patrick replied, "You mean the governor of the whole state of Iowa?"

Jacob nodded affirmatively. They continued to watch as only a handful of men stood in front of Colonel Stone, while the other line for the enlisted ranks grew.

"You know what," said Patrick. "I think I would look pretty darn good in one of those officer uniforms."

Jacob snapped his attention to his friend. "You can't be serious," said Jacob.

"Not sure yet," replied Patrick.

The young men continued riding to the livery to put up the horses. As they walked back to the campus, both men were mulling over their thoughts.

Thoughts of Georgia Hume kept Jacob from a sound sleep. He woke periodically, wrestling with his ideas on how best to address the marriage issue with the young lady. It would need to be addressed with her the next day. On the other hand, Patrick Quinn slept soundly with a clear plan hatching in his subconscious. The two men later trudged to breakfast, Patrick smiling and greeting passing friends, while Jacob appeared tired and detached.

After breakfast, Patrick said to Jacob, "C'mon with me, I'm going to take a walk."

The men walked, and Jacob paid little attention to their direction, but became alert when he realized that they were back at the town square, and he and Patrick had halted in front of Colonel Stone at the continuing enlistment rally. Jacob listened as Patrick spoke to Colonel Stone.

"Yes, sir, my dad is Aaron Quinn in Burlington."

The colonel spoke softly, "I know your dad, son. How is he?"

"Just fine, sir," Patrick replied.

The conversation continued to the point that Colonel Stone confirmed that the Iowa Legislature had given him the authority to hand pick officers who would serve under his command. The names of the men he chose would be sent to the legislature for immediate approval. At the end of the conversation, the colonel informed Patrick that he would be nominated as a lieutenant in the Iowa 25th Infantry. To Jacob's astonishment, Patrick and the Colonel shook hands, and Patrick was given a sheaf of papers to fill out and bring back the following day. Patrick turned around and grinned at Jacob.

"I'm going into the Army," said Patrick.

Suddenly, Jacob became aware that the colonel was speaking to him. "I said, what's your name, son," said the colonel.

Jacob turned and answered, "Jacob Roush, sir."

"Are you from Burlington, too?" asked Colonel Stone.

"Yes sir," said Jacob.

"Then your dad must be William Roush," said the colonel.

"Yes sir," said Jacob.

"Well, Mr. Roush, I know your father quite well, as we both had dealings with the Iowa Legislature, and if you have the same fine character as your father and mother, the Army needs leaders of character. I need a couple of captains in my infantry companies. Perhaps you would be interested in serving in one of those positions," said the colonel, as he looked directly into the eyes of Jacob.

Jacob's knees began a slow tremble, and he was speechless. For what seemed to be several minutes, but was in fact seconds, Jacob could not speak. At the end of that interval, Jacob mumbled that he would give it a try.

"I did not quite hear you, son," said the colonel.

"Yes sir, I would like to give it a try!" said Jacob.

"Good! Well then, Mr. Roush, here are your papers to sign, thereby making you a captain in the United States Army," said the colonel as he handed several pages of paper to Jacob. "Please bring them back to me tomorrow. When you come back, you and your lieutenant friend can then sit in as we continue to select enlisted troops for the 25th infantry."

As the young men walked slowly back to campus, in addition to wondering what had just happened to him, Jacob also remembered that he still had not had the courage to speak to Georgia.

Another fitful night passed, and the next day Jacob parted company with Patrick as Patrick headed for the town square. Jacob would follow him later. With a heavy heart, Jacob walked to the women students' dormitory and asked to speak with Georgia Hume. Georgia's bright, smiling face soon appeared, and she rushed to his side.

"What a pleasant surprise," she said. "I was not expecting to see you today."

Jacob looked at the eager young woman, and his heart broke. He quickly excused himself and went outdoors. He rushed behind a nearby bush and was sick. Georgia stepped out of the dormitory as Jacob straightened up and came from behind the bush.

"Oh, Jacob, aren't you feeling well?" she said.

It was over in less than an hour. Jacob had explained that he was too unsure of himself to get married, but that when he returned from his Army service, he would like to call on her again. Georgia Hume was no fool. She was sure of herself and could see that Jacob was not committed to a marriage anytime in the near future.

Steeling herself, she said, "Jacob, I love you. But every time we have spoken of marriage, you have evaded the commitment. I am letting you know that I will pray for you while you are in the Army, but I will not wait for you." Tears rolled from her eyes as she said, "Yes, you may call on me when you return, but I will not guarantee that I will still be single."

They both turned and parted on the steps of the dormitory. Jacob turned back once as he walked away, but the strong young lady did not once look back.

Later that day, Jacob and Patrick sat on the grass behind the uniformed Army men as the young men in the line at the front of the tables were interviewed and inducted into the army. Between his lack of sleep the previous night and an extremely sad mood, Jacob paid no attention to the proceedings and dozed. Patrick was like a terrier, his eyes darting to-and-fro, not missing any of the activities as the young enlistees were processed.

Jacob was rudely interrupted in his somnolence by a stout elbow banging off his ribs.

Patrick began shaking him, and whispered, "Jacob, look down at the end of the table."

Jacob's eyes followed Patrick's pointing finger, at the same time hearing a loud, gruff, and impolite sergeant's voice say, "You're not welcome here. We don't need your kind, now move along."

Jacob became alert, and studied the man to whom the sergeant was speaking. Jacob suddenly jumped to his feet and walked over to the sergeant. "May I ask what the problem is?" said Jacob.

The sergeant looked up and was none too keen to have Jacob butt in. But he also knew that Jacob was soon to be a Company Captain who might very well be his superior, so he held his tongue and said, "Yes sir. This here Indian just showed up and says he wants to be a soldier. Bein' an old Indian fighter myself, I don't fancy havin' one of them in the ranks," said the sergeant.

By this time, the adjutant had stepped up and was told the same story by the sergeant.

Jacob turned to the adjutant and said, "Sir, as it happens, I know this man and can vouch for his character. If it is all right with you, I would like to have him in my company."

Lieutenant Clarke turned, walked back, and spoke with Colonel Stone. He then strode back and said to Jacob, "Mr. Roush, it seems that you are to have an Indian in your company." Turning to the sergeant he said, "Carry on sergeant," and walked away.

Jacob then turned to the sergeant and said, "This Indian's name is Kon, and I would like you to register him as a sergeant in my company."

Fifteen minutes later, the three men had jubilantly greeted and hugged each other.

"Kon, you have no idea how glad I am to see you. You have lifted my spirits and made me feel alive again," said Jacob. "But tell me why you did this. Why would you enlist in the Army?"

Kon replied, "I have listened to our drivers, and I have listened to Mr. O'Connor, all talking about men owning other men. And I have listened to my parents talking about Indians having slaves. I also know what a great opportunity I was given to work for Mr. O'Connor. I have decided to fight to keep our country strong."

Kon was twelve years older than Jacob and Patrick, but the two younger men were wise enough to realize that having Kon with them was a definite experiential asset.

The entire regiment would muster again in Mt. Pleasant at the end of September, giving all three men time to return to Burlington and speak with their families. The mood in all three families was somber. None of the parents had expected their sons' decisions to enter the Union Army. Four Toes and New Rain had suspected something, as Kon had left town some days previous and had not told them where he was going. Aaron and Mary Quinn, through the years had grown used to new, daring developments in the life of Patrick, but nothing of this magnitude. Mary spent a great deal of time behind closed doors in her room, while Aaron pressed the option to Patrick of simply not showing up for the forthcoming military encampment.

William Roush was so angry about his son's decision that he threatened to never speak to Jacob again. After all, Jacob was leaving his father's business to tramp around the country as a soldier; certainly not a suitable career for a wealthy college graduate with a successful business to run. But of all the parents, Martha was the most devastated. The stress of thinking about her son going into a war made her physically ill, and she took to her sick bed. She would not speak to anyone and refused to eat. Doctors called at the Roush home nearly every day to care for

Martha, while William stood outside her sick room door wringing his hands. With the current developments, once again Jacob rued his decision. The same words, "What have I done," coursed through his brain almost constantly. His own father would not speak to him. His usual melancholy mood took a further downturn and remained at that point for the remaining two weeks Jacob was home.

The time for mustering with the 25th Infantry could not come soon enough for Jacob. But when the day arrived to leave and just prior to leaving the house, Martha came to her son. She held him in a tight embrace, kissed his cheek, and whispered in his ear, "Jacob, you must come back to your father and me, do you hear me?"

Jacob answered her, "Mother, I promise to write to you often, and I will come home!" With those words, Jacob turned and walked out the front door of the Roush mansion to meet Patrick and Kon for the trip back to Mt. Pleasant.

Chapter Three

Jacob's War

As officers, they were expected to bring their own horses, preferably an animal sound enough to serve them for as long as possible during their time in the Army. The leads on Jacob and Patrick's horses were tied to the back of the carryall. Kon was driving the rig. Aaron Quinn accompanied the three men as they drove in sporadic silence toward Mt. Pleasant. Aaron would return the rig to Burlington after leaving the three men at the encampment. The three families had finally resigned themselves to the fact that the men had each made a potentially life-threatening decision, and there was little any of the parents could do to change the situation. But Aaron still had words of parental advice for Patrick as the rig bumped along. He still held a slight hope that Patrick would change his mind, stay home, and enter the family lumber business. As he glanced at his oldest son, he shuddered, and a cold feeling came over him when he thought of the dream that Mary had told him she had experienced two nights ago. Aaron forced it out of his mind, and focused on the slowly passing scenery.

Aaron Quinn left the three men and drove away from the military encampment. On this 27th of September, 1862, the encampment was alive with the influx of primarily young men from Des Moines County, Henry County, Washington County, and Louisa County. The men were registered into their assigned military units. Jacob would lead Company D, with Patrick as one of his Platoon Lieutenants. Kon would serve as a sergeant on Jacob's personal staff. There were ten companies assigned to the Iowa 25th Infantry, with nine hundred seventy-two men making up the entire Regiment.

The whole month of October was spent attempting to mold young men into soldiers. Hour after hour the men were led in cadence marching, breaking into battle formations as if readying to meet an imaginary enemy. Rain or shine, mud or dry fields; all were immaterial. The instruction in drill and discipline continued. Shooting skills were honed. Officers were expected to train their own horses, and each time gunnery practice was held, the officers would ride their horses in close proximity to the firing line of the rifles and the artillery. The first time this practice occurred, several of the horses, including Jacob's and Patrick's, panicked and bolted at a gallop away from the noise. It was all the men could do to bring the animals under control and bring them back to the noisy area. But the horses and mules that would pull the artillery caissons soon became accustomed to the roar of the guns. The men grew accustomed to bland, often cold, camp food. Living in tents in the late fall, and learning proper outdoor toiletry in slit trenches made the men long for warm weather and hot food. Little did they comprehend that these simple pleasantries of life would not be enjoyed for many months. Blisters and sore bodies only made a soldier stronger – at least that's what the sergeants told them.

Discipline was ingrained by sometimes heavy-handed, older, career sergeants; men who had faced war and resultant battle death and wounding in Indian battles earlier in their careers. It was these veterans who tried to paint the proper picture in training to prepare young men for the harsh, grotesque realities of battle and war. It was these same wizened senior enlisted men who also trained the new officers, including Jacob and Patrick, while being very tactful to show the proper respect for superior rank.

When they were able to get a few minutes alone, Jacob and Patrick expressed doubt to each other about their ability to learn the proper battle procedures, but most importantly their doubts about leading men in a chaotic battle scenario. If the truth were known, both young men were scared. But they would never confide these feelings to anyone else.

Colonel Stone made his presence felt daily as he rode from company to company watching the training. At times he would call an officer to the side and offer advice and coaching. He too, had concerns about how the regiment would perform under battle conditions. One month of such training was grossly inadequate, but the men were needed at the front, and the difficult month of training soon came to an end. Several days were spent packing up the regiment while the training was completed, and early in November, the regiment marched southeast through Burlington to board troop boats on the Mississippi River.

Word of the regiment's movement far preceded them, and families and friends lined the streets as the army came through town. Families could only shout a tearful hello, and possibly pass a keepsake or a bit of food into hands as their sons passed by. After reaching the O'Connor Transportation landing, the blue-clad men soon boarded troop boats. Mike O'Connor owned these boats which had been contracted to the Army. Other specialized boats were used for the artillery, horses, and supply wagons. When all was ready, the regiment moved into the main channel of the river.

The upper Midwest of the country had been experiencing drought conditions for many months. As a result, the river was down considerably, and the piloting of the boats was treacherous. In the course of the next few days, there were many boat groundings, which resulted in men and cargo being off loaded at times to free the boats from the hidden sand bars. Progress was slow.

Arkansas had seceded from the Union in May 1861. But the Union retained several forts in the state after the secession. The fort at Little Rock was ultimately surrendered to the confederates, but one of the remaining Union forts was at Helena, sitting on the Mississippi. Under the safety of four huge Union batteries overlooking the river, the Iowa 25th Infantry landed at Helena, Arkansas on November 17, 1862. The regiment resumed rigorous battle training.

November 21

Dear Mother, It pleasures me to have a few moments to write to you. We have reached our new camp here on the Mississippi. We are next to a Union fort and feel safe with all the big guns located here. Our trip down the river was not pleasant, as we had to keep disembarking to lighten the boat's load to get past sand bars. I have made a few friends, and most of my men are from good stock. We have been told we will continue training here for a while yet before we move on. Say hello to Father and Edna.

Your loving son, Jacob

Later in November, Jacob and another captain, along with their respective lieutenants, were summoned to see Major Calvin Taylor at regimental headquarters. Major Taylor spoke to the officers.

"Gentlemen, I will be leading your two companies on a reconnoitering expedition. You need to prepare your companies to leave in two days. I'm going to refrain from advising you of our ultimate destination, but you must prepare for long days of marching."

A short discussion and questions followed the meeting before the men returned to their companies. In two days, the boredom of camp life and training ended as the two hundred plus soldiers, two wagons, and two brand new ten pound Parrott field rifle cannons, which had been forged at West Point, New York, filed out of camp, marching to the west-southwest. There was no hurry to the march, as their purpose was to discover and report on rebel opposition, and the strength of those rebel sightings. In addition, the mission was also meant to harden the troops to long hours of marching. They met no resistance the first day, but as they approached Lakeview, rebel sniper fire became more frequent. At each instance, the snipers were routed by a volley from the union troopers.

As the companies marched through the Lakeview area, they foraged food and any needed supplies from scowling citizens in the town and from farms they encountered. The companies marched further south, approaching Elaine. But a mile from the small town, the mounted scouts rapidly returned to the main body and reported to Major Taylor that the rebels had set up breastworks across the road. The scouts estimated that there were as many as fifty men manning the barricade, but they appeared to have no artillery.

Major Taylor sent the skirmishers out, and then split the companies to go down both sides of the road. After another half mile, the main body halted while two platoons were sent to flank the right and left sides of the rebel breastworks and lay in waiting. The force resumed their march after allowing time for the flankers to set up their positions.

When the breastworks came into view, the rebels behind the barrier began firing, but the range was still too great. The marching continued until a halt was called. Again the Union soldiers took up firing positions on either side of the road, while Jacob stayed with the main body of his company. The Parrott rifles were brought forward, rapidly spun around and loaded. The major ordered them to fire at will. The two cannons roared, and after three rounds, the range was found and the next shells landed on the breastworks. Two rebel soldiers were tossed into the air, killed by the impact of the cannon rounds. After another firing of the cannon, the line of rebels behind the roadblock quickly broke, with rebels fleeing in all directions. Union rifle fire from hidden positions on the flanks of the breastwork soon cut down many of the fleeing rebels, and the remaining rebels continued their flight.

Then there was silence, suddenly broken by cheers from the Union soldiers. The men quickly cleared the road of the rebel blockade, and the march continued with the column heading west.

A few miles west of Elaine, in late afternoon, high ground was found and the group posted pickets and set up camp for the night. The long marches were still somewhat of a novelty to the inexperienced men, so spirits remained high, especially considering their victorious experience earlier that day. Major Taylor sent word to both companies that their performance had been most professional, and that he was pleased. Suppers were eaten, and stories of the day were shared. Decks of cards, harmonicas, and Jew's harps were pulled from backpacks, and the music could be heard from various parts of the camp. Patrick had come to Jacob's tent and the two men talked. Neither man had been fired upon that day. Primarily, they talked about Army life and about their home and family. They also shared their concerns for days ahead and wished each other well.

November 29

Dear Mother, I hope this letter finds you well. We met and bested a troop of rebel soldiers a couple days back, and all men are accounted for and without injury. I have been thinking some of Christmas that will soon be upon us and remembering some of our family's fine times. I miss you and Father, but maybe this war will end soon.

Your loving son, Jacob

For the next few days, rebel snipers continued to ineffectively fire on the column, but there were no true skirmishes. Then one evening, the companies camped outside of Marvell. Guards were posted, and the camp quieted for the night. Reveille was sounded the next morning, and as the men drank their coffee and ate, the firing began. Rifles barked out, and minie balls shrieked and sounded like heavy rain as they passed through tree leaves throughout the camp. Jacob lay on the ground listening and watching, trying to determine from where the shots were being fired. He then got up and ran, shouting orders to his lieutenants to set up a defensive perimeter. With the help of the sergeants, D Company soon encircled half of the camp. A similar maneuver by the other company formed a defensive line around the other half of the camp. It soon became apparent that the rebels were spread around the camp, lying in tall grass. Aside from that grass, they were without cover. But the Union soldiers were not in much better shape to make their defense, even though they were on higher ground. The previous evening, there had been some half-hearted shallow trenches dug, but now, troopers had their entrenching tools out making hurried, deeper hollows to lie in for protection and from which to shoot. A steady return fire by the Union rifles soon suppressed some of the rebel fire.

The cannons were quickly brought on line and loaded with canister. It was hoped that the canister shot would rip away some of the tall grass while finding human targets. But even though the canister fire was devastating, the rebels refused to run. They continued to fire on the Union contingent. His aides had brought his horse, and Major Taylor rode the Union line giving orders. Momentarily, he gave the signal of lowering his sword and the entire Union line rose and the large blue circle began running forward to encircle the rebel line. The rebels responded with a fusillade of fire, which was only slightly effective, reaching and wounding several union soldiers. The white smoke was thick and acrid, and the noise was deafening.

Jacob found himself running forward with his troops, with sword held high. His mind had shut out all extraneous thoughts, focusing only on survival. With his troops abreast of him, he suddenly reached a rebel soldier pointing a rifle directly at him. Jacob's arm swiftly came down, and his sword caught the man's forearm, opening a wide, bleeding wound and breaking the rebel's arm just at the point that the rebel's rifle fired. The shot went to the ground. The rebel's shot was quickly answered by a Union soldier at Jacob's side. The rebel fell backward with a gaping hole in his chest. A multitude of similar actions were taking place all around him. He drew his pistol and fired at another rebel, who also fell. Ever so slowly, his brain began to process other activity around him, and he became aware that the noise was subsiding, and he watched the rebel forces fleeing from the area. The skirmish was over. Jacob looked down at the dead rebel soldier covered in blood at his feet and turned to the side and vomited.

With Kon standing close by, two older sergeants walked by and blithely said, "That's all right Captain, everybody gets to pukin' in their first battle," and they both laughed and continued on.

Kon moved to Jacob's side and said, "My father spoke to me about the battles with the soldiers when he was young. I guess it must have been much like this."

"I don't believe that anyone can ever get used to this, Kon," said Jacob. Several of the Union soldiers had been wounded, but there were no deaths. The companies finally broke camp and began their eastward march to return to Helena.

December 10

Dear Mother,

Please do not worry about me as I am safe and well. Our company met a small force of rebels a few days ago and successfully routed them. I am ashamed to admit that I was greatly fearful during the fighting, but I emerged unscathed. My men fought quite bravely. Patrick and Kon are well and send their regards. Please give my warmest regards to Father and Edna.

Your loving son, Jacob

***

Early on December 13th, word was received at Helena that the Union Navy had suffered a loss in Vicksburg, Mississippi. The Navy gunboat, USS *Cairo*, was involved with other ships in clearing torpedoes from the river off Vicksburg in preparation for an attack on Haines Bluff. But the *Cairo* fell victim to a torpedo herself. The torpedo was activated by an electrical charge sent by two rebel sympathizers hidden in some bushes on the bank of the river. This was the first time in history that a ship had been sunk by a torpedo ignited by an electrical charge. To an army in wait at Helena, it only served to enforce the fact that military troop travel on the river was not without peril.

***

Chickasaw Bayou

For the past two weeks, other brigades had joined the forces at Helena, swelling the Union troops to seventy thousand strong. The objective of this army would be to capture the city of Vicksburg, Mississippi. It was vitally important that the Union control the Mississippi, but heavily armed Vicksburg was standing in the way of making that happen. General Ulysses S. Grant was in command of this formidable army. He split the troops into two corps. He would lead one corps, and Major General William T. Sherman would lead the other, designated the XV Corps. After all preparations were made, on the 22nd of December, the Iowa 25th and other brigades making up Sherman's XV Corps boarded fifty-nine troop transports accompanied by seven gunboats. There were thirty-two thousand men being transported. The river fleet was commanded by Rear Admiral David Porter. The flotilla of river craft moved south on the great river, with Admiral Porter leading the boats down the Mississippi to Milliken's Bend, above Vicksburg, where the boats turned north, travelling up the Yazoo River. In the meantime, General Grant's corps marched on foot, south along the river, following railroad lines to Oxford, Mississippi, where he laid in wait, hoping to lure the confederates out of Vicksburg to attack his army.

The river craft landed late on December 24th, at a location called Johnson's Plantation, north and east of the city of Vicksburg, and camp was made. As Jacob tended to his horse and oversaw the formation of Company D's camp, his mind wandered to the date. Tomorrow would be Christmas, and he would spend his first Christmas in the Army, far away from home. He fought the melancholy feeling, pushing himself to stay busy in his leadership role. He found Patrick Quinn and wished him all the best for Christmas, and the two men embraced briefly. He then made sure that his lieutenants wished all of the men the very best for the holiday.

Christmas day was a day of rest and reflection for Sherman's thirty-two thousand men as they quietly celebrated the birth of the Christ child, while cleaning, inspecting, and readying their gear for the next day. It was the lonely Christmas of military men.

December 25, Christmas
Dear Mother,
I take pen in hand to write you a few lines on this Christmas day. I am well, as are Patrick and Kon. I offer my most sincere wishes that you and Father had a joyous Christmas. It appears we will not be fighting today, and I suppose that is the most we can hope for on this Christmas. You might not recognize me as I have lost some weight and have grown a mustache. Patrick teases me about that. If I do not have time to write

*before the New Year, I wish the best in the new year for all of us, and
hope this war ends soon.*

Your loving son, Jacob

The opposing force of Confederates under the overall command of Lt.
General John C. Pemberton was not about to give up their strategic city.
When it was learned that General Sherman's force had landed at John-
son's Plantation, Confederate forces were quickly moved to the area.
Sherman's force of thirty thousand plus men would face Confederate
Major General Carter Stevenson, who had fourteen thousand men. But
Sherman quickly found out that the numbers were somewhat immaterial.
The Union soldiers faced a formidable defense, both natural and man-
made. The terrain was an entanglement of heavy trees, interspersed with
swampland. Chickasaw Bayou, a four-foot deep stream that was fifty
feet wide and choked with trees also blocked the planned Union line of
attack. In addition, the rebels had built dense barriers of felled trees. The
battle would not be easy.

Jacob's company again found itself marching to the front. Jacob led
his men through the fetid swamps to the right side of the Confederate
line. He was part of General Frederick Steele's division which would
attempt to turn the rebels' right flank.

On December 28th, Jacob and his men bravely charged the rebel line,
but were quickly repulsed by withering artillery fire. Many of the Union
soldiers were wounded. On December 29th, General Sherman ordered a
prolonged artillery attack on the rebel positions in preparation for a full
Union assault. The artillery duel between the opposing forces lasted
nearly four full hours, but did negligible damage to the rebel defenses.
When the artillery barrage was over, the brave Union soldiers again
attacked the rebel lines.

Jacob and his men were involved in another attack and got as far as the rebels' advance rifle pits, but suffered losses, with many men wounded before they were forced to fall back. Jacob was exhausted. He and his men waded back through the swamp to higher, safe ground where he and the men collapsed on the ground to rest. That evening, General Sherman said that he was "satisfied with the high spirit manifested" by the troops. Two hundred eight Union soldiers were killed, and over a thousand were injured. The horrors of war were now firmly etched in Jacob's mind.

Patrick and Kon had also escaped injury and conferred with Jacob while they rested. Patrick's usual bravado was not in evidence. He had seen his fellow soldiers literally cut in pieces from withering rifle and cannon fire. Kon was even more stoic. The men spoke little and parted for the night.

The following day, there were no charges by the Union forces, and Jacob was able to move among his men, giving kind words and encouragement, and holding his emotions as he observed the men who had been severely wounded.

January 1

Dear Mother,

I wish you the happiest of New Year's days. We have not had to go fight for a few days. We are to move again, but I am not told of our destination. I had a dream last night that I was back home, helping Father at the store, and eating large amounts of food. I woke to a breakfast of biscuits, beans, and coffee. As you can imagine, I would much rather be at home. Please tell Father that my horse has performed most admirably in my travels, and seems calm in all the noise of battle. Many of the men have been sick. They tell us it is the swamp water, but I remain well.

Your loving son, Jacob

***

Arkansas Post

General Sherman's forces were once again on the march. On January 2, 1863, the force reached the mouth of the Yazoo River to join Major General John McClernand's forces. Admiral Porter would once again be moving the Army on the river. Jacob and the other junior officers soon learned that the boats were taking them to the Arkansas River, where they were to attack a fort known as Fort Hindman, near a settlement called Arkansas Post. The capture of this fort would ensure the safety of Union supply boats. The previous month, in December, a Union supply steamer, the *Blue Wing*, loaded with armaments had been captured on the river and taken to Fort Hindman. The fort must be taken to protect shipping and communication.

Jacob, Kon, and Patrick, along with thirty-two thousand other Union soldiers landed at Nortrebe's Plantation and immediately began moving toward the fort. By 5:30 p.m. the troops had reached their assault positions and held there. At the same time, Admiral Porter moved his gunboats into position on the river and began firing his artillery at the fort. He was assisted by Union artillery across the river. The sky filled with the bright explosion flashes and dense smoke. Jacob watched in fascination, knowing that a multitude of rebel soldiers lay dying, but that he and his men would not have to face those same rebels. And just as fortuitous, when the artillery barrage ended, it was too dark to advance.

The next morning, the artillery barrage resumed from the gunboats and Union artillery with the result that the guns of Fort Hindman were silenced. The infantry then began its advance. The rifle fire from rifle pits occupied by the rebels from Texas and Arkansas was nearly constant. Jacob was in a battalion on the right and moved against these rifle pits. The rebel bullets whined like giant angry mosquitos, and the thick white smoke hung in the humid air. Jacob, with Patrick nearby, led a charge against a rifle pit, killing a few rebels, but their group was repulsed under the steady rebel fire. Gathering his forces again, Jacob charged the rebel line a second time, but was thwarted again. He drew his men together to rest before receiving further orders. General McClernand was planning a final massive assault, using all the Union soldiers at his disposal.

But as the afternoon progressed, there suddenly appeared several white flags along the Confederate lines. Although the Confederate General, Churchill, later denied giving the order, the garrison at Fort Hindman surrendered to McClernand's army. The cheers of the Union soldiers erupted; the battle for Fort Hindman was over. More than four thousand rebels were captured and sent up river to union prison camps. The Iowa 25th suffered casualties including sixty men killed, wounded, or captured. Adjutant Samuel Kirkwood Clarke, two captains, and two lieutenants were killed in the battle. Jacob, Patrick, and Kon had survived, a fact that amazed all three of them.

February 1

Dear Mother,

We have been encamped here for several weeks near a place called Young's Point. The men are resting, but sickness still is abundant. They tell us the rainy wet and gloomy weather is not good for the constitution. I manage to stay well, but I sure miss the sunshine. Patrick and I talk daily, and Kon comes to see me frequently. It is good to have two fine friends to talk with. One of my men has given me a harmonica. I don't play it much cause my mustache gets caught in it. We had a bad go of it at a place called Arkansas Post. Many men were killed, but I guess God is watching over me. Regards to Father and Edna.

Your loving son, Jacob

Sickness had indeed become a problem in the camp. Colonel Stone gave orders that the Iowa 25th would hold drilling and marching exercises daily except on Sunday. He insisted that the men stay active in an attempt to keep them strong and less likely to be infirmed. The cold, damp weather brought colds and flu to the closely confined large group. The Colonel could be found walking among his men, encouraging them. He also made sure that all of the living quarters were policed as well as the entire camp area of the 25th. It was during this period that a large number of men at Young's Point died of malaria and other viruses, while the Iowa 25th only lost four men to illness, probably due to the watchful eye of their Commanding Officer.

***

Jackson, Mississippi

"I believe that we may yet have some nice spring weather," said Patrick.

He was speaking to Jacob as the men walked their horses amidst the Company D camp area. Their men were gathering up the last of their belongings in preparation for the march. The two corps under General Grant were moving toward Jackson, Mississippi, on this clear and sunny May day. This massive army had crossed the Mississippi south of Vicksburg and had been travelling northeast for several days. On May 9, Confederate General Joseph Johnston arrived in Jackson to assess the defensive capability of his troops in that city. He found that there were only six thousand soldiers fit to defend the city. Johnston ordered the evacuation of the city, but left behind a force to meet the Union army. On May 14th, the Union forces moved into the city.

The now-familiar sound of the rifle fire interspersed with the light artillery rose in volume as the men advanced. The rebels were in pockets firing at the Union soldiers as they moved from street to street. Most of the citizenry of Jackson had heeded General Johnston's mandate to seek cover in the countryside. Slowly, the rebels had had enough and moved out of the city, fleeing to fight another day. Sherman's men had taken the city of Jackson forcing the rebel army to flee.

General Grant, who had been traveling with General Sherman, hosted a celebration for the officers in the Bowman House, a hotel in the center of the city. While Jacob was required to attend, he did so mostly out of curiosity to meet other officers, including General Grant. Immediately following this celebration, the Union Army burned a great part of the city and tore out all rail lines leading west toward Vicksburg.

A large supply of rum had been found in the city, and the celebration by the Union soldiers lasted for nearly a day. Order could not be maintained, and the soldiers took advantage of the situation, pillaging the city. All facilities in Jackson that could reasonably assist the Confederacy were burned or destroyed. Jacob had watched as his troops burned a warehouse full of cotton. Finally, late in the night, when a light rain had stopped, Jacob and Patrick sat outside their tent talking.

"We've been mighty lucky, Jacob," said Patrick. "But I'm worried," he said. "I always wonder how much longer our luck can hold."

Jacob did not respond. The same thoughts had occurred to him. Kon walked up, sat down and joined them.

"With your permission, sir," he jokingly mocked Jacob.

The men chuckled. They had been friends for far too long and had been through the hell of battle together too many times to rest on officer/enlisted formalities, except in the presence of other soldiers. Somehow, Kon had gotten three cigars, and the men lit up. Although none of them smoked on a regular basis, they thought the situation warranted this indulgence.

"I got a letter from my Father today," said Patrick. "He said his coal buying operation is doing quite well, and he still says he wants me to join him in the business when I get back. And he said to tell you, Kon, that he needs you back to ramrod the maintenance department."

The men were quiet as they smoked their cigars.

"I wish I was home," said Kon.

On May 16th, Jacob was once again astride his horse moving in formation with the rest of Sherman's corps. His worn out regiment followed, plodding on the road west. As he rode out of the city, he looked around and saw only filth, fires still burning, buildings in rubble, and still unburied rebel fatalities of war. He had seen enough in his short time in the Army, and he was sick of it. He thought more and more of the river in Burlington, the small city there, and of his family. They were the same thoughts as all soldiers since the beginning of time. The XV Corps was moving west. They were returning to Vicksburg.

***

Vicksburg

His army was spread from Vicksburg east to Jackson, more than forty miles, with encampments at strategic points in between. Lt. General John C. Pemberton, the Confederate General directing this army, was faring poorly. His army was under attack from two directions. Union General Grant had crossed the Mississippi, moved northeast, and had captured Jackson. Leaving Jackson, Grant moved west and defeated Pemberton's forces at Champion Hill and Big Black River Bridge. Union General Sherman was northwest of the city of Vicksburg and was threatening to flank Pemberton's army. The rebel army was now only a fraction of its original size. Nearly three-fourths of his army had been lost in the two previous battles. General Pemberton had two choices. He could bring his depleted army back to the well-defended defense works surrounding Vicksburg, or he could amass his army, abandon Vicksburg, and escape to the south of Vicksburg. His commanding officer, General Joseph

Johnston, urged him to abandon the city and save his army. But when polled, Pemberton's general staff informed him that his army was in no physical condition to travel. He had little choice. He drew the army back into the heavily fortified city of Vicksburg, taking everything edible in his path, both animal and plant.

Vicksburg was well defended. Except for the area along the Mississippi River, the defense line circled the city, and consisted of varying level terrain of hills and knobs with steep angles. There were also numerous gun pits, forts, trenches, redoubts (small forts), redans (v-shaped defense works), and lunettes (protrusions in the defensive line).

Upon reaching the defense works on May 19, 1863, Generals Grant and Sherman deployed their troops strategically facing the Confederate defenses. The Iowa 25th, with Jacob, Patrick, and Kon, was positioned on the far right of the Union line, north of the city. General Grant ordered an attack on an area well away from the 25th, at an area known as the Stockade Redan. As the Union soldiers attacked, they had to cross defensive walls and an eight-foot-wide ditch. From their higher positions, the rebels cut down the Union line, easily repulsing the attack. General Grant followed this failure with an artillery bombardment to soften the rebel lines, followed by sending another division of men against the line. This attack was also repulsed by the rebels, at the cost of a rising number of casualties.

Word of these failures spread through the Union lines, thereby deflating the confidence of the men. How could this possibly be happening? The Union Army's most recent victories in Arkansas and Mississippi had proven that the Confederate Army was no match. Yet, here were seventy thousand Union troops poised to defeat General Pemberton's rag-tag army, and they were repeatedly repulsed. Jacob's regiment patiently, but anxiously waited, having already learned the fate of hundreds of their fallen brothers.

The Iowa 25th had been ordered to stand down while awaiting further orders. The men could eat if they had any edibles, and water was distributed. The men relaxed, but there was no comfort. The sticky heat was unbearable; so stifling that it was hard to breathe. They were spread out in small trenches in the full sun, with no shelter. Jacob overheard one of the sergeants saying, "It's too damn hot to play cards." For Jacob, it took no convincing. He could not remember ever being this uncomfortable. His mind wandered to his boyhood days of swimming in the river at Burlington. He longed to be home. Patrick was near him, but the two men did not speak to each other. It was too hot for the effort.

As the sun lowered on the 19th, the artillery bombardment began. Two hundred twenty artillery pieces and naval gunfire kept up a blazing storm from hell for the entire night. Citizens of Vicksburg had abandoned the city for the most part, and many were living in caves dug into hillsides, still behind the Confederate lines. The city was ablaze with fires. Pleas from the Vicksburg citizenry to the Union generals had saved several large homes in the city by virtue of using the stately old homes as hospitals available to both sides. Cannoneers made an effort to bypass these designated locations as they continued firing on the city. Cannon balls rolled down city streets, crashing into buildings. Other armament blew up on landing, leveling a few structures and injuring anyone foolish enough to have stayed in the city. But, astonishingly, considering the immense barrage, there was very little severe damage to the city.

All was relatively quiet on the 20th, and Jacob and his men were able to repair equipment, eat, and talk, knowing that another wave of attacks could be ordered at any time. Morale was up again after the men had eaten some of the food they had foraged.

The men were also able to walk around camp, and many of the men searched out friends from home. Jacob checked on the welfare of his men and continued walking about the camp. He stopped and listened to a group of men quietly playing popular and religious songs and singing when they knew the words to some of the songs. He remembered his mother's love for music as he stood and listened. He did not notice as Kon came up beside him.

As the musical group broke up, one of the men looked up, and stood and walked over to Jacob and Kon.

The soldier said, "Beg your pardon, Captain, but is this the Indian in the Iowa 25th?"

Jacob looked at the soldier and saw no malevolence in the man's eyes. Jacob answered, "The sergeant, who happens to be an Indian, is my friend. His name is Kon, and yes, he is in the Iowa 25th."

The young soldier then recognized the bluntness of his question and answered, "I'm sorry sir, and Sergeant Kon, I meant no disrespect. I simply wanted to shake Sergeant Kon's hand. You see, I too am a bit of an oddity in this here army. I'm a Quaker, and there aren't very many of us in the army. And I know for sure there aren't many Indians either. So I guess we have that in common."

Kon extended his hand and shook hands with the soldier.

"Where do you hail from," said Jacob.

"Up by Oskaloosa," responded the young man.

Jacob's mind immediately brought back sweet memories of the Quaker girl who had meant so much to him in college, Georgia Hume. Jacob asked the soldier, "What does your family do in Oskaloosa?"

"We're just simple farmers," was the response. Jacob and the young Quaker soldier talked for many minutes, while Jacob ached to ask the question that haunted him. They continued talking and the conversation turned to the huge mining enterprise near Oskaloosa. The area was now the largest producer of coal in the state and boasted over thirty different mines. The young man also told Jacob that area Quakers were drawing plans to start a college in Oskaloosa, but with meager funds, the school was really just in the idea stage.

Finally, Jacob got up the nerve and asked, "Do you know a Quaker family named Hume. I understand they are farmers in the area. Their daughter, Georgia, was at Iowa Wesleyan while I studied there."

"Oh yes, sir, I know the family. They attend Friends Meeting at our church," said the soldier.

Jacob then braced himself and asked, "Do you know if Miss Hume ever married?"

The soldier rubbed his cheek for a moment, as if he did not know how to answer. Then he said, "Well, sir, it's a kinda strange story. When she returned home, she seemed different. Kinda quiet like. She has had plenty of interested suitors, but she has not yet married. Well, I better get back to my company, or they will wonder where I am," he said. "Nice meeting you, Captain, and you too, Sergeant Kon," and the young man turned and walked away.

Jacob and Kon stood still for a few seconds watching the soldier return to his unit, and then walked on.

May 20, 1863

Dearest Mother, I am pleased to take pen in hand to tell you I am fine. Here at Vicksburg we seem to have the rebels surrounded. We certainly travel around the countryside. I have never suffered so from such hot weather before being here. The strength is just drawn out of me by this heat. I long to be home. I am surely tired of eating hardtack and beans, and so wish for one of your fine chicken dinners. I have received two of your letters while here, and am happy to hear about the goings on back home.

Your loving son, Jacob

That evening, the Army served beans, hardtack, and coffee for supper.

On the morning of the 22nd, the artillery resumed its massive chorus, with the barrage lasting for four hours. The Union attack followed, along a three-mile long front. While this action was taking place, Jacob's division moved into position on the far right of the line. Upon orders, Jacob moved his company into a position through a spring-fed ravine called Mint Spring Bayou. Blazing a trail through the tangled vegetation took most of the morning. Jacob and his men were exhausted. The effort of cutting vegetation in the intense heat sapped the men's strength, leaving them gasping for breath. By 3 p.m., General Steele's division, which contained Jacob's company, was in position, and General Steele gave the order to charge against the 26th Louisiana Redoubt. Jacob led his men forward. He glanced to his sides and saw Kon on one side, and Patrick leading his men on the other. The redoubt had loaded canister and the screaming metal flew all around. The smoke and especially the deafening roar of noise, once again caused Jacob's brain to shut down all circuits except those needed for survival fighting. In this mental state, the rifle fire all around him was no longer a source of concern. Jacob was able to crouch on one knee and take aim with his pistol at a rebel exposed on the redoubt wall. He fired, the rebel fell back, and Jacob rose and again moved forward. While men fell all around him, he continued moving ahead. At one point, he was staring directly at an artillery piece on the upper part of the redoubt. He could actually see the ball leave the barrel of the cannon as it fired. He kept moving forward. But as he turned to see the progress of his men behind him, he could see that his men were falling so fast that other regiments were refusing to follow and support his regiment's efforts. He turned back to the front, and his vision suddenly exploded in a flash of vivid red and yellow, followed by the light receding to only a pinpoint. He fell unceremoniously to the ground.

James Duermeyer

A musket ball had struck him on the right side of his head, and Jacob's world went dark and quiet.

Part Three

Anna

Chapter One

Anna Arrives

While the War Between the States raged in the country's South and Southeast, making enemies of friends and enemies of brothers, it was of little concern to Anna Maier. She was only concerned with making her presence known in Burlington in a most resplendent manner. She even sat in resplendence, in what would become the front yard of the property, on a brocaded crimson chair, while holding her silk parasol to shade her from the sun. Her house girl stood to the side of the chair should Anna require anything. Anna was focused on the activity of two hundred laborers who were working diligently to carry out her every whim while trying to build the house that would become the largest and most lavish in Burlington. Anna was overseeing every stone, piece of wood, and nail that went into the building of the house. Every few minutes, she rose from her chair, strode over to the general foreman, and in no uncertain terms pointedly told the foreman where a specific carpenter, or mason, or other craftsman was not carrying out his duties properly. This was the third foreman on the job. Anna had fired the first two, shrieking at them for some minor detail before severing their employment. The present foreman had been on the job for almost three months and had many times been on the verge of simply walking off the job. The constant pestering, criticism, belittling of his skills and his manhood, and the whimsical changing of the building plans was far more than what he had bargained for in taking the job. But he had a family to support, and the woman paid well, so he suffered the constant harassment in silence and refrained from leaving.

The architect had been contracted from a prestigious firm in St. Louis. He had taken a month to finalize the drawings, living in a Burlington boarding house until he could complete the plans and return to St. Louis. Each time he had brought the newly drawn or revised plans to the woman for review, she made changes, resulting in yet another revision of the plans. When she became unhappy with him, the woman would send a telegram to his firm in St. Louis. Thankfully, the firm had gained an acute perspective on Miss Maier through this unnecessary interaction and retained the architect, allaying his fears of being fired in reaction to the ranting and rambling telegrams sent by the woman. The firm also knew that they were being handsomely paid. The architect was overjoyed on the day that the woman had finally approved the house plans. Immediately after Anna had signed off on the final plan, he hurriedly caught a train and left town.

As the warmth of the afternoon sun became more apparent, Anna fanned herself with a richly colored oriental, hand-held fan, but she soon succumbed to her warmth-induced drowsiness, her eyelids drooped and eventually closed, and her mind wandered, replaying the events of the past year that had brought her to this point.

***

"Then it's settled," said Isaac Maier, and the two men shook hands. It was a very warm evening in June 1862, in Chicago. With their sleeves rolled up and their collars open, the two wealthy fathers sat at a table in the kitchen of the Marvin Stearn home. After many meetings between the two men and dinners attended by both families, a financial dowry agreement had, at last, been made. With the blessing of both sets of parents, the arranged marriage of Marvin's son, Luke, to Isaac Maier's daughter, Anna, could now be planned. The wedding would take place late in December, after the close of the Hanukah holidays. The wives joined their husbands in the kitchen, and a celebratory bottle of wine was shared.

Mrs. Stearn bubbled over in excitement saying, "I am so happy. My Luke will make a good husband to Anna, and she will be a wonderful bride and wife. Last night, as I gazed into the sky, I saw a shooting star, so this marriage must surely be blessed."

Florence Maier stared down into her glass of wine, keeping her own thoughts on what that shooting star might have meant. Florence Maier was not necessarily superstitious by nature. But she was well aware of the nature of her youngest daughter, Anna. She remembered distinctly, twenty years ago when Anna was an infant. She had gazed into the beautiful doll-like face of baby Anna. Anna had, indeed been a beautiful baby. But Florence had seen something else in the baby's eyes that only a mother could see. She saw a small fire burning in the eyes of the baby. It was an impudent look, and Anna had been far from a quiet baby. She had cried at the slightest discomfort. Florence and Isaac Maier had not gotten much sleep during the infancy of baby Anna. Even twenty years ago, they shared their thoughts on the forming personality of Anna and worried about the baby's obstinate nature. They had not experienced this personality trait in their other children.

As she looked at the glass of wine, Florence Maier's thoughts returned to the week of Anna's birth in 1842. She vividly recalled the details of when Isaac had paid yet another visit to his banker.

***

Isaac Maier was an extremely lucky second generation Jewish gentleman. His father had started a business in Chicago, trading in precious metals and selling jewelry out of the front parlor of his walk-up apartment. The elder Maier, with an astonishing talent for making money, was soon building a business that was known throughout most of Chicago as a fair and honest place for jewelry and precious metal. The family had grown along with the business, and upon the death of the senior Maier, Isaac had inherited a company free of debt, along with a large amount of money. It seemed that Isaac had the same business acumen as his father. Continuing in his father's tradition, the company became the largest jewelry and precious metal company in the area.

In addition to his love for commerce, Isaac also loved his children immensely. Upon the birth of each of his three children, he established generous trust funds that would become the property of each child when he or she reached eighteen years of age. For all practical purposes, with the size of the trust funds and their monthly income, none of the Maier children would ever have to work a day in their lives.

On a typical chilly, blustery day in Chicago, Isaac Maier was seated across the large oaken desk from his banker at the Chicago Fidelity Bank. One week prior to this meeting, Anna Maier had been born, the youngest and the last of the Maier children. She joined older sister Hilda, and brother Johan who were born three and two years earlier respectively. Isaac and the banker were drawing up the papers and funding the new trust fund for baby Anna. The funds would become Anna's when she reached her eighteenth birthday and would give her a handsome lifetime income.

Florence's thoughts of her family continued. The Maier family was raised in a strict conservative Jewish manner. The parents entertained their friends of influence with gala parties and the children were given the finest schooling and finishing that wealth could provide. It was expected that the children would retain the family wealth and marry only into other families of like worth. The son would be further educated, while the two girls in the family would attend finishing school to become debutants in wealthy society. They would attend a staggering number of balls and galas; all intended to make the young ladies well known in their sphere of wealthy family acquaintances. The girls would also have marriages arranged by their parents when they were of age. The girls would not recognize the seriousness of this aspect of their lives until they grew toward womanhood. They had received years of schooling and a disciplined home environment. Florence was amazed at how quickly the time had passed. To think that the marriage of her youngest child was now being discussed brought on these reminiscences.

Anna was the youngest of the Maier children. Anna had an older sister Hilda, and an older brother, Johan. Hilda's arranged wedding to a wealthy young man had taken place five years earlier, and she was now a mother, and fortunately, very happily married. Johan was nearly ready to complete law school at the University of Chicago and presently had no plans to marry. This situation also incensed Anna, who thought it was highly unfair that the boy in the family was not being pressured into a forced marriage and could choose his own spouse.

The family battle which had begun shortly after her parents' meeting with the Stearns' in June had become more intense. On this September morning, there had been another row before Isaac left for work.

"Luke Stearn is a klutz, a dunderhead, and I refuse to marry him," screamed Anna. "You cannot make me marry him. I hate him. We despise each other, and I refuse to even be in the same room as him!"

Every attempt by Isaac to settle this issue was met with haggish screeches from Anna. Florence, as usual, held her handkerchief to her mouth and sobbed. Among families practicing arranged marriages for their daughters, the marriage agreements between families were iron clad. There was no room for reneging on the contract. The consequences of such an action would be shunning by their neighbors and friends. Even in the case of a wealthy family, a family that failed to honor its commitment would henceforth be held in very low esteem, indeed.

Part of Anna's wrath had to do with the fact that the community now recognized her to be betrothed to Luke Stearn. Hence, she was now considered to be unavailable to other suitors. Her parents forbade her to attend any mixed social activities unless they were also attended by Luke Stearn. Determined not to be bridled, Anna would meet her girlfriends and discreetly go to places where young men might also be in attendance. But in most instances, Luke Stearn would also be there, spoiling Anna's plans to avoid him. Anna chafed at being referred to as "betrothed".

She began making her plans in secret. The headstrong young woman was determined not to marry Luke Stearn, and by any means she could devise, she would prevent the marriage from occurring. She would leave Chicago and go west. She had even decided where she would relocate. She had chosen Burlington, Iowa, because it was a prosperous and growing community that could be reached nearly the whole distance by train, and where she also thought that her parents would not be able to find her. She had also confirmed that in Iowa, a single woman could own property. This was in keeping with her plan. She kept a diary of her progress in making all the preparations necessary to relocate. The details were numerous, but most importantly, she had her trust fund, her own money, which meant that she had a steady flow of income for the rest of her life.

One day, after another heated argument with her parents over the pending wedding, she retired to her room. Her mother gently rapped on her bedroom door.

"Anna, I want to talk with you," said Florence.

Anna screamed, "I will not speak any further about this," and as her mother entered the bedroom, Anna moved into the adjoining dressing room and slammed and locked the door.

Florence Maier stood for a moment looking at the dressing room door, and then moved over to Anna's dresser. Her curiosity had been piqued when she saw some papers lying on top of the dresser. As she looked at them, she saw what appeared to be various bank papers, but protruding beneath the papers appeared to be a train ticket, which she hurriedly studied. Florence then quickly turned and left the room.

Later, when Isaac returned from work, Florence confided in him. That evening's dinner was very strained, with very little interaction between the parents and the daughter. As dinner was nearly completed, Isaac spoke.

"Anna, I want you to tell me the truth. Do you intend to continue this melodrama of refusing to marry Luke Stearn?" he asked.

Anna responded, "Father, I have made it very clear that I will not marry Luke Stearn."

Isaac picked up his napkin, wiped his mouth, replaced the napkin in his lap, and sat back in his chair. He then said, "I am greatly disappointed that you would not abide by your family's wishes, and in doing so, you will bring great disgrace to our family."

"I don't care," said Anna, "I will never marry Luke."

"Then how will you live?" said Isaac.

"What do you mean?" said Anna.

Isaac once again paused, and then replied, "I mean this. For most of your selfish young life, you have brought pain and anguish to your parents, and this situation of your marriage is the final example of your selfish arrogance. If you should not marry Mr. Stearn, and instead take some sort of action on your own, your mother and I shall have no other alternative except to disown you from our family. You will become dead in this family, and we will hold Shiva for you. You will never be able to return to the family. Is that what you truly want, Anna?"

Anna was stunned. She formed a mental picture of her mother dressed in black, sitting in their parlor observing Shiva for her. She never would have believed that her father would have the heart to say these words to her. She had walked herself into this trap, and she was now forced to finally concede to marry Luke Stearn, or to make her own way in the world. For several moments there was total silence. Then Anna slowly folded her napkin, placed it by her plate, stood up, and walked away from the table. Her silence sealed her fate.

With her railroad ticket in her purse, she carried her bag to the waiting cab the following morning. As she was preparing to leave, she overheard her mother telling the cook and the house maids to prepare the house for Shiva. The cab left with Anna aboard and headed to the Chicago, Burlington and Quincy railroad depot.

As the train wended its way southwest, Anna gazed out the window from her rail car seat and watched farmers working their harvests in the fields as she passed. She felt no remorse at leaving her family. She was now excited, knowing that she controlled her own destiny. It would have to be a cold day in hell before she would marry that dimwitted Luke Stearn.

In the following days, the Maiers held a funeral for Anna, with services at the cemetery. An engraved tombstone was placed on the empty grave. A notice was posted in the Chicago newspaper announcing the death of Anna Maier. Florence Maier held Shiva for Anna, intermittently weeping for this sad event in the Maier family. Disowning a family member was not unheard of, but was considered the last resort to preserve a family's standing and honor in an extreme, unsolvable family crisis. It would not be the last time that Anna was entwined in such a circumstance.

***

On the early October day of her arrival in Burlington in 1862, Anna breezed into the lobby, walked to the reception counter, and asked for the finest room available in the Burlington Hotel. The hotel clerk was somewhat taken aback, having a very attractive young woman, apparently traveling alone, asking for his best room. But her brash look, and the less than friendly piercing eyes, quickly broke down the hotel clerk's caution, and the room key was soon handed to her.

Anna's next stop was at the Burlington Bank. As she sauntered from the hotel to the bank, many local eyes watched the young woman as she moved down the street. Her clothes were obviously stylish and expensive, and her silk parasol twirled as she walked. Proper ladies who observed Anna either thought she was a very stylish aristocrat, or a high class lady of the evening. As there were no real aristocrats in Burlington, the ladies leaned toward their second opinion. Men who watched her had other thoughts, but simply stepped aside to let her pass, then furtively allowed their eyes to follow her as she walked away.

James and Johaan Stroud had followed their father, Peter, in his banking endeavor. Peter had semi-retired, turning over the day-to-day operation of the bank to the boys, and although he came to work every day and was still the bank's president, coming to work was more out of habit than necessity. But he did not want to give up the pleasure of chatting throughout the day with his myriad of good friends as they came in the bank to conduct business.

On this particular October day, Peter was in the bank, as were James and Johann. It was a quiet afternoon, with only two customers at the teller counter.

Anna strode to the tellers' counter as one of the customers was leaving and said to the teller, "I would like to speak to the president of this bank."

"Yes ma'am," said the teller, "I believe he is in his office. May I tell him who is here to see him?"

Anna replied, "No you may not! Simply tell him I wish to open an account at his bank."

Naturally, the teller was dumbfounded at the audacity of this woman, but he kept his composure and glanced to his side. Peter had been reviewing some papers at the end of the tellers' counter and had overheard the woman's conversation. Ordinarily, he would not talk to a new customer. He left that to his sons, or a senior teller.

But he was curious and gave a slight wave to the teller as he strode over to the teller's window and said, "May I help you madam?"

Anna retorted, "I wish to speak to the president of this bank, not some teller. Would you please go fetch him for me?"

Peter could hardly keep a straight face at the arrogance of this woman, but he said, "Madam, let me assure you, you are in good hands, since I am the president of the bank. Now, how may I assist you?"

Once again in her life, Anna was made to appear foolish by her arrogance, and her arrogance overrode decency and manners. She blundered on without acknowledging her rudeness.

"What is your name?" she demanded.

"My name is Peter Stroud, and I am the President of the Burlington Bank," said Peter. He continued, "May I ask your name?"

Even with the knowledge that she had appeared rude to Peter, Anna felt no remorse. But she put her hand forward and said, "My name is Anna Maier."

Peter held her hand momentarily, then said, "Would you like to come back to my office where we can discuss your business."

"Thank you, I would," replied Anna.

Peter read and reread the letters handed to him by Anna Maier. They had been written by a vice president of the Chicago Fidelity Bank. The letters divulged the details of the lucrative trust fund of Anna Maier, and the balance of a huge sum of money held in her name at the same bank. There was also a letter of extended credit. He also learned that she was only twenty-two years of age, and there did not appear to be any immediate heirs to her accounts. In other words, she was single and wealthy. Peter was impressed. Setting aside the arrogant nature of the young woman, she was obviously very well-to-do, and the Burlington Bank would certainly welcome such an account.

He heard himself say to her, "What are your wishes, Miss Maier?"

Anna responded, "Why, I wish you to wire my Chicago bank and transfer my funds here to your bank. I have many things to take care of and will need to have the money available."

"I assure you, Miss Maier, it shall be taken care of," said Peter.

As Peter and Anna walked to the front of the bank, they passed other offices. Peter stopped at one office and introduced her to a man and woman seated in the office.

"Miss Maier, may I introduce you to my son, James, a vice president in the bank. And this lovely lady with him is his wife, Alice."

The introductions concluded, and Peter walked Anna to the next office, where he said, "Miss Maier, may I introduce you to my second son, Johann, a junior vice president in the bank," said Peter.

Small talk followed, but Anna's interest was suddenly piqued. There was no mention of Johann having a spouse. Anna filed this away in her memory. In a few moments, as she walked away from the bank, she smiled inwardly and thought; that situation had gone well. She then made her way to the telegraph office and sent several messages, including a wire to an architectural firm in St. Louis.

In the next few days, Anna was seen at various places in the city conducting business. Most significantly, she paid a visit to the county surveying office. The business of surveying Burlington property in the initial years of the city had been done by Dr. Ross, but as the city had grown, so had the surveying business. A private firm had taken over those responsibilities, ultimately performing their work for the county. Anna had previously rented a surrey and driver and had purposely ridden the bulk of the streets and boundaries of Burlington. As a result, she knew precisely where she wished to buy property for building her home. She had selected a location on the north hill, overlooking the Mississippi. The large property appeared to be vacant, except for a small cabin in a state of some evident disrepair.

She strode purposefully into the surveyor's office and asked to see the person in charge of the office. A greying gentleman rose from his drafting table and addressed Anna.

"Yes ma'am, I am the manager. What can I do for you?" he said, all the while visually appraising Anna.

"I wish to purchase a piece of property, and I would like to know who the present owner might be," she answered.

While she described the particular property and its location, the surveyor drew a conclusion regarding Anna. His thought was that it was very strange that a young lady would want to buy property, and also strange that such a young person would have the financial means to purchase property. But he also looked into the young woman's eyes, and a chill came over him. There was something to be reckoned with regarding this woman, and he had no doubt that she would acquire what she wanted, by any means possible.

"Madam, the property you are inquiring about is owned by old Mitchell Sutter," said the surveyor. "He is an original settler here in Burlington, and an elderly gentleman who stays to himself in his cabin. He can probably be found there, but I have reason to believe that he will not sell his property. Other folks have asked him about it, and he always refuses their overtures."

Chapter Two

The Sutter Incident

The harvest festival, which many people were now calling Halloween, had ended some days before. In early November, 1862, Anna drove herself to the property of Mitchell Sutter. As she alighted from her buggy, she looked in all directions as she approached the decrepit cabin. Appraising the property once again, she looked around one last time, then rapped her parasol handle on the cabin door. She stood at the door, waxing impatient, and was almost ready to knock again, when the weather-worn door slowly opened inward. A stooped, elderly man, who appeared to have given up shaving and bathing some time ago, greeted her.

"Good day to you, sir," said Anna in her most pleasing and innocent demeanor. "My name is Anna Maier, and I have passed by your charming home several times, often wondering about the view to the river from your property."

Sutter answered with a grunt, "So what?" he said.

"Well, kind sir," said Anna, "you see, I do some painting in my spare time, and I am anxious to gain a perspective of a planned landscape painting of the vista view from your bluff."

Anna's lies swirled from her in a most easy manner.

Sutter locked his rheumy eyes on the young woman. There was something about her that told him to be cautious.

Again, he answered with a simple, "So, what do you want?"

Anna held her tongue, and resisted the urge to simply rap the man over the head with her parasol. The old man's impudence annoyed her greatly.

Instead she answered, "Sir, would you be so kind as to allow me to walk to the back of your property and gaze at the river and surrounding bluff. I am certain I could behold a scene for my next landscape, which would be marvelous."

Sutter again watched the woman, and uncharacteristically let down his guard. "I s'pose it would be all right, but then you need to leave me alone," he said.

"Wonderful," replied Anna. "Would you care to walk with me, and perhaps show me the best view? Here, take my arm if you need to."

Sutter was taken aback and stared at Anna for a few seconds, but then moved through the door. He took Anna's offered arm and leaning on his cane, he slowly walked to the back of the property. Anna could barely contain her disgust at the horrid unwashed smell of this filthy old man, but kept her smiling façade, chattering to Sutter as they moved among the trees toward the edge of the bluff. They were now standing no more than two feet from the edge, gazing out toward the river.

"Dear sir," Anna cooed, "I am speechless. What a wonderful vista you have. You must treasure this scene daily."

Sutter just grunted.

Not one to make small talk and waste precious time, Anna bluntly struck to the heart of her real intentions. "Mr. Sutter, I admire your property greatly, and I am prepared to pay you very handsomely if you would care to sell it to me."

She continued, trying her best to charm the old man, "Would five hundred dollars be satisfactory to you for the purchase of the property?"

Now Sutter knew why he had suspicioned this woman, and his anger rose.

"Now you listen lady, you come here givin' me this purty story about you paintin' and all, when all the while you just wanted to get my property. Well, it ain't for sale, and you need to git!" he said.

But Anna did not move. "Now, now, Mr. Sutter," said Anna. "I believe the property is for sale for the proper price. Why, for heaven's sake, I am even prepared to give you one thousand dollars for the property. Isn't that a wonderful price? Surely it would be foolish to refuse such a large sum of money," she said in her most deferential manner.

Anna's anger also rose. She could not believe this silly old man was standing up to her and offering resistance to her plan.

Sutter responded, "I believe I have made myself clear, lady. My place ain't for sale." And as he said this, he raised his cane and shook it in the air.

Anna became furious with the old man's actions. Her plans would not be stymied by the likes of this silly old fool.

She also raised her closed parasol and stoutly jabbed Sutter in the stomach, while saying, "You old fool, a thousand dollars is more than you have ever seen in your lifetime, and ..."

Her voice trailed off as she watched Sutter stagger a step backwards at being jabbed in the midsection by Anna's parasol. Without the aid of his cane, which he was still holding in mid-air, Sutter teetered backwards one more step and careened at the edge of the bluff for only another second or two. Then the mud beneath his worn shoes gave away. A small shout came from his lips while his legs slipped away and the rest of his body followed. He fell to the rocks far below, at the bottom of the bluff, at the river's edge. Striking the large rocks, the old settler died instantly. His cane lay on the ground at the bluff's edge where it had fallen from his gesturing hand before Sutter tumbled over the edge. Although it was her parasol jab to the old man that had caused this tragedy, Anna felt no remorse, nor responsibility. She bent over, picked up the old man's can and threw it over the bluff's edge. It clattered on the rocks below, coming to rest near the body of Mitchell Sutter.

The county held an inquest, led by the county sheriff, into the death of Mitchell Sutter. The old cabin was searched for clues, and in a steady, drizzling rain, the sheriff stood on the edge of the bluff on Sutter's property. He was gazing below at his deputy looking for clues among the rocks on the riverbank below. If the sheriff had only moved twenty feet farther south, he might have seen the marks made by the heels of a woman's shoes, but they were rapidly disappearing in the downpour. There was some suspicion in the case, especially since the county surveyor told the sheriff that Miss Anna Maier had visited his office to inquire about the property only the day before. The sheriff spoke with Miss Maier, but she avowed to have never met Mr. Sutter and to have no knowledge of the death. In the end, there were no other witnesses to question, and the case was closed with a report stating that indications were that the doddery old man had simply stepped too near the edge of the bluff, lost his balance and his cane, and accidentally fallen to his death.

Sutter had no relatives and no will, so the property quickly went to probate and was sold at public auction. Anna's final auction bid of one thousand, five hundred dollars had purchased the prime property on the bluff.

***

Anna roused from her half-sleep to observe that the workers were leaving for the day. She must have dozed for nearly an hour. She rose from the chair and stretched her cramped muscles as she walked into the partially completed shell of her house, going from one framed-in room to the next. She gazed on the beautiful colors of the exotic woods that had been shipped to the work site and were being incorporated into the ornate, wide, winding staircase. Her hands moved slowly over the beautiful, smooth marble pieces in the fireplaces and mantels. The marble had been imported from quarries in Italy. She looked up to see the multiple layers of crown moldings at the ceilings, and the many hand-made stained-glass windows which had been placed in their framed openings. Everything she saw gave her pleasure. But it was not pleasure in the artistic beauty of the craftsmanship; no, it gave her pleasure to know that no one in Burlington would have a home like this. She would have the biggest and most elegant residence in the city. And this gave her pleasure. She harrumphed to the construction foreman who silently watched her and then made her way toward what would in the future be the front door of the house. She stepped out and looked around. "You stupid girl," she shrieked to her house girl, "go get my buggy, I am going back to the hotel."

Every day followed a similar pattern, with Anna camped out in her chair at the front of the property, sporadically rising from her chair to shriek at the foreman or one of the workmen. And each day when the workers left the site, she would stroll through each room, imagining in her mind the activities that would unfold in each room in the future.

On the first floor, to the right of the long center hallway, she stood in the middle of what would soon become a grand hall, large enough to hold formal dinners followed by an orchestra-led dance. She could almost hear the orchestral music in her head, and lightly twirled across the floor of the room in her imaginary dance. Oh, she would be the grand dame of the city with her soirees. Then, she climbed the mostly completed, extraordinarily wide staircase, which had been especially made to ac-commodate the wide hooped-skirts so fashionable at the time. The staircase was constructed of beautiful exotic woods imported from various sources in Europe. She imagined the enthralling entrance she would make gliding down these beautifully stained, elegant stairs in her most expensive finery, for her dinner dances.

On the second floor, she walked through the partially completed rooms, knowing that the second floor would primarily be the family's residence, containing eight large bedrooms, each with its own fireplace, and a sitting room where her future children could play and be isolated from the downstairs adult gatherings. She would forbid the children from playing downstairs, or from entering the ball room. Those areas were for adults. That she had no husband, nor prospects of one, was of little consequence to Anna, for she had a plan. The construction of the house on the bluffs was merely the first phase. Once again, she brushed her hands over the intricately carved, Italian marble fireplaces and dressing tabletops.

Then Anna went out to the second floor, covered, screened balcony, and walked a short distance on the balcony to the rear of the house to the unique second floor private toilets. They would be the only second floor toilets in any home in the city. While outdoor toilets were still the norm, her home would also have an outhouse in the rear yard, but it would be used only by the servants. Anna walked by the small toilet room that would be used by men, and continued to the much larger female accommodations. Anna and her female guests would be able to simply walk upstairs to use this new, modern accommodation on the second floor, attached to the house. They would not have to go outdoors in inclement weather to use the toilet.

The ladies' toilet room was built overly large to allow ladies to be able to disrobe from as many as seventeen petticoats and the cinched corset and hang them to the side of the room while performing nature's functions. It was tastefully painted and decorated, and had its own gas lighting. The room also contained a "fainting couch", as it was common for ladies of the time, because of the large number of petticoats, and the beauty enhancing, yet internal organ strangling corset, to become over-heated and oxygen deprived to the point of fainting. It then became a necessity to retire to privacy to remove some layers of petticoat and loosen the corset in order to breathe freely and cool off. The refuse chamber was copper lined, an improvement that would help deter odors that resulted from wooden construction which absorbed refuse. The plumbing for these second floor toilets was attached to the wall and ran down the side of the house, ending in a covered pit at the rear corner of the house. A service company had been retained to come to the home monthly to remove the cover from the pit, and empty the pit by hand shoveling. Essentially, then, this was an enlarged, enhanced, double outhouse that had been purposely built at the rear of the second floor of the home. It would be like no other residential toilets in town, and Anna was sure that the social elite attending her social gatherings would think that she was ever so clever to have such marvelous accommodations.

During the construction of the home, horses and carriages would drive slowly by the north hill, bluff location. The construction project was the talk of the town, and people marveled at the grand stone columns adorning the front porch, the craftsmanship of the stone masons, the beautiful stained glass in a few of the upper windows, the beveled glass in all the other windows, and the long, grandiose, circular, paved drive-way being laid brick by brick that would accommodate a score of car-riages, and the façade-matching carriage house. Everyone knew that the builder was a single woman, only twenty-two years old, but other than those meager facts, this new resident to their city was a mystery. She kept mostly to herself in the hotel, or at the building site, and usually sent servants to run her errands in the city. It would not remain so.

Near the middle of October, 1863, almost a year after its initial groundbreaking, and with more than two hundred assorted craftsmen at Anna's disposal, Anna Maier's grand home overlooking the Mississippi from its prominent, picturesque location, was completed. Anna gave the home its name, "Flint Bluff." A hand-cast, molded brass sign, in a sure to be seen location at the entrance of the circular drive contained the words, "Flint Bluff, 1863," ensuring that anyone passing by knew the location and name of this extraordinary home.

Immediately upon completion of her home, Anna commenced her social debut. She began injecting and/or buying her presence and membership in every upper income social group in the city. She was soon known and admired by every socialite family in town. She had even learned that the wealthiest families in town attended the Methodist Church. Casting her Jewish lineage aside, she was soon a member in good standing of that church; good standing because the trustees of the church soon learned that her monetary contributions to the church were substantial. Anna had no interest in the church itself. She was there only to entrench her influence and reputation among the more powerful citizens, and her plan quickly unfolded. She was invited to more societal gatherings and galas than she could possibly attend, and wealthy families with eligible sons made diligent efforts to bring Anna into contact with these young men. But in this regard, Anna outpaced these families by devising her own plan. She envisioned a New Year's Eve formal ball like no other previously seen in Burlington, and she was spending long days going over the smallest details. She was personally involved, of course, with all these items, first of which was to draw up the list of the elite invitees. Included in the invitations would be a statement that the children of those families who were over twenty-one years of age would be permitted to attend the occasion with their parents. Anna was certain that the attendees would, therefore, include every young man of marriageable age from the wealthiest families in town. In private, she marveled at her own cleverness. This would be the first large social gathering in her new home, where she was anxious to impress the city elite with the beautiful, sheer magnitude of Flint Bluff.

Part Four

**Vicksburg
Aftermath**

Chapter One

The Siege

The artillery shelling continued for days. Not only were the Union artillery pieces positioned around the city for systematic bombardment, but the river was teeming with Union gunboats that also delivered their ordinance on the city. The Navy's gunboats fired over twenty-two thousand shells into the city and the Army artillery fusillade was even heavier. No Vicksburg resident was safe from death by the screaming metal barrages. The never-ending explosions of light, and ear piercing noise nearly drove Vicksburg residents insane. The residents had been told to seek shelter away from their homes. There was a ridge partially circling the city located outside the city and still behind the Confederate lines. Well over five hundred caves were dug into this ridge, and a diverse citizenry occupied these caves. Residents did their best to make the caves comfortable by bringing rugs, furniture, and even pictures to their adopted cave. This network of caves was dubbed "prairie dog village" by its inhabitants. But even within their relatively safe shelters, Vicksburg residents still could not escape the explosions of light and the terrible numbing assault of the noise of war.

With the river secure, Union steamboats by the score docked on the Yazoo River to disgorge more troops, food, ordinance, ammunition, and supplies for the Union army. After suffering nearly five thousand Union soldiers killed or wounded, General Grant was determined to sacrifice no more Union soldiers, and he reluctantly committed his army to a siege at Vicksburg. Seventy-seven thousand Union soldiers ringed the city and its defenses. They settled in by digging their own trench network outside the Confederate lines. As the siege lines became solid, the Confederates faced another problem. The Union dead and dying men, and the dead horses and other animals lying where they had fallen created an over-whelming odor in the full sun in May. Wounded soldiers from both sides continued to cry out for help while lying next to their dead comrades. The Confederates sent word to General Grant that they wished to have a truce, so that both sides could bury their dead and treat the wounded. At first Grant refused, but then capitulated, and the horrible aftermath of battle was cleared from the fields. Soldiers from both sides intermingled, talked, and traded mementos while assigned to this gruesome duty.

Within the city, the Confederate soldiers had little food. Without a proper diet, scurvy, malaria, dysentery, diarrhea, and other diseases were rampant among the men. Over half of Pemberton's force was sick or hospitalized. As the siege wore on, fewer horses, mules or dogs were seen in Vicksburg. As the artillery continued its deadly barrage, several wealthy owners of mansions feared that the shelling would destroy their stately homes. In order to save their houses, the owners sent word to General Pemberton and to the Union forces that they would volunteer their homes for use as hospitals. Large red crosses were painted on the roofs of those homes approved for use as hospitals. Casualties from both sides intermingled in these hospitals, and were treated as equals. As a result, the Navy gunners and Army artillery did their best to avoid directly aiming at these homes, thereby saving them from certain destruction.

General Grant's plan to "out-camp" Pemberton's army at Vicksburg was ultimately successful. On July 3, 1863, General Pemberton sent word to General Grant that he was surrendering. General Grant paroled the thirty thousand men under Pemberton's command, hoping that they would return to their homes and never fight again. This did not happen, though, as most of these parolees would return to fight in Tennessee in later battles. On July 4, 1863, the surrender documents were signed.

President Lincoln later announced, "The Father of Waters again goes unvexed to the sea." Some days later, General Grant also received word that the Union Army under the command of General George Meade had been victorious at Gettysburg, Pennsylvania. That victory came at a great cost of over fifty thousand casualties, with nearly seven thousand men from both sides killed. This event and the fall of Vicksburg marked the turning point of the Civil War. Thenceforth, the tide of the war would gain momentum in favor of the Union forces.

***

Mr. Duff Green, a prominent businessman in Vicksburg, had built a sumptuous mansion as a wedding gift for his bride, Mary, in 1856. The home stood majestically near the center of the city. The home was built for entertaining with large spacious rooms, including a ballroom. During the bombardment of the city, the home was struck at least five times by Union cannonballs. In order to save their beloved home, the Greens offered the use of their mansion as a hospital for the wounded soldiers. Soon the home was filled with wounded men. Union troops were confined to the top floor of the home, and Confederates housed on the main floor. The kitchen located on the basement level of the home continued to be used for food preparation. Other rooms on that level became surgery sites where hundreds of soldiers were treated. So many limb amputations were performed, that amputated arms and legs formed a huge pile in the side yard of the property before they could be properly disposed of. The floor of the surgery room was often awash in blood.

After the surrender of the city on July 4th, the government leased the home so that the treated soldiers could remain there for recuperation before being returned to their respective homes. While the home was used as a hospital, the family retreated to two caves they built in the side yard of the home. It was during the bombardment of Vicksburg, and while the family was living in the caves, that Mary Duff gave birth to a baby boy, and named him William Siege Green.

***

Kon was lying on a bedroll in the corner of a room on the second floor of the Duff Green mansion. The same dream had awakened him early this morning. In the dream, he was running forward toward the blazing guns. Beside him was Jacob, and close by to the right was Patrick Quinn. But as the dream continued, the spirit of the dead rose in front of him and drew a dark, woven robe across the scene. With the booming and crashing of gunfire all around him, the spirit then reached his hand forward to Kon and beckoned him to come with him to the place of the dead. The spirit's eyes glowed like the sun, but his skin crawled, almost a black color from thousands of crawling cicadas covering the arms and body of the deadly spirit. The apparition then spoke his name, and again beckoned Kon to follow him. As had happened many times prior, Kon then abruptly shouted, and awoke, covered in a thin layer of sweat. He slowly sat up, covered his eyes, and silently implored the spirits of the living to deliver him from this dream. He sat motionless for a moment before he looked up to see a nurse looking at him.

"Are you all right?" the woman asked. Kon shook his head, then nodded that he was fine. The nurse stood for a moment, smiled at Kon, and moved on.

It was now late June 1863. For over ninety days, Kon had stayed in the make-shift hospital in the Duff Green Mansion. His wound was not serious. On March 22nd, a stray bullet had pierced his boot and tore a chunk of flesh from his lower calf. The wound had become infected, but was now infection free; it had healed nicely. He had been discharged from the hospital some weeks ago, but did not leave. Kon walked the grounds of the hospital as much as possible, strengthening the wounded muscle. When he was not walking, sleeping, working, or eating, Kon stayed in one place in the Union ward; on a camp stool next to one of the beds.

The bullet had dug a five-inch long furrow on the right side of Jacob Roush's skull. The hair that was regrowing along the site of the wound was white. In the midst of his thick dark hair, then, was a streak of white hair. It would mark him for the rest of his life, until age would match the rest of his hair to that surrounding the wound. The scalp and head wound had healed well, but the man's brain still suffered the effects of the severe blow to the head.

Jacob lay in a comatose state in the hospital bed. He was alive, and yet, he was not. His eyes remained closed, he did not move, and he was fed liquids by placing a jointed metal tube down his throat. Kon sat daily on the small stool, in a meditative pose, listening to the sounds of the cannons in the distance and the crashing cannon balls some streets away. Occasionally, he would reach for the hand of his friend. Jacob's hand was warm, but there was no response from Jacob. Two or three times daily, a Union Army doctor would stop by Jacob's bed. Sometimes he would feel the young man's pulse and open Jacob's eyelids. He would then take a small wooden stick and draw it along the bottom of Jacob's feet and along the palms of Jacob's hands.

On this particular day, the doctor examined Jacob, and then turned to Kon and said, "Son, I don't know if this man will ever return to us. You might as well head for home."

Just as the doctor turned to continue his rounds, Kon spoke softly.

The doctor turned and said to Kon, "What did you say?"

Kon looked up slowly and said, "He will wake up."

The doctor wagged his head and said, "I hope you're right," and walked away.

Kon awoke early on the morning of July 8th. At first he was confused by the stillness, and further puzzled by sound that he heard. He quickly rose and walked out into the garden of the mansion. He looked up into the trellis and saw them. It was a pair of wrens staring back at him and scolding him. For the first time since he could remember, Kon was hearing birds. There were no guns firing; no cannons blasting the air. The outlying military units, to which the news of the Vicksburg surrender finally reached, were at last quiet. There was a calm surrounding the mansion, and he could now hear several jays sounding their raucous calls. The spirits of the living were speaking to him. Kon returned to the house and hurried to the upper floor again. As he moved to Jacob's bed, he could see that Jacob's eyes were open and looking directly at him. Kon took Jacob's hand and squeezed it. There was a weak, responding grip from Jacob. A tear fell from Kon's eye.

That night, Kon had another dream. Again, the gunfire surrounded him as he ran forward. This time there was no curtain of death trying to reach him. Instead, his dream replayed the March 22nd attack. As he ran forward, he saw Jacob and Patrick fall at almost the same time. In the next instant, his lower leg was painfully flung to the side, causing him to fall, striking his head on the ground. He lay dazed for several moments until his mind slowly cleared. He rolled over and rose to his hands and knees. He looked around and saw Patrick. He crawled toward Patrick keeping below the whining rifle bullets singing their death song. He reached Patrick, who was lying on top of Jacob and yelled at him, but Patrick did not respond. After concluding that Patrick was dead, he rolled him off of Jacob, revealing an ugly bullet entry wound just under Patrick's left eye. Turning his attention to Jacob, he then saw the long ugly wound on Jacob's head. Fearfully, he lifted Jacob's hand. It felt warm. He then leaned close over Jacob's face, placing his cheek up against Jacob's nose. He felt a warm breath touch his cheek. Jacob was still alive. The gunfire was far too strong for him to move around, and Kon lay down next to Jacob. Their attack had begun at almost four o'clock in the afternoon, and it would soon be getting dark. When at last darkness came, the guns fell silent and Kon stirred. His leg was aching terribly, but he rose to his hands and knees again. Under cover of darkness, he struggled to his feet, stifling a scream of pain caused by his wound. His pant leg was stiff with coagulated blood. Reaching down, he lifted Jacob's shoulders, and with Jacob's legs bumping along the ground, Kon slowly and painfully made his way back to the Union defenses. A sniper's bullet whizzed by him as he moved to the line.

"Don't shoot!" he rasped, trying to gulp air into his wheezing lungs.

A sentry responded, "Show yourself!" Kon moved ahead and was soon surrounded by Union soldiers as he collapsed from fatigue.

There was a new procedure being used to preserve the bodies of soldiers being sent home after a gruesome death on the battlefields of the Civil War. The first form of embalming had arisen out of necessity to enable broken bodies to be sent to their final destinations. A mixture of half formaldehyde and half water was pumped into the body to prevent the flesh from decomposing, and to prevent the horrible after-effects of this natural process. Patrick's body was subjected to this preservation procedure, and his body and many others were shipped north on the river by steamboat. The body would reach Isaac Newton Prugh's funeral parlor in Burlington, where he would make the preparations for the young man's funeral.

The Quinns held services for their son shortly after the arrival of the body. The same solemn activities were held hourly across a nation that had reluctantly become accustomed to strife.

***

As time passed, some days were better than others, but significant progress was being made. Jacob sat on his bed and repeatedly, albeit slowly, raised his arms to regain their strength and use. He was able to stand, but could only walk while being supported on both sides by Kon and a nurse. His speech had returned, but was sometimes disjointed and slow. When he was at last able to make himself understood, the nurses wrote letters for him, which reached a much relieved Martha and William.

On July 4th, when the patients in the hospital learned that the Confederates had surrendered the city of Vicksburg, there was no rejoicing. Every recuperating veteran in the Duff Green Mansion, whether Union or Confederate, only wanted one thing, to go home.

In Burlington, Iowa, when news was received of the fall of Vicksburg, the young boys in the parish at St. John's Catholic Church pleaded with the parish priest to ring the church bell in celebration of the fall of the Southern stronghold. The priest agreed that this, indeed, was an event warranting the celebratory ringing of the historic bell which had been brought to Burlington years prior by Father Mazzuchelli. The peeling bell was soon heard throughout the city, in celebration of the fall of Vicksburg.

August 1, 1863,
Dearest Mother and Father,
I remain in a hospital in Vicksburg. Kon is here with me. We were both injured while in a horrible fight here. But we are mending nicely. I am being well taken care of. Please do not worry. I am, however, sorrowful over the loss of Patrick. He was a good friend, and I will miss

him. Please convey my sentiments to his parents. I pray that we will come home soon.

Your loving son, Jacob

Jacob's rehabilitation went slowly. While Jacob recuperated, Kon had become a well-respected fixture in the hospital. He had appointed himself the maintenance man for the mansion, making repairs to the home and its fixtures, and assisting the medical staff with cleaning the home and moving patients. Kon also looked in on the Green family occasionally to see if there was anything he could do for them. Jacob was regaining his muscle control and coordination and could move slowly without help, while employing the use of a cane to steady himself. His speech was also improving, but his cognitive skills were slowest to recover. He still needed help writing letters, and with reasoning and solving problems, but still there was slow improvement. He continued to suffer from sharp, severe headaches, which immobilized him for several hours each time they occurred. He would suffer these headaches for many years. With the white streak in his dark head of hair, Kon would sometimes tease Jacob about somehow being related to a skunk, but Jacob did not mind and chuckled along with Kon.

In mid-November, the doctor who had patiently watched over Jacob's progress, stood by Jacob's bed and told him that he would soon be going home.

"Captain Roush, I want you home for Christmas. I think your progress would be improved if you were with your family in familiar surroundings. We have done all we can do for you here, so I am going to arrange for transportation for you and your sergeant."

Kon's normally stoic face showed a small smile.

"However," the doctor continued, "Sergeant Kon, you have proven yourself to be invaluable here in our little hospital, and I would certainly allow you to stay on as part of our staff if you would agree."

Kon's slight grin quickly faded. He was afraid he might offend the doctor and looked over at Jacob.

Jacob quickly spoke for Kon, "Doctor, Sergeant Kon is my right arm, and I would like him to come home with me. What do you say Kon?"

Kon looked again at the doctor and said, "Yes, sir, I would also like to go home."

"All right," said the doctor. "I'll go ahead and arrange for the transportation for both of you."

***

On November 19, 1863, the tall, gaunt, bearded man with the strange stove pipe hat stood before a crowd at Gettysburg, Pennsylvania, the site of one of the bloodiest battles in the history of the world. What President Lincoln said that day would be recorded in history forever. News of this speech at Gettysburg made its way by telegraph around the nation, and was published in newspapers read by the people of the United States. Newspaper copies reached the small hospital in Vicksburg, and they were read with very little emotion by the recovering soldiers who were able to read, including Jacob.

***

On the day of their departure, the doctor gave a letter to both Jacob and Kon. In essence, the letter stated that due to the severity and unknown recuperative time needed for full healing of their battlefield wounds, the Army was releasing them from further military activity. They would not be returning to the war.

Chapter Two

Home at Last

On the fifth of December 1863, Jacob and Kon were wished well by the doctor and nurses at the makeshift hospital and were driven by Army wagon to the Vicksburg wharf to board steamboats contracted by the Army for moving wounded and recuperating soldiers from both armies to their homes up river. The wharf area was alive with boats of all sorts, with a large number of Union soldiers arranging the distribution of supplies coming into the city. Many of those supplies would follow the Union Army as it made its way further east and north toward future battles.

The trip up the river to Burlington was uneventful. Weather permitting, Kon spent almost all of his time each day near the bow of the steamboat, anxiously waiting for a first view of home. Several stops were made for fuel and provisions, but the returning soldiers remained on the boat during these stops. No one wanted to be absent from the boat as it continued northward. Citizens in the cities where they stopped all cheered the steamboat as it landed, shouting their appreciation for the sacrifices made by the young men for their country. As the boat moved north, both Jacob and Kon marveled at the change in the scenery and the change in temperature, with most of the trees visible from the river having lost their foliage in the cooler weather, unlike the Mississippi area where they had been suffocating in unrelenting heat for the past several months.

There were Iowa soldiers from Keokuk and Fort Madison on the boat, and stops were made for residents of those cities to disembark. The next stop would be Burlington, and Jacob stood by Kon in a chilly mid-December breeze as the bluffs of Burlington came into view. As the boat neared the wharf in Burlington, a brass band struck up a lively tune, and a large crowd could be seen waiting for the boat. William and Martha Roush, Four Toes, and New Rain were among the crowd. They waited for other passengers to leave the boat, and then Jacob and Kon moved across the gangway. Martha hurried to embrace her son as William stood close by waiting to greet his son. Four Toes and New Rain hugged Kon. In a moment, though, the two men were drawn over to a small stage that had been set up on the levee. They were led up on the stage where a Union Army Officer stood next to several civilian gentlemen. In a moment, one of the dignitaries asked the crowd for its attention. When all was quiet, a clergyman was asked to give thanks for the return of the two men. A short prayer of thanks was given, followed by short speeches from city officials. Jacob and Kon looked at one another and each knew the other was uncomfortable with these formalities.

The final part of the ceremony was the introduction of the Army Officer, a Colonel.

After his introduction, he turned to Jacob and Kon and said, "Captain Roush, and Sergeant Kon, I come to Burlington today representing the State of Iowa. The Adjutant General sends his regards and wishes me to convey his regrets that he could not be here today, but he wanted me to read the following citation to both of you." The Colonel took a document from his inside coat pocket, unfolded it, and began to read it aloud so the crowd could hear.

"I take great pleasure in commending Sergeant Kon, and Captain Jacob Roush for their bravery and heroic actions during the battle for Vicksburg. Captain Roush led his men against the fierce resistance of the enemy, and was severely wounded in the course of the action. Sergeant Kon was by his side, and also was wounded in the action, but later was able to rescue Captain Roush by carrying him to safety. For these brave actions, I am promoting Sergeant Kon to Brevet Lieutenant, and I am promoting Captain Jacob Roush to Brevet Lieutenant Colonel. This document is signed by General Frederick Steele," said the Colonel. "Congratulations to both of you. You have served your country with honor."

The crowd yelled and applauded. Jacob and Kon made their way through the crowd, shaking hands with everyone until they could finally make their way home with their families. The two men were truly home at last.

Parked unobtrusively to the edge of the crowd was a glistening black closed carriage, harnessed to a matched team of gray horses. Unseen, peering out the window of the carriage, was the beautiful dark-haired woman who had recently completed the Flint Bluff Mansion. The carriage remained throughout the presentation to the two men, and then slowly rolled away from the crowd. Anna had seen enough to begin planning.

Part Five

The
Reluctant Union

Chapter One

The Introduction

Apparently quite a number of men had the same idea. The duck blinds dotted the riverbanks on both sides of the river. The icy blasts of wind from the north had driven the waterfowl south in their migration toward their winter destinations, resulting in a large turnout of duck and goose hunters to their respective blinds. There would be no shortage of waterfowl for the Christmas dinner tables of the hunters. On this late Saturday afternoon, the two men each had shot enough birds for their family dinners.

Mike O'Connor had welcomed Kon back to the transportation company as if he had never left, and Jinks and Kon were soon carrying out their activities together again. Of course, they were now men, and Jinks was married, so their activities had toned down considerably from those when they were younger.

"Do you think much about the war?" said Jinks. "I mean, was it really as bad as everyone says?"

"It was worse," said Kon, "and I try not to think about it. I thank the spirits that I was able to return home." Kon was not comfortable talking about the war, even to his best friend. "I'm going to head home and take the birds. My mother will want to begin cleaning them. I want to go to Roush's and see Jacob. I worry about him," said Kon.

"I'll go with you," said Jinks. "I haven't seen Jacob for a while."

The two men stopped at their homes and then walked up North Hill together to knock on the Roush's door. After a moment, William Roush opened the door. This surprised Jinks, as he knew the Roushes had house servants.

"Well now, here are a couple of men I would welcome any time. Come in, come in," said William. "Jacob has been asking about you scoundrels."

Just then Jacob, leaning on his cane, came around a corner with a big grin on his face.

"Kon and Jinks. What a great surprise, come on in the sitting room," said Jacob. "From the looks of you, you must have been down to the river. Did you have any luck?"

"Yep, we've got enough birds to feed the whole town," said Jinks.

The men all laughed.

A servant soon appeared with coffee for all the men while they talked. After the small talk was done, and the coffee cups emptied, Jinks stood up. "I've got to get home guys. Edna will wonder what has happened to me."

Jacob responded, "Tell Edna I said hello. I hope you're keeping my sister happy," and again the men all laughed.

A few minutes after Jinks left, Kon was alone with Jacob.

"Do you still have the headaches, Jacob?" asked Kon.

"Yes, but they are not as frequent," said Jacob. "I think I am actually doing pretty well. God is looking after me."

"I have asked the spirits of the living to take away our bad dreams," said Kon. "I seem to have less bad dreams. I hope this is the same for you."

Jacob replied, "You are a good friend, Kon, and your prayer must be working because I am sleeping better. I only have trouble sometimes when I can't seem to make the right words come out when I am thinking and talking. I laugh when it happens."

The two men talked for a few minutes longer, and Kon finally left to return home.

Martha had been upstairs when the visitors were downstairs and now came to see Jacob. "Oh, I'm sorry I missed Jinks and Kon. Did you have a nice visit?"

"Yes Mother, they make me feel better when they come around," said Jacob.

"Dear, I have wanted to mention to you that we received an invitation to a New Year's Eve party. There is a new young woman in town who, apparently, is very well off and has built a magnificent home a couple blocks over. You have probably seen it. She calls the home, Flint Bluff," said Martha. "We are all invited, William and I, Edna and Jinks, and you. Isn't that wonderful?"

"Yes, I've seen the house. But, Mother, I really don't feel well enough to be going to a New Year's party," said Jacob.

"Well, it's a few days off yet, dear, so you don't have to make up your mind quite yet," said Martha.

Jacob could ascertain from his mother's conversation that it was quite possible he would be going to a New Year's Eve party that he had no interest in attending.

Anna had spent many hours poring over the details of the New Year's ball. She had limited the invitations to be sent only to the "top forty" families in the city. But even with this limitation, she was sure that she would have over a hundred attendees. She had browbeaten the servants to put the home in a fantastic, sparkling condition. Ornate, yet beautiful decorations had been strategically placed throughout the home. Anna had hired the finest chef and food preparation team to prepare a sumptuous feast to be served prior to the dance. The orchestra had been hired and would arrive from St. Louis the day before the festivities to practice in the mansion's great hall. No detail was overlooked under Anna's fastidious scrutiny. Tables were set up in the great hall, the sitting room and the parlor. They would be quickly removed following the dinner to make room for dancing and socializing.

***

"Yes, Mother, I do feel better, but I am still reluctant to go to the ball with you and Father," said Jacob. "I would prefer to simply curl up in front of the fireplace with a book."

William spoke up then, "Jacob, I think your mother wants to show off her son to society. It will certainly make her, and me, happy to have you come with us. After all, Edna will be there with Jinks, and the Quinns especially want to visit with you. Who knows, you might make a few new friends."

Jacob knew that he would only tolerate the festivities and was not convinced that he would enjoy himself. But he loved his parents and really did want to see the Quinns, so he relented and said, "I guess I'll have to find a dress cane for the occasion."

The staff of the Flint Bluff Mansion still was not accustomed to the shrieking and barking out of orders by their employer. Miss Maier was like no other employer they had worked for. She was a dynamo without reins. If possible, they stayed out of her sight, but that was nearly impossible, as the woman raced from room to room, confirming, changing, and rearranging items that caught her attention. It was two p.m. on December 31, and the guests would begin arriving at six p.m. Wine and cocktails would be served, followed by dinner at eight p.m., with the grand dance to follow. Finally finding everything to her satisfaction, Anna left the staff to complete the final preparations and retired to her room to prepare herself. Recalling her shopping trips to St. Louis in the fall, she opened her closets to reveal the beautiful dresses, undergarments, and accessories that she felt would accent her figure, and place her well above the guests in terms of appearance. Her servants drew her bath water, and following the bath, she applied the latest scented powders, colognes, and skin enhancements. Anna was in no hurry. She had no intention of returning downstairs until all the guests had arrived. Only then would she make her entrance.

By 6:30 p.m., the guests had all arrived. The reactions of the guests had all been similar. They marveled over the beauty and craftsmanship of the mansion. After entering the main double door entrance, the first thing they saw was the marvelously intricate detail of the wide sweeping staircase. Mahogany, teak, maple, black walnut, and red oak all blended into the staircase creating a feast for the eyes. It could very well have been something out of a palace. Guests' eyes then turned to the exquisitely colored Persian carpets and the tapestries on the walls. The Belgian cut glass, gas chandelier was larger and more brilliant than anything they had seen. The furnishings and paintings throughout the home were beautiful and undoubtedly priceless. It was readily apparent that the owner had worked with the finest decorators and not spared any expense. For the guests, just seeing the home was worth coming to the ball. They would talk about it for a long time. Anna knew this would be the reaction, and she gave the guests time to study the home before she made her entrance.

At last, she was ready. A very subtle, unseen signal was given by one of the house staff members to the orchestra leader, and the soft, romantic music began. Guests became silent and let their eyes travel to the grand staircase. Anna lifted her skirts ever so slightly and flowed down the steps. Every gentleman's eyes were fastened on the beautiful dark-haired young lady as she smiled slightly and descended the stairs. She was dressed in a royal purple, velvet, sleeveless dress, with a rather risqué low neckline. A priceless cameo was pinned at the low point of the décolletage to mask a portion of the very visible cleavage. A choker strand of iridescent pearls circled her neck. Matching pearl earrings and two strands of pearl bracelets wrapped her wrist. A pair of ivory combs secured her upswept hair. An ivory colored shawl was draped across her shoulders and arms. That should probably have been enough, but not for Anna. She also displayed a large gemstone ring on each hand. And even though the weather was very cold outdoors, she carried a coquettish fan along with her handbag. As she looked around at her guests' faces, she was, indeed, pleased with her entrance. It was exactly the reaction she had sought. She began mingling among the guests, and the conversation level rose again among the guests. Of course, the conversation was much the same in each knot of guests as they conversed about the grand entrance of their hostess.

Time passed quickly, and Anna made her rounds laughing and making small talk with everyone. At one point, she made her way to the Roush's. William had previously met Anna when she had come into the store with her house servant. He therefore made the proper introductions to Anna of Martha and Jacob. Jacob had suffered a trip to Fort Madison recently to purchase the appropriate dress military uniform commensurate with his brevet award. He looked very dashing in the Lieutenant Colonel's Army dress blue uniform. Jacob was somewhat taken aback by Anna's beauty and felt awkward while making small talk with her. Momentarily, Anna moved on to speak with other guests. Periodically, she would slip away from her guests and speak to staff members who were making the last table preparations. At her instruction, name cards were discreetly shifted around the tables by the staff.

At precisely eight p.m., a small gong was carried and sounded by a servant to announce dinner as he walked among the guests. The attendees then began looking at the three long lines of tables to find their respective name card. As the guests stood at their chairs, it was soon evident that the Roush's and the Stroud's would be seated very close by

Anna Maier at her place at the head of the main table. The mayor of the city was seated on Anna's right, but directly on her left was the handsome young Army Lieutenant Colonel with the intriguing streak of white hair. Martha and William sat next to Jacob. While the mayor held Anna's chair for her, Jacob leaned on his cane and watched. His mother was beaming. Jacob, however, was finding this situation to be uncomfortable. He certainly did not want to be the center of attention.

As the food courses were served, conversation was light-hearted, and everyone seemed to be enjoying themselves. After all, it was New Year's Eve. Everyone except Jacob. His head had started to throb so fiercely that he was almost nauseous. And for some strange reason, Miss Maier kept directing conversation to him. He recognized Anna's ploy to get him to open up and talk more, but Jacob kept watching her eyes. There was something in her shining eyes that beguiled him while at the same time warning him of the woman's conniving character. His discomfort was only heightened.

Dinner ended, and the staff quickly cleared the tables and disassembled them for removal. The sitting room and parlor were now available for the guests. The men who smoked adjourned to the parlor, and the other guests wandered around the sitting room and ballroom, quietly conversing with friends. Some time passed until many of the lady guests began whispering and giggling to each other. Apparently, a few of them had availed themselves of the toilet facilities on the second floor, and a new topic of discreet conversation had begun. Husbands who used the facilities next to the ladies' room were soon let in on the secret by their wives, and guests would laugh quietly as each small group ascended and descended the opulent staircase.

Finally, the guests were ushered into the ballroom, where Anna took her place by the orchestra. A chord played by the musicians got the attention of all guests.

Anna then spoke, "Ladies and gentlemen, my new friends. I am so pleased that you could all come to my little party. I had so wanted to meet all of you, and this gave me that opportunity. I hope you enjoy yourselves for the rest of the evening."

She then introduced the orchestra leader, and said, "One of my favorite musical pieces that I have always enjoyed is a polka entitled, 'The Jenny Lind Polka' by Anton Wallerstein. I would like to start our dance with this song. Mr. Mayor, would you be so kind as to be my partner for this dance," said Anna.

The music began and Anna and the mayor led the rather brisk dance. They were soon joined by many other couples. Anna gracefully changed partners to meet all the young, available men. The dancing went on for hours, but at last it was approaching midnight.

Jacob's head still ached, and his balance was wavering. He had finally found a chair away from the dance floor, in a library room at the back of the house where it was a bit quieter. He stared out the black windows, knowing that far below was the Mississippi River. It gave Jacob peace to know the river did not change. It would be there forever.

Anna had searched for her missing guest and had now made her way silently to Jacob's side in the library.

"Colonel Roush, you are being a recluse," Anna said. "Might I give you a penny for your thoughts?"

Jacob rose from his chair and was at a loss for words. "Please forgive me. I was just thinking that I probably should go home. I am not feeling well."

Anna replied, "I am so sorry to hear that. But I surely must insist that before you go, you have one dance with me. Now you cannot turn down your hostess on such a grand night," she said.

"Miss Maier, I truly do not wish to offend you, but you may have noticed that I am not at my physical best. I would not want to embarrass you at your own party," said Jacob.

"I promise you, I do not embarrass easily," said Anna, and she began to lead him to the ball room.

Just then, the orchestra leader announced that it was midnight, and the musicians began playing "Auld Lang Syne." Anna stood on her tiptoes, and kissed Jacob on the cheek. "Happy New Year, Jacob," she said.

A bit red in the face, Jacob responded, "Thank you, I hope you also have a happy new year."

"Oh, I will," she said, "I will."

Anna led Jacob to the orchestra, and when the celebration had died back, she announced to her guests, "I have a favorite waltz that I would like to end our party with. That waltz is 'The Tales from the Vienna Woods,' by Johann Strauss. I promise I will end all my parties with this song. Thank you all again for coming. I don't know about you, but I have had a wonderful time."

She then turned to the orchestra leader and nodded. The beautiful strains of the Strauss waltz began, and with Anna leading, she danced slowly with Jacob. William and Martha smiled from across the room, where they, too, joined the guests for the last dance of the evening. As the music ended, the guests braved the cold and moved to the porches of the palatial home to watch the celebratory fireworks that were ignited at the rear of the house on the bluff's edge. Everyone expressed their awe as the multi-colored rockets soared out over the river, loudly announcing the start of the new year. It was a spectacular closing to the gala evening's events.

As her guests filed out of the house and the carriages rolled out of the driveway, the servants closed the front doors of the house while Anna climbed the staircase to prepare for bed. As she thought back over the evening, she was thrilled that her house-warming and New Year's gala had gone so well, and she began thinking about the next phase of her grand plan.

Chapter Two

Jacob's Dilemma

The ride home from the New Year's Eve party at Flint Bluff in the Roush carriage was anything but quiet. An exuberant Martha could not stop talking about what a wonderful time she had had at the event. William leaned back in the plush seat and closed his eyes, but made a proper conciliatory acknowledgement to Martha when it was needed. Jacob was quiet, absorbing his mother's comments, but he began to consider that his mother might be making some of her comments as if she wanted him to agree with her, especially when she commented several times on what a gracious, beautiful young unmarried woman Anna Maier seemed to be. On that point, Jacob kept his own thoughts. He was unsure of the underlying character of Miss Maier, but he had to admit, she was certainly beautiful and charming.

Jacob's recuperation was nearly complete by the end of February, and he was now walking without the aid of the cane. He began to accompany his father to the mercantile and was becoming more involved with the business. But his heart was not always in the job. He loved his father and wanted to please him, but he was unsure that he wanted to spend the rest of his life running the Roush Mercantile. Almost daily, he quietly weighed his options.

Under the guise of blossoming friendship, Anna Maier paid a near-weekly visit to the Roush home. Ostensibly paying a visit to her friend Martha Roush, Anna would sit in the Roush parlor sipping tea and talking and laughing with Martha. These visits were timed to ensure that Jacob was at home, and invariably Martha would call Jacob in to join the two women. While Jacob was always reluctant to join his mother and her friend, the conversations were lively and good-natured, and he saw these meetings as a pleasant diversion to the day. If William happened to be at home, he might also join the group for a lively card game. It was after a few of these visits had taken place that Martha made her first reference to marriage.

"You know Jacob, I believe Miss Maier has taken a fancy to you. Have you noticed the way she looks at you?"

Jacob replied, "No mother, I haven't noticed such a thing, and frankly, I am not in the least interested."

Martha frowned slightly at Jacob. "Now dear, don't get huffy. I simply was thinking that your sister Edna is married, and she and Jinks are very happy. I only want you to be happy, and you are old enough to start thinking of such things."

Jacob did not bother to answer, but instead went to the kitchen for a glass of water.

The visits to the Roush home by Anna Maier continued. But even with more time spent in her company, Jacob had reservations about the character of the young woman. But Anna had no such barriers. She had set her sights on the handsome son of one of the wealthiest families in town. She would have her way, and she had plenty of time to make it happen.

Continually weaving her seductive web, it was always Anna who encouraged Jacob to attend the myriad of social events in the city. By now it was common knowledge among the city's elite that Miss Maier had indicated her intentions regarding Jacob Roush. They were seen in each other's company at all the finest parties and events. Anna always wore a large smile as she leaned on Jacob's arm. But Jacob usually was very subdued; outwardly appearing happy, but subdued.

***

It was called a May Fest. Brother and sister, Horace and Bella Bailey, had invited all of the young people in their social circle to their parents' home. Naturally, Jacob and Anna were invited. It was to be a festive event with plenty of food and games on the lawn. A croquet course and a badminton court had been set up on the back lawn, with enough lawn chairs for everyone. Servants distributed hand-churned ice cream as fast as the group could eat it. Couples strolled the grounds of the Bailey mansion, while others talked, ate, or played games. Anna did not let Jacob out of her sight and insisted on staying by his side when talking with friends. It was a fun gathering and gave everyone a chance to catch up on friendships and the gossip of young adults. A highlight to end the event would be the maypole dance. An equal number of ladies and men each grabbed a colorful streamer from among the many hanging from the top of the pole. The ladies danced in one direction around the pole while the men danced in the other direction. As the streamers wrapped around the pole, they finally could not be wrapped any farther, and the dancers, while grasping the end of their streamers stopped. It was at this point that the game dictated that the men must give a kiss to any lady who was standing next to him. The odds of Jacob standing next to Anna at the end of the dance were very long. But it happened. Complying with the rules of the game, Jacob leaned over to kiss Anna. But as he did so, Anna let go of her streamer and put both her arms around Jacob's neck, and kissed him full on the lips. She held this position for several seconds, long enough that other couples noticed and began good-naturedly teasing and laughing. As the couple parted, Jacob's face turned quite red.

Anna just laughed and said, "Why Jacob, I believe you are blushing."

As he drove Anna home, he was deep in thought. He had enjoyed the party up until the final May pole event. He was unsure of himself and thought maybe he was making too much of an innocent kiss. But as he clucked to the horse to increase their speed, Anna spoke.

"Jacob, do you care for me?" she said.

Jacob was quickly brought out of his daydreaming. What kind of question was that, he thought.

He stammered. "Yes, Anna, I do care for you."

She replied, "Well, that's nice, but you have a funny way of showing it. Honestly, you haven't said ten words since we started for home."

"I'm sorry," he said. "I'm just a bit preoccupied."

They rode in silence for a few minutes, with the horse keeping a slow pace until Anna said, "Jacob, you know I care about you. In fact, I am in love with you." Anna then giggled, "You know Jacob, not too long ago, if a man kissed a woman, he was obligated to marry that woman. Did you know that?"

"I guess I have heard that before," Jacob stammered.

"Stop stammering, silly boy. Don't you think it would be a good idea if you married me?" said Anna.

Jacob was flummoxed to the point he could not answer. Finally he simply said, "I guess I have not thought about it."

Just then the horse passed a great deal of hay-enriched gas, which certainly broke the mood. Both Jacob and Anna had to laugh.

But as Jacob walked Anna to her door, the mood again became serious. She reached up and kissed Jacob on the cheek. She then said, "Jacob, you need to think about marrying me. And you need to ask me quite soon. I have plans for us, Jacob." And with those words, she turned and opened the door and went inside, closing the door behind her.

Jacob slowly drove home in the early evening, all the while sifting through his thoughts. She could not have made it any plainer. Anna had just proposed to him. She had told him they were to marry, and he needed to formally ask her. He was astounded by her bold actions. In many ways, her audacity frightened him. Marriage was never his intention. He was not ready to make that commitment. At home, he tended to the horse and put the cart in the stable. It had turned into a worrisome evening. He told his parents that he was tired and that he was going to his room to read and retire for the night.

At breakfast the next morning, before William and Jacob went to the mercantile, Martha asked Jacob if he had enjoyed the previous day's party. He said that he had enjoyed himself, while he buttered his toast.

"Were you able to talk with all your friends?" Martha asked.

"Mother, I said I had a good time, and yes, I was able to talk with everyone, even Patrick's brother, Michael, and his sister, Mary. They asked me about what happened at Vicksburg. I guess people just don't understand that I would prefer not to talk about the war."

William thought for a moment and said, "Well, Jacob, you are a link to their brother whom they miss greatly. It stands to reason they would want to talk to you about Patrick's last days."

"You're right, of course, father," answered Jacob. "But I have something else weighing heavily on me now, and I guess you need to know what it is."

For the next several minutes, Jacob related the conversation he had the previous day with Anna Maier. As he expected, Martha was jubilant. But he quickly dispelled her hopes, telling his parents that he had no intention of marrying Anna Maier. To further worry his parents, he also said that he just did not know what he wanted to do for the rest of his life. William's jaw dropped, he grunted audibly and slowly got up from the table saying, "I guess it's about time I go to work." Ordinarily, father and son rode to the store together, but today Jacob said that he would walk to work.

It was a fine, warm, sunny morning. The trees were leafing out fully, and birds were singing. It was the kind of morning to lift a man's spirit.

But Jacob did not notice the glorious morning. As he walked to the mercantile, Jacob weighed his options. He finally came to the conclusion that he was not going to marry yet, and he formulated a plan. As he continued walking, he remembered a conversation that he had had with a young Quaker soldier.

Chapter Three

The Mines

His bandana was wrapped tightly around his face. But each time he swung the heavy pickaxe, chunks of coal came from the vein, accompanied by fine black coal dust that permeated the bandana, all of his clothing, his face and his eyes. Periodically, he would lay the pickax down and pick up the large shovel. He would then shovel the coal that he had removed and dump it into a small ore car that could be pulled by one man. Jacob and a partner were working in a tunnel mine. In the area southeast of Oskaloosa, Iowa, where the majority of the mines were located at that time, there were both strip mines and tunnel mines. The strip mines were worked by steam shovels and steam driven drag-line machines. But the miners who were lowest in hiring order had to work in the more dangerous tunnel mines. As one of the junior men, Jacob labored daily in a tunnel for the Consolidation Coal Company.

Each day when he left the mine and boarded the horse-drawn company wagon to return to Oskaloosa and the run-down boarding house on the west side of town, he would take two baths. The first one was at the old pump behind the boarding house. He and the other four miners who lived there took their coats and shirts off, no matter what the temperature might be, and poured buckets of cold well water over each other to rinse off the coal dust. It had not been too bad in June, when the mine hired him, but now, in early September it was a bit cooler. Jacob did not mind, though. He understood when old Goldie Cathcart, who owned the boarding house, had told all of them that she didn't like to take on miners for boarding, "because they're just too damn dirty." But, she needed the income from the boarders who held steady jobs, so she charged the miners an extra seventy-five cents a week to do their laundry. And she did not want them coming into the house until they had gotten some of that "nasty black dust" off of them before they made their way to the bathtub in their communal bathroom. When any men came to the door to inquire about a room, she gave them all the same Goldie Cathcart speech.

"I don't want any of you bringing any old whores in here, ever. I don't allow gambling, but you can play cards. You can have a drink if you like, but if you ever get rowdy, I'll call the sheriff and have you thrown out. Be on time for supper, or you don't eat. Them's the rules. If you've got an animal, you can use my stable, but you have to buy your own horse feed and clean out your own stall."

Goldie's cooking was highly regarded, and she included a lunch with the cost of her boarding, always hand packed by her. She was just like a strict mother to all of the young male boarders. Goldie was a "pistol," but the miners loved her.

The steady clanging crunch of the pickaxe breaking the coal vein's contents was like a slow, cruel metronome in Jacob's head. The work was back breaking and monotonous and required little mental skill. Jacob's mind tended to wander when he was chipping coal.

He thought back to June 1864, when he had left home. He was still ashamed of how he had left. Rather than face Anna Maier and his parents, he simply left a letter for his parents, telling them that he would be gone for some time and not to worry about him. He explained that he was trying to sort out the paths of his life. He would write to them when he was settled. But he did not keep his word. He had not written to them and still did not consider himself "settled." He knew his parents would worry. He periodically told himself that he would write them a letter soon.

Unbeknownst to Jacob, William and Martha knew exactly where he was. Mike O'Connor's teamsters made weekly runs to Oskaloosa picking up coal for use by the riverboats at the Burlington wharf. One of the drivers had seen the miners leaving the Consolidation Coal Company shaft one day while waiting for his coal to be loaded, and as the miners removed their bandanas and hats, he saw the dark-haired young man with the distinctive white streak in his hair. It could only have been Jacob Roush. He mentioned his sighting to Jinks O'Connor.

On the following run to Oskaloosa, the driver carried a note from Jinks, addressed to the mine owner. When the driver returned, he brought a response from the mine owner confirming that there was a miner named Jacob Roush working at the mine. After Jinks told him, Mike O'Connor shared this information with William and Martha. The parents were relieved to know that Jacob was safe, but wisely chose to let time take care of resolving Jacob's restlessness. It was all William could do to keep Martha from getting in a buggy and "high-tailing it" to Oskaloosa to see her son.

Early in November, Jacob was working in a drift mine shaft with a partner, a young nineteen-year-old lad named Elmer Burke. They were doing concentrated blast mining. Jacob was shoveling the coal into a tram car, and Elmer was using a single jack to bore a hole for a dynamite charge. Elmer completed setting the charge and began unrolling fuse cord from a spool in his hands. Jacob grabbed the tram car rope and pulled the cart toward the mouth of the tunnel, yelling "fire in the hole" to alert anyone else in the vicinity of the tunnel to stay away. But Jacob was in front of the tram car and did not see that his partner had played out too much fuse. As a result, a large coil of the fuse lay on the floor of the tunnel. Elmer also was not very careful when he was laying out the fuse, because he walked all over the fuse, breaking the seal on the safety coating of the fuse in various places. Elmer then cut the fuse and lit the end. When the fire reached the coiled fuse, it ignited the fuse of the adjoining coil through the broken safety coating, thereby fully bypassing a third of the planned length of the fuse. This greatly cut down the burn time to reach the charge.

As the two men continued pulling the ore car and walking to the entrance of the tunnel, there was a huge roar and shocking blast of air, dust, and coal which slammed into the men and the tram car. The tram car hit Jacob in the back, knocking him to the ground, and the blast hit Elmer in the back, also knocking him down. Both men were dazed and lay still for a moment. They slowly rose to their hands and knees and swung their heads and looked at each other.

"Elmer, I am never going into another mine with you," said Jacob.

Elmer swung his head to the side and looked at his back side and said, "I don't reckon I'll ever go into another mine neither." The back of his pants had been shredded from coal bits as they struck him, and blood was flowing from the numerous puncture wounds on his posterior.

Elmer was patched up and would live to tell the story of his careless blasting experience, but he decided that one large scare was enough, and he never did enter another mine. Jacob made sure that his own future tunnel partners had a bit more experience than Elmer.

As with all such mine mishaps of the time, an investigation was completed by the Iowa Mine Inspectors. Their report was short. It read,

Mr. Elmer Burke, a laborer in Consolidation shaft no. 6, failed to take seriously the established blasting procedures in setting said charge. Insufficiency of fuse resulting in his negligence hence caused said blast. It must be noted that Mr. Burke is no longer employed by the Consolidation Company. I have also informed the shaft foremen of a need to more fully train the below-ground crews.

B.L. Lewis, Inspector

It was not long after this incident that Consolidation found itself in need of a bookkeeper, due to the drunken and unsavory activities of its previous bookkeeper. Simon Williams, the local Oskaloosa operations manager for Consolidation Coal Company, and also the man who hired labor for the mines, remembered a man that he had hired back in June. He remembered the man because he had been an officer in the Army, had gone to college, and had a white streak in his hair. He wondered at the time, why a man with this intelligence and talent, and who did not fit the mold of the usual roughnecks working in the mines, wanted to work in the mines. But since labor was always in short supply, he had hired the man and put him to work digging for coal.

Sometime later, to the great relief of his parents, Jacob did write home, and explained that he was getting along fine, that the work was extremely hard, but he was content for the present. He made no mention of Anna Maier in any of his letters. He did mention that he had regained all of the weight that he had lost during the war, thanks to the hard work and the great food provided by his landlady. He also apologized to his mother when he mentioned that Goldie's pies were the best he had ever eaten.

And in a letter received by the Roush's in November, he told them that he had gotten a new job. He was now the bookkeeper for the company and would not be working in the tunnels again. While the Roush's were glad that Jacob would no longer be underground, "like a gopher," as Martha said, they still missed him and hoped for his return to Burlington.

***

On a bright Sunday afternoon in December 1864, a week or two before Christmas, Jacob had dressed carefully in his best clothes and saddled his horse in Goldie's stable. He headed west out of town to a farm for which he had obtained directions. Less than an hour later, he rode to the front gate of a well-maintained, small, two story wood-frame farmhouse. A small waft of smoke was curling above the brick chimney of the house. There was a hitching bar where he tied his horse as he watched a busy flock of hens rummaging in the trace of snow on the ground outside their coop at the side of the house. He could also see a corral with eight draft horses munching from shocks of hay and a large barn behind the house. Four big pink pigs lay in the sun just outside a brooding house near the barn.

Shortly after he rapped gently on the front door, Georgia Hume opened the door. Her honest, country, good looks stopped Jacob's breath. A swarm of pleasant memories flooded his mind as he stood outside the screen door looking at this lovely girl.

"I saw you ride up, and I didn't even recognize you at first. Jacob, what a wonderful surprise," she said, and gave him a small hug. "Please, come inside out of the cold."

Jacob entered the living room of the home. He looked around the room. The furnishings were very plain. The only picture hanging on one of the walls was a picture depicting Jesus Christ and his disciples at the last supper. The furniture appeared to be hand-made of oak and pine. A thin, braided rug covered the center of the floor in the room. It was readily apparent that this was the home of a hard-working, non-ostentatious family that was very content with their way of life in the country. There was a low fire in the fireplace.

Georgia then introduced him to her mother and father. Georgia's father gruffly acknowledged the introduction. It was plain to see that he was not pleased to meet Jacob. The final introduction was to a younger brother. After further small talk, Mrs. Hume suggested to Mr. Hume and her son that they go to the kitchen for a few minutes. Georgia was left alone with Jacob. It was then that Jacob studied Georgia and could see that she was pregnant. His heart fell. He was immediately saddened and nearly speechless. Georgia could see what had caused the change in Jacob's expression.

"How have you been, Jacob? I am so happy to see that you survived that terrible war. What have you been doing? You must tell me everything," said Georgia.

Jacob regained his composure adequately enough to tell her briefly about the war experience, omitting most of the details. He then told her that he was working as a bookkeeper for the mining company.

"Do you think you will stay with this job, Jacob?" she asked.

"I'm not sure," he said, and went on to explain that he continued to feel restless and had not made up his mind what he wanted to do for a lifetime career. He also mentioned that his father wanted him to join him in the family business.

After an awkward silence, Jacob worked up the courage to say, "I presume you have married?"

"Yes, Jacob, I married quite some time ago, and we are expecting our first child in the spring. My husband's family farm is quite near here, and he is over helping his father today. I'm so sorry you can't meet him. He is a wonderful man."

"I'm glad for you, Georgia. I'm glad you are happy, and I am glad for the news of your baby. I can see that you are well and happy."

Jacob stayed perhaps longer than he should have, but the couple talked and laughed, remembering their days together at college. Georgia walked him to the porch as he was leaving.

Jacob could think of nothing further to say, but he turned to Georgia, and said in a whisper, "I'm sorry, Georgia."

Georgia reached up and kissed Jacob on the cheek. "Goodbye, Jacob," she said, and turned and went into the house.

As he rode back to town, Jacob recalled the day he had told Georgia he was going into the Army. She had told him that day that she had loved him, but that she would not wait for his return. She had been true to her word, and yet, in his heart Jacob had hoped to be able to return to a fondly remembered relationship. He rationalized that he had no one to blame for a failed romance except himself.

***

Jacob buried himself in his work. He spent the majority of his days at his desk, and the clock meant nothing to him. With his increase in salary, he was able to move into the hotel and had a clean room to himself. The food at the hotel was not nearly as good as Goldie's, but he enjoyed the privacy afforded by having his own room. He was content with his situation in life, but deep in his inner core, something kept gnawing at him. He feared putting a name to it, but deep down he knew it was just plain loneliness. He missed his family, and he missed his friends. A glimmer of what was most important in his life began to surface, and over time, Jacob was maturing.

Chapter Four

Jacob's Return

On March 4, 1863, a dapper, curly-haired actor by the name of Booth attended the second inauguration of President Abraham Lincoln. He was invited to attend by his secret fiancée, Lucy Hale, who was the daughter of John Hale who would become the nation's ambassador to Spain. Mr. Booth kept a diary. After the inauguration, he wrote in the diary.

"What an excellent chance I had, if I wished, to kill the President on Inauguration day."

***

It had now been nearly a year since Jacob had initially left home. He had gained great favor with the Consolidation Coal Company to become a trusted financial key in the company. His bosses were mentioning another possible promotion in the future for Jacob.

In May 1865, the city received the exciting news that the Civil War had ended. Confederate General Robert E. Lee had surrendered his army of Northern Virginia to Union General Ulysses S. Grant, at the McClean House in the village of Appomattox Court House, Virginia. The event had occurred a month earlier on Palm Sunday in April of 1865. The news brought a wave of unpleasant memories to Jacob's mind, but he said a prayer of thanks that the war was finally over, and that he had lived through it. He then said a second prayer for his fallen friend, Patrick Quinn, and all of the other soldiers who had died in the conflict.

***

On April 11, 1865, President Abraham Lincoln told his wife Mary about a dream he had had a few nights before. He told her that he had been asleep in the dream, but had awoken when he heard subdued sobs, as if many people were crying. In his dream he walked from room to room in the White House to find the people who were in distress. In the dream he finally entered the East Room and was shocked to see a catafalque, upon which rested a body wrapped in funeral vestments. Around the body were a group of soldiers and people in mourning.

Lincoln asked the people, "Who is dead in the White House?"

He was told it was the president, who had been killed by an assassin's bullet. President Lincoln told his wife, Mary that he had been annoyed by the dream ever since it had occurred.

On April 14, 1865, while attending Ford's Theater in Washington, D.C. to watch the play entitled, *Our American Cousin*, President Lincoln was comfortably seated in a box overlooking the stage. He was accompanied by Union Army Officer, Major Henry Rathbone and his fiancée, Miss Clara Harris. The shadowy form of John Wilkes Booth gained access to the box of the President and his guests, and shot the President of the United States. The President died shortly afterward, and the news raced across the country. A shocked nation went into sad mourning. When the news reached Burlington, the bell at St. Paul's pealed a mournful tone. Sadness prevailed, at least in the northern states of the nation. Veterans of the Civil War, such as Jacob and Kon, fondly remembered their Commander in Chief.

***

The spirited animal was beginning to falter, and its breathing was heavy. Jinks O'Connor had to slow the horse to a walk to let it regain its breath and restore its strength. He had taken the best horse that was in his stable, but he had ridden it too hard. He could now see buildings in the road ahead. He was almost to the settlement of Oskaloosa.

Jacob was poring over a list of payable invoices when the outer office door opened. He paid no attention, as the office was generally full of people coming and going to conduct business, and the door was continually banging and slamming. But in a moment, he looked up to see Jinks standing at the front of his desk. Jacob jumped up, surprised, and quickly shook hands and hugged his brother-in-law.

"Jinks, I'm so glad to see you. What brings you north?" said Jacob.

"Hello, Jacob. I'm mighty glad to see you too. I just had to come and find you," said Jinks. He self-consciously twirled the brim of his hat in his hands.

"Well, sit down here and tell me all about what is going on at home," said Jacob.

"Well, I guess that's why I'm here," said Jinks. "I'm afraid things aren't going so well at home. You see, Mother Roush is in a bad way. She's mighty sick, and the doctor doesn't know how much longer she can last. She and your father are asking about you."

"What do you mean, mother is in a bad way?" said Jacob. "What's wrong with her?"

"I told you the doctors don't know exactly what her ailment is," said Jinks, "but they keep talking about something called cancer, and they don't know how to fix it. Your father and I think you might want to come home pretty quick."

A horrible weight hit Jacob's soul. His mother was gravely ill, and he was not there to help her and his father. There was no question about what his reaction would be.

Jinks arranged for a sturdy, light wagon and a fine stout team. The men cleared out Jacob's hotel room and loaded the wagon. Jacob bid goodbye to his bosses at Consolidation, and the following morning the men were underway for Burlington. The team of horses was kept at a steady trot, conserving their strength by alternating that gait with a periodic walk. They were making good time. Their only stop had been in Mt. Pleasant, to water and grain the horses, and get food for themselves.

Edna and his father were by her bedside when he walked into his mother's bedroom. Self-consciously, Jacob walked slowly over to his mother's bed. Martha looked up, saw him, and smiled. Jacob bent over and kissed his mother on the cheek, and she hugged him around his neck. When she finally let go of him, he straightened up and glanced at his father and Edna. They both greeted him warmly.

Later, when William and Jacob were alone, Jacob said, "Father, what is wrong with mother? She does not appear sick."

William replied, "Jacob, there is something growing inside of her. The doctor says it is slowly killing her, and there is nothing that doctors can do for her except to give her medicine for the pain." Both men retrieved their handkerchiefs, wiped their eyes, and blew their noses.

They sat together for a long time, until Jacob finally said, "I have been a fool. I hope Mother forgives me."

"She forgave you a long time ago, son," said William.

Martha lived for another two weeks, during which time Jacob and Edna spent all their free time with her. The mother and her children talked about all of the good times they had had while the children were growing up, and the stories they had told each other, and the sights they had seen together. On her good days, Martha's eyes sparkled when the stories were told, and she laughed along with her children. A nurse who had been hired by William sat to the side and laughed along with the Roushes as the stories were told. Periodically during the days and nights, the same nurse would tend to Martha's needs, and ensure that pain medication was administered.

The July 4, 1865, fireworks celebrating the nation's independence had gone on sporadically throughout the previous day, but it was not a time for celebration at the Roush mansion. Martha had died three days before on July first, at age fifty-five, and the family and a multitude of friends were holding services for her at Aspen Grove Cemetery. Everyone who had come into contact with Martha Roush in her lifetime knew her as a kind, generous lady with a good sense of humor. She was loved, and the turnout of mourners reflected that love.

As the crowd filed past William offering their words of sympathy following the service, the family moved toward their carriage. One of the last persons to shake William's hand was Anna Maier.

"Please accept my most sincere condolences to you, William. Martha was a wonderful lady," said Anna. William silently nodded his acknowledgement. "And it is so nice to see you home, Jacob," she said. "I pray we'll see more of each other in the future," she said as she smiled slightly and walked away.

***

He watched his father as he moved about the store. There was a distinct change in William. He carried his grief openly, even several weeks after Martha's passing. For all practical purposes, Jacob was now running the business. His father's heart had been broken by the death of his beloved Martha, and he took no real interest in the day to day operation of the mercantile. He came to work out of habit, but even in his diminished state of mind, he often told Jacob how pleased he was that Jacob had come home to help him, and he told his son just as often that he loved him.

The only time that William showed a spark of his former character was when the two red-headed, nine-year-old rascals, Mark and Gregory, the rambunctious grandsons that he loved dearly, charged through the doors of the store to greet their grandfather and uncle. During those visits, William laughed and rough-housed with the boys and gave them candy treats. This was the William that Jacob remembered dearly. The death of his mother, and the immense grief of his father, weighed heavily on Jacob. His world as he knew it was under siege. Before his eyes, he was seeing the not so gradual shift in the hierarchy of the Roush family. He began to see that the responsibilities for the family were slowly shifting to his shoulders, and it frightened him. As he had done so many times in his life, he wished to avoid responsibility, but the sight of his pained father would not allow that. At that instant in time, he resolved that he would remain, and become the head of the family, skillfully running the family business. As he continued to gaze at his father, he wondered if he was up to the task.

***

Jacob was more than up to the task of taking over the Roush Mercantile. His familiarity with the family business, coupled with his military discipline, college training, and experience working with the coal company had fully prepared him for the challenge. Under his quiet guidance and leadership, the business flourished to the point that a new smaller store was added to the west side of the city, and another store was opened in Ft. Madison. Jacob also bought out two of his smaller competitors in the city and closed their operations. For dry goods, food supplies, clothing, guns and hardware, there was no place with more merchandise and a wider array of goods.

The Roush family financial worth rose accordingly. With the twins in school, Edna O'Connor also worked at the store. She had learned the bookkeeping from Jacob and excelled in that aspect of the business.

William was true to his word and had turned over full management of the business to his son; however, he still came to work, but found that he was comfortable just wandering the store, greeting old friends, and helping out at the new ice cream counter that Jacob had put into the store. He loved to watch the young mothers bringing their children in for a special ice cream treat. At times, he could be found behind the ice cream counter dishing up cones for his favorite youngsters. And of course, his favorite youngsters were his rowdy, energy driven grandsons. They always had an ice cream treat ready for them as soon as they entered the store. He truly believed that they were his reason for living.

With his rugged good looks and, of course, his family's position, Jacob was considered the city's most eligible bachelor. He was invited to innumerable social events in the city and attended some of them. A relationship resumed between he and Anna Maier, but he could just as easily be seen at social gatherings with other young ladies. He enjoyed himself and remained noncommittal.

Anna, meanwhile, was reexamining her tactics. Her plan had not changed. By any means, she would marry the most eligible, attractive, wealthy man in town, and that was Jacob Roush. She stretched the moral, socially acceptable limits of how a young woman could court a young man. She had no qualms about asking Jacob to accompany her to social engagements. She also had no modesty when alone with Jacob and allowed him to kiss her freely. She also bought small gifts for him, asking nothing in return, and would appear unannounced in the store to take Jacob out of the store to get a cup of coffee. William always watched in amusement as Anna grabbed Jacob's arm and led him out of the store for lunch or coffee. He remembered fondly how grand it had been to walk down the street with Martha on his arm.

Jacob had grown used to Anna's behavior, so much so that he rather enjoyed some of her attention. Other than the fact that he felt himself being somewhat pressured by Anna at times, he had not seen anything malevolent in her behavior or personality to alarm him. Whether consciously or unconsciously, Jacob found himself growing fonder of Anna Maier.

As fall moved into early winter in 1865, Jacob spent more time with Anna. Edna and Jinks teased Jacob, reminding him that at twenty-five, he was not getting any younger, and he ought to think about marrying Anna, since they were already spending so much time together.

One afternoon, Jacob was sitting in a duck blind on the riverbank with Kon and Jinks.

Jacob blurted out to Kon, "Kon, what do you think I should do about getting married? I know that Anna wants to get married. Do you think I would make a good husband, and do you think Anna would make a good wife?"

This was so out of character for Jacob to ask a question like that, that Jinks could not help but laugh out loud.

"Oh, keep quiet, Jinks, I'm asking Kon," said Jacob.

Even Kon had to smile. Kon was twelve years older than Jacob, but he recognized his limitations.

"Geez, Jacob, I'm a fine one to ask. I'm not even married," said Kon. "But I do know this. You are my friend, and you are a fine man and will make a good husband and father. You must do what your heart tells you to do. I will not comment on Anna, because I don't know her well enough. Oh, and one more thing, don't listen to Jinks, 'cause he's full of goose shit," said Kon.

The men were laughing so hard that their chance of being quiet and bagging any waterfowl was spoiled for the afternoon.

The same evening Jacob was sitting in the living room with his father, and he asked William almost the same question as he had asked his friends.

"Father, Anna Maier would like to get married, she has told me that. But I have not asked her. What do you think I should do?"

William was humbled and flattered by the question. He did not expect to have Jacob ever ask his advice on this subject, so he took his time answering.

"Jacob, you know that when I was a young man Martha and I did not have a choice. Our families arranged our wedding. Thank God that we loved and respected each other, and we were happy to be married. But in your case, you have a choice. If you love and respect Anna, and she feels the same way about you, then I would advise you to ask her to marry you. Frankly, I don't care who you marry. But for selfish reasons of my own, and for your future happiness, I would like you to promise me that before I die you will get married. That would make me happy, and I know Martha would be happy if she were here to see that. Who knows, I might like to see a couple more grandkids running around this old house someday."

Jacob nodded his head and looked at his father and grinned. "I think I can make good on that promise," he said.

Chapter Five

Esther Blue Wing

Initially, Kon had told no one of his discovery. For weeks, he had been watching a group of flat bottom fishing boats moving back and forth across the river. There were usually two of the homemade wooden boats, each carrying four men, two of whom were rowing. At times, a woman could be seen in place of one of the men. The boats would come from one of the river's many islands and enter a small inlet that led to a marsh. The occupants of the boats would then fish for a few hours, snare waterfowl, and return to the island. This may not have been unusual, since many of the islands had people living on them, usually without owning the property. But what intrigued Kon was that the occupants of the small boats appeared to be Indians, wearing westernized clothing as well as some garments of Indian design.

One day in December, Kon approached the marsh on foot and made himself visible to the fishing party. One of the older men walked over to Kon and greeted him. The older man spoke broken English, but was easily understood. Kon learned that the old man's name was John Red Hawk. He and this party of Indians came from Minnesota. They were part of the Prairie Island Dakota Sioux people. Each winter, they were allowed to hunt off of the reservation and would travel south on the Mississippi River to avoid the harsh northern weather. They did not always come to the same place each year.

Soon the other men also gathered around Kon, and he explained to the older man that he lived here among the white people and even had an occupation. This so astounded the men that they could not stop asking questions.

Among this small group was a middle-aged woman. She stayed to the side of the group, cleaning fish, and stripping feathers from a duck they had caught. She listened to every word spoken by the men, and she carefully looked at Kon. From the conversation, she knew that Kon had assimilated into the white world, and she also surmised that he had white man's wealth. She carefully made a beckoning motion to the older man, who walked to her. They talked for a moment, and the man rejoined the other men. The conversation continued, but then the older man invited Kon to join them at their camp for a visit.

Kon was delighted. He was as fascinated with the lives of these Indians as they were with his, and he eagerly joined the group as they rowed the two boats to the island. He watched as the men carefully hid the boats by covering them with branches after bringing them up onto the island. The group then walked through the trees and brush on a well-concealed path, traveling up a hill to a small clearing at the mouth of a large cave. Kon was amazed. The location looked so much like the cave his mother and father had lived in, and he did not even know this location existed. Since there was no fear of other Indians raiding them, or danger from white settlers, the camp seemed relaxed, with its main purpose being fishing and hunting.

There were approximately forty Indians in the communal group, with five or six children scampering around the camp. Kon noticed there were only a couple young men in the group. The cave seemed to be the main lodging for the group, and was spacious enough that it contained several smaller caverns. Thus, it was large enough for privacy if it was needed. There was a communal cooking fire outside the cave, and ashes showed the existence of another fire at the mouth of the cave. Several of the women were tending the cooking fire and preparing an early evening meal. Kon was asked to join the group for dinner. The men ate together, with the women in a group behind them, serving the men.

After the meal, the men moved closer to the fire that had been renewed at the mouth of the cave. The conversation was never ending. The Sioux wanted to know all about Kon's experiences with the Sauk people, but were even more interested in the world of the white people that Kon inhabited. The stories flew around the campfire. Kon learned that this small group of people lived at a place called Prairie Island in a land called Minnesota. That was their reservation provided by the government. In the winter, the location became bitterly cold, with much snow. This prompted many of the group to move further south down the river so that they could hunt, trap, and fish during the colder months. Several of their people chose not to make the winter journey to the south and stayed at Prairie Island. The men also told Kon of their experiences with Indian agents, and the Christian people who came to see them, and who tried to take away their ancient spirits, making them learn strange words from a book they called the Bible. These Bible people also gave white man names to the people in addition to the Indian's own name. That is how Red Hawk became known as John Red Hawk. So, the group had been westernized to the extent that they wore mostly western clothing and spoke some English, and many of them had double names.

In the dimming light, Kon could not always see all of the men and women, but at one point during the early evening, he had noticed a younger woman among the women sitting behind the men. He also saw the older woman who was with the fishing party speaking to the younger woman. During the campfire discussion, he learned that John Red Hawk was the leader of the encampment, and the older woman was his wife. Their daughter was the younger woman Kon had noticed.

As the evening passed, it became apparent that the Indians were making no plans to take Kon back to the other side of the river. Courtesy dictated that he would be spending the night with the Sioux people. As the hour grew late, people began drifting away from the fire, going back into the cave to sleep. A small handful of men remained with Kon, still telling stories. Kon was enjoying himself, but was extremely tired. Finally, John Red Hawk said he was tired, and asked Kon to accompany him. He led Kon to a small alcove and told him this was where he was to sleep. He was given blankets as a cushion to sleep on and for warmth. He also told Kon that he and his wife and daughter were further back into the cave and would see him in the morning.

Kon lay awake for a few minutes thinking about all the wonderful stories he had heard, and the life these new friends led in the north. He was glad he had accompanied them to the island.

He had been asleep for some time when he was nudged in his sleep. Kon roused awake, and only then did he discover that there was a woman sharing his blanket. She was snuggled up next to his side. Kon turned his head and could only make out dim features in the ebbing light bouncing off the cave walls from the small fire at the cave mouth. But he knew this had to be the young woman he had seen earlier in the evening. She was awake and touched his cheek.

Kon was startled, and knowing that John Red Hawk and his wife were nearby, whispered, "Who are you?" followed by, "What are you doing here?"

She replied, "My name is Esther Blue Sky, and I am here because my father and mother told me to come to your side. I am your gift for the night."

It was not uncommon for an Indian tribe to provide a visiting male guest with a woman to share his bed. But Kon did not know this, for he had never lived in an Indian environment other than with his father and mother. He was quite speechless as the young woman began gently massaging Kon. Kon was now wide awake and was about to leap up and run out of the cave. But instead, he calmed down and grabbed the woman's hands. He was not sure what to do next. He very nearly threw caution to the wind and let nature take its course. But it just did not seem right that he should take advantage of the situation. He relaxed his grip on the woman's wrists, but was still unsure of what he should say to this woman.

He finally said to her, "Esther, is this something you want to do?"

Esther responded, "Oh yes, I have watched you all night, and I wish to be by your side and make you happy."

About two more minutes was all it took for the rest of Kon's caution to fall, and nature did, indeed, take its course with the couple entwined between the blankets. The noises of pleasure emanating from the couple were heard by Esther's mother from her place not far from them. The old woman smiled and drifted off to sleep.

As the first light filtered through the trees, Kon sat at the opening of the cave and watched a brazen turkey on the far side of the clearing scratching along the tree line. He reasoned that if any of the men were up and about, the turkey would be in the Indians' stew pot that evening. The Indians did not drink coffee, and Kon was really missing his morning caffeine. He always enjoyed his coffee as he sat around the maintenance shop with his mechanics prior to going to work for the day.

After the formalities of last night, if they could be called formalities, it was now permissible for Esther to be seen with Kon, and she suddenly appeared at his side. Kon quickly looked at her, as he still had not seen her in full light. He was shocked! Esther had the clearest blue eyes he had ever seen. He had never seen an Indian with blue eyes. It was beyond Kon's comprehension that for generations, white men had intermingled with the Indians, especially the trappers who sometimes wintered with various tribes. A long dormant gene for blue eyes which had passed from generation to generation had suddenly made itself known with Esther's birth. This was so unusual that the baby had been revered and had been given a name fitting of her eye color. Besides her eyes, Kon could not help but notice that Esther was truly beautiful. Her wardrobe consisted of a mix of western clothes and Indian garb. She wore a rainbow colored, freshwater clam shell on a thong around her neck and a beautiful beaded belt at her narrow waist, over a cloth shirt and skirt which matched her eyes. Deer skin moccasins covered her feet, and a beaded leather strand held her hair away from her high-cheeked face. To Kon, she was the most beautiful woman he had ever seen.

At the conclusion of breakfast, Kon prepared to return to the other side of the river with a fishing party. He could not help seeing Esther's mother continuing to cast glances his way, and it was not long before John Red Hawk strolled over to talk to Kon.

"Esther's mother had a dream last night," said John Red Hawk.

Kon didn't say anything out of respect for the older man.

"She said it was a good dream. It was about you." He went on. "The spirits told her that you would marry our daughter."

That got a quick reaction from Kon. He had been looking past the old man at the river, thinking that he needed to get home. But suddenly he jerked back and looked the old man in the eyes. He thought the old man might be playing some kind of game with him, but still he did not say anything.

Then the old man said, "The spirits also told her that you and our daughter will have many children."

That was enough, thought Kon. He needed to get across the river.

"John Red Hawk, I thank you for your hospitality. I have enjoyed meeting you and your people, but I must go now."

The two men shook hands, and Kon turned to join the boat men and fishing party. But before he had taken two steps, John Red Hawk said, "I look forward to seeing you next time."

And of course, there was a next time, and many visits after that. Kon had told Four Toes and New Rain about his experience, leaving out the intimate details, and told them that he was going to ask John Red Hawk's permission to marry his daughter. His parents were delighted. Kon made regular visits to the island every day he was not at work. He took a terrible ribbing from his best buddy Jinks, but Edna and Mike thought it was a blessing that Kon had found a girlfriend.

"When are we going to see this Indian woman, Kon?" teased Jinks. "I'll bet you don't even have a girl over there. You're probably just going over to keep the raccoons company."

"Well, one of these days you'll see," said Kon.

For the past three visits, the negotiations took place after the noon meal. Kon was worn out from all the talking and considered giving up. John Red Hawk would not give his consent for Esther to marry Kon without a dowry. That was the subject of the spirited debate and negotiations. In truth, John Red Hawk was just playing with Kon. His wife had made it clear to him that Esther was to marry Kon, so John Red Hawk was just having fun frustrating Kon. He enjoyed the younger man's company, and this was a way to keep him coming back to the island. But at the end of January, when Esther's mother told him to stop teasing Kon, John Red Hawk finally had to give up the game. Kon thought it was odd that John Red Hawk, with a twinkle in his eye, had finally settled on one hundred U.S. dollars, a bolt of sewing cloth, and a new shotgun and shells for hunting birds. At various times during the negotiations, the stakes had been much higher. Esther had stayed within earshot of all the negotiations and knew her father had been toying with Kon. But when the agreement was reached, she was extremely glad it was over.

John Red Hawk and Esther's mother spoke to Kon and Esther at great length. They had made the decision long ago that their daughter would somehow be assimilated into the white men's world instead of living within the limitations of a reservation. They believed that Kon had been sent by the spirits to take their daughter to his world, and they were ecstatic. But Kon had a multitude of details to work out for wedding their daughter.

One detail had been nagging at him for quite some time. One day, in the afternoon, he approached Mike and Jinks, and announced to them, "I want another name." Neither Mike nor Jinks knew what he was talking about.

"What do you mean, you want another name," said Mike.

"I want two names," said Kon. "I only have one name, and you have two names or even three names. You see, I'm getting married, and I can't have my family without a name."

Both Mike and Jinks jumped up from where they had been sitting in the transportation office, and almost simultaneously let out a giant, "Whoopee. You're getting married?" they said.

"Yep," said Kon.

The back-slapping started, and the manly teasing kept up for several minutes, with all three of them shouting and laughing.

When the raucous behavior subsided, Kon said, "Now if you guys are done, I would still like your opinion on this name problem. What do you think I should use for a name?"

Frankly, Mike and Jinks were stumped. They had never heard of such a problem. They thought everybody was born with two names, except Indians, of course. They had no idea what an Indian might do to get another name.

"C'mon boys, we're taking a walk," said Mike, and led them to the shop of an attorney he had consulted in his business dealings.

After he heard the story, the attorney laughed, but then said that the problem really was not too hard to fix. He told them they would need to go to the county clerk's office and file for the new name. After the filing was done, it would go to the mayor's office for approval. If it was approved, that would become the legal name of the applicant. After they received this advice, the three men returned to the transportation office.

"So what do you think you want for a name?" said Mike, as they sat in the office.

"I'm not sure," said Kon. "That's why I was asking you guys."

"I think this requires some serious thinking," said Mike, and he brought out a bourbon bottle and filled three glasses.

Kon almost never touched alcohol, but he knew that to get his friend and his boss to help him, he would need to partake of a sip. He made a note to go very slow, knowing the O'Connor reputations.

For an hour, the three men batted around names. They were getting nowhere, but getting tipsier as time went on. Kon was still sober, managing to pour most of his drinks into the corner spittoon when Mike and Jinks weren't looking. They had only just come to the conclusion that the name Kon would remain to become his first name.

Finally, Mike said to Kon, "You know, Kon, you can have any name you want. Is there someone that you admire that you might like to have the same name? Is there any name that you're partial to? Think about anybody that you might have known, or somebody you respect," said Mike. "What do you think?"

A thought suddenly occurred to Kon. His mind went back to a time when he had been lying in the mud dodging Confederate bullets in Jackson, Mississippi, and after the battle was over, he and the rest of the muddy, but victorious brigade had trudged along the road back to Vicksburg. As they had walked along, a figure on horseback, followed by six other riders, one of whom was holding a United States flag, came toward the men. Among the walking men, the talk immediately revealed the identity of the Union Officer. It was General Ulysses S. Grant, on a fine black horse, in his best uniform, with his sword by his side. The general had removed his hat and was waving to all the soldiers as they walked back to Vicksburg. Kon remembered that scene, thinking that it was an honor to have had General Grant greeting the weary foot soldiers as they made their way on the road. He had thought that the general must be a good man to take the time to greet the war-weary infantry men who had just taken Jackson for General Grant. He told this story to Mike and Jinks.

"I want the name Grant," said Kon. "I think that would be a fine name. What do you think?"

"I think you could sure do a lot worse, and probably not much better," said Mike. "But what about the Ulysses part of the general's name? You want that too?"

"Well, why not?" said Jinks. "I think your new name should be Kon Ulysses Grant. That's got a real official sound to it. What do you think, Kon?"

"Grant, Grant, yep, I like that. I'll tell Esther that she will soon be Esther Blue Sky Grant," said Kon, and he shook hands with Jinks and Mike, who were finishing off the bourbon bottle. Kon headed out the door to file the new name at the county clerk's office.

There was another detail concerning the wedding that had been nagging at Kon for several days. He needed advice again. He went to find Toby Barth at the livery stable. As he neared the smithy's shop, he heard the unmistakable ring of a hammer striking a hot metal shoe on a well-worn anvil. But it was not Toby coercing the metal, it was Bobbin. Now nearly twenty years old, Bobbin could run the blacksmith business just as well as his father, and he had the imposing physique to prove he had swung a heavy hammer thousands of times.

"Hello, Kon. What brings you here today?" said Bobbin.

"I came to see your father. Is he around?"

Bobbin replied, "He's in the back room there. Probably taking a nap," and he chuckled.

Kon walked to the little office door at the back of the shop and gently knocked on the door. He heard a sharp bang, which alarmed him, so he opened the door gently. He then spied Toby getting up off the floor and an overturned chair on the floor next to him.

Toby grinned and said, "My own damn fault. I shouldn't have been leaning back on that chair before I nodded off a bit. Kon, good to see you. What have you been up to? Did I hear something about you maybe getting married?" The men shook hands.

Kon laughed, "Yep. I guess it's true, and I wanted to talk to you about that."

Toby looked quizzically at Kon. "Don't ask me nuthin' about marriage. All I know is it's OK for some men, but not so fine for others. Thank the Lord, I still have my Lizzy, though."

"Well," said Kon, "it's not exactly about that. You see, I need to figure out how to get married."

"What do you mean, how to get married. Why, you just go to the courthouse and get a license, and get a preacher man to marry you up. It's as simple as that," said Toby.

"That's the problem," said Kon. "I don't have a preacher man, and I don't know if any of them would marry an Indian couple. That's why I came to see you. I know you go to church and are friendly with that Reverend Salter. And he doesn't seem to mind that you are not white. Do you think he might marry an Indian couple?"

Toby answered, "I sure think he would do it. Let's go talk to him."

The two men trudged up to Fourth Street and found Reverend William Salter in the small office of the church. He looked up from the papers he was examining and saw Toby. "Toby, how are you?" he said and put out his hand.

Toby shook the minister's hand. "Do you know…" was all Toby said before Reverend Salter said, "Sure, I know Kon, but Kon, we've never formally met. How do you do?"

Kon immediately liked this man, and could see that Toby trusted him. "I'm fine," said Kon.

But now, he was at a loss on how to continue this conversation.

Toby helped him out. "Reverend Salter, my friend Kon has a problem, a good problem. You see, he wants to get married, but he doesn't know anyone to perform the ceremony."

"And he wonders whether or not I would conduct the marriage, is that right?" said Reverend Salter.

"Yes sir, you've got it," replied Toby.

Kon felt a bit helpless as he listened to this conversation go back and forth without him.

Reverend Salter turned his full attention to Kon. "Kon, I would like to ask you a couple questions, would that be all right?"

"Sure," said Kon.

Reverend Salter began, "Kon, I know you probably have not had any formal Christian education, so I will make this as simple as I know how."

What Reverend Salter could not know was that Kon knew some of the tenets of Christianity from his association with white people, and from his days in the Army.

"Kon, did men make the heaven and earth?" asked Reverend Salter.

"No sir," answered Kon. "Men can't make those things. They were made by spirits, or God."

"Good, you believe in a higher presence," said the minister. "Whether you call it spirits or God, I don't believe that's important at this time. Let's just say we both believe in something far more powerful than either of us. Kon, are you familiar with the Ten Commandments?"

Again, Kon answered the question, "Yes, I have heard of them."

This surprised Reverend Salter a bit. "Can you tell me what any of them are?" he asked.

"I have heard soldiers tell me that you should not kill another man. You should not steal. You should not tell lies about other people, and you should go to a church on Sundays. We would talk about these things as we were marching during the war," said Kon.

Reverend Salter then said, "You know Kon, I have married people that did not know as much about our beliefs as you do. And if you obey those commandments you just told me, I would consider you to be a good man. I would be happy to marry you and your intended. Would you like to be married in our church?"

"Yes, sir," said Kon.

The men began making plans for a small private wedding which would be held in the Congregational Church in the near future.

The last detail of getting married that Kon wanted to resolve started a story that stirred the whole city. Kon had diligently saved his pay from his job and had a respectable savings. But it was not quite enough. Kon wanted his own house. He did not think that a man of his age who was married should continue to live in his parents' house. Kon knew of two settlers' homes that were for sale. The occupants were adventuresome sorts, who wanted to leave Burlington and head further west and start over again. That evening, he told Four Toes and New Rain of his day. The older Indians were not sure that he was doing the right thing by changing his name, but they were pleased that Kon would remain as his first name. They also did not know what to think about a wedding in a white man's church. In truth, they had never had a wedding ceremony, even in Indian fashion. They had simply been thrown together by circumstances many years ago and had been living together ever since. Neither of them had ever been in a white man's church. But their wish to have their son be happy and do the right thing overrode any concern they might have had.

Kon then gently told his parents about his final detail. He wanted to buy a house. That would mean that he would move out from under the roof of his mother and father. He knew this would sadden them. He told them that he would like to look at a couple of houses that were for sale. But he was not sure that he had enough money to buy either of them. He asked his father for advice. The discussion between the man and his parents lasted for quite some time, but Four Toes finally prevailed.

He said, "Kon, I want to think about what you have told me. New Rain and I will talk to the spirits and ask for guidance. Let us wait for seven days, and we will talk again."

Chapter Six

Four Toes' Treasure

During the seven day interval, Four Toes was a busy man. He made visits primarily to his friend Peter Stroud who accompanied Four Toes to attorneys' offices and various county offices. In addition, the two men moved about the city in a carriage. At one point while they were together, the two men rode out of town on two horses, with a pack mule being led behind them. They told no one except the attorneys what they were doing, keeping their activities to themselves.

At the end of the seven days, Kon returned to his parents' home for dinner, and he had a surprise with him. He had gone across the river and brought Esther Blue Sky to meet Four Toes and New Rain. New Rain was delighted. The evening went well. After dinner, Esther went to the kitchen with New Rain to help New Rain. Four Toes and Kon went to a corner of the living room to talk quietly.

"The spirits have spoken to me," said Four Toes. "They have given me a plan. Your mother and I would like to have you live with us in this house, but I know it is too small for all of us. Also, I fear the big river flooding this house in a season with much rain." The old man continued. "We have several acres of land here. You remember that many years ago, Mike O'Connor gave us this property. I know that Mike would like to have this land to enlarge his freight yard. I will talk to him about returning the property to him."

Kon could not believe what he was hearing. His father was actually thinking of leaving his home, the old original trading post for the settlement of Burlington.

"Father, why are you doing this?" said Kon. "Surely it is not because I talked about having my own house?"

With a twinkle in his eye, Four Toes then began a rather lengthy story. It was a story that Kon had never heard before, and he gave his father his rapt attention.

Four Toes told Kon that at the close of the Black Hawk War, Four Toes had taken refuge in the cave southwest of the future settlement. He had lived in that cave by himself until he was joined by New Rain. He had explored every inch of the large, deep cave, thinking that at some time he might have a need for a place to hide from soldiers if they came looking for him. But as Four Toes told Kon, he was not the first man to have set foot in the cave. In his explorations of the cave, Four Toes had made a discovery. Where the casual explorer of the cave would never have found it, Four Toes had found two, medium-sized metal chests. They were buried, and he might never have found them, but an overhead grouping of stalactites in the cave dripped a steady, small stream of water over one of the buried chests, washing away the sandy soil under which the chest had been buried, and forming a translucent glaze over one of the chests. The second chest was discovered when Four Toes was unearthing the first one. Four Toes had broken the old rusty locks to discover that the chests were full of gold coins. Four Toes told Kon that over a period of time, he had moved the coins out of the cave and had hidden them in a different location.

Kon had never been told this story, and it was all he could do to hold his tongue. He was not even sure that his father was entirely truthful, or whether he was even completely lucid. But why would he make up such a story if it was not true?

Four Toes continued telling Kon that nearly thirty years ago, when Peter Stroud opened the first bank, Kon had gone with him and New Rain to the bank.

Kon interrupted. "I remember that. It was the first time you and mother took me to the village from the cave."

Four Toes nodded and continued. "On that day, I gave Peter Stroud one hundred of the gold coins to put in the bank. Peter is a good friend, and he never told anyone about my coins. He told me that the coins must have been placed in the cave by men from a faraway land called France. Those men had come up the big river exploring to find things to take back to their land across the sea. Peter also told me that each of the coins was worth five United States dollars. But I never told Peter that I had many more coins. But Peter did something very special for me. In the days that followed the opening of the bank, he took me to the assay office and helped me fill out a claim for the land around the cave. But because I was an Indian, I could not purchase the land. But Peter Stroud claimed the land, and had the assayer man put the deed in Peter's name. About a week after that, Peter had the new deed, and he came to get me, and we both went back to the assayer office. Peter then signed the deed over to me, giving me the property. I paid him for the land after we left the assay office. So, I own nearly forty acres around our old cave."

"Why didn't you ever tell me about this?" asked Kon.

"It was never important enough to talk about," said Four Toes. "Even New Rain did not know about this until I told her last week. And some-times knowing a secret can cause problems."

Four Toes continued his story. "Last week, I told Peter Stroud about the other coins. I told him that I wanted to put all the coins in his bank. I took Peter to get the coins, and we packed the leather bags of coins into Peter's bank bags, loaded them on a mule, and brought them back to the bank. So they are now safe in the bank." Four Toes then said, "Peter and I have visited with an attorney to make sure that the coins could no longer be claimed by anyone else. The lawyer has told us that the coins are mine forever. Peter has told me that there were nearly two thousand coins, worth ten thousand United States dollars."

Kon nearly fell off his chair. "Ten thousand dollars!" he said. "Father, you are a rich man," said Kon.

"Riches mean little to me. New Rain and you mean more than riches to me. But I told you I have a plan. I want to build a small home for New Rain and me on our property. And I would like you to build a house for you and your family on the same property. In this way, you can be close to your mother and me."

"I don't have enough money to build a house," said Kon. "I will have to ask a bank to lend me money."

"No Kon," said Four Toes. "The bank will take your money for their use, and make you pay them far too much. My plan is that you will use your own money, and I will give you the extra money you need. But just like the white man's bank, you will have to pay me back the money you use."

What a time it had been these past two weeks. He had gotten permission to marry Esther Blue Sky. He had gotten a new name for his family. He found out that his father was a wealthy man. And he was going to build a new home. It was overwhelming to Kon. He told himself that he must be the happiest man in Burlington. The following day, as he rowed Esther Blue Sky across the river to her people, the couple made their final plans.

The spirits had told Four Toes and New Rain that this was a favored time. So, on the afternoon of New Year's Eve 1865, a small assemblage met in the Congregational Church on Fourth Street. William Roush, Jacob Roush, Peter and Maria Stroud, Mike, Jinks and Edna O'Connor, Four Toes and New Rain, and John Red Hawk and his wife watched Reverend Salter marry Kon Ulysses Grant and Esther Blue Sky Grant. The first Christian wedding joining two Native Americans in Burlington was taking place. At the completion of the formalities the entire entourage boarded one of Mike's small boats and crossed the river to the Sioux encampment. John Red Hawk, as the senior member of the Indian camp, then proceeded to perform a Native American ceremony signifying and celebrating the marriage of his daughter to Kon. The ceremony was beautiful with its singing, chanting, and dancing.

Reverend Salter was greatly interested in the life of these people and carefully watched the ceremony. He later admitted that he had enjoyed himself immensely. Kon Grant and his bride, Esther, then returned to Burlington to join his parents in their home, while progress was being made on the construction of the two new homes on the property of Four Toes. Some of New Rain's dreams would later come true. The new house would be sorely needed, as Kon and Esther would eventually add a total of seven children to their family.

Chapter Seven

Other Plans

Once again, she was deeply enmeshed in each and every detail of the upcoming event. Anna was browbeating each servant, making sure that her New Year's party would once again be the city's event of the year. Since the turnover among her servants was always high, virtually none of the current staff members had helped with a previous party, thereby necessitating Anna's intervention in each detail. Anna could never understand that her constant meddling and criticism drove away help almost as fast as she could replace them. At the appointed time this evening, the city's elite would begin arriving for the Flint Bluff New Year's Eve gala.

At six p.m., the guests, dressed in their resplendent finery, began arriving in carriages in the long circular drive of Flint Bluff. They entered the home and were waited upon by the staff. As usual, Anna would not make her appearance until all the guests had arrived. She was still upstairs primping and making the final adjustments to the dress gown she was wearing. The cost of the dress, which had been purchased in St. Louis for just this occasion, was enough to build a modest house. Even Anna knew she had spent far too much for the dress, but her ego would not allow anything less. The rich, bone colored silk dress had real pearls sown to the front of the dress from the waist to the top of the bodice. With her hair carefully coiled upon the top of her head and held in place by exquisite combs, she chose to offset the white of the dress and pearl adornment with an extravagant ruby necklace, earrings, and bracelet. Her shawl was a deep red silk to match the jewelry. The look was dazzlingly beautiful, and Anna preened in front of the full-length mirror in her room.

The look would tantalize a certain man, and that was the plan. Tonight, she would put a stop to her intended's hesitation. The servant attending to her only wished at this point that Anna would soon go to her guests.

To the quiet murmurs of her guests, Anna finally made her entrance. The eyes of disapproving female guests, with their obviously approving male escorts, followed Anna's steps as she glided down the ornate staircase. She strode confidently to the orchestra's alcove, and bid good evening to all of her guests. When cocktail hour was concluded, the guests moved to the tables, found their individual name cards, and were seated. Once again, Jacob found himself seated next to Anna.

As the soup was served, and the guests were eating, Anna leaned over toward Jacob, allowing her low-cut dress to work to her advantage. She then whispered to Jacob.

"I intend to announce our engagement tonight."

Jacob had just taken a spoonful of soup, and suddenly dropped it, clattering on the edge of the bowl, and then down onto the floor. Several sets of eyes around the table turned toward him as he made his apology while a servant picked up the spoon and brought another to him. Anna only smiled and patted Jacob on his arm.

The conversation around the dining table went on as usual, but Jacob was not hearing any of it. His head was buzzing as he tried to realize what Anna had just told him. What was he to do? He had considered being married to Anna at times when he was alone, but had never gone so far as to ask her for her hand. They had associated on a social basis, and he was fond of her. But marriage?

The dinner of baked, wild pheasant was not to Jacob's taste. But the discussion around the table was lively. Jacob said little and was content to listen to the other conversations. After he calmed down a bit following Anna's previous statement to him, he caught himself rather enjoying an occasional furtive look at Anna. He marveled at how beautiful she was.

At the conclusion of dinner, the tables were cleared and taken away to make room for dancing. Anna took the arm of the mayor, and the refrain of the 'Jenny Lind Polka' began the evening's dancing.

As Anna moved around the dance floor, courteously dancing with as many of the men as possible, she enjoyed discreetly listening to as many of the women's conversations as she could while seeming oblivious to the gossip she was hearing behind her back. Inevitably, she came at last to Jacob.

"Have you been avoiding me, Jacob?" she teased. "I have been trying to catch up with you all night."

"On the contrary, Anna. I have been in the corner just watching you. You are quite the butterfly, and a very beautiful butterfly," said Jacob.

"Well, well, Jacob Roush, aren't you the flatterer," she said. "Now come and dance with me. And I must warn you that once I have you dancing, I do not intend to let you loose, maybe forever."

Little did Jacob realize how prophetic those words would prove to be. True to her word, Anna kept Jacob by her side.

They danced most of the rest of the evening, until Anna took him by the arm and guided him to the back of the house to the library. She closed the doors behind them and immediately kissed Jacob.

She then said, "Jacob Roush, I want you to tell me why you have not asked me to marry you. And I want you to tell me right now!"

Anna had a habit of putting Jacob on his heels, and he was teetering as she spoke. She did not even give him any time to answer, and said, "Don't you want to get married in your lifetime?"

Jacob answered, "Yes, I do, but I just don't know when that will be."

She answered, "Well, let's presume that it will occur in the very near future. Now what is wrong with marrying me?"

"Nothing, I guess," said Jacob.

"Then it's settled. We are going to get married. I believe that spring would be a great time for the wedding, what do you think?"

This was all going way too fast for Jacob to even think about any such details, and he stood staring at Anna. What in the world was happening? He was speechless.

Anna continued. "Now, would you have any objection to me announcing our engagement tonight?"

He said quietly, "I...I guess not."

"Now, see, that was not so painful, was it," Anna cooed.

Anna took Jacob's hand and led him back to the ballroom. Getting everyone's attention, she spoke to her guests. "Ladies and gentlemen, I wish to thank you all for coming to my party. I hope you had a wonderful time. And now, before we have our final dance, I have an announcement. Mr. Jacob Roush has asked me to marry him, and I have accepted." A cheer went up from the guests and they filed by Anna and Jacob offering their congratulations.

The evening ended in its usual manner, with the final waltz, 'Tales From the Vienna Woods' being played by the orchestra. Jacob did not even remember dancing to that music. He was befuddled, to say the least.

Jacob stayed behind after the guests had filed out the front door and headed for their carriages. "Anna, are you sure we should be getting married?" he asked.

"Jacob, we have been over this many times. Of course, we should get married. You were meant for me, and I was meant for you. Now stop being silly and go home. I'll see you tomorrow. If it is not too cold, we could take a sleigh ride. Pick me up at two o'clock." She guided him out the front door.

It all seemed so easy when she said it, but Jacob still had trepidation about being married. Frankly, he was a bit afraid of the responsibility, and he got an uneasy feeling from listening to Anna tell him about what a wonderful life they would have together. There was something in Anna's personality that frightened him, but he could not put his finger on whatever it was.

For the next three months, the couple was seen at every social event in the city. Anna held numerous small dinner parties to enable her social circle to better get to know Jacob. Jacob took it all in stride, but could not help feeling that his life was being managed to the point that it was now out of his hands. His escape was his work and his close friends. Whenever he was not at the store, he found great joy in fishing or duck hunting with Jinks, Kon, Horace Bailey, and Johaan Stroud.

In addition, he had taken up the game of poker. Jacob had converted an unused store room on the upper level of the store to a small apartment, adding an outside stairway entrance. Horace Bailey had taken over his father's business and enlarged it by building a new factory for manufacturing furniture. Horace had donated some blemished furniture which would normally be thrown away or reworked, and the men could play cards, smoke their cigars and have a few drinks and not bother anyone else. The men called their little game room, "boys' town."

If he was not with his friends, Jacob would be found escorting the lovely Anna. Not that the situation was so bad, of course. The couple was regarded to be the high society darlings of the city, which caused considerable kidding by Jacob's friends. Each time the couple was together, Anna had a list of wedding preparation minutiae for Jacob's discussion and input. To Jacob, this wedding planning went far beyond boring. And whenever he had an opinion, Anna would go ahead with what she wanted to do anyway. But one of the details was troublesome to Jacob, but only for a short time.

One day while the couple was sitting at the table in the Flint Bluff dining room going over more wedding details, Jacob had just begun to sip on a hot cup of coffee while listening to Anna.

She said, "You know, Jacob, we have never talked about our finances. Should we do that now?"

Frankly the subject had not entered Jacob's thinking at all. He knew that Anna had her own finances, and he had his own. He had assumed that when they were married, the funds would remain segregated, a common practice when wealthy people married.

"I presumed that we would each continue to keep our own separate funds," said Jacob. "Isn't that what you had thought best?"

"Yes, I suppose that would be best," she said, "but now and again I might need some extra pin money. You would not object to helping out when new items are needed for the family, would you?"

"Of course not," said Jacob, as he sipped his coffee.

"Now about the property," said Anna. "You know, of course that this is my house. If you have no objections, I would like to keep the property with me being the sole owner. But of course, I will put you in my will to inherit the house should something happen to me. Does that meet with your approval?"

Jacob was shocked. He really had no strong feelings on the subject, but the manner in which she stated it disturbed him. It was as if he would become a tenant in a home that really was not his. He thought this was odd. He had presumed that once they were married, they would share ownership of the home. He sat looking into his coffee, but finally lifted his head.

"That's fine, Anna, and we will also keep my property separate with me retaining sole ownership of it. That makes the finances ever so much easier."

Now it was Anna's turn to be shocked. She had opened a door that she could not reclose. Jacob's father, William, had already given Jacob far more property and holdings than she had. Jacob had shrewdly added to these holdings. He and his father owned the mercantile outright and all its property and merchandise. Jacob owned the property of the other stores, as well as being partners in several other enterprises including the bank and other holdings. His wealth far exceeded hers. This discussion, and her clever plan to keep Jacob from ownership of the house, had not gone as she intended. And yet, Jacob had surprised her. He once again proved that he would not necessarily be beguiled into complying with her every plan. Anna had just forfeited her own access to the funds of the wealthiest bachelor in town by voicing her own silly, selfish plan. Inwardly, she was crushed.

Anna rose from her chair. "Very well, Jacob. That will be fine. But I do feel a small headache coming on, so perhaps you should come back tomorrow. I should lie down for a while."

As he got his foot into the stirrup and swung his leg over the back of his horse, he pointed the horse toward the mercantile and couldn't hold back a small chuckle. She was a high-spirited, somewhat devious woman, and he was beginning to understand her.

They were married in April 1866, and were gone until the end of June. Their honeymoon trip was spent sightseeing by private compartment on railroads to the east coast. They visited Chicago, where Jacob was introduced to Anna's siblings; Hilda, who was married, and Johan, who was now engaged. Although Jacob asked about seeing her parents, his entreaty was tactfully ignored, and they continued their honeymoon without meeting with the senior Maier's. Their travels took them to Philadelphia, Boston, and New York. Jacob's mouth hung open as his cash was distributed in the many clothing emporiums in New York. He had to keep telling himself that it was their honeymoon, and that this would never happen again. He also had to admit that being with his beautiful wife, seeing her laughing and happy was a great joy. He, too, was happy.

Chapter Eight

1867-1876

Plans had been in the offing for several years, and construction finally began on a permanent railroad bridge across the Mississippi River at Burlington. The hurdles were many and formidable. Just building a bridge across such a large span of water was only a small part of the engineering for the bridge. In this case, the water was always moving. Stabilization of construction equipment to build the cofferdams for construction of support columns was quite a feat in itself, but American ingenuity and perseverance prevailed. In addition, the bridge had to be constructed so as to allow river traffic to pass either under the bridge, or the bridge itself would have to somehow move out of the way of the passing boat traffic. Thus, the bridge was built so that a section of rail bed and track could pivot on the top of one of the columns, thereby opening a gap for boat traffic to pass.

In 1868 the railroad bridge was completed. The first train to cross the bridge included a private sleeper car occupied by a large group of railroad moguls. A ceremonial celebration was held on the Burlington side of the river after the crossing. Trafficking of goods and services for communities and states west of the river would never be the same. Any article needed for further settlement of the nation's western regions could now be brought more quickly and directly by railroad. Business in Burlington benefitted from faster railroad distribution. The Roush Mercantile also was able to receive merchandise and supplies more expeditiously, thereby enabling Jacob's business to grow and prosper.

One day in 1873, when Jacob picked up mail at the postal office for the Roushes, before going home for the evening, he sorted the mail to separate the business mail from the family mail. In so doing, he found a rather nostalgic letter. The return address was from Mr. Clarence Hume. Immediately, thoughts of Georgia filled his mind. But with the manner in which their relationship had ended, he could not help but wonder about a letter from Georgia's husband. When he tore the envelope open, there was a letter and an invitation. The invitation was from the Society of Friends in Oskaloosa. He was being invited to attend the inauguration of the new William Penn College, a Quaker school, built under the sponsorship of the Society of Friends. The letter was handwritten by Georgia, and said only, "I thought you might like to attend the college's opening. I hope this finds you well. Georgia." Jacob smiled at Georgia's thoughtfulness, but with memories swirling through his mind, he ever so slowly, resignedly dropped the letter in the trash.

***

The men loved it. Jacob and Kon sat on the front porch of Flint Bluff in 1876 with a visibly pregnant Esther watching the brood as it swarmed around the porch laughing and screaming, sometimes crying, sometimes crawling on the adult laps, and then jumping down to join the rest of the children. Three of the Roush children, James, Ruth, and Marcus were being visited by the six Grant children. The Roush baby, Helen was in the house with Anna. The Grant children, Moses, Sarah, Mathew, Mark, Luke, and Joann were all distinguished by their long, straight black hair. So far, Esther's blue-eyed gene had not made an appearance in their children, but they were hoping the baby Esther was carrying might be the one to have the haunting blue eyes.

This get-together occurred roughly every other Saturday afternoon, weather permitting, and was held either at Flint Bluff or at the Grant acreage. And as usual, Anna was conspicuous by her absence.

When Jacob took the children to the Grants, Anna would always claim to have a headache and stay home. It was just as well, because the children were then free to swing from ropes in the hayloft of the Grants' barn, climb the windmill, and ride the horses; all activities that children love, but anxious mothers might not care to see. When the visitors arrived, New Rain helped Esther prepare a large amount of food to feed all of the hungry little mouths, while Kon, Four Toes, and Jacob sat on the porch. Four Toes and New Rain would marvel at the happy throng of children running under foot. Many years ago, New Rain's dream spirits had revealed this very scene to her. But each time when the Roush children returned home, Anna waited for them in the foyer and would march them immediately upstairs into their baths to wash off "the country smell."

Anna spent a great deal of money on the children. They had only the finest clothing and toys. She spent hours fussing over the clothes that little Ruth would wear. She made sure that the boys were always clean and neat. She preferred that the children stay indoors, playing in the upstairs family room so that they did not soil their clothing. She was determined that her children would not be like the other ragamuffins running loose around the city. She smothered them with her money and tried to isolate them from other children as she was able. But she was not always able to keep them indoors and away from other children.

When the Roushes and Grants got together at Roushes, the scene was quite different. Anna would remain in the house, claiming a headache and the need for her to be attending to the baby. All of the children remained outdoors, chasing each other around the exterior of the house, and playing games in the street in front of the house. Lunch was served by servants on tables set up on the rear porch overlooking the river. The children were still too young to venture down to the river without an adult with them. So, sometimes the two fathers would take the youngsters to walk along the riverbank to look for souvenirs, shells, turtles, or crawdads. Jacob and Kon were at peace, watching the children playing on the bank beside the river that they loved.

A great many discussions had been held between Jacob and Anna to allow the mingling of the children of these two very diverse families. Jacob could not begin to count the number of times that he had heard Anna say, "I will not have any heathens in my home. Those Indians and their children will not step foot in my house! Is that clear?" Nor could he count the times he had heard, "I don't know why you associate with a heathen. You have no need to take our children to some Indian camp," (referring to the Grant acreage). It had taken all of Jacob's fortitude to get Anna to accept the fact that Kon was a dear friend who had saved his life in the war, and that it was great fun for the children to play together. She had finally accepted the get-togethers, but she would not lower herself to be part of them.

This attitude, of course, was not lost on Kon and Esther. Without being told, they knew Anna's attitude regarding their family. But because of the deep friendship between Kon and Jacob, it was accepted that Anna would not be a part of the intermingling of the families. But Anna did not fool anyone. Periodically she could be seen peeking out the windows at the boisterous children as they played their games. It was her own selfish attitude that kept her from joining the fun.

It was this same attitude that had boxed Anna into another corner. While she had met the influential community leader, Johaan Stroud at his bank when she came to town, she had been unable to nurture a friendship with him and his wife, Alice. On the occasion that the Grant children came to Flint Bluff, the Stroud children, who lived nearby would be escorted by either Johaan or Alice to join in on the children's fun. Then Alice or Johaan would sit on the porch with Jacob and Kon, talking, laughing, and watching the herd of children playing. Anna desperately wanted to ingratiate herself to the Stroud's, but could not swallow her pride and join the group. Because of this, in front of Jacob, she would refer to Alice Stroud as "that commoner woman." However, "that commoner woman" was highly regarded in the city, and her family wealth far exceeded Anna's. Anna was aware of this fact also. It was all so frustrating to Anna.

Not surprisingly, the intelligent Roush children were thriving in private schools. While the family certainly was not Catholic, the children attended a local private Catholic school; a school with a more stellar reputation for learning than that of the public schools. A generous monetary contribution to the local Catholic diocese assured a place for the Roush children in the school. As soon as they were old enough, however, the children were sent to St. Louis to private academies for middle and high school. Because the children were away from home so much, they developed a keen sense of independence and self-sufficiency. These traits would serve them well in their adult lives, but greatly frustrated their mother. Anna was used to generally being in charge of all family affairs. So when the independent-thinking children came home on breaks from school, there was always friction between one or more of the children and their mother. By their love for one another, and dependence upon each other in times of strife with their mother, the children took these incidents in stride. The four siblings formed an impenetrable shell around themselves to such an extent, that their feelings for their mother could not be described as love between mother and child. It more closely could be described as respect, but it was respect only because Anna was their mother. Even though they loved their father dearly, they all harbored a wish to leave home when they were able. Her children's defense mechanism was not lost on Anna. It infuriated her to no end, causing her to attempt to even further control their lives.

Anna's unmitigated arrogance suffered another setback in 1878. A wealthy jewelry merchant in Burlington, George B.P. Carpenter was finishing a mansion called 'Prospect Point' for his family. For some time, Anna's home had been the premier home overlooking the river. But Prospect Point was far more prestigious than Flint Bluff. Prospect Point had such touches as built-in shutters, skillfully fitted to the home's butternut woodwork. There were hand-made writing desks, with elaborate inlaid decoration. The china closets held priceless imported ceramics and china. At least one ceiling lamp was imported from India. Only the finest Irish linen adorned the tables. The home was huge, with Swiss influence in the Gothic Revival architecture. In short, there were no other homes in Prospect Point's class. The Roush's attended parties held at Prospect Point, and Anna would overhear other attendees commenting on the sumptuous home and its furnishings. This made her livid. On their way home, Jacob would inevitably hear Anna's venting about the Carpenter home, and how it was not nearly as tasteful as Flint Bluff. Jacob knew Anna was wrong, but he wisely refrained from comment, knowing that Anna no longer had the city's most prestigious home. This did not bother Jacob in the least, other than the fact that he would have to listen to his wife's ranting about the situation.

Chapter Nine

The Steeple Incident

In 1884, the Catholic Church was expanding in Burlington. The second Catholic Church, St. John's was nearly completed. Construction was progressing, and the impressive, tall steeple was being laboriously built by construction workers.

James Roush and his sister Ruth were away in St. Louis attending school. The youngest Roush children, Marcus and Helen were enjoying an outing with their classmates from the private Catholic elementary they attended. The school had asked for the mothers of the children to accompany the classes on a field trip to watch the workers putting the final touches on the St. John's steeple. This would then be followed by a picnic on a grassy field next to the church. The children were spellbound by the sight of a young man sitting on a rope sling seat high up on the side of the steeple. The worker was nailing cedar shingles to the steeple. The children, their mothers, and the convent teachers were sitting in the grass on blankets eating their picnic lunch, talking and laughing among themselves. Suddenly, there was a sharp bang. All eyes looked up to see that one of the ropes holding the young man working on the steeple had broken. As they watched, another loud bang signaled the breaking of the final rope holding the young man in the air. Karl Alfred Funkquist, a twenty-one-year-old Swedish immigrant who had been in Burlington for only two years, fell to his death as the picnic gathering watched in horror. The following day, the *Daily Gazette* carried the article of the young man's tragic accident. It stated that the young man left a widow and a four-month-old son.

The shocking scene inflicted upon the youngsters at the picnic was more than Anna could abide. To her thinking, Marcus and Helen should never have had to witness the gruesome death of the man on the steeple. She felt that the Catholic Church should be held accountable for subjecting her children to such a horrendous sight. That evening, Anna confronted Jacob and told him that she wanted to sue the Catholic Church.

"Anna, the incident was an accident," said Jacob. "The church cannot be held liable for the equipment used by the builder. I will not support you in your wish to bring forward a legal suit."

"If you will not support me on this, Jacob, I have no use for you! I will do this myself," said Anna.

The following day, Anna appeared at an attorney's office and demanded that the lawyer draw up the necessary papers to file suit. The attorney talked and cajoled Anna. He knew there was no basis for filing such a suit. Their talk went on for over an hour, and finally the attorney lost his patience.

"Mrs. Roush, I have listened to your pleas, but I have also told you that there are no grounds for such a suit. I am respectfully informing you that I will not represent you in such an endeavor. Therefore, I am wishing you a good day," said the attorney, and escorted Anna to the office entrance.

Anna was so infuriated that she considered striking the attorney with her parasol. Instead, she made it very clear that the attorney and his family would no longer be welcome at any social function in the future at Flint Bluff. As she stomped down the street away from his office, the attorney heaved an inward sigh of relief.

***

It was after this incident that a widening schism began to form in the marriage between Jacob and Anna. She would not get over the fact that Jacob had not supported her in her wish to press forward a frivolous lawsuit against the Catholic Church. The carrying of this grudge, and the resultant spats between the two adults upset Jacob greatly. He began spending more time at the mercantile, and there were many nights, that rather than go home and listen to Anna's carping, he simply stayed overnight at his apartment above the store. When he was at home, the couple slept in their separate bedrooms.

Perhaps it was witnessing such an unfortunate death, and the stress of a failing marriage that brought on another new circumstance in Anna's life. She began having a dream that repeated itself every few nights. In the dream, she was standing at the edge of the bluff behind Flint Bluff. She was calmly watching the riverboats gliding north and south on the river. As the dream progressed, she felt that her life had turned out wonderfully. She was married to a handsome, successful man and had four beautiful children. She was the leading matriarch of the city. Then she contemplated how much better her life was than the other women in town, and she openly grinned in her sleep. As the dream continued, a sense of calm pomposity enveloped Anna. But it did not continue.

In her dream, as she stood gloating at the edge of the bluff, she was struck by something hard between her shoulder blades. She turned to see her attacker, and as she turned, a high-pitched, banshee-like, screeching laugh commenced. As she turned fully, she saw the ghost-like apparition standing a few yards away from her. The gossamer ghost was still laughing, while wildly waving a cane in the air.

The apparition then shrieked, "I will see you dead!"

The visage was of the man she had killed, Mitchell Sutter. Sutter continued his eerie cackling laugh while drifting to-and-fro before Anna. The dream only ended when Anna startled awake and immediately sat up in her bed. The visage of Sutter hung in the air at the foot of her bed, slowly fading from view. Anna was shaking and damp with perspiration. Returning to sleep was impossible, and she remained in a sitting position in bed until the first fragile rays of daylight broke the hold of the night-time dark.

Chapter Ten

1890-1900

Even with a severe case of paranoia, Anna was not giving up her place in society. The dances, celebrations, and social gatherings still were held at Flint Bluff. As ever, Anna was the gracious, yet cold, hostess. She had not lost her skill in hosting elaborate soirees. While not well liked or respected by some of the other elite wives, no one wanted to miss a party at Flint Bluff. The guests all knew each other and had a fine time socializing and dancing to the orchestra, and over-indulging in the rich, tasty meals prepared by the home's staff. Anna was in her element at these events, flitting among the guests, wishing well to the attendees. Men's eyes still followed her around the ball room and dining room. She was still a beautiful, well-structured woman whom any man would relish escorting around the dance floor. She maintained her love of music and was the first in the city to have one of the new phonograph machines. She placed the machine in the ball room of the home and quickly purchased a large library of recordings. It pleasured her greatly to play her music in the ball room in private. She would turn the crank on the side of the phonograph to wind it up, move the arm to the recording, and begin swirling around the ball room dancing with an imaginary partner as the music played. Her favorite tune did not change, and she repeatedly played her recording of *The Tales from the Vienna Woods*.

The Roush children continued to mature and pursue their individual interests, while being not so subtly guided by their mother. James, the oldest son had completed his law school studies. He had joined a prestigious law firm in St. Louis. At a social gathering for the firm, he had met the daughter of one of the senior partners and was now engaged to be married. Of course, Anna was delighted that her oldest son had found a suitable marriage prospect. At twenty years of age, oldest daughter Ruth was now ready for marriage. Even after her own negative experience with her parents, Anna believed it was her duty to select a suitable husband for her daughters. After openly defying her own parents regarding the same subject, she still would not allow her own daughters to select their own spouses. Anna had carefully come to the conclusion regarding who would be her future son-in-law, the future spouse for Ruth. Anna was determined that Ruth would marry Joshua Stroud, whom she considered to be worthy of marriage to her daughter. After many heated discussions between Jacob and Anna regarding this arranged marriage, Jacob trudged off to carry out his wife's wishes.

Jacob's heart was not in this activity. On the point of arranged marriages, he was completely at odds with Anna. He felt that arranged marriages bordered on slavery. The process took away the freedom to choose one's spouse.

"It's barbaric," Jacob said under his breath as he trudged toward the bank.

He was still trying to figure out what he was going to say to his friend, James Stroud, as he opened the polished bank door, and made his way to James' office.

He sat across the desk from James Stroud as the two men drank coffee and talked small talk. It was the same desk that had belonged to James' father, Peter, and the same desk where Peter and William Roush had shared discussions and coffee. James' son Joshua had an office down the hall, and this young man was the subject of discussion between Jacob and James. At twenty-three, Joshua was three years older than Ruth, and as an heir to the bank, and in the eyes of Anna, he was considered a suitable suitor and husband for Ruth. As a result, Anna had insisted that Jacob speak with James to arrange for the marriage of the couple.

Jacob, however, knew that Ruth and Joshua had grown up together and were fond of each other. He did not know how strong their feelings were, but he did not believe that the discussion between the two fathers would involve much negotiation. That is the main reason he had given in to Anna. The two men talked and joked and finally arrived at the key subject.

"Give me a moment, Jacob. Let me get this straight. You are asking for an arranged marriage for Ruth and Joshua, and you want my concurrence. Is that right?" asked James.

"Yes," was the simple reply by Jacob.

"My God, Jacob. I thought arranged marriages went away with the Pilgrims. Do you seriously believe in them?" asked James.

"Well," Jacob stuttered. His head ached. "Sometimes an arranged marriage might serve a satisfactory purpose. As a general rule I don't champion such an endeavor..." Jacob looked like he was about to say something more, but closed his mouth and lowered his head.

"I believe I get the picture," said James. "Anna had a hand in this, didn't she?"

Jacob lifted his head and looked at his friend. His silence answered the question.

James smiled. "Jacob, I will not go along with the arranged marriage, but I see the jam you are in. I also know that the youngsters are fond of each other. At least that is what I am led to believe by Alice."

James paused for a moment and then said, "Tell you what. If Joshua believes that he should marry Ruth, he certainly has my blessing. But if he is against the union, then that is the end of the matter."

James then suggested that they bring Joshua into the discussion, and called him into the office.

James addressed his son. "Joshua, Mr. Roush and I were wondering when you are going to get around to proposing marriage to Ruth."

James grinned conspiratorially at Jacob. Jacob felt sorry for the young man being put on the spot by his father. But he need not have worried.

The feelings between Joshua and Ruth must have been stronger than either of the fathers knew, because Joshua answered, "Well sir, if I have the permission of each of you, I will take care of the situation forthwith."

Jacob and James looked quickly at each other and burst out laughing.

Joshua Stroud and Ruth Roush were married in early 1891.

***

While the older children were now comfortably ensconced in their personal lives, there were more personal problems associated with the two younger children, Marcus and Helen. They had each inherited a rather belligerent personality trait from their mother. Marcus's attitude often led him to have fist fights with other boys, and on a number of occasions he had to be quietly removed from the firm grasp of local constabulary by Jacob's paying assigned fines, paying for property damage, and making substantial contributions to various police benevolent funds. When of age, Marcus had begun attendance at St. Louis University. A pattern that had evolved during his high school years soon emerged even stronger at the university. His habits of never studying his lessons, chasing girls, and pulling tasteless pranks rose to a new level because of his liberal use of alcohol. It did not take him long, therefore, to become well known to the university provost office. Jacob made nearly monthly trips by rail to St. Louis to rectify Marcus's latest misguided venture. Each time Jacob made the southern trip, he sternly lectured his son. But each time as he spoke to the boy, he saw the black shadow of arrogance in the eyes of Marcus. Marcus was on the verge of being administratively removed from the university.

On the contrary, Helen was a kind, gentle girl, who as a child had played quietly for hours with her dolls and other toys. She was a sweet young lady who adored her older brothers and sister. The older children doted on Helen, sharing secrets with her and watching over her on the rare occasions when the children were outdoors. With the older children now having moved away, Helen was left at home without the support of her siblings. With her father at work all day, she had only her mother for social interaction. She was lonely. She loved school and was delighted when she was old enough to be sent away to private school. She attended an exclusive private school in Davenport, the Bernard Academy, for only the wealthiest of families. The city had a thriving synagogue which dated from 1861. The Jewish church sponsored this exclusive co-educational middle and high school, but accepted students of other faiths. Helen loved the interaction with young people her age at the school. She immersed herself in her studies and was a high achiever in all of her classes. She was proud of her accomplishments and considered herself an equal to any other student in the school. Even more important, though, was that Helen was maturing and beginning to think independently. She was learning to stand up for what she believed.

When the reports of grades were distributed, with copies sent to each student's parents, Helen's report always contained high marks. Invariably, the instructors would also make note of Helen's deportment, stating that Helen was respectful and well behaved. The instructors always said she was a delight to have in their classes. These remarks on her school reports meant a great deal to Helen. She was proud of them. But to Anna, they meant something entirely different. Because Helen had been such a quiet, and somewhat withdrawn child, to Anna these remarks by her teachers meant that Helen was still being quiet and withdrawn; not spirited enough. Anna would find out later that this was certainly not the case.

Helen's streak of independence was being constructively modified at school. While it would serve her well in later life, it was a constant source of friction every time Helen returned home from school for a visit. Quite soon after her arrival home, mother and daughter would come to loggerheads. The subject was usually that Anna believed that Helen should be, or do, something according to Anna's directions, while Helen believed that she could accomplish the same goal by doing it her way. Clothes were always an issue. Helen was a beautiful young lady, but truly did not care about her appearance or clothing, whereas Anna was always dressed in fine clothing. Helen wanted to spend as much time with her local friends when she was home, but Anna more often wanted Helen to stay home. There were numerous such petty arguments throughout the day when Helen was home. They would usually end with Helen retiring to her room, or simply walking out the door to meet her friends. When this happened, there were even nights that Anna told Helen not to come back home, and she would lock the doors to the house. Of course, these were nights when Jacob was not home, as he would not allow such nonsense. Helen did not mind being locked out, as she had numerous friends where she could spend the night. In the morning following these lockouts, when Helen returned to the house, Anna's guilt would overcome her actions, and she would be waiting at the front door to welcome her daughter with kisses and attention. As heartless as Anna could be, Helen was still her daughter. Helen eagerly waited for these vacation breaks to end so that she could return to Bernard Academy and her studies and her friends.

In the summer of 1893, to avoid the friction with her mother, seventeen-year-old Helen stayed in Davenport. She had volunteered to tutor younger students who were having difficulty with their studies. The rabbi and the school staff welcomed the help of this stellar student to assist some of the other struggling students. Helen had found her calling. She loved her summer job at Bernard helping the other younger students with their studies.

One of Helen's students was a young Catholic boy whom she tutored in arithmetic three days per week. He was a bright, rambunctious lad who simply did not choose to focus, although he had the ability to grasp the mathematical procedures. Because the boy was so bright, and because the family was not well to do, the youngster was being subsidized by the church to attend this school. Each day, as they finished their lessons and just before it got dark, the young boy was picked up at school by a rather good-looking young man. Helen soon learned that this man was the youngster's older brother. Each day that the man picked up the boy, the conversations between him and Helen became more lengthy and animated. His name was Nicholas Wentz, but he explained that everyone just called him Nick.

Nick Wentz came from an honest, working family environment. His father was an accountant who worked for the Rock Island Railroad, which had a large hub in Davenport. Nick had studied commerce for two years at the St. Ambrose Seminary and School of Commerce. But because the family could not afford more schooling for him, twenty-one-year-old Nick was now in an apprentice program with the Rock Island Railroad. He had been assigned to the security department of the railroad and was learning the interesting and sometimes dangerous job of a railroad detective. He loved his job.

The young couple's relationship blossomed all that summer. But Helen was aware that in the fall she would be starting college. She had mentioned to her father that she would like to stay in the Davenport area and attend Augustana College. During a break in the summer, Helen returned home and discussed her plans with Jacob and Anna. Being suspicious of an underlying motive for her daughter wanting to stay in the Davenport area, Anna had made up her mind that Helen needed a change in location.

"You will not be going to that Swedish college in Rock Island. No daughter of mine will go there, and that is final," said Anna.

Jacob said nothing. Helen had discussed her relationship with her suitor, and her plan for college with Jacob, and he knew his youngest daughter was clever. He held his tongue, smiled inwardly, and listened to the mother and daughter.

"But mother, I prefer to attend Augustana. Many of my friends will be going there in the fall," said Helen.

By now, Anna suspected there was some other reason for Helen insisting on staying in Davenport, and she would not even consider such a request.

"Apparently you were not listening young lady. You will not stay in Davenport. Our discussion is done!" said Anna.

Helen hung her head and sighed. "All right mother, you win," said Helen. "I will go to William Penn College in Oskaloosa, and that is not very far from home."

Anna looked at Jacob with a slight smirk. "Do you not have anything to say about this?"

"No, Anna, I do not. Personally, I do not care where Helen goes to college. But if you do not want her in Davenport, then I would say that William Penn is a good alternative," said Jacob.

"Then it's settled, Helen. You will attend this William Penn place, and I'm not especially happy with that arrangement either," said Anna, and she stalked out of the room, inwardly gloating that she had once again gotten her way.

When she was gone, Helen looked at her father, and they both smiled. As it happened, Nick Wentz's railroad training would involve passing through, and stopping over in Oskaloosa every two weeks on the railroad. Helen had revealed this fact to Jacob when she had told him of her plan. Anna had walked into the web of her daughter's plan and did not even know it.

Helen began her education studies in the fall at William Penn College. She would begin to fulfill her dream to become a teacher.

***

It was a bitterly cold winter day. The temperature had not risen above ten degrees, with a whining north wind howling all through the night before. On that day, in the winter of 1895, during Helen's first year in college, eighty-six-year-old William Roush died peacefully in his sleep. The doctor had summoned Jacob the day before to be by his father's side.

William's last words were, "I'm going to see Herta." Tears of sorrow clouded Jacob's eyes.

Several small fires were built at the grave site to thaw the ground, and two days later the burial of William Roush took place at Aspen Grove Cemetery. On a crisp, cold, but sunny day, hundreds of mourners paid their respects at the service. A cherished soul and an original settler who had contributed greatly to the community had passed on. At a local attorney's office several days later, the last will and testament of William Roush was read. The business was divided between his two children, Jacob and Edna, and the senior Roush home was left to Jacob, while Edna received a like value in cash and other investments. Neither Martha nor William would ever have thought of not equally dividing their children's inheritance. It was all very simple in a loving family.

Anna had not attended the funeral of her father-in-law. They had never had a close relationship, but more importantly, she had now been experiencing severe pains in her hip joints, especially in cold weather.

She had seen doctors and had been told that her condition was called arthritis. She was now fifty-five years old and was forced to use walking canes when the pain was most intense. Anna felt this condition was entirely unfair, and that she certainly should not be subjected to any "commoner's disease." When the pain was at its worst, Anna remained in her room. But even in her painful condition, Anna was still making plans. Of utmost importance to her at this time was commencing the arrangement plans for the marriage of her youngest daughter, Helen.

When not bothered by her ailment, Anna was scheming in earnest. She had made a trip to Davenport to visit with the synagogue's Rabbi. The purpose of her trip was to bribe the Rabbi into revealing the names of some of the wealthy congregation members who had sons of marriageable age. The Rabbi initially refused, but when Anna offered a great sum of money for a much needed building project at the church, several family names were confidentially given to Anna. This situation was made all the more ludicrous by the fact that Anna had not stepped foot in a Jewish church in years and was, in fact, a member of the Burlington Methodist Church.

Anna then hired a private investigator to gather information about the families. Armed with this information, Anna narrowed the potential families to two, whom she believed were fabulously wealthy. While Anna remained comfortably ensconced in her Davenport hotel room, she sent messengers to the homes of the two families to arrange meetings with them. At the arranged times, she paid social calls on the two residences. Her first stop was at the Schmitt residence, the home of Charles Schmitt, a wealthy building contractor. Anna and the Schmitt's spoke for nearly two hours, until she was finally told by Charles Schmitt that she was "archaic."

"I thought that arranged marriage nonsense was long gone," said Charles. "I see no reason to force my son to marry someone in whom he has no interest. I will not be a party to this archaic, selfish plan."

As he showed Anna to the door he said, "Good day, madam."

Anna was livid. She believed she had never been treated so shabbily in all her life. "The nerve of that buffoon," she thought to herself.

The following day she called on the Goldman residence. Archibald Goldman was a well-known private financier. His acquaintances, most of whom were also his drinking buddies, called him Archie. He and his family lived extravagantly in a large home overlooking the Mississippi River. But the investigation by the private investigator hired by Anna did not reveal certain facts. What Anna did not know was that Archie Goldman was on the verge of losing that ostentatious home and everything in it. Even his family was unaware that Archie's creditors were circling him like turkey buzzards, and he did not have the funds to pay them off. His financial dealings had not always been on the up and up, resulting in his present situation, and even a possible lawsuit that could result in his incarceration for a lengthy tenure. He was seriously considering his options, including fleeing from the city and his creditors. He was a desperate man.

Anna's conversation with the Goldman's went smoothly. Unlike her dealings with the Schmitt's, Anna began to take a liking to Archie and Mrs. Goldman. When the true nature of the visit was finally divulged, the wheels in Archie's diminutive brain began turning.

"Now as I understand it," said Archie, "it is common in these circumstances that the girl bring a sizable dowry to the relationship. Isn't that so?"

Anna now knew she had the fish on the hook. "Yes, that is usually appropriate," she said.

The discussion and negotiation continued for two hours. Pictures of their respective offspring were shown to each other, coffee and brandy was served, and the negotiation figures went back and forth, while Archie consumed more brandy than coffee.

"Now you must understand, Mrs. Roush, that I really have no incentive to enter my son Robert into such an agreement unless you give me proper motivation," said Archie.

"I had believed that we had come to an agreement of fifty thousand dollars; half of which would be paid immediately, and the other half to be paid ten days prior to the wedding. Isn't that your understanding, Mr. Goldman?" said Anna.

"Well, you know, Mrs. Roush, there are going to be other unforeseen expenses in setting up this wedding and household for the children." Archie had to bite his cheek to keep from smiling. "I believe that the final figure should be seventy-five thousand. Forty thousand up front and thirty-five just before the wedding. I believe I can draw up a quick little contract for us to sign. I'll go get paper and pen."

Anna felt that she had somehow been outsmarted in the negotiations, but her arrogance deceived her into believing that she was the winner in the overall scheme. Anna had never lost at anything. After all, hadn't she successfully arranged an excellent marriage for Ruth a few years ago? Now, she had found what she believed to be an extremely wealthy young Jewish man for Helen to marry.

Anna was ecstatic. The contract was signed, and she returned to Burlington. She later wired the forty thousand dollars to Goldman's bank. Such a large withdrawal from the bank could certainly not go unnoticed. It was not long before James Stroud talked discretely to Jacob, but Jacob was at a loss as to why Anna would have taken such a large amount of money out of her accounts. He would bide his time to learn of the plot.

At Thanksgiving in 1896, Helen was unable to come home. She was involved in a teaching project at William Penn College, and did not want to make the trip home and then immediately return to school. Jacob decided that because his daughter was not coming home to Burlington, he would make the trip to Oskaloosa and have dinner with his daughter. And because Jinks planned to go hunting on Thanksgiving, Edna decided she would accompany her brother to visit her niece in Oskaloosa. The trip seemed to go much faster having someone to talk with, and Jacob was glad for the company of his sister. During the rail trip, Jacob swore Edna to secrecy and told her about Helen's beau, Nick. After their arrival, the threesome settled into a comfortable booth in the Downing Hotel dining room, which was serving a delicious Thanksgiving dinner. Helen had thought that she would be eating alone on Thanksgiving Day and relished the company of her father and aunt. As they ate, they talked about anything that came to mind.

Finally, Helen said, "Father, I believe that Nick is going to ask me to marry him." Jacob and Edna looked at each other, and the brother and sister knew what the other was thinking. Both of them knew that Anna would never approve of the marriage of one of her children, unless she had personally arranged or approved of it. They also knew that with Nick's family's means and religion, she would never approve of Helen's marriage to Nick Wentz. Both Jacob and Edna expressed their joy to Helen. They followed this with a lengthy caution to Helen that she would soon be in for a very difficult time with her mother. On the return trip to Burlington, Jacob and Edna tried time after time to formulate a plan to help Helen, but in the end they failed.

At Christmas break, Helen returned to home in Burlington and once again spoke confidentially to her father. She revealed to Jacob that Nick Wentz had asked her to marry him, and that she had agreed. Nick had completed his apprenticeship and was now a railroad detective. Helen pleaded with her father to smooth over the news of the engagement with her mother.

On the day after Christmas, Jacob felt that he had finally found an opportune time to speak with Anna about Helen. The three of them had enjoyed a fine dinner and were sitting together in the living room.

"Anna, Helen is nearly twenty-years-old, and I think we should be giving some thought to her getting married. Helen has some ideas on the subject that she has shared with me," said Jacob.

Anna's head jerked up from her reading, and she stared glaringly at both Jacob and Helen. "I do not want to hear any scatterbrained ideas from either of you. And yes, we do need to talk about the subject. I have wonderful news. A marriage has already been arranged. Therefore, the matter is settled."

Anna then went into a lengthy one-sided conversation, telling Jacob and Helen the plans for Helen to wed Robert Goldman. She revealed that a portion of dowry had already been paid, and that plans were being made for the wedding to take place the following summer. Neither Jacob nor Helen could grasp the audacity of Anna's remarks. It was unbelievable that such an important life event in Helen's life would be taken over completely by her mother without input from either her husband or Helen.

"But mother, you don't understand. I have agreed to marry a wonderful man who loves me. I do not wish to marry someone I have never even met," said Helen.

"Well, you just need to tell whoever it is that you've been involved with that you will not be marrying him. I have already paid a substantial dowry to Mr. Goldman's family. You will be marrying Robert Goldman, and that will not change!" Anna's voice rose toward a shriek as the argument continued. Jacob now fully understood the reason for the substantial bank withdrawal that Anna had made.

"I am not 'involved' with anyone, mother. I am in love, with an honest and loving man, and his name is Nicholas Wentz," said Helen.

"Honest! Honest! Bah!" Anna screamed. "Honesty will not get you the finer things in life. It will not allow you into society. It will not make other people look up to you." By now she was shaking her cane in the air. "Wealth and money, that's the only thing people pay attention to. Do you think that anyone would pay any attention to you if you were not my daughter? You must marry within a better class of people, and that is what I have arranged. Your wedding to Robert Goldman will take place in the spring. Now get out of my sight!"

Jacob jumped up from his chair. "Anna, you have gone too far this time. You cannot intervene in every facet of your children's lives, especially to demand that one of your children marry a person for whom they have no interest. I have sat back through all the years of our marriage watching you manipulate people and events to your personal interest. I also did not put a stop to your manipulation in Ruth's wedding to Joshua. Thank God, those two were already in love. But I will not allow Helen to be pushed into an arranged marriage to a partner of convenience. As far as I am concerned, she has my blessing to marry the man she loves."

"I've heard enough of your sniveling," said Anna as she stared at Jacob. "Mark my words, both of you. Helen will not marry Mr. Wentz!" She turned and leaning heavily on her canes, slowly made her way out of the room.

The battle continued to rage for the next four days while Helen was home from school; ironically, the very same type of discord that had occurred between Anna and her mother many years ago.

Anna watched from behind a curtain in an upstairs window as Jacob kissed his daughter and helped her into the carriage that would take her to the train to return to school in Oskaloosa. This marriage matter was far from being over, Anna thought, and she continued making plans.

Chapter Eleven

The Attempt

Upon her return to school, Helen narrated the situation to Nick as it had unfolded while she had been at home. Nick thought this was the strangest story he had ever heard. But as he was spending more and more time arresting rather unsavory people in his job, he also knew that people were capable of all types of abnormal behavior. Having never met Mrs. Roush, he could only speculate on what a mean-spirited person she must be.

"Helen, you must be very certain that marrying me is what you want to do. You know that your mother will never forgive you," said Nick.

"Oh, my dear Nicholas. Of course, this is what I want to do. In fact, I would like for you to find out where a Catholic boy and a Methodist girl can be wed. I will be completing my teacher training in just a few more weeks, and I would like for us to be married as soon after that as possible," said Helen.

***

Anna had bribed and browbeat the stable hand, Homer Broyles. She had told him that she knew of the unsavory places where he hung out at night. She also told him he would be fired unless he gave her information that she wanted. Anna knew that Homer was an associate of some rather rough looking characters, as she had seen him several times walk to the end of the driveway in the evening to meet them as they went to frequent the seedier gin joints.

After two days, the stable man came to the door of the house and asked to see Anna. The maid took him to the parlor, where Anna was sitting. His boots, covered with horse dung, left a disgusting trail and distinctive odor as he walked.

She looked up as he entered. "Well?" said Anna.

"It will cost you seventy-five hundred dollars. Twenty-five hundred for me, and five thousand for Willie," said Homer.

"Fine. I will give you three thousand dollars now, and you will get the rest when it is finished," said Anna. "Now get those stinking boots out of my house.

***

Charlie Mason was a fine, well-respected man. At forty-years-old, he was almost old enough to be Nick's father. He had been a railroad "dick" for nearly twenty years and knew almost all of the tricks crooks used in trying to steal from the railroad. Nick thought the world of Charlie, and they got along much like father and son as they made their rounds watching over railroad equipment. Nick had been permanently assigned to work with Charlie, and they were attached to the Oskaloosa Rock Island office.

It was nearly midnight on a cold clear January 3rd night in 1897. The two men were hidden behind a stack of rail ties while they watched a tool and equipment shed. The shed had previously been broken into and burglarized. Charlie had heard from an informant that there might be another break-in on this night. Charlie and Nick were lying in wait to catch the criminals.

As it neared one o'clock, Charlie said, "Let's get out of here, kid. I think my ass is frozen shut, and I don't think they're gonna show." The two men came from their hiding place and began walking toward the roundhouse, where there was always a pot of hot, syrupy, rancid coffee to warm them up.

It was over almost as soon as it began. The two thugs jumped from between the box cars and swooped down on Charlie and Nick. As the shouting and fist fight ensued, lights went on in a nearby caboose, where a watchman had been sleeping. One of the thugs had pulled a knife and was attacking Charlie. But Charlie was strong and fit. He gave the thug a thrashing until the thug was breathing his last. But with the last bit if energy, the thug's knife struck home. The thug and Charlie were both dying, locked in a deadly combative embrace. Nick and the second thug exchanged blows, but the second thug was no match for Nick, and he was about done in, but managed to turn tail and flee. As he escaped Nick's grip on his hand and ran, Nick heard a small metallic clinking noise. Nick was spent too, so he did not give chase. As the old watchman came running with his lantern casting a glow in the cold night air, Nick leaned over Charlie and the thug. Charlie Mason, a true hero to Nick, had expired.

Nick turned to the dying hit man. "Why did you do this? Who are you, and what have we ever done to you?" said Nick.

The dying man moved his lips ever so slightly. Nick leaned closer to hear him utter his last mortal words, "Roush woman."

Nick took the lantern from the old watchman and walked back to where the fight had taken place. He searched the ground for nearly fifteen minutes before he found what he was looking for. He reached down, picked it up, and put it in his vest pocket.

The dead hoodlum was identified by police as William (Willie) McNutt. He was a deadbeat, no-account hoodlum who frequented the wharf bars from Ft. Madison to Muscatine and always seemed to turn up in petty thefts, robbery, and muggings. McNutt was known to take on "work contracts" of a scurrilous nature. It was a mystery to the police as to his purpose in being in Oskaloosa, and why he and his partner would want to jump two railroad detectives. Nick Wentz was not so sure it was a mystery.

At the end of January, Jacob, Edna, and Jinks made the trip to Oskaloosa to observe the wedding of Miss Helen Roush to Mr. Nicholas Wentz. The wedding took place in the First Congregational Church and was presided over by Reverend Paul Gibson. Reverend Gibson thought it was one of the strangest stories he had ever heard, when two weeks before, Helen and Nick had called on him and asked him to marry a Catholic boy and a Methodist girl. This would be a first for the minister, but since his church was founded on the principle of religious tolerance, and the ceremony would be private, he consented to marry the young couple who were clearly in love with each other.

It was a beautiful, simple service, with Edna blubbering quietly through the ceremony. While Jacob, Edna, and Jinks stayed overnight at the Downing Hotel, the newlyweds blissfully consummated their marriage in the Honeymoon Suite at the Lacey Hotel two blocks away. They did not come out of their room for two days.

Ironically, Helen accepted a teaching position in Burlington at the private Catholic school that she had attended as a child. She was one of only two teachers on the staff who were not Catholic sisters. It was also unusual that a married woman would be allowed to teach school. But this rule was more common in public schools, and the diocese had no such rules. Nick's request to transfer to the Burlington office of the Rock Island Railroad was honored, primarily as a reward for the brave detective that had nearly been killed along with Charlie Mason.

Jacob was extremely happy. Helen and Nick would be moving to Burlington, and he had a wonderful surprise in store for them. He had discussed his plans with Edna, and she was also looking forward to having the young couple close by.

Chapter Twelve

Another "Death"

Anna was livid. Not only had she learned that Helen had married Nicholas Wentz, but the previous day she had received a letter addressed to her from Mr. Archibald Goldman. She sat and reread the letter.

February 14, 1897
My Dear Mrs. Roush,
I trust this letter will find you enjoying good health. Unfortunately, it is my solemn duty to carry out such a menial task as to send you this letter to remind you of our mutual contract.
It is my understanding from my sources that your daughter, Helen, was wed in Oskaloosa some three weeks ago. Please be so kind as to inform me if this is not correct.
If this is indeed true, it would appear that you have reneged on our contract. Be that as it may, I must remind you that there is a matter of thirty-five thousand dollars that you promised to pay to me by virtue of your signature on our agreement. I shall expect to receive payment in this matter forthwith, and no later than two weeks hence.
If you so choose to ignore my plea, I shall be forced to retain a solicitor, reveal our agreement, and demand payment in a court of law.
Archibald Goldman

Once again, by her own arrogant, misguided scheming, Anna was boxed in with no escape, by Archie Goldman, a con man with nefarious skills far superior to her own. She certainly did not want the distasteful business of her contract with Goldman to reach the city's societal ears.

She would be forced to pay the man. The money was wired to Goldman's bank the following day. The quiet withdrawal of thirty-five thousand additional dollars from Anna's accounts was confidentially reported to Jacob by James Stroud. But this time, Jacob was quite sure he knew the reason for this monetary transaction. With Helen marrying the man she loved instead of the man Anna had arranged for her to marry, Jacob surmised that there had to be a financial obligation to pay a second payment to Goldman. He was quite sure of this because the money transfer had gone to the same bank and account; an account in the name of Archibald Goldman. He also knew that Anna was bound to be in a foul mood for the next few days, and he took the opportunity to work late and stay in his apartment at the store for a couple nights.

During those nights that Jacob was absent, Anna again had the recurring nightmare wherein the ghostly form of Mitchell Sutter appeared in her dreams, continually shouting that he would "see her dead!" Each time the dream occurred, Sutter seemed to become more aggressive, wildly waving his cane in the air and staggering around Anna's bed. The dream frightened Anna until she awoke, moaning and covered with perspiration.

She was also beginning to believe that she had begun walking in her sleep. Upon awakening some mornings, she found her walking canes in a different location from where she had placed them the night before. Anna began to dread going to sleep each night. She began to rely on sleeping powders provided by her physician to aid in her sleep and subdue the nightmare. They did not always work, and Anna finally conceded that she could not escape Sutter's grip on her sleep.

The former home of William and Martha Roush was only two blocks from Flint Bluff. Jacob was extremely happy that Helen and Nick were moving to Burlington. As a wedding gift, and to express his joy of having the couple near him, the William and Martha Roush home which had stood vacant since the death of William, was swarming with craftsman, painting and refurbishing the old mansion. Jacob broke the news to Helen and Nick that the home was now theirs. He was so proud to see the old house once again coming to life, and to know that his daughter would start her life in the fine old home of his childhood.

***

A few days later, Anna was rudely interrupted from an afternoon nap as she reclined blissfully on a chaise lounge in her study. Her house maid was shaking her awake.

"Mrs. Roush, Mrs. Roush, you must wake up," said the servant as she gently shook Anna's shoulder.

Anna roused and looked at the servant. "What do you want, you stupid woman? Can't you see that I was sleeping?"

"Mrs. Roush, you must come quickly. He's back," said the maid.

"You are not making sense," said Anna. "Who is back?"

"It's the stable man, Homer," said the maid, "and he appears to have been drinking. He is demanding to see you immediately."

Anna hobbled to the front entryway.

"What do you want?" she said to the stable hand.

Surprisingly, Homer Broyles was dressed in traveling clothes and had a small valise at his feet. He did, indeed, smell like he had been imbibing of spirits.

"Well, well, Mrs. Roush, and good day to you," said Homer. "I believe that what I have to say might more wisely be said in private."

Anna just stared at him. "Whatever you have to say can be said where you stand. Now what is it you want?"

"You have hit the mule square between the eyes. It is about what I want," said Homer. "You see, I don't much think that you would want me to be spreading around town what I know about your plan to kill that railroad dick. And since I figure somebody might come looking for me, I plan to leave town. That is, after you write me a little draft on your bank for ten thousand dollars. And that, dear lady, is what I want. So why don't I go with you while you look for something to write on. Then I'll be on my way."

Anna just stared at the stable hand. Blackmail! She could not believe it. With everything that had gone wrong, here was this unpleasant man demanding that she pay him off. She thought for just a few seconds. "The report I have heard is that the police said that there were two men at the rail yard in Oskaloosa. You were the other man, weren't you?" she said.

"So what if I was?" answered Homer. "Just get me my money and I'll be gone."

Anna had to smile inwardly. "So you admit you were involved in the incident. That changes the picture, I believe. Now, I am quite sure that you do not want me to inform the police that you were the second man. Therefore, I believe that we have a bit of a stand-off here. Neither of us wants the whole event to become known. So, I do not believe that I will pay you your blood money."

"Blood money is it?" said Homer. "Listen lady, the blood is on your hands. I didn't kill anybody, and I only ended up on the receiving end of the other railroad dick's fists. Nice try, Mrs. Roush, but I would not even go to jail for that. Now go get my money, or I will air your dirty laundry!"

For a long time, Anna just stared at the disreputable stable hand. She knew she had to carry out his bidding. She turned and slowly walked back to her study. She returned in a moment with a signed paper to be presented to the bank, folded it up, and threw it at the man. Homer picked it up off the floor, unfolded it, read it, and doffed his hat. "I never want to see you again," said Anna.

"Can't say for sure, ma'am," said Homer, and he turned and walked out the large front door.

***

The business with the stable hand was the final humility. She would now take action on her own. A memory was painfully etched in Anna's brain; a memory of an event that still pained her, but which had happened almost forty years ago to her. For the next few days she was busy planning. She took the train to Ft. Madison and made a call on the rabbi at the Jewish temple there.

"Mrs. Roush, I simply cannot do your bidding. While it is an old custom in some European communities, this is America. We just don't do this sort of thing here," said the rabbi.

He had been arguing with Anna for over an hour. She had told him that she wished to declare her daughter, Helen, dead to the family. She was demanding that the rabbi conduct a full Jewish funeral service for the daughter, to be held in Burlington. Anna had even demanded a burial in Aspen Grove cemetery in Burlington. The rabbi continued to protest.

"Rabbi, I happen to know that your congregation is not doing well. Financially, your church is going to collapse unless you receive emergency funding," said Anna. "I am prepared to give you the money your church desperately needs to bring it back from the edge of bankruptcy. But only on the condition that you perform this service for me."

The Rabbi had no choice. As distasteful as this woman was, his small flock of followers was in danger of losing their church. He could not have that. In the end, he agreed to Anna's terms.

In the next few days, the Burlington 'Gazette' carried a small obituary item. It read:

Roush, Helen, born 1876, daughter of Mr. and Mrs. Jacob Roush, died unexpectedly Tuesday evening. The family will be holding a private service officiated by the Ft. Madison Jewish Temple on Sunday. Only the immediate family will attend. Burial will be at Aspen Grove Cemetery. Friends of Mrs. Jacob Roush may call upon her following a seven day period of Shiva.

Nick Wentz brought the newspaper home and showed Helen the obituary. He thought it must have been a rather strange blunder by the newspaper to print such an item. But when he showed it to Helen, she stared at the page and tears began falling from her eyes, landing on the newspaper before her.

"Darling, what is wrong," said Nick. "It's just an error by the newspaper."

Helen whispered, "I was afraid she would do this," and she explained the ramifications of what being declared dead in a family meant, versus what Nick had thought was just a mistake by the newspaper. When she was finished, Nick folded his lanky arms around his wife, kissed her, and held her close.

"I never knew how cruel one family member could be to another family member," said Nick.

That Sunday, a lone black buggy, draped in black, followed the funeral home's black wagon being pulled by a matching pair of gray horses as it wound its way to Aspen Grove Cemetery. The buggy was driven by a hired driver and contained Anna Roush and the rabbi from Ft. Madison. A graveside service was held, and an empty coffin was lowered into the ground, next to a small limestone marker inscribed, 'Roush, Helen, 1876-1897.'

Following the funeral service for Helen, a black wreath was placed on the front door of Flint Bluff. Anna, attired in black from the veil covering her head to the black shoes on her feet, sat at a parlor window that could be seen from the street. Passersby could see Anna sitting still at the window. For seven days, Anna Roush sat at the window, ensuring that anyone passing knew that her daughter had died. And yet, behind her back, everyone who knew Anna also knew that her daughter Helen was alive and well and living in the old Roush mansion. If they felt anything from seeing the woman in black at the window, it was sympathy for Jacob and Helen. As for feelings about Anna, most of her estranged friends simply thought she had gone insane. In truth, Anna probably had crossed over the ill-defined line between the world of the rational and that of the delusional.

Jacob could no longer abide Anna's behavior. What his wife had done regarding their daughter was not the behavior of a loving mother. He spent very little time at home. Even when he was there, the couple spent no time together. They did not eat meals together nor sleep together. Jacob spent most of his time reading in the study or sitting outdoors on a bench overlooking the river, or on a bench in the front of the house, reading, and waving to neighbors as they walked by.

For company, Jacob acquired a small German schnauzer puppy, which he named Fritz. Fritz adored Jacob and followed him around the house and pattered behind Jacob at the store. Whenever she spied Fritz, Anna shrieked at Jacob to "get that filthy animal out of my house." Each time this occurred, the schnauzer would cower under Jacob's legs and growl.

Jacob normally would reply, "Now Anna. You know that if Fritz goes, I will also go. Is that what you want?"

This would usually silence Anna's hysterics, but Jacob kept Fritz close by to avoid Anna's wrath.

Anna's nocturnal nightmares became more regular. They also inten-sified, becoming more terrifying to her. Instead of just one ghoul in the form of Mitchell Sutter, there were now two specters ghoulishly dancing in her dreams. The second ghostly visage had no face and remained to the side and behind the Sutter image. The sleeping powders only mini-mally helped her to sleep. The lack of sleep was adding to her irrational behavior. Jacob could not help but pity his wife, but he did not know the specifics of her sleeplessness. The attending doctor was also at a loss for an explanation. He stated that Anna's hip pain would be subdued easily by the sleeping powders. Anna had told no one of her nightmares.

Chapter Thirteen

The Investigation

He was sitting in the round house drinking coffee with one of the train crews as they waited for their train to be readied for departure. The men were telling stories and joking with each other. The swirling cigarette smoke rose along with the steam from the hot coffee. One of the men had brought in some home-made cookies his wife had baked the night before, and the men mumbled around the delicacies in their mouths as they talked. It was a partly cloudy, but still somewhat cool day at the end of March 1897. The warmer temperatures had eliminated any late season snow on the ground. Nick was enjoying his cookie and the stories told by the older men.

A gust of cool air followed the lawman as he came through the roundhouse door.

"Close the door old man," said the train crew engineer. "You're letting too damn much cold air in here!" He was a friend of the visitor.

Sheriff Nathan Wolf was a large man. He was a good three inches taller than Nick Wentz, who also was taller than any of the other men at the table. All the men seated at the table knew and respected the sheriff. By virtue of his reputation, the ne'er do wells in Burlington also gave Nathan Wolf a wide berth. They did not want to end up at the business end of his sap or his hard fists. By appearance, the sheriff was a young man who did not present such a formidable picture. He was all business, but usually had a grin on his face, which could vanish in a second if the man was provoked.

The sheriff poured himself a cup of the acrid, thick coffee from the overworked, sticky brown urn. "How are you boys? Don't you train guys ever have to work for a living?" said Wolf as he grinned and sat down at the table. He joined into the conversation and took the one remaining cookie that was laying on waxed paper in the center of the table. The conversation went on for another ten minutes before a yard mechanic popped his head in the door and told the train crew that their train was ready to roll. The crew finished their coffee and headed out into the train yard to climb aboard the rolling stock.

The sheriff turned his attention to Nick.

"I was hoping to find you here, Nick. I picked up two guys last night, drunk as a couple of skunks, who got in a fight in a bar. They pulled knives on each other, so I brought them both in for a free night's lodging. I've still got them, and I want you to come with me while we have a little 'Come to Jesus' meeting with them. Have you got time?" asked Wolf.

"Sure, the boss is gone," said Nick. "He went over to Ottumwa for a couple days on a case, so I can break away from here. Let's go."

The lawmen entered the sheriff's office, and the sheriff pointed out the two men he had brought in the night before. They were too far away for Nick to make out their features. A third man, who was still sleeping off a drunk from the night before, was snoring in one of the sparse bunks in another cell.

"One of those two characters told me something last night when I brought him in. I want you to hear the same thing, and then we will talk to the second man. If you don't mind, just keep your mouth shut, and I'm not going to tell them who you are. The sheriff walked back to the cells and opened the cell holding one of the prisoners. He brought the man into the private, gray-walled interrogation room where Nick was waiting. Wolf shoved the man into a chair across a wooden table from Nick and the sheriff.

Tom Barrett was an opportunist, local bum, whom the sheriff knew quite well. He had spent many nights in the Burlington jail, almost always for intoxication, but once in a while Barrett resorted to petty theft to feed his need for booze.

"All right, Tom. I want you to tell me what you told me last night. Let's talk about the money," said the sheriff.

A surly Tom Barrett, curled his lip, looked at the sheriff, and said, "I don't know what the hell you're talking about."

Wolf knew that would be the answer. He said, "Now Tom, we can do this the easy way, or I can make it a bit more exciting. What would you like?"

"I'd like you to go suck an egg," said Barrett.

It happened so fast that neither Nick nor Barrett saw it coming. Wolf drew the sap from a side pouch of his pants, and the blackjack loudly crashed onto the table, smashing two of Barrett's fingers, breaking them instantly. Barrett howled in extreme pain and clutched the maimed hand. He began sobbing loudly.

"Now Tom, shall we think about this again? Tell me what you said last night, when I asked you what had started the fight between you and Broyles," said the sheriff. The sap was still in his hand, and he slapped his other palm with the sinister black leather-wrapped device.

Barrett eyed the blackjack as he continued moaning. "I told you we got in a fight over money," he said.

"Why did you get in a fight over money?" asked Wolf.

"Because the bastard had too much money, and he wouldn't even buy me another drink. So I got mad at him, and we started fighting."

Wolf eyed Barrett. "You haven't told me everything yet have you Tom. How much money did Broyles have?"

Barrett was studying his maimed fingers. "He had a whole damn wad of bills."

"Where would Broyles get money like that, Tom," asked the sheriff.

"I don't rightly know, but he said something about a railroad dick and an old lady named Rose, or Rush or something. He was so drunk, he didn't make much sense. But he still wouldn't buy me another drink. He's a horse's ass!" Barrett continued his moaning while he rocked back and forth in his chair, holding his maimed hand.

Nick then spoke up. "Sheriff, I'd like to ask this man a question."

"Sure, go ahead," said Wolf.

Nick reached in his vest pocket and pulled out a ring. He put it on the table in front of Barrett. "Have you ever seen this ring before, Mr. Barrett?" asked Nick. The ring was distinctive. It was silver in color and had an engraved snake design that swirled around the ring. Two small red gems represented the eyes of the snake.

Sheriff Wolf had never seen the ring before, but figured the railroad detective knew what he was doing so he stood back and watched.

Barrett looked at the ring and then looked up at Nick and the sheriff. "Yeah, I've seen the ring before, but I want to make a deal. I want to get out of here as soon as we are done talking."

The sheriff then took the blackjack and gently rapped it on the table over and over. He then said, "Here's your deal. You're going to do five days in my beautiful jail for being drunk and fighting. And I'll overlook the fact that you also had the knife. And that's as good as you are going to get." Wolf then struck the table again, but this time it was much stronger and louder.

"All right, all right," said Barrett. "The ring belongs to Homer. He's had it for a long time, but he said he lost it. Is that what you want to know?"

The sheriff and Nick conferred in the hallway outside the interrogation room. Nick told the sheriff the circumstances of his finding the ring. Then Wolf took Barrett back to his cell and returned to the interrogation room with Homer Broyles. This time, Nick was not in the room. He waited unseen, outside the door of the interrogation room, where he could still hear the conversation.

Again, Sheriff Wolf shoved the prisoner into the chair opposite the wooden table. "Now then, Homer. We're going to have a little talk."

"You mean you're going to have a little talk. I ain't flapping my gums," said Broyles.

"Homer, I'm giving you a warning. I want proper respect, and I want the right answers when I ask you questions. Do we understand each other?" said Wolf.

Broyles just stared venomously at the sheriff.

"Where did you get the wad of cash that I took off of you last night?" asked the sheriff.

"The tooth fairy gave it to me," sneered Broyles.

The next thing that Broyles knew, his head had struck the table after Wolf's black jack struck him on the side of his jaw. Blood flowed from Broyles' mouth, and he spit a tooth onto the table. The side of Broyles' head began showing the first signs of what would become an ugly yellow and purple bruise.

"Where'd the money come from?" asked Wolf.

"The old lady gave it to me," he answered.

"What old lady?" asked Wolf.

"Old lady Roush. She's crazy," said Broyles. "I fixed one of her carriages, and she handed me this wad of bills. I wasn't about to say no to her."

The blackjack struck again, but not nearly so hard. It was more like a painful attention-getter on the side of Broyles head.

"Now Homer, you just lied to me. So let's try that answer again," said the sheriff.

"I told you, the old lady gave me the money," whined Broyles.

"Well, that may be true," said Wolf. "But she didn't give it to you for fixing any damn wagon. She gave it to you to kill someone, didn't she?"

Homer Broyles suddenly was alert. This was not just about him and Barrett getting in a fight, and he knew now that he had better keep his mouth shut. "I didn't kill anybody. What are you talking about? You've got the wrong man. What killing?"

The sheriff then moved just inches away from Homer Broyles' face, and said, "You killed a railroad detective up in Oskaloosa, didn't you Homer!"

Broyles lurched in the chair. "You're full of shit, sheriff. I haven't been in Oskaloosa for a long time, and I sure as hell didn't kill any railroad dick."

The blackjack hit Broyles so fast he did not even see it coming. Broyles' hand, which had been on the table, now had a thumb that stuck up at a right angle from his hand, and he was howling in severe pain.

"Just a couple more questions, Homer," said Wolf. "Were you in Oskaloosa at the end of January?"

"No," answered Broyles.

"Did you attack and kill a railroad detective while in Oskaloosa?" asked the Sheriff.

Broyles swung his head back and forth.

"Did Mrs. Roush pay you to kill the railroad detective?" asked Wolf.

"No, I already told you no!" said Broyles.

Nathan Wolf just grinned. "That's all I wanted to know. Just stay put," he said, and walked out of the room.

A few seconds later, the sheriff reentered the room with Nick. As soon as Nick saw Broyles, he recognized him as the man he had fought with in the rail yard in Oskaloosa. Broyles also recognized Nick, and now knew that he was in real trouble.

"Recognize this man, Broyles?" asked the sheriff.

"Never seen him before," said Broyles.

Whap! The sap hit the table in front of Broyles, startling him and making him jump in his chair. The sheriff then reached in his pocket, and put the silver ring on the table. "Ever see this ring before?" asked the sheriff.

"No, never," replied Broyles.

The sheriff then struck the man several times with his fists. When he was done, Broyles' face looked like hamburger, and one of his eyes was swollen shut.

"Broyles, I'm going to lay this out for you," said Wolf. "Old lady Roush hired you to kill that railroad detective. Then you hired Willie McNutt to carry out the plan. But your buddy Willie got killed, and he killed Charlie Mason, the wrong railroad detective. How am I doing, Broyles. Have I got it right so far?"

Broyles looked at the sheriff, and gave the slightest affirmative nod.

"You might have gotten away with your end of the plan, but you dropped your ring, and then you weren't smart enough to get out of the state with the money," said the sheriff. "Screwing your buddy out of a drink last night wasn't very neighborly of you, and that's where I came in. Isn't that right, Homer?"

Again Broyles nodded his head. "But at least I didn't kill that detective," he said. "Hell, he wasn't even the guy that was supposed to be killed. It was this guy here," he said and pointed to Nick.

"No, you're just an accessory to murder. You might not get to hang, but you'll rot in Ft. Madison prison," said the sheriff. "Let's go," and he took the prisoner by the arm and led him back to his cell.

When the sheriff returned to the interrogation room, he found Nick slumped over in a chair with his head down and his elbows on his knees. The sheriff placed a consoling hand on Nick's shoulder. "I'm sorry,

Nick. I didn't know that Anna Roush was this involved with the death of your partner."

"I had an idea," said Nick, "but I chose to ignore it for my wife's sake."

"I'll go see Judge Wilcox tomorrow and get an arrest warrant," said Sheriff Wolf. I'll wait for a day or two before I serve it. No need for you to do anything else."

"OK. Thanks Nathan. I guess I better go break the news to Helen," said Nick.

"If you think you have to, but please don't be telling anybody else."

The two friends shook hands, and Nick slowly walked out of the sheriff's office.

Chapter Fourteen

Incident at *The Ill Wind*

There was probably another reason the grungy tavern was originally named "*The Ill Wind*," but as of late, the name definitely fit. Nothing good ever happened in this despicable tavern nestled among seedy, run-down businesses, which in their finer day may have catered to the commercial fishing trade on Lake Michigan. But now, this area on the Chicago lakefront was home to only the underbelly of humanity, the types who flourished on cheap booze, disease-laden prostitution, petty gambling, and violent crime at the end of a switch-blade knife. Even the police did not frequent the area at night unless they were called out. Then they would show up in a group of no less than six men.

On the evening of March 14, 1897, *The Ill Wind* was frequented by its usual scurrilous crowd of low-life characters. The smoke was so thick in the tavern that it could be cut with a knife. The onslaught of rancid smells was the first thing any unfortunate visitor to the bar would notice. Stale beer and urine odors intermingled with the whisky vapors. All of these smells were entrapped within the cigar and cigarette smoke, which nightly added another greasy nicotine layer to the walls and ceiling of *The Ill Wind*. Heavily rouged whores sat at random tables against the walls, passing the time filing their nails, each with a cigarette hanging from the corner of her mouth. Unshaven, foul-smelling men with malice in their hearts stood at the bar nursing their poison of choice. Most of them had money for only one drink before the large, heavily muscled bartender threw them out for taking up bar space. Only the desperate frequented such a place.

In a corner at the back of the tavern was a suspended gas light fixture. It cast a smoke-hampered dim light over an ancient circular wooden table, which was emblazoned with numerous cigarette burns and assorted nicks and gouges. In the center of the table was a small pile of coins and bills. Six mustachioed and bearded ruffians, all wearing well-worn, stained hats, sat around the table while one of them dealt another hand of poker. The game that night was five card stud. Antes sat in the middle of the table, and the pot was "right." The dealer threw out a hole card to each player, followed by an up-card to each player. A jack of clubs was the highest card showing on the table, and the bets proceeded. All six players stayed for a third card. The second up-card was dealt to all of the players. The man with the jack was dealt a ten of clubs, and his jack/ten of clubs was still high on the table. Two players folded. The bets were placed again, with jack/ten betting, and then raising for a second round of bets. Another player folded. Marcus Roush and two other players remained. One of Marcus's opponents was a well-known thug. His reputation for "roughing up" patrons of the bar and the poker games was heeded by most men who knew him, and he was generally avoided. A third up-card was dealt. The ace of spades landed in front of Marcus, and the ruffian with the jack/ten of clubs received the nine of clubs. Another player folded, leaving only Marcus and the ruffian with the possible straight flush. Marcus now bet because he had an ace showing. He checked. The ruffian across the table from Marcus looked up and studied Marcus's face.

"What's the matter, pretty boy," said the man. "You scared of these little puppy paws? You better be, 'cause I've got either a flush or a straight flush looking at you. I'll bet two dollars."

Marcus was down to his last few dollars. He sat for a few seconds, and then reached into his vest pocket. He drew out the two dollars and placed it in the pot. "I'll call you," he said.

The ruffian across the table said, "Well, do you now. We'll see about that. I'm raising you another two dollars."

Marcus didn't have another two dollars.

Again he sat for a few seconds, and then said, "I don't have two dollars."

He reached into his pocket and withdrew a switch blade knife.

"This knife is worth more than two dollars," he said, and he threw it in the center of the pot.

At this point, the ruffian knew that he was beat. He didn't have the necessary club hole card. His hole card was red. All he had was showing on the table; the four clubs with the jack/ten high. He had failed to bluff Marcus into folding. Since he had been called, he violently threw the red card on the table. Marcus had another ace as his hole card, but hadn't needed it. He threw his hand into the pile of discarded cards. Slowly, he then leaned over and collected the cash in the center of the table. It was nearly two a.m. and the bar was closing. The card game broke up.

The unsavory characters slowly filed out of the broken-down tavern and headed their separate ways. Most of them would return the next night for the same hopeless routine.

Marcus left the tavern and began walking. The dark of the night was accompanied by the soft lapping of the small waves coming in for a rest from the lake. Marcus trudged back toward the run-down flop house where he had been staying. He had been lucky this night. He had thirty-seven dollars and some change in his pocket. He would be able to pay his rent. He was tired and not paying attention to his surroundings. Suddenly, two men jumped out of the darkness and grappled with Marcus.

"I want all my money back, pretty boy," said the ruffian who had been Marcus's opponent at the poker table.

Somehow, Marcus broke free and drew his switch blade that he had regained with his poker winnings. Marcus pushed a button on the knife, and the blade shot free with an instant metallic click.

"Go to hell," he growled at his assailants.

The attackers also held their own knives, and in a few struggling minutes, it was over. Marcus lay mortally wounded and had been stripped of everything of value on his person.

The police were notified the next day when Marcus's body was found by passersby. Marcus was known by the police because of his previous brushes with the law. They found nothing of value on the body and sent it to the city morgue to eventually be buried in a pauper's grave. But they did find a slip of paper with a note scribbled on it. It read:

Aunt Hilda, 5502 Wellington Avenue, Chicago

Mrs. Hilda Sterm was later questioned by police, whereupon it was discovered that Marcus Roush was her nephew, the son of Hilda Sterm's sister, Anna Roush, of Burlington, Iowa. Hilda made arrangements for Marcus's body to be shipped to Burlington. She also sent a telegraph message to her brother-in-law, Jacob Roush, at the Roush Mercantile in Burlington, informing him of the death of his son.

Chapter Fifteen

The Fall

It was nearly nine p.m. on the fifteenth when Jacob received the telegram at the store, informing him of the death of Marcus. He debated with himself whether to immediately go home and tell Anna, but he knew she would already have retired for the night. Instead, he finished up some paperwork and climbed the stairs to his apartment above the store. He poured himself a generous bourbon and sat by the window looking out at the city lights, and the lights on slowly moving boats on the river. He critically contemplated how he could have been a better father to his children, especially to Marcus. He then did what any loving father would do in the circumstance. He wept.

At eleven p.m., Jacob gathered Fritz in his arms and with Fritz in one arm and reins in the other, he rode his horse to Flint Bluff. At home, he poured himself another bourbon, took it to his room, drank a portion of the whisky, then disrobed and crawled into bed. A fitful sleep came upon him.

The doctor had specifically warned Anna not to vary from the dosage he had prescribed for her. Laudanum was a highly powerful opiate which he prescribed for Anna's hip pain, and to help her sleep. But she had taken a triple dose of the opiate along with her prescribed sleeping powders that evening. She was sleeping deeply, but the hallucinatory nature of the laudanum ensured a high amount of activity in her mind. Her dreams flowed at a frenetic pace. The nightmare then began. Mitchell Sutter and the other ghost with no face occupied her imagination. They were both now screaming at her.

"You will die, you will die," they repeated, while Sutter waved his cane wildly above his head. The visage of a railroad train rolled slowly across the field of vision behind the second man. It was the dead railroad detective, whom Anna had never seen in real life.

Still in deep slumber, Anna rose from her bed. Her subconscious willed her to pick up her walking canes. She then sleepwalked toward her bedroom door. She was angrily pursuing the two nightmarish figures of her dream. Her psyche demanded that she put an end to the ghoulish visages. As she opened and walked through the bedroom door in her sleep, she began madly waving her canes above her head. In her mind, Anna was now screaming at the two men as she chased them. But the sound coming from her mouth was just a low, droning mumble that repeated itself over and over. Anna continued sleepwalking toward the center of the wide hall on the second floor of her house.

The mumbling sound and the clattering of Anna's canes alerted the terrier, Fritz, as he was sleeping at the foot of Jacob's bed on the opposite side of the house. His salt and pepper hackles rose, and a low growl came from his throat. He quickly leaped from the bed and squeezed through the bedroom door which Jacob had left ajar. In his stiff-legged terrier gait, he trotted toward the center of the second floor, where the terrier spied a figure in the blackness, madly waving two canes in the air. He immediately sounded his alarm, with four shrill barks. The barking roused Jacob, who rose from his bed, wrapped a robe around himself and peeked out the bedroom door. A maid, from her bedroom at the back of the house, was also roused by the commotion, and she peeked out into the hall.

Fritz began barking in a frenzy. At just that moment, while still asleep, Anna's right foot slipped over the topmost step of the grand staircase. The loss of balance, while bringing her subconscious to a higher alert level, still did not wake Anna. Her right foot lost contact

319

with the top step, and she lurched toward the second step, as she began to awaken. It was too late. When her right foot contacted the second step, her knee buckled, and she hurtled downward, turning over and over down the beautiful, wide, grandiose staircase. She died upon impact. Her neck had been broken in the fall. Both Jacob and the maid ran down the stairs to Anna's side. Anna's nightmares would no longer eerily invade the privacy of her mind. The maid quickly dressed and ran out the front door, making her way to Edna and Jinks' home. Jacob sat on the floor at the base of the stairway, holding his wife's head in his lap, slowly sweeping her hair from her face. For the second time in a matter of hours, Jacob wept over the passing of a family member; this time, the wife to whom he had been married for thirty-one years.

Edna and Jinks were a blessing for Jacob. They handled all of the details associated with the two family deaths. Mother and son were buried at the same time in the Roush family plot at Aspen Grove Cemetery. Sadly, only a handful of Jacob and Edna's friends showed up at the services. During Anna's lifetime, her true, loving friends were few.

Chapter Sixteen

The Final Years

He sat in a chair near a front window where he could see anyone on the sidewalk in front of the house. As his mind wandered, he thought about the past few years, and how fast the time had flown. It was now early summer in 1907. Jacob remembered his sixty-seventh birthday like it was yesterday. When his health began to be a factor, he listened to the advice of his doctor. With Edna's concurrence, they sold the mercantile business. In a very unusual term of the sale, he demanded that he be given an honorary place on the board of directors of the new business, mostly to satisfy his own curiosity on how the new business managers would operate the mercantile. The new owners had chuckled when he also demanded that he would retain his apartment above the store until his death. He gave up the business, but he refused to give up his enjoyable weekly poker games in the apartment with his friends. It was at these poker games that he would sinfully smoke a nice cigar against his doctor's orders, and take a nip or two of bourbon.

As he waited, Jacob's mind wandered to all the marvelous changes that had taken place in technology in his lifetime. The year after Anna died, the Burlington Country Club opened, and shortly after that, he had taken up the game of golf. He enjoyed being out in the fresh air, but did not care much for the game. He was fond of quoting Mark Twain, who said, "Golf is a good walk spoiled." Hence, he only played golf to spend time with some of his friends. He remembered when the power plant was built, and when he had had the house converted from gas lights to electric lights. He laughed to himself as he remembered when the house had been converted to indoor plumbing with public sewers. What a marvelous invention that had been. He watched as one of the new Oldsmobile automobiles clattered down the street, and thought of how he would miss seeing the beautiful teams of horses moving in a stately trot up and down the streets. He still had not given up his carriages and horses. He loved them too much. His eyes caught movement at the sidewalk, and he slowly rose from his chair to meet his visitors.

Tuesday and Friday mornings were his favorite times of the week. His two "girlfriends" would soon be coming to see him. As he spied them coming down the sidewalk, he shouted to the cook in the kitchen that they were coming. He watched as nine-year-old Rose skipped along the sidewalk ahead of her mother. Helen was pushing an empty stroller. Three-year-old Victoria insisted that she was too big to ride in the stroller, and instead, could walk beside her mother and the stroller. Hence the pace of the three was rather slow. Jacob teased his two granddaughters, calling them his girlfriends. Rose always corrected him and said that they were not girlfriends. They were just girls.

Giggling and laughter permeated the home as the two girls and Helen crossed the threshold. The girls ran to the kitchen, where they knew a treat awaited them. The cook had the cocoa already in cups and fresh cookies were on the kitchen table. Jacob loved these times when he had a chance to talk to Helen and watch his grandchildren grow. He had devoted himself so much to his business that he had failed to watch these same growing years in his own children. He regretted that. But God had given him another chance with Helen and her children. He marveled at the strength and beauty of Helen, his youngest daughter who had had the inner strength to stand up to Anna for the sake of her love for Nick, and for what she believed was the right thing to do. And now Jacob watched as she raised her own children with love and understanding. He was grateful, absorbed every nuance of the experience, and was extremely happy.

***

It was a harsh winter in 1907-1908. The newspaper said it was one of the coldest winters ever recorded. But the whole family would once again come together for Christmas. Ironically, the Roush family had started out as believers in the Jewish faith. But the whole clan had moved to Christianity over the years, primarily due to the proximity to places of worship.

William and Martha's original Roush mansion would soon come alive with the sounds of a family enjoying each other's company. Helen and Nick would be hosting the Roush family get-together. Edna and Jinks Quinn and their twins, Mark and Gregory, and their families; James Roush and his wife and family were coming from St. Louis; along with Ruth and Joshua Stroud and their family. Kon and Esther Blue Sky Grant would also join the family gathering. As Jinks' best friend, and the man who had saved Jacob's life, Jacob and Jinks had long ago "adopted" Kon and Esther into the family.

Santa Claus had come the night before, and the children knew there were presents for all of them. Their anticipation could not be contained much longer. After light refreshments were served, permission was given and the noise level took a pronounced leap as the children scrambled to find brightly wrapped presents with their names on them. Wrapping paper flew around the parlor, and the noise was joined by the sounds of crying dolls, pop guns, and train whistles.

Unnoticed in a far corner, Jacob winced as he coughed several times.

When the cook said she was ready, everyone sat down at the beautifully decorated tables. Edna's cook, assisted by Jacob's cook and maid, began bringing the food to the table. Before everyone began eating,

James Stroud said grace. Then Jacob slowly got to his feet, and everyone looked toward the most senior Roush at the head of the table.

Jacob's hands shook ever so slightly, and his voice wavered a tiny bit as he said, "I would like to give thanks that all of the people I love in this world have come together to enjoy Christmas." The family quietly murmured their own comments. "But I also want to offer a toast. I offer a toast to Marcus and his mother. We miss them in our midst. May their spirits be finally at peace." Glasses quietly clinked around the table, as Jacob slowly regained his seat.

The tables, pushed together to accommodate all of the family, groaned under the weight of all the food and drink. The younger children sat at their own table nearby, giggling and poking each other with their sticky fingers. The mischievous O'Connor personality showed itself again in two of the O'Connor grandchildren as they secretly put spoonfuls of mashed potatoes in some of the other children's coat pockets. Pumpkin pie and whipped crème covered the faces of several children. The older adults sat back and watched the shenanigans of the children, clearly enjoying the personification of free will and the innocence of youth.

From early morning until far past bedtime, the walls of the old Roush mansion reverberated with the conversation of the family members, and the giggling and squealing of the grandchildren. After the youngest children were put to bed in one room with the maids watching over them, the adults went to midnight church service.

It was bitterly cold that Christmas eve. The clouds of steam blasted out of the nostrils of the horses as they pulled the carriages to the church. Everyone was wrapped in blankets and robes, and talked cheerily as they moved to the church. Sitting in his usual pew, Jacob relished the beautiful music and words of his favorite Christmas carols sung by the congregation.

Later, everyone had finally bedded down for the night. Jacob, Jinks, Kon, and Nick smoked cigars in the study at the rear of the house, with two windows ajar to provide a bit of fresh air. James was with them, but refrained from smoking. A fire was cheerfully crackling in the fireplace, and each man held a small glass of bourbon in their free hand.

"It has been a wonderful Christmas, Dad," said James. "I even hate to head back to St. Louis in a day or two."

"Well, you could move your law practice up here to Burlington," said Jacob, and the other men nodded and mumbled their agreement.

"No, the wife and in-laws would scalp me. Er, no offense, Kon," said James. He was red-faced in embarrassment.

"None taken," said Kon as he chuckled.

The men finally were coming to the end of their stamina, and they all moved off to find where their families were sleeping.

"You can stay here tonight if you want to, Father," said Helen, as she watched Jacob struggle into his coat and hat.

"Nonsense," said Jacob. "The walk in the fresh air will do me good. It's only a couple blocks."

"OK Father, we'll see you tomorrow," said Helen. Jacob had told no one, but he knew he was sick. He coughed deeply several times as the cold air penetrated his lungs.

Jacob had contracted an aggressive flu, which now had progressed to pneumonia. Although he had already become more frail as the years had passed, it took nearly three weeks for the flu and subsequent pneumonia to finally drown Jacob. The doctor had given Jacob drugs to help him sleep with no discomfort. Edna, Jinks, Helen, and Nick were by his bedside when his body stopped functioning. At sixty-eight years of age, he exhaled his last soft breath, on a clear, cold, late January afternoon in 1908.

Chapter Seventeen

The Will

This was certainly not the joyous occasion for the gathering once again of the children of Jacob and Anna Roush. The enjoyment and merriment at Christmas, only a matter of weeks ago, was lost at this moment in time. On a blustery March day, Jacob's children, James, Ruth, and Helen, along with Jacob's sister Edna were seated in the office of their father's attorney, Edwin Brightwell. Brightwell was a rather pompous old fellow, but he had been a good friend to Jacob Roush. He had handled the legal requirements of Jacob's business, and also family matters requiring legal attention. He was well aware of the status and holdings of the Roushes.

Brightwell started the proceedings. "Ladies and James, thank you for coming here today. I will try to make this as short as possible. Rather than read all of the legal terms required for the will to be certified by the court, I will attempt to summarize the pertinent details. As you all know, Jacob Roush was an extremely wealthy man. With the exception of a donation to Iowa Wesleyan College, the Methodist Church, and other assorted charities, he has made provisos for selected staff who worked for him at the mercantile, and for the house servants. The bulk, then, of his estate, which after selling his business, is primarily in liquid assets, is to be divided into four parts. The smaller portion is to go to Jacob's sister, Edna for her use as she sees fit, and to ensure that her grandchildren attend college. The other larger shares are equal in value, and are to be distributed to Jacob's three surviving children, James, Ruth, and Helen."

Sealed letters outlining the specifics of the exact monetary numbers and conditions, if any, were handed to each of the beneficiaries to read later in private. Jacob had enclosed a handwritten note to accompany each letter when he had drawn up the will some years before.

"Now, I have one other piece of business that needs to be taken care of," continued Brightwell. "There is the matter of a hold-over clause from the will of Anna Roush. As you may already know, Anna spent her money very freely. When she died, she left her remaining assets to Jacob. Those assets have been included in his estate, which you are each receiving. But Jacob and Anna's house was never community property. Anna built the house and retained ownership of it throughout her lifetime. And that is where this hold-over clause comes into effect."

By now, the Roush children were confused. They had all assumed that Flint Bluff had been owned jointly by their parents. But they also knew of the haughty arrogance of their mother, so they were not surprised at this last bit of information.

Brightwell continued. "I'm sorry, but I must now get rather personal with your family affairs. You all know that your mother ostracized Helen from the family, even declaring her to be 'dead'. As a result, when she had her will drawn up, Anna was only truly concerned with the disposition of Flint Bluff, the home that she was so proud of. Therefore, she requested a specific clause in her will. I will read that clause."

"In the event of my death, my beautiful home, which had been my anchor and my source of pride and inspiration, will be passed ONLY to my three oldest living children."

"Now I must be blunt with you three," said Brightwell. "Anna's intent was that under no circumstance was Helen to be given any right of ownership of Flint Bluff. That is why this clause was placed in the will. I argued with Anna over and over not to do this, but you know your mother. She would have it no other way. But she could not foresee the death of Marcus, and when he died, there was no time to change the will's provision. Therefore, I have taken the matter up with Judge

Wilcox, and we have come to this conclusion. The clause is very specific in saying that the home will go to the three oldest living children. I believe that your mother boxed herself in with this language in the will. In the eyes of the law, therefore, Helen, your mother's sham of declaring you dead and holding the subsequent funeral was just that – a sham. You are very much alive. Therefore, the inheritance of Flint Bluff is to be divided between the three of you. I hope this meets with your approval."

The three Roush offspring looked at each other with their mouths hanging open and a look of total surprise on their faces. From behind them, where she was sitting, their aunt Edna had heard the whole conversation of Mr. Brightwell. She suddenly burst out laughing. Initially, she was ashamed and covered her mouth with her handkerchief. But then, James burst out laughing and was joined by Ruth. The laughter was contagious, and even Mr. Brightwell's face broke out with a large toothy grin. Everyone in the room had, of necessity, dealt with Anna's haughty, arrogant, personality. The irony was lost on no one. Before she died, she had boxed herself into a course of action by virtue of the language in the will; which, in the end, had gone quite contrary to Anna's wishes. It was an example of justice served after the death of the antagonist. The happy chatter of James, Ruth, and Edna continued, but Helen was quite embarrassed by the whole matter.

"Don't be so self-conscious, Sis," said James to Helen. "Instead remember what mother had done to you. This is sweet revenge!" Helen smiled, but still felt a bit strange with all the attention paid to her.

James stayed in town for a few more days, and the three siblings explored ideas on a course of action for the Flint Bluff property. His stay also gave Helen time to develop an idea. The discussion bounced back and forth between the three heirs.

"I certainly do not want the house," said James. I have all the money I will ever need in my lifetime. Frankly, I never want to set foot in Flint Bluff again!"

Ruth spoke up. "The three of us are very lucky. Father has provided for all of us to want for nothing. I also have no use for Flint Bluff. As far as I am concerned, we can sell the house, or even give it away. The memories of living in that house are not among my favorites. What do you think, Helen?" she asked.

Helen looked closely at her brother and sister.

"Well, I have given this some thought, and I have a plan. But I don't know if you two will agree." Helen paused. "Maybe it's not such a good plan after all."

"Well, let us decide that," said James.

"All right, here is what I have been thinking about. You both know that since I stopped teaching at St. Paul's, I have been volunteering at the church and helping with the finances in the office. Because I am around the priest and his staff so often, I overhear a great deal about the parishioners. Some weeks back, I heard about a devout family which is part of St. Paul's church family. Their name is Harrison. Mr. Harrison works on the railroad. The family has ten children."

"Wow," said James. "What does the guy do, own the railroad?"

"No," answered Helen, "and that is just my point. The family lives on the edge of poverty in a small, four room house down by the railroad tracks. Seven of those children are their own. But the other three are orphans that the Harrisons have taken in, because the children have no families. They have been doing this for years. Each time one of the foster children is adopted, the Harrisons bring in another poor child to help. In addition, each week, the Harrison's host a free hot lunch at their meager home. Poor people in the neighborhood come by the home and are given a hot lunch. It isn't much; usually a bowl of beans and a piece of bread. But for some of the people, this is the only meal they will get all day. I do not know how this poor family manages to set aside enough money to care for extra children, or feed the hungry in the neighborhood. The Harrisons don't have the money to care for the foster children, or give away free food. In short, the Harrison's are saints. The other day, I overheard the priest say that all of the good work of the Harrisons may have to come to a halt. Apparently, they are just stretched too thin. They are now in danger of losing their house." Helen paused and listened to James and Ruth talk for a moment, and then she continued.

"After hearing their story," said Helen, "I have an idea. I would like to sell the house to the Harrisons so that they can continue working with foundlings, and their feeding of the poor."

Ruth asked, "But how can you do that. They don't have the money to buy a house."

"I propose that we sell the house to them and the St. Paul parish, to be co-owners of the house, for one dollar from each of the parties," said Helen.

"Oh my goodness," said Ruth. "Mother will spin in her grave!"

James just smiled and shook his head from side to side. "Being a lawyer, I thought I had heard it all. But Helen, you have risen to first place in my list of stories. I think this has to be the strangest idea I ever heard."

Helen pursed her lips, and her shoulders sagged.

"Wait," said James. "You didn't let me finish. The strangest idea I have ever heard, yes, but also one of the kindest, heart-felt gestures I have ever heard." He sprang from his chair. "Ruth, I don't know about you, but I like the idea. As long as we can be assured that the house will be used for that purpose."

Ruth responded, "Well, none of us want the house, and we never really want to go back to the house, so I also agree. Let's give it to charity."

"James, that is why I think the house should also be in the name of the parish. So that the house will be used for the church's purpose, as well as giving the Harrisons a place to live and help the community," said Helen.

The three siblings had made their decision. Two days later they were back in Mr. Brightwell's office. In addition, the St. Paul's parish priest, Father Thomas, joined the meeting. The discussion went on for quite some time. The priest was literally in shock. He said, "I am stunned beyond words at the kindness and generosity of you three people. I have had a dream to one day have a Catholic foster home for children. The city needs it terribly. With the strange workings of the Lord, my dream has come true."

"I'll have the necessary papers drawn up for everyone's signature," said Brightwell.

The following day, the papers were signed by the Roush children. Accompanied by the parish priest, they then made the trip to the home of the Harrisons. The Harrisons lived in a run-down wood frame, two bedroom house. All the boys slept in one bedroom, and the girls slept in another. Peter Harrison and his wife slept in the cramped living room; one on the couch and the other on the floor. One bathroom served the twelve people. The house had certainly seen its better days. But some-how, the generous and loving couple made do, and all of the children thrived in the loving atmosphere.

The Harrisons knew Helen quite well, as she had taught some of their children. But they were somewhat leery as they saw a contingent coming to their door, especially with the priest. They were imagining the worst.

Helen introduced her brother and sister to the Harrisons. James then spoke up. "Mr. Harrison. I have a wonderful surprise for you. Would you be inclined to trust me for just one moment?"

Peter Harrison was very confused. He wondered what could be happening. But the priest and the two women were smiling. He responded, "Yes, I don't know what this is about. But of course, I will trust you for a moment."

James turned to Father Thomas. "Father, will you please allow me to have one of your dollars?"

Father Thomas knew what this was about, and he quickly produced a dollar from a coin purse in his pocket and handed it to James.

James said, "Mr. Harrison, do you have a dollar you could give me? Remember that I asked you to trust me, and believe me, giving me a dollar will be well worth your time and money."

Peter Harrison could only gape at the smiling man. What in the world could a well-dressed man like this want with a poor man's dollar? And why had he asked the priest for a dollar? He paused, but finally reached in his pocket, pulling out a well-worn coin purse. He carefully opened it, drew out a very worn paper dollar, and handed it to James. James then reached inside his coat and took out a piece of paper. It was the deed to Flint Bluff.

"Mr. Harrison, I would like to present this document to you. It is the deed to Flint Bluff. You and Father Thomas have just purchased the property formerly held by me and my sisters. You will live in the home, and with the help of the church, you will be able to continue your foster home in a much larger house. Oh my, please forgive me. I guess that I should have first asked; would that meet with your approval?" said James.

He smiled as Peter Harrison read the deed over and over.

"Father, is this man being honest with me?" Peter asked the priest.

"Indeed he is," said Father Thomas. "I, too, had trouble believing these people. But it is the truth. Your family and the parish will work together to make this a fine foster home."

Mrs. Harrison came and joined her husband, while a couple of noisy, jabbering children skittered past the group. When the situation was explained to her, Mrs. Harrison broke down and cried. She could not stop crying, but went from person to person hugging them all in turn. Flint Bluff was indeed going to a worthy family and a worthy Christian cause.

A few days later, Helen and Ruth watched as an old horse drawn wagon brought the few personal items from the Harrison home to Flint Bluff. The Harrisons had little to bring with them to the mansion, but because all of Anna's furnishings remained, nothing was needed. They stood in the vestibule of Flint Bluff, watching the darting children carrying in assorted bags and boxes. Each time the children went up the stairs, momentarily they would be seen sliding down the banister of the grand staircase. Other children were playing tag and running from one end of the ballroom to the other. Helen and Ruth watched in amazement to see all of this activity. It was gratifying for them to see the home finally being enjoyed.

"And to think," said Helen. "Mother would never allow us to be on the first floor of the house, let alone in the ballroom. What would she have thought about this scene?" Both women could not stop giggling as they hugged each other.

Epilogue

Weeks later, the first of the weekly soup lunches for the underprivileged was held in the great ballroom at Flint Bluff. Father Thomas helped the Harrisons ladle out soup and dish out slabs of corn bread to the needy.

On other days, the grand ballroom at Flint Bluff, into which Anna Roush had forbidden her children ever to enter, was alive with screaming laughing children. In addition to the Harrison children and the foster children, surrounding neighbor children came to play at Flint Bluff. As on so many other days, the children were roller skating round and round the ballroom, bumping into each other, falling down, screaming, crying, laughing and giggling. They were enjoying themselves immensely.

Mrs. Harrison stood against a wall of the ballroom, intermittently cranking the old phonograph so that the children had music while they skated and played. As the old recording turned, the beautiful melody of "The Tales from the Vienna Woods" once again filled the vast ballroom of Flint Bluff.

Coming Soon!

MARKET TIME CONSPIRACY

JAMES DUERMEYER
BESTSELLING AUTHOR OF *FLINT BLUFF*

He came from a humble background, a farm kid with the ethics and core values that are so prevalent in the Midwest. Following high school, Buddy Miller joined the Navy during the Vietnam War, and while serving on a ship in Southeast Asia, an incident occurs that will affect him for the next decade. With courage, he faces and manages the disability of PTSD and confronts the ghosts of his past…

James Duermeyer tells a rare story—a glimpse into the life of a man facing his worst nightmare. It is a wonderful, heart-felt story that gives the reader a look into the disability of PTSD. But the story is much more than that. It is a story woven from a young boy's growth into manhood, war, friendship, humor, perseverance, entrepreneurship, genius, and most importantly love.

On Sale Now!

On Sale Now!

A DANGEROUS LAND TRILOGY
BOOK 1

For more information
visit: www.SpeakingVolumes.us

www.ingramcontent.com/pod-product-compliance
Lightning Source LLC
Chambersburg PA
CBHW030920260626
47169CB00002B/337